going to the sun road

National Park Road Series Books

Buffalo Road: A Yellowstone Park Love Story

Going to the Sun Road: A Glacier Park Love Story

NATIONAL PARK ROAD SERIES

Fall in love with some of our most precious, public national treasures. Unlike many other federally funded institutions and buildings, our parks have been preserved and protected for anyone and everyone—of all ages—to use and enjoy.

The wisdom of setting aside these lands goes beyond their natural beauty, wildlife habitat, recreational and family enjoyment and special memories created, to another benefit and bonus— more essential than ever today—knowledge. They store knowledge and answers in undisturbed layers of deep time.

Answers to understanding how our planet functions, past and present. Clues to the beginnings and process of life on earth and being able to see what "green" and "natural" truly mean. From mountain building—or destroying—volcanoes, to microscopic primitive life forms that color hot springs, to the architectural evidence of ice sheets and glaciers that carved the land and shifted rivers around, they teach that earth is not static, but continually shifting, changing and recycling in ways we still need to fully understand to make good decisions for the future.

Each book introduces a park with such a unique personality it becomes a main character—with its background of complex forces that shaped its present: from the geologic upbringing of the region, to climate shifts and stresses that molded, to stories of the First People to adapt to the ever-changing land. Though works of fiction, the historic and prehistoric beginnings are carefully researched to enhance the tour of roads and paths in, around, and leading to the heart of the present day park.

You will be guided by another love story, an entertaining light romance, with more new friends to share the trip and the laughter.

4

going to the sun road

A GLACIER PARK LOVE STORY

Bett Bone

NATIONAL PARK ROAD SERIES- BOOK 2

edmonds, washington

GOING TO THE SUN ROAD: A Glacier Park Love Story

Copyright © 2018 Bettina Carter

all text and photos © Bettina Carter

ALL RIGHTS RESERVED

Published by Bettina Carter , Edmonds, WA 98026

https://bettinacarter.com

 bettbone@outlook.com

ISBN 13:978-0-9983576-4-5 trade paperback

ISBN 13:978-0-9983576-5-2 kindle eBook

Library of Congress Control Number : 2018906617

Product of the United States of America

FOR TERRY

for all his helpful advice,
not only thoughtful, but honest;
for traveling up the
Going-to-the-Sun Road with me—
even on foot when it was closed—
and for being my big brother
all my life
Thanks OWB !

prologue

IF I ONLY KNEW HIS NAME!

Thoughts paced in her head faster than the glide and pause steps of her satin slippers, measured to the wedding march.

But the handsome savage was so deliciously dark, tall and dangerous…who needed a name?

Jennifer McCallum controlled the little skip in her nerves and step, trying to restore the dignified demeanor she wanted to project. Or as dignified as a lady barely topping five feet could effect; one told she looked like a southern belle doll on collectors' shelves.

Jenny wanted off that shelf.

Taking another step, Jenny lowered her eyes and checked her appearance. Satin gown smoothed, lace gloves over a perfect manicure, bouquet in place, everything just as she expected of herself—neat, elegant and organized.

Except for her unruly emotions.

Why had she never been able to keep them from tilting her to such dangerous extremes?

A few more flower petals crushed beneath her elegant slipper, she cast another glance down the aisle as she glided forward, closer and closer to the altar.

Oh, he was a feast for the eyes. Raven hair, brows, eyes, all hard-carved hot male face and body. She did know he was a ranger at Glacier National Park. She had never been there, but she would see it all soon.

And … she expected to thoroughly enjoy it.

Heat and moisture began to gather where her hands clasped her bouquet and along her spine. Jen hoped she didn't start glowing, as her southern ancestors would say. She wished

9

the music would let her glide a bit faster and stir up a cooling breeze.

But she hesitated a little too long for the next beat of the music.

You would think she could have at least gotten his damn name before this started! It was embarrassing, if not annoying.

Sighing, she squared her shoulders, raised her chin and took a quick step to get back into rhythm.

Well, it would just have to wait.

Only one more giant step left.

She would just have to call him 'Handsome Savage' for now.

After flashing him a dazzling, seductive smile, Jenny modestly lowered her head over her bouquet, taking her position before the altar.

The music faded, everyone in place, the crowd rustled then quieted behind them—except for the child's voice chirping, "What they doin'?" before being shushed.

"Dearly beloved," the minister began, "we are gathered here today ... "

Jen studied the bouquet clamped in her hands, trying to loosen her death grip on the arrangement before she crushed the fragile stems. She breathed deeply, slowly, drawing the subtle calming fragrance of the dewy blossoms into her lungs. She took a quick peek at him from the corner of her eye. as the minister began a long series of remarks on the auspicious occasion, barely hearing his words. Her nerves were alive and snapping, standing so close to him.

Catching her surreptitious look, the devil gave her a wicked smile that curled one side of his carved tan face, and each of her tiny toes. Suddenly Jen felt as dewy as her flowers.

Several times during the ceremony, she felt the heat of her Handsome Savage's gaze on her, pulling her glance to him. The eyes that trapped hers were as dark, intent, and dangerous as hot lava boiling her blood. Those molten eyes didn't restrict themselves to her face, either, consuming all of her. She felt their molten flow cover and sear every inch of her body, sending ripples of heat and excitement skittering deep inside. Jen barely managed to keep from fanning herself with her bouquet, glowing like an ember now.

The ceremony was beautiful and moving. The handsome couple seemed lit from within with joy and delight in each other, oblivious to all the tears and happy sniffles of the spectators.

After a kiss that surely seared the bride down to her toes, and left the guests wondering if the passionate couple remembered their presence, the bride and groom, now man and wife, finally turned to the crowd with huge dreamy smiles.

The dark haired best man turned an amused, still heated, gaze on the petite maid of honor, offered his arm, and escorted Jen back up the aisle behind the happy couple, without melting her on contact. It was, however, a very near thing. Even the flowers in her bridesmaid's bouquet were singed brown around the edges and decidedly limp. And she still didn't know the damn savage's name!

So this was the woman that his buddy said had cried all over him, like a broken water spout, at their first meeting.

Sounded like a female to avoid like a plague.

Turning as the wedding music began, he had waited beside his buddy for Garrett's bride to arrive at the altar, preceded by her best friend—The Flood.

She wasn't crying now. Though, he judged, she might make some grown men do so. Not himself, of course. And she had nothing to do with the way his head was spinning. It was the wedding. He hated weddings. His nostrils flared slightly as he studied her preparing to come down the aisle.

Petite, but it was more accurate to call her a miniature—a perfect copy of a lushly curved lady in her fancy full length gown. Posed like the one atop a wedding cake. The brunette was a tiny doll with china blue eyes, dark hair and lashes, pretty pink rosebud lips, hour-glass shape, and tinted porcelain skin. But skin he could warm to his touch, all silken, soft, fragrant, and flushed. She would taste a lot sweeter than any cake—with or without frosting.

He shifted his chin, the damn tux choking him. He had sworn he would never wear one, especially near a wedding—even as an observer. But Garrett was his best bud; he would suffer through it.

To distract himself from the unnerving leg-shackling words of the ceremony, he locked on the little maid. Spent his time slowly undressing the beauty mentally, and making sure she knew it.

Felt it.

Enjoyed it.

Maybe she would be too distracted to drown someone in tears when it was over.

There was not a soul at the wedding, or in the whole county, that didn't know what had brought the bride and groom together earlier that year. Their first meeting had been the subject of front page banner headlines. An angered buffalo had inadvertently introduced Garrett and Dana—though Dana was, mostly, in absentia. But fortunately, that near tragedy in Yellowstone Park had turned into a story of true love and romance, and today's fine fairy tale ending—and new beginning.

Though the good 'ole Montana boys would never express such mushy thoughts out loud. Their sentiments, their cheer for the outcome, was expressed teasing the groom with one last bawdy bit of wedding night advice, and a final bone-smashing back whack, before wandering off eager to kiss the bride and get the party started.

Garrett was finally alone with his best man, and couldn't resist laughing. "Nice tux."

"Only for you. Only this once. Never ask me again, bro."

"No need. Once in a lifetime occasion."

Sipping their drinks, they stood together surveying the crowds enjoying the reception, gazes landing over where the bride and her maid-of-honor were deep in conversation.

"Always knew you'd fall for this marriage business, Garrett. Such a boy scout and family type."

"It wasn't about being a marrying type, friend," the grin fell from Garrett's face, his voice turned rough and quiet, "It was not being able to bear losing her for a life that would just be existence, instead of a joy every single damn day." Eyes locked on his bride, his smile came back like sunlight striking a snowy mountaintop.

Casting a glance back over his shoulder, Garrett watched his silent buddy shifting, fidgeting, avoiding his gaze. He almost laughed out loud at his friend's discomfort. Close for decades, they had shared some deep and private thoughts, but usually only sitting around a campfire in the dark, with a few six packs and only the light of glowing embers and the stars above to shadow their feelings and faces. He knew emotions were things his friend liked to kick sand over and bury like dangerous embers, before they could burn him.

Working Montana road crews as summer jobs in high school, hard muscle building work, every minute outdoors, appealed to both of them. Soon they spent their free time together, also: camping, hiking, horseback riding high mountain trails, and fishing clear, rushing rivers. They'd talked about it all, the sports, school, career plans, and women. And on some occasions, more.

His buddy was scowling about one of those talks now.

"That little one always emotional like that? Always crying?"

"Did you at least give her your handkerchief, you ass?"

"Never carry them. I have no use for weeping women."

"She's just happy for us."

"So am I. I think," his best man grudgingly admitted, "But I'm not causing a flood over it. Women!"

"Hah," Garrett hooted. "You love them!"

"Temporarily." He flashed that very successful, wicked grin, adding, "And ... I always leave them smiling."

"Temporarily," Garrett muttered under his breath. "Don't bother casting your eye over there, pal. Jenny is like a sister to Dana and a real sweetheart. You break her heart and I would have to act the brother and break that pretty face of yours. Maybe a few ribs. How about an arm? I'm glad to hear she is too emotional for you so I don't need to warn you to keep it friendly with her."

"Too bad I have to be up at Glacier early tomorrow. I won't have time to do more than bend that heart a little, anyway."

With another slow and thorough study of the petite brunette, he turned to Garrett and grinned much like a wolf that had spotted fresh prey.

Uneasy, Garrett hoped he was just being taunted. He hadn't heard the promise he was looking for yet.

"Shame on you, Jen," Dana laughed, shaking her finger. "Not very PC of you."

Jen tore her eyes away from the men and gave Dana a blank stare. "PC?" How had the conversation switched from hot males to... "Computers? What?"

"PC," Dana repeated. "As in politically correct."

After a continued blank cobalt stare, Dana added, "Garrett's best friend is full blooded Native American."

"Native American? Native American!" Jen gasped, slapped her hand over her mouth, blue eyes wide and horrified above. Her neck seemed to cringe into her shoulders as a flush rose up her face. Even her voice rose. "You mean the man I've been calling a savage?"

13

Hands waving helplessly, she stuttered rapidly, "Oh my god. I didn't mean. I didn't know. You know I don't ever …It wasn't a slur. I just meant he's hot. I don't divide people. You know that, Dana. Oh god, I'm an idiot. Quit nodding. At least," she finally wound down, "I didn't say it to his face. But that doesn't make it any better. Even if it wasn't intentional."

Sighing she turned to gaze at the man that so fascinated her, realizing she was even more intrigued.

Dana felt a little bad teasing Jen when she knew Jenny only divided people into either good or mean individuals—with a special category for hot males. She turned with Jen to study the pair of them, her husband and his best friend. They were being eyed in return.

Formal tuxedos didn't begin to disguise the tall, lean, outdoor-honed bodies of the two men. Tailoring only emphasized broad shoulders, as did the western-style silk vests for their hard-bellied waists and lean hips. The two were a study in darkness and light, standing there together, both in contrasting coloring, and some personality traits. Each was terribly handsome and charming in his own way.

Her husband, Garrett, was tallest, though his best man carried himself with a bearing and dignity that disguised any height difference until they were seen, as now, side by side. Her man had thick blond hair like a golden palomino, an open friendly face, and denim blue eyes that mirrored the bright Montana skies.

The best man was black eyed, raven haired, with sharp predatory angles to his face and smile, as exotically dark and dangerous as Garrett looked bright and open. Both males the type that had women falling at their feet, though Garrett would apologize and help the lady up politely. His best friend, Dana had heard, would smirk and take advantage of her prone position, or step over her and stroll away. And never look back.

Dark and light, that's what she saw. Sunlight shimmering off thick shaggy blond locks of Dana's good guy, and rich raven-black hair, on the dark, wickedly handsome bad boy. When she turned to speak to Jen she saw a matching wicked gleam in naughty blue eyes.

"Jenny ... Jen ... hey, hello?"

"Huh? Oh, sorry, what were we talking about?"

"We were discussing," Dana prompted amused, after watching her friend savage, with her eyes, the very man she had called by that name, "your inappropriate language."

14

Jen huffed, tiny fists braced on satin hips, sucking in an indignant breath.

"I just meant he looks like he would be savage in bed!" she nearly shouted, then clamped her hand over her mouth, flushing at the gasps and turned heads. Turning her back and edging closer to Dana, she whispered furiously, "Savage in bed. You know, as in passionate, sinful, sensual, wildly exciting and deliriously decadent. There was nothing ethnic about it!" Jen nodded righteously, flushed a bit and frowned accusingly at her glass of spiked punch.

"Ah, of course," Dana nodded soberly, then just had to chuckle. Jen had such a bold, brash mouth for such a tiny doll, her shield guarding a too tender, too generous heart; though there was no pretense her temper could flare to full size. "Relax. I remember that time we discussed that being too politically correct was almost an insult, and racist, because it meant you had to first see people as a specific category, rather than as an equal individual, just to parse your words correctly. And I'm with you. For everyone to be seen and respected as an individual based on their personal merits, not any ethnic, or other category." Dana giggled, "Remember that time in college that you told that nineteenth century history professor that you thought the reason early Europeans out West denigrated Indians was because they were jealous of their beautiful tans and toned bodies?"

Jen muttered, "I still believe that." Motioning toward Garrett's best man, she challenged, "I mean is he gorgeous, or what?"

"They both are," Dana agreed, "but, just beware, my friend. According to Garrett he is a notorious…'rakehell' is the word, I believe, in those books you are always reading. But good luck, girl," Dana laughed over her shoulder as she turned and left as her new husband beckoned. She turned and called out something else, but Jen had other concerns on her mind.

"Hey! Dana, wait! His name…?"

Too late. Jen stomped a tiny foot, grumbling to herself, and decided to make a break for the restroom before refilling her punch.

It was only after she had washed her hands and was looking in the mirror applying more lip gloss that her eyes popped wide open as she remembered what Dana had called back to her.

Had she said, "Don't worry, I'll make sure he is not offended?" No! She wouldn't mention… would she? Dana had warned Jen that married people told each other everything, and if

Garrett knew about her PC error, he wouldn't tell his friend, would he? Embarrassed, Jen decided the only safe course was to avoid the arrogant dangerous man—except for discreet peeks at that luscious, and yes, beautifully tanned body.

Still a little concerned what his buddy had in mind for Dana's, Garrett was about to say something when his new wife joined them.

Despite her tumble of auburn curls, and the laughter that seemed to live in her green eyes, the new Mrs. Hearth, his wife, had a cool, confident beauty. She was tall, with a lean, lithe athletic grace, despite the lace covered sling reminder of the buffalo goring, when she had saved the child of a stranger. A renowned national gymnast as an orphaned child, she was undeniably talented, beautiful, brave, and now all his. His Dana, his life.

"Stop leering at my wife! I might have to forget we're friends," he growled, though he really couldn't blame his friend. She was a lovely, laughing sight as she approached them.

"Mm-mm, that is one gorgeous woman, even if she can't cook. You are lucky, pal, that I didn't see her sooner."

Garrett wasn't about to confess how many times he almost did. His friend had been on temporary ranger duty in Yellowstone last summer when Garrett had been taking Dana there to woo her. And he had made a complete idiot out of himself trying to avoid her meeting his handsome, charming friend.

"Too late now," his smile was as smug as his voice. "Why do you think I only let you meet her twenty minutes before the wedding? At least married woman are safe from you." Slipping his arm around his wife as she reached him, Garrett planted a brief but possessive kiss on her lips.

After sharing some comments, Dana asked, "Ready to cut the cake and get our pictures taken, honey?"

"I'm ready for anything." Mischief danced in his denim blue eyes.

Matching his mood, she told his best man his job was to go corral Jenny and meet them at the cake table for their group picture, adding in a huskier tone, "I'll take care of this guy."

"You are wanted."

The dark, liquid drawl, took her by surprise and sent a shiver down Jenny's spine.

16

She turned to face a broad male chest, and took a step back, a deep breath, and dared to look up into that painfully handsome face and chirp, "Hi. I'm Jennifer McCallum," she held out her hand, with her best smile.

"I know." He smirked. Ignoring her outstretched hand, his lean fingers wrapped around her bare upper arm instead and he started towing her over to where people were gathering around the cake table.

Well! The arrogance!

Trotting along awkwardly in her high heels to keep from being dragged behind his long loose strides, she caught a breath and tried again in as polite a tone as she could manage, "And you are...?"

"Glad to see you finally quit weeping."

Oh! What was wrong with a few happy tears at a wedding?

Temper started to overcome the desire she had felt for the insufferable man. Now that she had caught him—well, technically he had caught her—she wasn't sure she wanted him after all. Just as she was about to try and yank her arm free he stopped, and she plowed into the hard solid wall of his back. Catching her with an arm around her waist, he pulled her up tight beside him.

Oh, he was hateful. But he did smell wonderful. Whatever his name was!

When she started to struggle, he smiled down at her, eyes dark and full of sin and charm, he motioned toward the photographer.

"You are too beautiful not to look perfect for the pictures, little wren," he murmured.

Ohhh...

"So, what did you think? Did you enjoy it?" Dana called, eager to hear Jen's reaction. It had been a month since Dana's laughing voice had last asked her that same question.

What did you think? Did you enjoy it?

It had been the day after.

After Thanksgiving, after Dana's wedding, after that dark and wicked best man, that Jen had met for the first time, had escorted her to the cabin. Alone.

She had not thought anyone had seen them, or intended to invite him in. He had just reached around her, pushed open the door to the guest cabin and his arm around her waist had pulled her in, around, and closed the door with her backed against it.

17

Suddenly she was face to face, toe to toe, in the near darkness of a single lamp, alone with her handsome savage, and her nerves didn't seem to know whether to shudder from danger or excitement, though dangerous excitement was what it felt like most. She didn't dare breathe or her satin covered breasts would brush his chest—his hard, muscled chest.

They were that close.

Jen was tempted to draw that very deep breath as he leaned down, his breath brushing her face, dark eyes intent as if he was waiting for something from her.

One forearm rested by her shoulder against the door. He brought his other hand up slowly, stroked it across her bare shoulder, and curled his lean fingers around her nape. When she didn't move or speak a glint sparked in his eyes that should have warned her, before his fingers pushed into her hair and mischievously ruffled her hair until her careful coiffure came undone, dark curls tumbling to her shoulders.

He watched closely as one long strand unwound and the hairpin clinging to it slide off and fall from her bare throat along the curve into the deep vee of her cleavage. His eyes followed and fastened there before he gazed up and with a wolf's grin murmured, "Shall I get that for you?"

Before she could answer, he send his lips on the trail of the errant pin, gliding down the path it had followed from her naked throat, down the upper curve of her breast to the hollow ...

She gasped in a deep breath, leaving him no room to search further, her hand reaching up to rest against his chest, but as he raised his head, she didn't push, mesmerized by the silkiness of his hair as it brushed against her jaw.

"No?," he whispered. Another wolf's grin. "Then maybe a consolation prize?"

Time was suspended as his dark unreadable eyes softened as they silently searched her face. She could feel his breath against her skin, smell his wonderful combination of aftershave and potent male, sense his lips coming closer. Before she could protest, his mouth came down on hers, but with heat, and tender enchantment, rather than ravishment. And even Jenny knew that the soft sound that came from deep in her throat didn't sound anything like a protest.

She would give him another minute—or an hour—before she complained, feeling her body melt against the door at her back and meld to the lean strength embracing her.

But his lips slowly left hers, to brush across her check, before he pulled his head back, studied her dazed eyes a moment then he stepped away from her. He drew her gently away from the door, and she willingly followed.

Before she could catch her breath, he opened it.

"I'll let you go now, little wren."

No! Please don't, she almost cried out.

"See you in Glacier, " he added and was out the door and down the porch!

But her dignity did require one thing. Standing on the threshold, hands fisted on her hips, she called out, "Wait. What is your damn name, anyway?"

He turned, bowed, and said, "Savage. Handsome Savage," in a perfect imitation of Bond. He laughed with delight when the door slammed and locks rattled to the tune of an angry mutter.

"Jen? I said did you enjoy it?"

She had pretended she hadn't understood the question, then. Now, hearing it again, the day after Christmas, recalled all the sensations and emotions that wretched nameless man had stirred.

And all the regrets.

Oh, she had plenty of excuses, it had been an emotional day from the start. She had been so happy and hopeful for Dana; so alone when Dana's new husband had led her away, followed by too plentiful champagne, slow sexy dances, reckless laughter, and dark, sinful eyes like hot lava flowing slowly over her. And ...

"Well?" Dana's voice startled her back from dark eyes, and relentless, restless dreams and desires. "Did you like your Christmas present?"

"Oh. Right. Sure. And yours?"

"Loved it. Hey, you will never guess what Garrett got me for Christmas. A cook book! Can you imagine?" Dana's laugh sounding delighted.

But Jenny, the gourmet cook that had tried for years to teach Dana how to boil water without burning the pot, could not — actually—imagine what the poor man had been thinking. Fortunately, Dana was too excited to wait for her friend to come up with a polite response.

"Listen to the note he attached to it. 'Dear wife —This is not a hint but a gift to prove to you that you are more talented than you think. You can do anything. What is a cookbook but a collection of formulas to combine items to get a chemical reaction that results in a product. My theory is that any woman that cooks is already part scientist, and any budding scientist female is a natural born cook. So accept my challenge? Your faithful lover and believer'."

"Isn't he a dear? And he gave me these cool measuring cups shaped like chemistry set vials and beakers. And ... I baked a cake! And he ate it!"

"Wow, Dana. Must be true love. Congratulations, girl. Now I think on it, he does have a point. We limit ourselves sometimes, and can handle more than we realize. It's just a matter of trying and seeing things from a different viewpoint. That is a gift! How sweet. "

She had missed Dana so much, even her crazy science passions and lectures. Maybe Jen should accept the challenge herself, not to shortchange or limit herself. She should pay attention, listen when Dana went on one of her binges. Learn something and appreciate the friend she missed so much. What could be so hard about trying to follow her friend's enthusiastic ravings when she got on the topics of geology and prehistory. It wouldn't hurt to have a new perspective. Jen vowed to try harder and not just roll her eyes when they went to Glacier this summer.

"By the way, Jen, did your wedding pictures arrive?"

"I got them last week. They are fantastic, your photographer was great! I especially liked the candid shots she took. The one of you two dancing as the sun set is exquisite."

"I love that one, also. I'm very pleased. I told her she could use me as a referral, anytime."

"She deserves it. But, I do have one complaint. Couldn't she have photo-shopped me slimmer?"

"Oh, Jen, don't be an idiot! You look fantastic and you know it. Though you do have kind of a funny look on your face in one of the group photos of the cake cutting, but it's still cute."

The one when her face and mouth had been startled into an 'oh' when everyone else was smiling 'cheese'. Yes, Jen would not forget that one—

"Another thing, Jen. I'm making reservations and need to know where you want to stay at Glacier Park. Did you know you can stay in real tipis on the Blackfeet reservation side, instead of a ..."

"No! I mean, I'll pass on the tipis. I would prefer a hotel with room service and long soaks in a bathtub. You know how much I need my luxuries, Dana. But, whatever hotel you choose is fine as long as it has a tub instead of a shower."

"Okay, I'll book the Many Glacier Hotel for us. It has a great location with plenty of luxuries. I will save the tipis, which I am informed the correct name for is 'lodges', for a romantic night away with Garrett when he arrives end of that week."

"Perfect plan. Anything else you need to know, or I need to do?"

"We're going horse backing riding, do you have cowboy boots?"

"No. Gosh, I guess I'll just have to go shopping." Jen's sigh didn't fool Dana for a moment.

"Your #1 passion. You are welcome, for the excuse," Dana laughed. "Oh, Jen, I do miss you, so much. I'm glad we are still taking our annual vacation. Garrett, the dear, is all for it. And," she added, "he figures we will have the worst of the girl chatter and happy tears over with by the time he joins us."

Throat suddenly tight, Jen managed to get out a faint, "Me too. I miss you Dana, you are the best … well, you know…"

Dana knew, getting emotional herself. It would be a long winter wait before they each saw their best friend again. Dana cleared her throat, and brightened her voice,

"Hey, Merry Christmas to you and have a real Happy New Year. Oh! I almost forgot," Dana's voice changing from strained to teasing. "Garrett said someone asked me to tell you Happy New Year and was checking to make sure you were still planning to be at Glacier Park next summer, but I promised not to say who. Gotta run now. All my love and Garrett's too. Bye for now."

Well, at least now Jen could guess the name of that mysterious someone, thanks to a photographer's caption on that cake photo. Standing, crushing Jen to his side, was a wickedly grinning, dark eyed rake, named 'Mr. T. Ravenwolf': Best Man, Park Ranger, certified hunk, dangerous male, and clearly a name challenged guy. Jeez! She wondered how long it would take to learn his first name. Picking up her magnifying glass and the picture from her coffee table, she settled back to study it.

She had a long, cold winter to wait, to guess, fantasize, and regret. But most of all wonder what he was thinking about her—if he was thinking about her. Did he hope she was still coming to the park—or wish that she wasn't? She wasn't sure what to read into that hit and run kiss.

21

It was a mystery. One to wait on along with the many Dana promised her, along with spectacular scenery, and a terrific time getting to know Glacier.

Glacier National Park was waiting and resting under an old familiar presence—a deep white blanket—much thinner and softer than the ice that had covered it for tens of thousands of years.

Over two million years ago the great Ice Ages began, invading and shaping the landscapes, retreating then returning and scouring away the evidence of their prior visits on each trip over land. It was believed once that this had happened four or five times during that chill time. More recent data from cores drilled in undisturbed ocean sediments had shown continental ice sheets were much busier than once imagined, with maybe twenty rounds of advance, retreat, with warmer interglacial periods in between, in roughly 100,000 year cycles.

Great sheets of ice marched across up to thirty percent of the earth's land surface—so impossible to imagine—but the evidence of their power to sculpt and carve was written all over the face of Glacier National Park in northeastern Montana, where the sheets dipped down from Canada unaware they had crossed some future international border.

The great ice sheets not only shaped the land beneath their crushing weight, but changed the unglaciated lands around them. Animals and plants either adapted and survived, migrated, or died. Rivers and streams found their courses blocked, diverted, or totally changed forever in flow, and direction, some being sent off to seek a new home in a different ocean portal. Continually creating new life patterns, pathways, and perspectives.

The most recent glaciation peaked around 18,000 years ago, creating an ancient glacial lake just south of the iced over Park, when an ice lobe flowing down into Idaho damned a river now known as the Clark Fork. The melt waters off the ice sheets backed up with icy water into a massive lake that filled the valleys to the southwest down past Missoula. Mysterious parallel lines in the high hills circling Missoula Valley, left its residents looking up from the valleys, puzzling over how they had been made—never guessing they marked numerous ancient shorelines.

But an ice dam will eventually float, and then blast apart. Ancient Glacial Lake Missoula broke its dam and escaped in explosive, raging, ravaging floods—Mega floods they are called— emptying the natural chill reservoirs dozens of times between

15,000 and 13,000 years ago. Blasting west through Idaho and Washington, as they rushed to the Pacific Ocean, the high velocity floodwaters rerouted and gouged the gorges of the Columbia River, and created massive wounds on the landscape that would mystify scientists for half a century.

When the great ice sheets retreated from the park that would be named for them, they left a few glaciers laying around. They also left the exotic scenery of their scouring, plucking, grinding work in high cirques, mountains in shapes of razor thin fins, peaks with horns, arêtes with hanging valleys dripping waterfalls, and the long glacial troughs running down both sides of the divide, now filled with long blue fingers of lakes.

In the freshly scraped bedrock and mountainsides there was an even greater story to be told. There was a mystery of earth time so deep and ancient it laughed at the mere two million year blink of ice age time.

And it was a mystery still not completely recognized or solved.

A mystery that had lain hidden beneath the miles and tons of ice now slept beneath the restful deep winter blanket of snow that it would nestle under until summer.

Waiting.

chapter one

THE FIRST THING THAT HIT them was the smell.

If there were an ether to make one feel like they were in the land of gods, it was the smell that rushed into their car. The aroma that rushed into their veins and through their senses with a primeval burst of life and joy. It was the richly layered pine, spruce, and cedar essence that reached deep within to welcome. It was air from a long forgotten time, breath that swelled like a rich meal, a force that could be felt, but never captured in pictures, that made the soul feel new, and fresh, and real.

Coming from a world of artificial scents and flavors, bouquets without fragrance, vegetables with little taste, this all encompassing richness—the smell of the untamed forest wrapping around and inside them—was a scent, a flavor, an experience as deep and rich and ancient and sweet as heaven must smell.

Before even showing their pass at the west entrance gate, the minute they had slowed in line to wait, the elusive scent enticed them. Dana and Jenny had rolled down their windows in anticipation—and been unexpectedly blessed.

For moments, the only sounds in the car were of deep breaths, and the hums of happiness as they savored, before sucking in another nourishing breath. They gorged on the smell, hyperventilating, turning to grin at each other, bursting into joyous laughter. Their Glacier National Park experience had begun with the scent of the magic to come, on the west end of the road called Going to the Sun.

Soon they were greeted by waters that framed the left side of the road for ten miles along Lake McDonald. A long finger of deep water, larger, but similar to other finger-like lakes gouged out by grinding glaciers on the flanks of the divide, it had filled with ice-melt waters that crashed down streams and avalanche chutes from scraped and scarred peaks as the ice sheets receded. Each late spring it refilled with the burden of winter snow and remaining alpine glaciers.

Colorful canoes were visible on a lake that was showing her calm and shiny mood that day under a bright sun, though the weather could change suddenly and dramatically almost anywhere in this park. Picnic tables spaced in the forested fringes along the bright blue-hued waters captured happy family groups enjoying themselves in the dappled shade and sunny refuges along the scenic shores. The far shore was richly furred with forest, rippled on the horizon with the mountain peaks that stretched into Canada. The sky was another vast blue lake above.

Jenny saw a young boy waving a tapered branch in front of the silhouette of a man and pointing excitedly at the lake. She could just imagine the child begging, "Daddy, can we go fishing like that man? Can we?", as he jumped up and down.

At another space a curly-haired toddler in brightly colored shorts and sandals knelt on a bench. He twisted a quick glance over his shoulder checking for adult surveillance before scooting onto the table, snagging another potato chip, and rapidly scrambling back down again. Jen laughed at the antics.

"All the kids seem to be having so much fun! This must seem like heaven to the ones that live in cities."

"Yeah." Dana's voice was soft and wistful, her eyes on the road, reminding Jen of the normal childhood joys that Dana had missed as an orphan and foster child. The only summer camp that Dana had attended was a gymnastics one. That had at least given her a successful career, and a sports family for awhile.

"Hey, let's pull over a minute and look at the lake," Jen suggested suddenly. They found a wide graveled turn out and scrambled down a path through the trees to a pebbled shore. Jen was glad she brought her camera; the view was enchanting. Dana was immediately fascinated by the pebbles washed by gently lapping waves at the water's edge. She kneeled down mumbling to herself.

"Time to play tourist, Dana. Look up and smile for the camera."

Dana glanced up with a grin as delighted as the children they had seen, holding up her hand to show a palm filled with rocks as if displaying treasures. That was so typical of her friend, Jen thought fondly—a photo of Dana with rocks and a big delighted grin.

"You have rocks in your head, girl," she teased.

Unfazed, Dana admitted it was true. She had signed up for a course in geology next semester at Montana State in Bozeman, and was eager to start learning more.

"Okay, quit picking up rocks. Yes, I know they are pretty, but hold still just a moment."

Jen stepped back, squatted, changed position, trying to get the perfect picture. She wanted to get the full scope of the lake and mountains framed behind Dana, but knew she would be killed if she didn't get the handful of rocks in the shot also. She scooted back a few more feet against the rise of the tree-studded bank.

Capturing the essence of the scene was not all that easy. There were too many lovely shadings of color in the lake and backdrop, and she wanted to get them all. To color a picture like that would take almost every blue and green tint in a box of crayons. The lake alone was swathed in bands of cornflower, periwinkle, sky blue, and a robin's egg blue, with a soft milky aqua tint she couldn't name. Also turquoise, she added to the list. It was awesome, if she could only fit it all in.

Small tips of land peeked out along the shoreline to frame the shot, where, depending on their distance, bright green, blue green, and deeper spruce tinted trees touched the water. Multi-layers and levels of mountains were stacked behind in indigo, cadet blue and dark charcoal striped with white bands and patches of snow.

And, Jen had to admit, the pebbles under the translucent edge of the water and in Dana's hand, were even more colorful in surprising tints of brick red, magenta, soft tan, dark gold, jade and sea foam greens.

"Would you take the damn picture, Jen!" Dana gritted out through a grin that was looking tense. "My legs are cramping from trying to squat like this after being in the car so long."

"Okay, but don't move yet, I want a couple shots and a close-up of you and your rocks."

Jen knew how to handle her friend.

When Glacier National Park was newly minted, and the first railroad tracks had been stretched across the nation along a northern route, the owners of the Great Northern Pacific railroad had used the park and the natives to promote their line.

Like the other national park lodges in the early 1900s, the great lodges of Glacier National Park had been built by private money, for commercial reasons.

In 1910, when Glacier became a National Park, it had only one hotel accommodation for tourists. The Lewis Glacier Hotel of early days is now known as the Lake McDonald Lodge.

The vision of Louis B. Hill, president of the railroad, created the opportunity for many to travel to this new recreational and remote wilderness national treasure. He created access from his rail line, accommodations to meet the needs of his clients, and a marketing campaign to draw the wealthy of the Eastern seaboard west instead of touring Europe.

The Great Northern Railway created a logo that boasted a Rocky Mountain goat encircled by the catch phrase 'SEE AMERICA FIRST'.

By 1913, his Glacier Park Hotel was completed in conjunction with a rail station at the eastern edge of the Park. It remains today with an abundant sweep of lawn leading from the tiny station, along a wide walkway lined with floral beds leading to the front of the hotel, the vision of the high snowy peaks inside the park stand sentinel behind. Now, as then, visitors are greeted with a taste of the local culture with a Blackfeet Lodge (tipi) near the entrance. The sweeping circular drive also now holds the famous red touring buses, restored by the Ford Motor Company, that later took tourists across the Going To The Sun Road after its completion.

By 1914, Hill had built the Many Glacier Hotel and a network of nine chalets for visitors to travel across the Continental Divide by horseback and boat.

In 1915, famous author Mary Roberts Rinehart journeyed three hundred miles east to west through the Park on horseback following the linked chalet network, and wrote a travelogue of her personal experiences, enthusing about 'The Call of the Mountains' and encouraging all to 'go ride in the Rocky Mountains and save your soul'.

Jen and Dana's next stop was at the Lake McDonald Lodge, just to take a peek at it, and use the facilities. But they were instantly charmed and distracted by its cozy lakefront setting surrounded by cabins, and the vintage restored red and black Ford touring cars called "jammers" parked outside. They immediately added that tour experience to their future to do list.

As they stepped down to the entrance from the parking area—the back door as the lodge fronted on the lake where early tourists had to arrive by boat—they saw a totem pole. A sight very welcoming and familiar to them, but more a symbol of the west coast Salish people than the Kootenai just west, and the Blackfeet east of this current park that used to be part of their homeland—on either side and across the continental divide—the "Backbone" of their world.

But it was clear the decor was meant more to be an early 1900s concept of an exotic luxury lodge along the lines of the Great Northern's Swiss style, with just touches of "western" accents. Columns and beams were large trees, furnishings were in the handmade Arts & Crafts style, and the requisite "antler" art was over the fireplace hearth. It was a small, cozy gathering space, but the girls hurried through to where the lake sparkled out back, beyond the flowerbox decked terrace of the original lodge entrance.

Stairs led straight down a heavily wooded bank to where a tour boat was loading on the lake, but Dana wandered down the winding, iron railed concrete ramp that swung left to line a creek, as it rushed to enter the lake. The woods and rushing water reminded her of Washington, her former home state. She was wishing now she had booked them here, on the side of the park so like her former Pacific Northwest.

Except for the rocks.

The creek bed was also lined with vastly varied, colored and striped pebbles and boulders. Dana leaned over the railing, studying the banks of the creek.

"Look, Jen, I wonder how they got all these gorgeous colors?"

A towheaded lad stopped at the rail, peered under to see what they were looking at. He twisted a face up to Dana covered with cheerful freckles, and smears around mouth and cheeks that were the bright blue tint only found in snow cones.

"My mommy says the angels painted them like that," he solemnly informed her.

Jen cast Dana a warning frown over his head only to find that they were two of a kind, with the young fellow's next words.

"But she says that about everything I ask," he gave a shrug of frustration. "I bet she prob'ly just doesn't know." Brightening, he boasted, "But I'm going to find out for myself someday!"

Dana laughed, ruffled his hair, "There you go, pal! That's the way." She smiled innocently at his mother when she came to corral her wayward son before they missed the tour boat.

"Really cute kid!" Dana commented, green eyes sparkling.

"Really curious kid, you mean, which is what you like about him. His poor mom 'prob'ly' ran out of answers long ago. Fate should get even with you, Dana, by giving you kids that ask a thousand tough questions a day."

"Then it's a good thing I'm going back to college for a couple years before having any. By the way, Jen, sneaky way to ask a personal question. For your curiosity, I plan to turn into a baby factory when I turn thirty-two, and pump out one a year. And Garrett will have his future construction crew for Hearth Homes."

"Or Dana has a field crew for her science expeditions," her friend teased wryly.

"Actually," Dana paused, serious for a moment, "I hope we turn out little individuals and have the sense to let them be whatever excites them most. Both Garrett and I are following our dreams. That's the legacy we want to give to our kids."

"That's the way, pal." Jen echoed smiling, her lips a little wobbly, her big blue eyes suspiciously moist.

Dana grabbed her in a quick hug, then threatened to dunk her in the lake if Jen started one of her tear fests. She took her back into the lodge thinking Jen would get her balance back with a little shopping in the gift store.

When they left the lodge parking lot, to rejoin Going to the Sun Road, the lake was behind them. Now trees crowded close and tall on both sides, arching high over the two lane road to create a rich, cool green tunnel.

Jen rolled her window down, so she could breathe in more of that exhilarating scent. It all seemed so novel, so unique, just having trees so close, instead of razed back and trimmed so distant like ones on urban and suburban streets. And huge trees, at that! She felt her face relax into a smile. It was so rich and peaceful. . . She tried to capture what she was feeling. Finally realizing that it reminded her of that same sense of hushed reverence she had felt in some of the old cathedrals her parents had dragged her through on a vacation to Europe.

Maybe, she mused, it was the primeval forests, the trees arching high overhead pointing to heaven, that had given the builders of those tall arched spires their design idea. This drive made her feel humble and small beside these great forests, but not in an insignificant way. It was an honored-to-have-the-experience kind of feeling. But no indoor chapel could match this feeling; no incense could ever be as rich as this scent. Jen did not consider herself very religious, but she could feel the reverent spirit in these woods.

Her quiet wonder was interrupted when the trees broke for a pull out area to the left, and Dana pulled the car over so they could climb down to view the churning chute of icy aqua waters rushing over the ledges at McDonald Falls.

Jenny hadn't expected this drive along the road through Glacier to be such an immediate visual, sensual, and spiritual treat. When she had seen the map, with just the one road all the way across the park, she hadn't said much to Dana, but she really hadn't seen what the big deal was. And no way was she doing major hikes everywhere, even for her best buddy! That's what Dana had Garrett for.

They'd already had a scenic drive, over a hundred miles of it, on their way up from Missoula, though Jen couldn't claim to recall much of it. She had been focused on catching up with Dana, her main reason for being here. They hadn't seen each other for what felt like ages, since Dana and Garrett's wedding last Thanksgiving.

That time, without the friend she has been closest to throughout her twenties, since they were college roommates, had been a revelation. Jen had not realized what a driving force her energetic, curious friend had been in directing her own life. Jen enjoyed her job, but it was just a job to her. Her passions were more focused on her house and gardening and learning the skills of a gourmet cook—though she had no desire to be a chef. She suspected she was a natural born homemaker, but as a single woman, that had been less than fulfilling. Dana had always been the one with all the plans, suggesting all the activities and experiences, all the adventures they had shared together. Dana had been the driving force, and Jen had coasted along in her wake, her life full with her job, and her home, and ... Dana's plans. And they'd had wonderful fun together, even though their personalities were so different, they were as close as sisters. And Jen knew she had 'lived' much more fully because of Dana's influence, but with her 'planner' gone, Jen realized she had never got around to charting out a course of what she wanted to be or do next. It was more than being lonely without her best friend, it was being alone with herself and asking 'who are you?' and 'what do you want for yourself?'. The only answers she had been able to come up with so far were that she wanted something more—more what she didn't know. So Jen was happy to be back on Dana's plan again for a while, while she thought things over, and she realized the events of the last year had changed her, made her more open and seeking those elusive answers.

Jenny had been thrilled to see how happy and healthy and improved Dana was after the accident last summer. But despite the long separation of close friends, it hadn't taken five minutes for them to be as chatty and easy with each other, as if they had never been apart.

So the first hundred and fifty miles had gone by almost unnoticed. Jen still hadn't understood what was supposed to be so special about the mere fifty mile scenic drive through Glacier Park, though she did want to see a glacier. She had seen news reports that they were all breaking up and melting way faster than expected, due to global warming. She'd heard the last of Glacier's were expected to be gone by 2030, or sooner. So she understood why Dana had wanted to come to this park, this year. Plus, it was close for Garrett to join them later.

But now Jen was starting to get it—the novelty of the park and Going To The Sun Road. Already her senses had been challenged, stimulated, with smells deeper than she had breathed before, sights of the lake so filled with color that they seemed photo-shopped, hardly possible of being natural. Even her spiritual senses had been tweaked.

And now the chaos of sound created by something as simple as water, bolstered by the strength of glacier melt water, smashing its way down the angular slabs of rocks at McDonald Falls, made it all seem even more invigorating and refreshing. So far they had seen less than a third of the road.

Quite frankly, she had been looking forward to the trip more for the chance of a different kind of sensual stimulation—one with dark hair that seemed to have name issues. But Jen was really getting into this place, especially when she could see all this stuff, and feel it, without having to get out and be really rustic and go hiking.

And she had barely sensed yet, hardly touched, what many considered the real drama and beauty of Going to the Sun Road, and the flavor and character that was Glacier National Park.

Or what a name-challenged ranger might add to that experience.

"Shirley." The short, paunchy ranger nodded and canted one hefty haunch onto the corner of the office manager's desk, uninvited. But as he spoke to her, his spiteful eyes and annoying voice were focused on Ravenwolf passing by.

As usual, the uniform of the owner of the annoying voice and habits was coming untucked. He refused to acknowledge that his butt and gut had grown too large for his former size, and continued to try to squeeze it all in. But his tightly stuffed shirt just made a smoother slide for his pants to skid off his belly.

"Earl." Shirley growled an acknowledgement.

The one piece of Ranger Earl's uniform that was squarely in place was his Smokey the Bear hat, which sat firmly on his head, though he had been indoors a good two hours. The hat looked as if it hadn't budged for years, and rumor had it that he never removed it, even when he slept. Earl knew it made him look more impressive, taller, or, at least, more something. It also covered the bald spot on his head.

Shirl suspected the man's head had gotten as fat as his girth and the hat would have to be cut off someday. He was not a popular, or well-groomed guy, but he was so close to retirement that the park staff just gritted their teeth and marked days off on their calendars, just waiting for that heavenly day.

"Shirley," it spoke, "did you ever wonder why the only area we have trouble with women sunbathing topless is in Geronimo's area?"

Rude, crude, racist, and insufferable, that was good 'ole Ranger Earl—the man that seemed to think his first name was some kind of title or entitlement. Not for the first time did Ravenwolf's fist itch to retire the man early, if not permanently.

"I suppose that's why Yellowstone sent him back to us, huh?" The ass continued to try and egg him on. "Doncha think, Shirley?"

Ravenwolf didn't even glance his way, continuing to ignore him, keeping his curled fist at his side as he headed for a back office.

Shirl ignored him also, except to tell him to get his fat ass off her desk and quit messing up her papers.

But she couldn't help but hide a secret smile. It was ancient history now, but there was a grain a truth in Earl's words. It had only happened once, long ago when Rave was just a new young ranger, but the juicy story had been told the length of the park and become almost a favorite legend among the other rangers.

Poor Ranger T. Ravenwolf was just a babe-magnet, too pretty in his bad boy way for his own good. But Shirl loved Rave like a son, and it was a toss up whether or not she flattened Ranger Earl first, before Rave or someone else did, or the man retired and got out of her face.

Rave had never mentioned the incident that had gained him so much unwanted notoriety. But the 'lady' tourist... well, that was a different matter! For some reason she had been so proud of her failed enticement of the handsome young uniform that she had bragged to every one in the park lodge bars, seeming thrilled to link her name with his in scandal—if not able to link with him in any other way.

As she told it, she had been enamored of the handsome young ranger and had wheedled his schedule out of some unknown person, probably Earl, and followed him around. She always appeared on the remote backcountry trails that he preferred to patrol on horseback. Unable to get any response but a polite, if distant, courtesy from him, she had changed her tactics, more determined than ever.

She had spread herself provocatively on a glacier he had to pass, dressed only in a bikini swim suit bottom, topless. She laughed saying how excited and hot she was waiting for him, or she surely would have frozen off her ass! She dramatically told the story, in a Southern drawl that became more false with each telling, of how she feared she might overheat, and be responsible for melting off a glacier. But she was, with batted eyelashes, so determined to get her man. When he arrived, and his shadow fell over her, she gazed up those braced legs, muscles lean and hard beneath that manly uniform, and claimed she had nearly dissolved with lust on the spot!

"Mr. Big Ranger Man", she had told him, breathlessly, "why don't you just lie down here with me and let me give you a little wildlife adventure." But that annoying man had just dropped a ticket on her, mounted his horse, and ridden away!

She had ended her story with a pout and another furious flutter of lashes.

That, Shirl recalled, was the tamest version of the tale the female had told. With a few more drinks, her comments had gotten increasingly lurid, her drawl melting into an alcoholic slur, but in none of her stories had the Ranger said or done anything to encourage her, outside of being guilty of being irresistible in a uniform, apparently—or preferably, out of it.

Rave, completely disgusted and afraid the woman was going to destroy the job he loved, immediately went to the superintendent, pleaded his innocence, and requested a voluntary transfer to other parks while the rumors died down.

That must have been almost eight years ago, but still the rumors persisted each time Rave returned to Glacier, his home park—mostly thanks to 'ole loud mouth Earl.

And the local girls, to her dismay, including Shirley's own nieces. The girls were all crazy for the handsome single ranger, and had a tendency to get underfoot. But when Rave was in uniform and working in the park, he was never anything but professional, courteous, polite, and honorable to all the tourists, local or not, male or female.

But off work, and out of uniform…?

Then Ranger Rave was no better than he had to be!

And there weren't many limits for a bachelor as hard and handsome as sin. He sure loved his women—in quantity. He went through them in swaths; he was a healthy, lusty young male.

But Shirl still liked the lad, and felt a little sorry for him having to deal with all the groupies he collected.

She knew he didn't want them crawling all over him and following him when he was trying to work. It frustrated, even angered, him at times, but he had to remain polite on the job to protect his career. He'd prefer to work away from the crowds in the deep back country stations and areas he loved, but in his uniform, with those great looks and broad shoulders he was a poster boy for public relations, too pretty for the park to let hide. And not only was he a hunk in uniform, but as he was part Blackfeet, the reservation that bordered Glacier on the east, he was an ethnically perfect public relations dream come true.

Folks came to the park to explore and enjoy its natural beauties, and there was no question that Ranger T. Ravenwolf was one of them. And the park officials knew it. Dressed up in his crisp, creased uniform, leanly muscled, his proud native heritage chiseled on the bones of his face, he was a real crowd pleaser.

It wouldn't be the first time the park had benefited from that kind of promotion.

In 1937 the U.S. Dept. Of Interior put out an official booklet for Glacier National Park with all the rules and guidelines for the park along with info on tours, accommodations and what to do and see—the website of its time. One of the headings, right after 'Flora and Fauna' was actually one that said 'Ideal Place to See American Indians'!

Shirl had seen it—on the earmarked, highlighted copy Earl had put in Ravenwolf's mail slot.

When The Great Northern Railroad financed the lodges and chalets in the new Park, to attract high-end customers to their northern cross-country rail route, a major promotional draw in the early 1900s was the way passengers were greeted when they stepped off the train at East Glacier.

Across the great lawns that stretched between the station and the lodge, the walkway was lined not only with flower beds, but the local native Blackfeet tribe, billed as the Great Plains Warriors and Hunters of the Buffalo, waiting to greet them in full ceremonial dress.

A unique Wild West welcome, the native people were on display for their exotic clothing and color, their songs and drums, feathered headdresses, beadwork, tipis, and dances. It was an unforgettable production.

Fortunately, over the years, a healthier, more respectful and mutually beneficial relationship developed between Glacier Park and the Blackfeet. Having been on the land long before it became a park, they had retained unique rights within the park, and retained the reservation lands that bordered it on the east, though some issues were still unresolved.

The Blackfeet now ran many of the concessions for the park, such as shuttles, boat trips, and jammer tours that included educating visitors, instead of being displayed for them. The lodges had a popular "America Speaks" storytelling program by the Blackfeet that also enriched the relationship and deepened knowledge of the land and its early people.

Six miles past where Lake McDonald quit shouldering the Going to the Sun road, Dana pulled into the Avalanche Creek Campground to park and find the trailhead.

They had wanted to travel the historic road from west to east this first time, on the way to their lodgings on the eastern slope of the divide. They hoped to get a sense of the park, its highlights, and hit a few spots that afternoon, before crossing to their lodge on this shortened day of their arrival. Then they could plan their days with their guidebooks and maps, and the ideas and materials they gathered as they passed through.

They thought about skipping the popular Trail of the Cedars nature hike. As women from Washington State who'd seen the Olympic Rain Forests, they didn't expect to see more impressive cedars. But Garrett had strongly advised Dana that they at least stop and check it out their first day, pointing out that the short seven-tenths mile loop would be welcomed after all their time in the car getting to, and across the park, and saying he knew Dana would want to see at least part of Avalanche Creek, even if they didn't continue on the longer hike to Avalanche Lake that day.

And he was right. Dana did so miss the sights and smells of her former home. Besides the red cedar and hemlock forests were important as one of the distinct habitats found in Glacier.

Jenny groaned as she tried to pull herself from the car. She'd become so stiff after the long plane ride and drive, she could barely straighten up. They hadn't stopped long enough at Lake McDonald to get loosened up. "I'm not sure ... "

"It's an easy, nature trail. The first part Is only a short loop. Trust me," Dana encouraged watching Jenny try to unbend. "It will be good to stretch your legs, you'll see."

"If it's so very short and easy why are you taking a backpack and all that water?" Jenny asked suspiciously, twisting from side to side to get some blood flowing.

"Because once you stretch out you might want to continue on up to Avalanche Lake, like we discussed."

"We did? And did we discuss how far Avalanche Lake is?" Jenny knew they had, but the idea of hiking, and the actual doing it, were two things in major conflict right now while she tried to stomp more feeling back in her feet.

"The Trail of Cedars loop is handicap accessible, you'll fit right in," Dana teased, knowing once she got Jen going, she'd enjoy herself.

"Did you tell me how far it was to the lake yet?"

"No. "

"Okay," Jenny sighed, "I'm in for the easy loop, no promises on the rest."

She followed Dana stiffly to the trailhead and onto the boardwalk and stepped into the forest.

This small stand of forest had miraculously managed to avoid the patchwork of forest fires that had greedily eaten their way through the park over the years. This stand had survived for centuries, dating to the early 1500s, with some of the stately old-growth giants at least five hundred years old. One couldn't help but pause and wonder at all that had changed over that expanse of time while these wise old trees stood aside and watched quietly.

Jen felt like she was home. She sucked in a deep breath of rich, damp earth, scents of moss and cedar so familiar and soothing. The multi-story layering of cedars, hemlock and black cottonwood created a dim, cool retreat where light seeped in to dance yellow freckles on a tree stump or spotlight a lacy fern. This was just like the forest in the Pacific Northwest, and it immediately replaced her travel weary spirits with a budding sense of fun and adventure.

"Just like home," she spoke softly, sharing a smile with Dana.

"I miss those woods." Dana replied with equal quiet reverence. "Did I tell you that when I was in the hospital I sent that sweet little German girl, Gretchen, a postcard of the huge trees in the Olympic National Park? I invited her to come so I could take her there someday."

"Do you think her parents will let her come, she's still pretty young?" Jenny tried to remember how old the child that Dana had saved from the buffalo at Yellowstone would be now. Nine or ten, maybe?

Jenny started moving through the forest, letting Dana set the pace.

"You know, I wouldn't mind getting back over there myself," she admitted. "I don't know why I don't get out in the woods more, when they're all around me."

"Because you don't have me to goad you to do things you like," Dana paused just a moment before adding, "Like hiking the measly little three miles to Avalanche Lake."

"Three miles! Roundtrip?"

"Well, no-o-o, but the hike only has about a four or five hundred foot elevation rise, so that's a pretty easy grade. Then you get to come down the other three."

"I don't know ... "

"But that's to the head of Avalanche Lake." Dana said quickly. "The foot of the lake is closer, only about two miles, and you can look up to see an old glacial cirque above the lake, Garrett said. Higher above that is where one of the remaining great glaciers feeds the avalanche chutes the lake is named for. Did I mention I read an article that said they now are afraid all the glaciers are melting away?"

Jen smiled behind Dana's back. She had seen the news and had known that Dana would find a way to use it as a prod on this trip. "You are such a manipulating goad, Dana."

"Goat?"

"Stubborn as, but I did say G-O-A-D. "

"Well, that's okay, I'm good at that." Dana gave her friend a wicked grin. "And did I happen to mention that Garrett's ranger friend is the one that said not to miss this trail? He spends a lot of time here." Her green eyes sparkled with amusement as Jen's blue ones widened then narrowed with a scowl.

"Change that. Manipulating goat is what I said!" Jen muttered, then sighed and surrendered. "Okay, I'll try the two miles to the foot of the lake, which was probably your plan all along. But be prepared to carry me back." Jenny threatened.

"The trail follows Avalanche Creek up so maybe I'll just tie a rope to your waist and float you back down."

"I am so-o-o glad you are my best friend because I can't even imagine what you do to enemies."

"Hey, I've just missed you so much, Jen, I could hardly wait to torture you again. "

"No doubt." Jenny grumbled, and couldn't help laughing.

No doubt about it, Shirl's thoughts were still on her favorite ranger, as she busily sorted through the emails and memos on her computer. It didn't hurt to have a modern native hunk like Rave showing off the uniform for the park service. No one wore it better. She was proud of him. Shirley, and many other of the local park staff were of Blackfeet, or other, native heritage

Still, there were those old-timers around from other parts of the country that still fumed and resented when anyone else was allowed a job in their former all white, all male, club. But only a little longer, Shirl breathed a prayer, with an impatient sigh.

"Is he gone yet, Shirl?" The stage whisper brought a guilty flush to her wrinkled, but soft cheeks. "Sure," she turned to where he stood in the shadow of the hallway. "Come on out...Geronimo," she added with a chuckle.

"That horse's ass," he said, much less forcefully than she would have. "I don't know why he does that. I don't look anything like Geronimo. I'm taller, my face is narrower and longer," putting a palm against that lean cheek, he asked eagerly, "Speaking of longer, how much longer do we have to suffer him?"

"Just one more long, miserable, month until he retires," she sighed.

They rolled their eyes in unison, expressing a 'that long, huh?'.

"So," Shirl couldn't resist teasing, "how many hot babes did you let burn their boobies for you today?"

"Not funny, Shirl. "

"It is to me."

"That happened centuries ago! Am I ever going to live that down? It wasn't even my fault, which I admit I have plenty of, but it really… Well, I guess I did earn my own bad rep, even if that one isn't on me. But, you! With that sense of humor, you are one warped woman. Did I ever tell you that?"

"Yesterday. The day before. The day before that."

"Okay, enough. Besides, I am a reformed man now."

"Oh, please! Don't expect me to buy that goat, Rave!

I remember when your father was a young boy he received the name Raven Chases Wolf, though he changed it when he left the rez for awhile, to Ravenwolf for a family name. But I swear, I really think it is time to have another naming ceremony for you. We should name you Wolf Chases Women All the Time."

"Warped woman!" He laughed. "I told you I was reforming. I'm serious, Shirl. I'm getting older now."

"Time to settle down, Rave?" She asked with a snort and a disbelieving arched brow.

"Well, now, whoa there, Shirl. Let's not get hasty. I was just going to point out that I can't run as fast in my older years to catch so many girls. So I'm going to settle for one at a time, now."

Shirl threw her head back in a great happy laugh that filled the whole room with pleasure.

"Now that I will believe when I see it !"

Rave just gave her that dazzling wolf grin, that hadn't aged or lost a bit of its deadly attraction.

"And since you mentioned women—I'm off the schedule tomorrow, so… What? You are shaking you head," he said warily. "I'm not going to like this, am I?."

"Sorry, pal. You were marked off the patrol schedule for a few days, but we had to pull a crew in to do some emergency damage restoration to a trail from that rock fall."

"Who volunteered me as a grunt this time?" he sighed, more resigned, than angry.

"Your most favorite guy," Shirl smiled a little weakly.

"Listen, Shirl, I'll work the laborer crew tomorrow, but don't let anyone touch the other days I've got logged off. I have two lovely ladies that should have arrived today—quit rolling your eyes—that I need to escort around."

He ignored her muttered, "Two? Of course, I'll just bet you do!"

"You remember my buddy Garrett Hearth, don't you? The one you said was a good example I should follow? Well, it's his bride, and her best friend."

"Oh, bring him by. I'd love to see him again and meet his new wife. I always liked him!"

"You loved him! You wanted to trade me for him, don't deny it. Well, he isn't coming. Not yet anyway. He plans to try and get here in a week before they leave, so I need time to..."

"He sent his wife to you alone?" She asked horrified. Then realizing her joke had hit a sensitive nerve for even teasing that his best buddy couldn't trust him, she apologized immediately.

"Sorry, Rave. Really. I know how close you two are, that was out of line. I promise I'll guard your other days off for you like a mother bear."

"Which you are," he teased, all forgiven. "Thanks, Shirl, I appreciate that. You deserve a big kiss, mama bear."

Laughing, she held up a hand in self defense, pretending to fend him off.

"Please, don't! I might have a heart condition that..."

But he swooped in laughing, planting a big smooching kiss on her soft cheek, whispering, "Thanks for keeping me sane, sweet woman."

Just then Ranger Earl strolled back in, hitching up his pants, and futilely tucking his shirt back in.

"Can't you keep your sex life out of the office, Geronimo?" He growled as he passed through.

"Hey, thanks for the compliment, Earl!" Shirley shouted after him, then turned back to Ravenwolf with a pleased smile. "I just don't know why he does that. You look much more like Wolf Robe to me," she said with a flutter of eyelashes.

He cupped a palm across his hard jaw, "Maybe a little longer here in the face, but, yeah, and at least he was Blackfeet," Rave agreed, "which reminds me," he set his hat back on his shining cap of blue-black hair. "I need to be getting up to Piegan Pass."

Pausing at the door as he left, he raised his voice to broadcast level for Earl's benefit, and called out fervently.

40

"Goodbye, my little passion flower! Until later, sweet, soft, sensuous mistress of my soul and heart."

He left Shirl rolling with that happy laugh of hers following him out the door. She was one great woman and a pal. He never would have survived without clocking Earl, without her.

Even old Shirl was not immune to the man's great looks and charm, or experiencing a tingle from those hot, succulent lips. Reaching up to pat the spot where his gift had landed, she regretted she couldn't cut out the spot he kissed and sell it on Ebay.

She would retire a very wealthy woman if that were the case!

Ravenwolf was not certain if he was relieved or a little upset. He was unhappy to have to call and delay and upset *his* buddy's plans, but wouldn't mind another day to prepare himself for *her* friend.

He put his sunglasses on to shield his eyes from the sun; but they didn't do anything to protect him from the memory pictured in his mind. Never before had a simple stolen kiss scared him right out a door.

It was probably just something he'd eaten.

chapter two

"HEY, WHERE IS YOUR camera, Dana? I thought you were going to take pictures to email to your little German friend."

"I do! I want Gretchen to see all the sites in Glacier. Especially the old growth forest. I guess yours is also back at the car?"

Backtracking the short distance they had gone to the parking lot, they decided to start on the other side of the loop this time. They noticed the section they'd been in had been cleared of some of its undergrowth, from old campsites or picnic areas.

They followed the signposts to the other trailhead for the Trail of Cedars and were immediately rewarded. Here there were no trails but a wooden boardwalk suspended above the boggy ground. It kept tourists on the path and protected the natural forest floor and native plants. Except for the boardwalk and viewing platforms, it had more of the feel of a five hundred year old woodland.

Ferns and mosses were abundant, sloppily intermixed with uprooted and ancient trees that had finally surrendered and fallen to the ground to become rich habitat. These decayed and rotting old trees were known as nurse logs as they provided nutrients and a platform for algae, mosses, mushrooms, and seedlings—a fertile nursery for the next generations growing up in the forest. As the older giants fell, they also opened up the canopy to light and air to aid the youngsters in their growth spurts. Soaring grandparents were intermixed with the varied height and sizes of all their generations of descendants.

As similar as it was to the Pacific coastal old growth forests, everything was on a smaller scale and lacked the rich, fecund intensity and density of vegetation of a temperate climate rainforest. But they relished the perfume of moss and cedar, the towering trees, thick of trunk and impressive to anyone unfamiliar with giant record trees of thirteen to twenty feet in diameter that lived in the Olympic Rainforest National Park—but each park they saw had its own unique personality.

Jen couldn't contain her pride in her home state when she heard some tourists from the mid-west exclaim how dazzled they were by the size of the biggest red cedar they had ever seen!

"Cedars can grow larger than any other tree except the giant sequoias," Jenny smiled and volunteered to the tourists. "They have that unusual bark that reminds me of a pin-striped suit that is peeling. The coastal natives used the bark for clothing and baskets, and hats, and their canoes were hollowed from those broad trunks. But most of all, don't you just love that smell?"

The tourists, delighted with their pretty and friendly blue-eyed tour guide, sucked in deep breaths and agreed heartily.

"We have some two and three times that big in my state, Washington." Jen continued, proudly. "You should come on over and see them sometime. The big ones are in our national parks, but these are like the little ones we have in local parks and playgrounds in the western part of the state," she finished, getting a little too carried away with her enthusiasm.

After saying goodbye to the friendly couple, she turned to see the wry smile and the raised eyebrows on Dana's amused face.

"Well," Jenny smiled a little sheepishly, "some playgrounds. I didn't say every playground. I even had a cedar seedling planted in my front yard last fall after you left, so I can see it from my kitchen window. It's only six feet tall now but someday ..."

"Cool. Someday it will be fabulous, Jen."

A way further along the boardwalk they came to a strange stone wall outcrop that lined one side of the area, covered in moss, and weeping water constantly, almost like an elaborate water wall fountain in a garden, but this one was a natural feature. The interpretive trail sign indicated that water seeped from the rock's fissures even in the dead of winter, creating icy spikes. Dana positioned Jen so she could get a few photos of her with the forest and weeping rock behind.

"We should rechristen this 'Jenny's Rock'," Dana said over her shoulder as she moved aside for Jen to take her photos.

It took a few more moments before Jen caught on—Weeping Rock—Jenny's Rock.

"You are so dead, Dana! I do not weep all the time."

Then she laughed.

God, she had missed Dana. Even her sick jokes. Especially her jokes. They hadn't had a chance to tease each other like siblings in so long. Thank goodness her pal had made it through her injuries and surgeries so Jenny could get back to insulting her, all in fun, of course.

Though, so far, Dana was scoring all the points! But she looked so strong and healthy on the trail ahead, Jenny sighed happily anyway. She noted that Dana didn't swing her left shoulder as freely yet, but at least that annoying sling was finally gone, and that was so reassuring and truly fantastic! Of course, Dana's athletic legs were as sleekly muscled as ever, so Jen foresaw a lot of huffing and groaning to keep up with her in the days ahead.

The boardwalk zigged and zagged around the five foot diameter cedar trunks, and then a nurse log suckling the toddlers of a future forest. Occasional decks with bench seats jutted off, to allow restful appreciation, or enable room for a special photo of the tall, stately trees, the creek rushing behind, and maybe a few folks you were experiencing this with in the foreground. Though people were really too short to fit in if you wanted a good picture up the branches toward somewhere in the sky where the tree ended. But getting someone in the shot helped give some scale and perspective, for the bragging rights on those precious, all important vacation photos taken in this novel place and time.

Taking another detour on the boardwalk, Jen found another great photo opportunity, and her chance to score a point teasing Dana. A massive tree had given up its grip on the earth, falling over and sending its thickly tangled and twisted roots up in the air forming an almost perfectly round, and solidly textured wall higher than a man was tall.

"Dana, stand in front of this root wall. This will be a great picture." Once she had her friend positioned, she raised her camera saying, "Of course this is what should really be named for me. They call it the 'cookie tree root'. Smile big now for the camera, say…. 'Dana can't cook to save her life!'" Jenny snapped her shot just as Dana grimaced.

"Okay, Jen! You got me that time. Point to you," Dana grinned.

"Ah, but I got mine on film! So I score a point every time we look at it." Jen crowed. Then, suddenly, Jen's lips tightened, trembled, her eyes flooded with moisture. She turned quickly before Dana could see, heading blindly up the boardwalk, taking deep breaths until she could regain control of herself.

Jen had had a sudden memory of sitting in a hospital, unsure whether Dana would survive, remembering a photo she had taken of Dana that morning in Yellowstone before the tragedy, and fearing it might be the last picture she ever had of her best friend. She sucked in another breath, trying to swallow the aching lump in her throat.

Now she had a new picture to put beside that one in her album—a new vacation shared together—and she was so damn thankful her friend was here so she could give her a bad time.

But, of course, she couldn't be caught weeping, or she would never hear the end of it from Dana. Thank God.

Hearing the sound of rushing water ahead, Jen noticed the glimmer of water beneath much of the creek side vegetation where overflow waters formed quiet ponds out of the swifter currents. By the time they reached a bridge that crossed in front of the waterfall spilling out of Avalanche Gorge, the sound of rushing water had become a roar.

On the bridge, looking up into the torrent, it was clear this was not a simple waterfall but a narrow, clogged set of upward climbing chutes that the water was smashing through with raw violence and an incredible fury of sound. The sheer energy of it was exhilarating—and a little terrifying—with the level of barely leashed power slamming endlessly through the gaps.

Jenny watched funny little birds playing around the channeled water, then gasped when they seemed to fly right into the torrent. Feeling sick like she did when a bird flew into a glass window, she bit her lip, afraid she'd see nothing but a bundle of limp feathers flushed down stream. To her relief and amazement, the birds popped right back out and dove in again.

"Did you see that?" she gasped. "Dana, did you see those birds?" Jen shouted over the water and pointed them out to Dana

"Water ouzels." Dana hollered. "Those little dipper birds are pretty cute and crazy, aren't they?" She turned back to her study of some rock formations beneath the bridge, pointing down, leaning closer to Jenny's shoulder to speak. "What do suppose those greenish black rocks are down there? They aren't grainy enough for granite. Do they look like mudstones to you?"

Jen leaned forward, frowned, tried to give the rocks her most serious study. She leaned back and eyeballed them some more, her lower lip pushed forward thoughtfully.

"You know, Dana, I think those look exactly like ... Well, like ah ... Like wet greenish black rocks." she finally admitted.

Fortunately Dana couldn't hear her over the roar of water.

Finally surrendering the chaotic thrill of standing on the bridge in the face of the outpouring to the other tourists waiting to cross the bridge and see up into the gorge, they moved on. Dana scanned an interpretative sign by the trail, and when they got far enough away to hear each other, told Jen that it said that the gorge had been formed by ice age glacial melt water chopping down through the bedrock, and that the water action was still reshaping the stream's channel."

"Huh," Jen said, making Dana think she was boring Jen again, when her friend surprised her by commenting.

"Pretty spooky. Look how hard that water was smashing down today even, and to think it does that 24/7 for every day, every year? Whoa!" Jen shuddered. "And it's so loud! I can't even begin to get my head around what it must of looked like, and how it sounded to have ice sheets trying to wash out there. Trying to squeeze through that narrow gap?"

Dana blinked a few times at her friend.

"Yeah, pretty damn amazing," she murmured as she took the lead on the path, seeming unsure if she was talking about the gorge, or its affect on her pal.

"Let's go up here, so we can look down on it. See it again."

Turning to her left, Dana led a still thoughtful Jenny along a split rail fence that guided them up a bark and log terraced slope that climbed steeply, challenging calf muscles. Switchbacks brought them back above and along the side of Avalanche Creek, on the rim of the gorge.

Above the gorge they could see that the water crashed down one level after another, like a stair step waterslide—only deadly. The sound of the waters' deep power was a steady undertone roar, without any gentle sounds of splashing, turned on full blast in a steady gushing white-water torrent. The water ricocheted off staggered ever narrowing rock walls, squeezing it into a deadly force that scoured rock as smooth as polished satin in the destructive channel.

Even Jenny thought the wet polished rock walls were stunningly beautiful, not just for the power that cut and polished them, but in their unique shape and color.

They were as sleek and smooth as the peeled red wood of a madrona tree, only a darker, richer red tint, mixed with purple where wet, to a dark mahogany. The path the creek had carved deep into the rock as it swirled and smashed escaping downslope had sculpted shapes that reminded her of modern furniture where a big waveform replaced the normal angular shapes. But while it

46

shaped rock smooth, there was nothing gentle in its tumult. Anything softer than rock was peeled, stripped, and slammed into shreds, like the logs caught in a jam in the middle—limbless, fleshless skeletons—as if the churning waters were piranhas.

Moss, ferns, delicate foot tall seedlings of red cedar and western hemlock clung desperately to the rim of the narrow gorge, seeking the moisture of the misty spume, daring to lean out into the open space for light and air, in a bid for survival.

It was beautiful, deafening, powerful raw nature, with no warnings or guardrails to protect the unwary.

But, thinking of raw nature, there had been one warning Jen had seen coming up the steep hill. A sign:

EXTREME WARNING GRIZZLY HABITAT

Dana," she turned to find her bent down tracing her fingers over a flat red rock in the path. "When does ... What are you doing?"

"This is the weirdest thing. See how these tan lines mark this rock?"

"Probably dirt." Jen answered impatiently. "So when does this trail loop back?"

"No it's not dirt, it's part of the rock. You know what this looks like? Oh, my gosh. It looks like mud cracked red clay that petrified!"

"Right. Hmm. It does, actually. Cool. Anyway, how much further on the loop?"

"Oh. Back at the bridge." Dana tried for nonchalance. "We're on the other trail now."

"We already passed it?" Jenny demanded, planting her feet in the middle of the trail, hands braced on her hips, elbows out and armed.

Dana knew that danger signal well and tried a diversion. "Well you seemed so intrigued by the gorge, and having so much fun watching those cute little dipper birds, that I didn't want to drag you away just because ... "

"Yeah, right!" Jenny was enjoying herself, but she wasn't about to admit it. Now she thought about it, she should have realized herself they were no longer on the handicap accessible loop when they had hiked up around that steep slope. She had been distracted by the bear warning sign. Who wouldn't be?

"Did you see that grizzly habitat sign?" Jen demanded.

"Relax." Dana reassured. "What you should worry about is that most of the fatalities in Glacier Park are actually water-related. I read it in a book. Slipping on wet or crumbling rocks near water is responsible for a lot of drownings. So just watch your step and don't fall in. You'll either freeze or get smashed to bits."

Great! Now that was in the easier-said-than-done category on this part of the trail. Especially if a grizzly charged you suddenly from the trees. You wouldn't even be able to hear them coming.

Big horizontal slabs of rock, lurched up a toe catching few inches on the trail along the steep, thundering gorge, with big weathered trees clinging to the top of them, thick roots tangling every direction curling around and between the rock slabs seeking any tiny bit of dirt they could find.

Dana stepped over the snarled roots commenting that they reminded her of the veins on muscled arms, all popped up and straining to clutch at anything to hold the trees on the rim in a death grip.

"How poetic!" Jen snorted. "They look like snakes writhing all over the place to me." Her fears shortening her temper.

Jenny's scowl almost made Dana laugh, but she bit it back, knowing better.

Jen didn't look like much of a threat in her petite size coordinated L. L. Bean hiking outfit. Light cocoa khaki walking shorts matched a pocketed vest and hat. Even her socks were a color coordinated cocoa with a top stripe in the bright geranium tint of her t-shirt, its rich coral-red only emphasized the stormy cobalt eyes above.

Her frowning china doll face was framed by rich dark brunette curls that were peeking out beneath her cap to see what all the trouble was. She looked more like a cute dressed up kid.

But an angry one at the moment, Dana noted.

For all her small size, the girl had a temper that could probably uproot some of these ancient trees. Fortunately, Dana knew Jen probably wasn't really furious this time, just annoyed and taking the chance to get even with Dana for her teasing. But her friend knew she could get the much taller Dana to shake in her boots when her temper was up, so Jen used it to advantage. Glancing off to the side, Dana muttered just loud enough to be sure she could be heard by the little tyrant.

"Boy, I bet Rave isn't going to be very happy when he hears how you were playing park ranger and trying to ship those tourists off to a different park in Washington to look at trees."

Jenny moved a threatening step closer, but kept enough distance between herself and her half-foot taller friend so she didn't have to cant her neck back to glare at her. It totally ruined the effect.

"You're trying to blackmail me now?" She stamped her foot for emphasis, then winced and recognized she needed to save her feet for when she gave in. "You would blackmail your best friend that you haven't seen in months," Jenny's voice rose dramatically, "just to hike further up this trail?"

"Absolutely!" Dana laughed, enjoying the show.

"Fine!" Jen snapped, turning quickly to hide her grin, taking the lead on the trail.

She was enjoying herself, and they had already climbed up part of the elevation. Her smile faltered when she came to a steep downhill slope into a boggy bottom where feeder rivulets joined the creek. Resigned, she continued down where she could get another close up look at the raging creek. It was more like a narrow raging river here, with tangled log jams and big bands of gravel beds dumped erratically, and probably constantly shifted by the force of the water that was a clear, icy green here, as crisp as the woodsy scented air.

'Rave', Dana had called him, Jen thought, as she tightened her teeth and calves to start back uphill to regain all that precious elevation they had just lost.

Finally, Jen had a useable name for him! Rave. It fit the dark, dangerous mouth watering man that Jenny recalled. She really hoped she didn't blush when she saw him again for the first time. All those hot nights of hotter sex that she had fantasized with him since she had last seen him ... Well, they just better not show up on her betraying face. She suspected the arrogant male was well aware of the effect he had on women and would move in for the kill if he spotted any interest on Jenny's part.

Wouldn't that be fun?

No, she captured that thought and reeled it back in. She was interested—very—she just wanted to make sure he didn't know that. In fact, she wasn't sure if she could hardly wait to see him and pretend that she didn't. Or more worried he wouldn't notice or remember her. And she was equally worried that he would ravish her—or that he wouldn't! What if ...

"HEY! Slow down!" Dana yelled from far behind and below her. "We need to stick together. Are you watching out for bears?" she shouted.

Lost in her memory, Jen hadn't realized her hiking speed had increased with the quickening of her pulse and the heat that rose along her cheeks—and elsewhere.

"Bears," Jenny snorted to herself. Of course not! She'd been worrying about something much more dangerous—wolves. Just then a slight breath of breeze rustled through the dense undergrowth beside the trail and Jenny jumped, feeling the hairs stiffen on the back of her neck.

Trying to act casual as she scanned around and listened to every little shift of rubbing leaves or brush while she waited for Dana, Jenny looked up at the trees along this section of trail. She'd heard that black bears liked to climb trees. She studied the outlines of the trees carefully, looking for dark lumps that might be baby black bear cubs that could have a pissed off mommy hanging out down here with her.

They had climbed higher. Most of the trees were now the soaring Western Hemlocks that could grow a hundred feet and had those distinctive funny looking tops. The tips of the hemlocks were all drooped over to one side, looking like a Christmas tree that had a way too heavy star it couldn't support on top.

Oh yeah, look for bears. No, Jen didn't see any but that didn't mean that they weren't there hiding in the bushes—or trees. Did black bears hang out in grizzly habitat? Or were they scared of them too?

"How much further, do you think?" she shouted down to Dana, just to make noise. Maybe she should whistle. What if that was a bear come-on? She couldn't seem to find any moisture in her mouth to use, or think of any songs to whistle except for Christmas carols looking at all the trees. Did bears believe in Santa? Never mind.

"I could sure use some water," she hollered instead.

When they rejoined, Jen thought she had never tasted sweeter water or more reassuring company, until Dana asked, "Are you hungry? Do you need some food?"

"NO!" Jen yelped. "Don't go waving any smelly food around out here!"

"Oh, I left the food in the car," Dana answered calmly. "I didn't want to attract any unwelcome company. I just wondered if you were too hungry to keep going and wanted to turn back?"

Now she asks! Jen thought, but really wanted to see the lake now that they had come so far. And more pointedly, she knew Dana would want to come back if they didn't finish the hike today.

Jenny knew she didn't have the guts to pass that 'Extreme Warning' sign again.

They continued on through the forest and brush. Jen graciously allowed Dana to lead this time. Dana had much more close-in experience with wild animals. Besides, she was much taller and would be able to spot and scare a bear much easier than Jenny. People—things—had to get to know Jenny before they were scared of her. Jen had two secret weapons: she could rage at them, or drown them in tears. But bears wouldn't know that at first glance.

"We are supposed to make noise as we hike," Dana wisely informed her, "so the bears hear us and we don't startle one."

As they climbed steadily, Dana spoke loudly over her shoulder relating what Garrett had told her about the unique fish of Avalanche Lake.

After the Ice Ages, when the glaciers and melting ice sheets chopped down into bedrock and permanently reshaped and gouged the creek into steep waterfalls, spawning fish were no longer able to get upstream to the lake. It was too steep and dangerous for them to climb.

The Westslope Cutthroat Trout were not only a unique species, first noted in the Lewis & Clark journals, but the ones in Avalanche Lake were even more so now. They had been isolated all alone in Avalanche Lake for over ten to twelve thousand years, without any contact with new fish. This had caused them to turn into their own unique genetic species of Westslope Cutthroat specific to the lake above.

"I know it's not glamorous like endangered polar bears, so it doesn't get much attention, but Garrett said there are several unique species of fish native to Glacier that were almost wiped out when some areas were stocked with non-native fish until they realized they had to stop and protect them in the '70s.

"Anyway, the fish of Avalanche Lake can't be found the same anywhere else in the world. Pretty cool, huh?"

It was pretty cool, Jenny thought, that they had been separated and spared all the ravages, living in isolation.

Jen understood the theory. Unfortunately she had learned the concept of damaging invasions of isolated populations from a much more dreadful situation in history classes.

When Europeans crossed over to the New World, they brought a host of illnesses with them that decimated the isolated native populations in America. The Cortez expedition alone let loose a beast that spread through not only those communities they visited, but across all the vast trading networks. Many fur trapper journals noted coming into unexplored wilderness territories and seeing Indians already carrying the scars of smallpox, and passing villages where everyone had died of some disease. As more trappers and settlers invaded, diseases ran rampant again and again. Some estimates said a third of the native population was killed. Others estimated it could have been half or more. Any amount was a horror, Jenny thought.

She thought of Rave's native heritage and how he was a survivor of the ravages that had been brought to his people. She wondered if she dared ask him about that? Or would that be an insult from someone with her European ancestors? Though her Scots ancestors had also suffered invasions, plagues, and starvation. She shook her depressing thoughts off, there was no way to undo any of the past, only to learn from it. And to appreciate each day, and this was surely one of the most beautiful, she thought becoming aware again of her surroundings. There was nothing like a good bear threat to make you really enjoy being alive on such a day!

The creek finally shepherded the girls to its source, and the vista opened up at the foot of Avalanche Lake. A vast semi-circle of mountain cliffs faced them with the lake at center stage.

"Oh, Dana, this is gorgeous!" Jenny breathed.

"It sure is." Dana stepped away from the trailhead and found a spot to lay out a plastic sheet so they could sit cross-legged and enjoy the view.

The mountains on three sides of the lake doubled their impressive looks in its shimmering blued-green mirror. After consulting her map Dana pointed out the cliffs of a pair of mountains that rose to over eighty-five hundred feet on either side, channeling the lake between them in a valley that ran southeast before them like a straight finger pointing toward its head.

To their right was Mount Brown, to their left was Bearhat Mountain that hid a high lake behind it near Logan Pass. Between Logan Pass and Gunsight Pass, to the south, ran the Crown of the Continent Divide that backed the lake and the high platform where a once massive glacier hid.

They were unable to see the remaining Sperry Glacier crouching high above the head of the lake, but its evidence was everywhere. The carved lakebed ended in a headwall of its past glacial cirque, completing the center of the cliffs that framed this glacial valley. The headwall showed clear signs the Sperry Glacier lurked above with the scars of its drainage trailing down the cliff face in long weeping tears. Chutes, denuded of trees torn away with each avalanche, created moist crevasses open to sunlight with their own lush vegetation starting in early spring.

Jen settled and gazed at the serene scene. There were no houses to clutter the lovely lakeshore. No roads or colorful cars to glint brassily in the sun. Just this dazzling view looking as beautiful as the day the lake had been born, whether there was anyone watching then to appreciate it or not. She felt the magic of the natural scenery start to settle into her soul.

She was here, with Dana, and they were going to have so much fun seeing and sharing all this together. Sighing, she leaned back on her hands, thinking, I'm really here at Glacier at last! The hike and the warm sun relaxed her muscles, while the joy and beauty of what lay before her had loosened all the knots and worries in her mind. She closed her eyes a minute, so calm she thought she might even doze a bit, Dana's voice a muffled sound in the background.

"What did you say?" Jenny yawned.

"Look at the bear." Dana repeated.

Jenny rocketed halfway to the sky, before landing and turning to Dana and realizing she was looking through a pair of binoculars and pointing at the head of the lake, a mile away. She put a hand over her heart to hold it in her chest while it recovered from its massive dose of adrenaline after being lazily limp just moments before.

"Here, take a look," Dana passed up the glasses, "you can see a great big grizzly bear in that middle chute about half-way up. Even the high-country bears come down in the early spring and summer and eat their way up the juicy roots and tender shoots of the avalanche chutes as they ripen uphill in tune with the elevation, following the snowline up."

Jenny took the glasses, her hands still shaking, eager to see her first grizzly out of a zoo, that is ... Without having to get up close and ... tasty.

"Okay, so where is that glacier?" Jen asked after the bear moved out of sight, still safely up in the chute.

"Sperry? Well, it's receded a lot over the years, but I'm not sure you could ever see it from here recently, just the amazing results from when this valley was plowed." Lowering her binoculars, Dana turned to her eagerly, "We could go see it. I really want to. It's shrinking!"

Jenny eyed her warily. "I sense a catch."

"It's just up there, above those cliffs at the head of the lake, against the side of the divide. "

Jenny's eyes traveled slowly up and up in the direction Dana was pointing, the path the grizzly had taken, rolling her eyes dramatically down to fix them on Dana.

"It's only about another three thousand or so feet up," Dana teased, "but you're right, there is a catch. You can't get there from here."

"Well, thank goodness for that!"

Jenny pulled off a shoe and sock, rubbing her foot while Dana described how they could hike down, drive back down the road a ways, then spend most of a day hiking back up to one of the only two remaining backcountry chalets to spend the night. The next morning they would need to hike further to reach the glacier field.

"Unlike Granite Chalet, Sperry Chalet has been renovated inside and has all the amenities that you could want, Jen," Dana continued when she got no response. "I saw a picture of it in a book, it's really rustic, but charming, and they serve meals ... "

"Or, how about this?" Dana changed tactics, "they have these great trail rides where they take you to the Chalet on horseback. Maybe we should do that?"

Jen turned to her, eyes wide and horrified. "But Dana, I forgot to pack my cowboy boots or hat!"

"Oh, well, yes." Dana tried not to laugh. She suspected if Jen had the items they were purely for fashion, and useless for a real trail ride. "That's a big problem I know, but...," she stopped as her friend held up her hand.

"Wait. Just hold it right there, Dana. I have an even better idea. A really great idea. Why don't you and Garrett go up there and spend a honeymoon-type night at the Chalet when he gets here? You can take lots of pictures of the glacier and bring them back down to show me. I'd be happy to find something else to entertain me for a few days."

"Or someone!" Dana leered, ducking to miss the sock that was launched at her. "Hey, better get that back on. We better beat feet if we don't want to be here all night."

They made good time down the trail until they reached the area where they had to climb up as much as down, and Jen stumbled to a halt exhausted.

"Just point me to the escalator," she panted, stopping for a long drink from her almost empty water bottle.

"Come on Jen, this hike was listed under 'Easy'. It's not much further. And then you can just sit and ride and sightsee until we get to the hotel." She saw an excited alertness come to Jen's eyes, and figured she must be thinking of a long hot bath. Then Dana noted the direction of Jen's glance. A ranger with glossy dark hair stood among the trees ahead, with his back to them, chatting with some tourists.

"Not him, Jen. Too short." Dana commented wryly.

"I know," Jenny huffed, before realizing it was too late to act uninterested and pretend she didn't know who, whom, or what, Dana was referring to.

"So, have you heard from Dana yet?"

"Yeah. The girls got there today. Dana just called. Sounds like they think they've arrived in heaven."

"Near enough." Rave felt a wave of warmth at the words. Pride. No matter where he was assigned, he always thought of Glacier as his—not just his park—but his. Home.

Shifting his phone to the other ear, he emptied his backpack out, automatically logging and checking his gear as he repacked, adding emergency rations and water to depleted stores. Positioning a light rain poncho on top of the pack, it was ready for his hike and anything he might encounter, expected or not. His smile thinned as he sat for a moment.

"Listen, I'm afraid I have a scheduling problem, Garrett. Sorry, buddy." Scrapping a hand through thick dark hair, he silently cursed Ranger Earl. "They snagged me tomorrow to do an emergency job crew as laborer for a washed out trail."

Garrett just laughed. "You never should have put our days of wild youth on road crews down on your resume, pal."

"Yeah, well I can't seem to get a break or reform my reputation from those days. That's for sure. I'm still a hard labor grunt the park calls on. But I'm getting older, more aches and pains, and I've reformed my wild ways."

"Since when?" Garrett snorted.

"Since your wife is coming to town," Rave taunted. "I want to focus all my considerable talents on her, of course. Nothing like a lovely green-eyed redhead to turn a guy into a one-woman man."

"Sure worked for me," Garrett agreed. "You try it and I'm afraid I'll have to hunt you down."

Rave grinned, unconcerned. "Well, if that's the way you feel, 'ole buddy, I guess I'll have to find myself a cute little blue-eyed brunette to turn my talents on instead."

"Just watch yourself. You supposed to guide the girls away from the wild animal encounters in the park, not be one of them."

"Well I can't claim to be a perfect gentleman, but I can be tame," Rave teased. "Anyway, I'll try to keep your wife from tangling with any bears or mountain lions."

"Good. Don't forget to protect Jen from the wolf."

"Wolves?" Rave laughed.

"Wolf, Ravenwolf. You hear me, buddy? Go easy. And don't worry about the girls tomorrow. They're so glad to see each other again they won't miss you."

Rave kept his own disappointment at the delay to himself, saying, "Just tell Dana to leave me a voicemail on where they will be so I can catch up with them. Talk at you later. Bye, buddy."

chapter three

""'THE GOING TO THE SUN ROAD, is a national treasure as an historic and engineering landmark. Completed in 1932 with the tools and skills of a past century, the road was literally carved into the side of the near vertical cliffs in places, by skilled stone masons with tools and supplies brought up by mule train, in order to scale the Continental Divide without destroying the natural beauty of the environment. The European methods of the time would have chopped the glacier carved landscape into a dozen or more switchbacks, whereas the National Park Service's determination to protect the wilderness required a patience of time and budget—sixteen long hard years to complete the fifty mile road—but they forever preserved the beauty of the natural sculpted works of the last ice age.'"

Jen paused to take a sip of the ice cold soda she'd grabbed when they got back on the road. Before continuing to read aloud from the brochure as Dana drove. she leaned forward first so she could look up at the rim of bare mountain cliffs they were approaching up the deeply forested McDonald Valley. Just ahead the forest opened some and she saw cars slowing for a sharp right turn to begin crawling up one of those cliffs. The impact of the words she had just read caught in her throat. She wasn't sure she was ready to hang off a cliff like a mountain goat!

Good thing Dana was driving, she thought, until she realized she would be on the side hanging over the plunge. She lunged over the back of her seat to grab her camera and some more water for her suddenly dry throat, while they were still on solid ground, and she didn't need to worry about rocking the car.

Jen freely admitted she was a bit of a wuss about really steep heights.

So what was she doing at the Crown of the Continent, of all places?

Turning and settling back into her seat, debating a moment before locking herself back into her seat belt, she looked over and saw the sparkle of excitement that lit Dana's eyes and smile as they slowly took a sharp hairpin turn up to the right. For a moment only the sky filled the windshield, then a ragged rock face, then they were climbing up the side of the cliff, with the whole McDonald Valley they had just passed through falling away on their right. Oh yes, this was why they were here. There was nothing that nourished her buddy like rocks and cliffs.

"This must," Jen cleared her throat, nervously jerking her eyes away from the increasing sheer drop off. "This must be what they call The Loop, the only switchback on the road." She picked up the brochure and started to read out loud again.

"'There is only one switchback on the road, known as The Loop. In 1967 fires burned on the west side of Logan Pass along the entire Garden and Glacier walls. In 2003, Glacier experienced its worst fires since it opened, with fifteen percent of the park burning, most on the west side. The 2003 Roberts Fire burned almost to the shores of Lake McDonald, and the 2003 Trapper fire near The Loop jumped the Going to the Sun road. Notice the patchwork where the recovering vegetation' ... yikes!" Jen stopped suddenly after glancing out, and way, way down. "This is scary. Oh... but stunning! Look down there, it's like an emerald valley . .
.

"No! Not you, Dana! You watch the road! I'll look, until I get too dizzy." Rolling down her window, Jenny started shooting off a panorama of pictures for Dana. The term "patchwork of vegetation" hardly suited the beauty of the U-shaped valley. Moist emeralds, varied greens and yellows of moss and lichen, jade and grass greens of deciduous trees, bushy shrubs, mixed with the dark spruce of recovering conifer stands, darkening into deep forests as they stretched west between snow crusted mountains that seemed shorter the higher they rose. Patches of meadows, flowing in and around the rest, coating the slopes like rich, touchable, textured velvet beneath the stark wall of cliffs that curved around to contain and hide this jewel of a valley from the east. The beauty was so breathtaking Jen almost forgot they were climbing along one of those stark cliff walls, until she pulled the camera away from her eyes for a moment, gasped and pulled her head away from the window, trying to edge as far toward the center of the car as her seat belt would allow.

Jen needn't have worried too much about Dana trying to crane to see the emerald valley and not focusing on driving the narrow two-lane paved road that had only a rugged, picturesque natural stone wall, barely higher than the wheel wells, on the outer rim.

She should worry though about Dana's enchantment with the vertical cliff wall that rose only a lane away from Dana's face on that side of the car. She could see her friend's hands just twitching on the steering wheel, eager to reach out and run themselves over the cliff face like a lover, but there was no space to pull off. Each time the traffic paused for a road crew repairing a stretch of retaining wall, Dana rolled down her window and took a few quick shots of that fascinating rock wall.

Her actions focused Jen's attention. The wall did look close enough that Dana should just be able to reach her arm out the driver's window and touch it, and there was supposed to be a whole car lane in-between. If she had been worried about climbing the side of the cliff, now she fretted more about being underneath it.

Jenny winced when a vehicle suddenly popped up around a curve heading toward them at what seemed a reckless speed, expecting at any moment the top of their van would slam into the rock overhang as they tried to squeeze between them and the cliff, launching them all into space to smash a thousand or more feet down into the valley.

"Do you suppose they have many horrid traffic crashes on this road?" Jen asked faintly.

"From what Rave told Garrett they seem to lose people on this road more from their deliberate acts, individuals flaunting safety precautions, like stepping past the retaining wall to take a picture, than vehicle accidents." Dana responded calmly, casting another admiring glance at the cliff wall.

The dark fine-grained and weathered rock had huge sheets and spalls that had fallen off, showing creamy chunks and swirls of fresh stone underneath. Jenny held her breath as they had to stop and wait under another huge ledge of rock jutting out, seeming to hang just a few feet over the top of the car. Dana, thrilled, leaned out her window taking pictures straight up at it, before she had to continue driving on. Jenny sighed with relief and continued reading the history out loud, interrupted by Dana's excited comments about the rock.

"Did you see that stripe? Jen did you see that funny swirly thing in the rock back there? I wonder what that was?"

"Did you see that steep and deadly drop on my side of the road, Ms. Driver?" Jen responded tartly. "Hey! Look out in front of us!"

Jen realized her nerves were making her a testy, crappy passenger, but she couldn't seem to help herself. Dana probably wanted to gag her, but the cloth might be put to better use as a blindfold. Though Jen knew she would be unable to keep from peeking.

A rude lump of mountain poked out across the road as it curved out of sight in front of them, with a small, dark, arched tunnel carved inside the rock.

"How do they find the damn road?" Jen wondered to herself.

"What's that?" Dana asked, slowing before the tunnel.

"I was just reading in here that this road gets thirty to sixty feet of snow in the winter and hundreds of avalanches that have to be plowed each spring before they can open it all the way across. So, how the hell do they find the road on this cliff, under all that snow to plow it?"

How indeed?

"We will have to ask someone. I know it's only open up here from late June, or early July to about late September to mid-October. I sure have a lot of respect for the crews that plow it open, but I would not want to be one of them," Dana said with emotion as they entered the dark tunnel, with only a tiny arch of light that seemed to open out onto space, instead of land, to guide them out.

"Oh, my ..." They both whispered and gaped in unison at the views framed by the arch as they emerged from the tunnel.

If it had been scary, or stunning, or fascinating, climbing a cliff rising over an emerald glacial valley before, now it was...pure magic.

Dana was at a disadvantage, she had to focus on her driving, while Jenny gasped with delight. The tunnel did nearly open onto air, as the road veered left along the cliff as it began its curve back around a massive cirque.

"No wonder Garrett said we should start on the west side, Jen was saying. "It's like going through the tunnel and coming out in wonderland, in another time and place," She commented with quiet awe. completely forgetting her recent fears..

As the road curved around the cliff, far ahead they saw one of the red and black jammers. The old touring car increasing the sense of dislocation and fascination of another time, though the ancient setting was the jewel. The exquisite beauty and power of the Garden Wall—a charcoal rock fin spearing the heavens— rimmed the magic scene. A dramatic stage, a dazzling experience for all who had crossed the Going to the Sun Road in the last eighty-five years and for those to come. If there had been nothing more to see in the park than just this one sight, Jenny thought, it would be enough for a national treasure all by itself. More than enough!

"There, Dana," Jenny pointed to a small area big enough for a car or two to park near the rim, "quick pull over. You have to see all of this!"

When they pulled over to view the waterfall that looked like a twisted ribbon of lacy silver falling down stair steps through an amphitheater of emerald; the masterpiece lit by the slanting rays of the late afternoon sun, they were dazzled by the sight.

If they could have seen straight through the Garden Wall marking the Continental Divide to the opposite side, they would have glimpsed a dark haired ranger at Piegan Pass facing their way, only miles away, thinking of them.

It was a magical place, but not quite that magical.

He had parked at Siyeh Bend just east of Logan Pass, high above where the Going to the Sun-Road turned and headed steeply down to the Jackson Glacier Overlook. Tossing his backpack and his wide brimmed uniform hat on, Ranger Ravenwolf headed across to the north side of the road to the trailhead that would lead him up to check conditions on the trail up Piegan Pass.

It was four and a half miles to the top of the pass, an easy hike for him despite the sixteen hundred foot elevation gain. Not a heavily traversed trail, as it could get strenuous for hikers coming the other direction out of Many Glacier, it would give him plenty of time for his private thoughts on the way back, while he took care of his job.

Crossing Siyeh Creek, his only company was a mule deer that looked up at him from a meadow, then lowered its head to continue its feast, seeming to brush his intrusion off with a flick of her long ear. He noted she looked fat, healthy, and happy, before climbing out of the meadows into the steeper slopes of a spruce and fir forest. Her calm presence also indicated there probably weren't any predators in the immediate area, though he always stayed on alert. As the trail switched its way back and forth, he watched the ground for washouts or fallen logs that might have impeded the path since his last check. Splitting off to the left as the trail forked after a mile, he paused a moment after another mile and a half to scan the open meadows and glance up the trail to Siyeh Pass, before heading left to continue up around the base of Cataract Mountain to the barren summit of Piegan Pass, named for one of the Blackfeet Nations.

A rain shower was starting so he only lingered there for awhile enjoying the views from seventy-five hundred feet, before starting to backtrack down to his car. Stopping to take a shot with his digital camera to record the current conditions of Piegan Glacier, he stared at it for awhile where it crouched on the eastern side of the Garden Wall, and let his thoughts drift to a particular tourist he hoped to see soon.

The sound of Garrett's subtle warning was still in his ears.

"Go Easy."

It would have felt like a subtle threat only months ago, but now he could accept it as a reminder. No one wanted little Jenny hurt.

But Rave did want her.

And planned to have her.

His rule book had just changed a little since he had first met the feisty brunette at Dana and Garrett's wedding.

He recalled his thoughts that day when he'd caught her eyes consuming him. He'd seen that look many times. Women tended to fall at his feet. It wasn't bragging really, at least not recently, just fact. He knew it and used it to his own satisfaction, like any healthy, lusty young man. And he was never going to get trapped in a life like his parents had. He had wild oats and never lacked for a lady dying to sow them for him. He let them. This one wanted him, he was sure of it, and he would accommodate her with great pleasure. His and hers.

When he fist saw her she was as petite and cute as a little blue-eyed doll, and probably brainless, he had initially thought. He knew now that was not true. She'd had curves that hadn't looked too dainty or fragile. Curves he had wanted to get his hands and mouth all over. That night. And she had known it. He'd seen the blush rising up her bare shoulders and throat as she quickly shifted her gaze to the minister as the bride and groom began to speak their vows.

He had been a little surprised, then amused by her resistance after the service. Playing her little hard-to-get game, no doubt. He didn't mind. Enjoying her feistiness, he found that the more she fussed, the more it aroused him. He liked her spirit, she'd be a handful of fun. Two handfuls.

And he had gained a secret weapon—information.

One of the girls he'd dallied with in the past was at the wedding. Trying to get his attention away from his fixation on Dana's pal, she had scornfully told him she'd heard the little brunette call him 'A Handsome Savage'. She thought he would be offended and turn his attention her way.

But he had thrown back his head and laughed. He loved it. Yep, she wanted him and she thought he was handsome. He wished they would hurry and get all this wedding fuss over so he could tease and tempt her with that knowledge.

Then she had let him have one taste of her lips, and nearly bewitched him with her fresh, sweet taste. It had scared him into backing away. He'd gone right out the door, expecting her to beg him to come back, giving him back the control. But the little tempest had sworn at him and slammed the door in his face.

Hmm. Hadn't expected that. Any of that. Maybe there was a lot more to this woman than showed. And the curiosity had him hooked. But his reaction to her also had worried him a bit. He was an experienced man, he should have forgotten her and moved on long ago. It was probably just an anomaly. His buddy getting married had most likely just shook him and put him a little off balance that night.

Still, he hadn't been able to get her completely out of his mind, and he had tried.

He had even finally given up on all his easy women he was so distracted. But It was time to grow up and slow things down a notch.

And he wanted the one that got away.

He'd just wait, take a little vacation from females, and capture that little brunette when she showed up in Glacier. He would need to figure out her game and play it a bit, but he would satisfy his lust and curiosity before she went home from vacation. That should provide a pleasant diversion and get the woman out of his system.

He had changed his plans back then, realizing she would need his undivided attention when she came that summer. It was all just a game.

His plans for Jenny had changed again earlier that spring. Rave had gone on a backpacking and fishing trip with his old buddy Garrett, just like they had done ever since their days together on summer road crews.

At dusk they had cleaned their catch and settled around an open campfire that Rave had carefully ringed with flat stones. The logs had burned, popped, and crackled down to a slow steady flame, wood smoke drifting in the air, embers hissing softly in the quiet of evening. Fillets of fresh trout sizzled in a cast iron skillet on the edge of the fire, and wrapped corn cobs and potatoes baked nestled in the coals. The soft hiss and simmer of the fire and cooking food, the plop and gurgle of a tin coffeepot starting to percolate, had been the only sounds in the comfortable silence of long standing friendship and shared camping trips.

As the stars began to speckle the sky, the rich scents of frying fish, corn, and coffee cooked out of doors made the mouth water, the well used muscles relax, and the perfection of the day's hiking, fishing, and camaraderie complete. After they had finished eating and cleaning up the pots and plates with water and sand, they settled back on the logs to sip dark coffee, gaze into the hypnotic flames of the campfire, and talk quietly of whatever came to mind.

For Garrett that was his new wife Dana, of course. Somehow the conversation had traveled on to Jenny, their friendship, and the events—the near tragedy—of last summer. It was clear Garrett deeply loved his wife. It was also clear he had thought he had lost her after his first contact with her.

"No one expected her to live," Garrett said, his voice rough, grim, and quiet as he stared, unseeing, into the blue flames licking across the red embers of the dying fire. "I truly believe that if it hadn't been for Jenny, Dana would have died in the hospital, never opening her eyes." He raised his own denim blue eyes, darkened with shadows and emotion to Ravenwolf's, staring seriously into them as he stated, "That little gal willed her to live. I believe it's what kept Dana alive."

Rave didn't recall ever seeing his buddy's easy going eyes ever so serious, except when he said his wedding vows, so he didn't snort in disbelief, though he thought it unlikely.

"Think so?" was all he murmured.

"You don't know what Dana's childhood was like. She was an orphan, always alone, never adopted by her foster families, never feeling wanted. Alone even with people around. Sure she was a child gym star, but that was all about needing to belong somewhere, to be cared about by someone. But fans don't love like family. It was always hollow. Until college, and Jenny.

"Jen snapped her up and made Dana her best friend, then claimed her as her sister. She gave her a bond and a tie that she had searched for all her life. So I know, without a doubt, that Dana couldn't, wouldn't, die and abandon someone who had given her that." Garrett voice trailed off into the quiet of the night, seeming to drift softly into the spaces between the stars.

Sobered, and humbled, Rave thought of his own raw, disconnected childhood. His confusion and lack of concern about who he was or if he even wanted to belong in this hard, angry world. He had been an orphaned soul, even with a living mother and the drunken sot he saw sometimes in the gutters of Missoula and was supposed to call father. Wanting the means to run away from his life, he had joined a road repair crew the summer before high school, and met an open faced and open hearted guy named Garrett. Rave understood what a true friend could mean to a lost soul; how one person could call to everything decent left inside, and change a life, and give that rare gift of hope.

"You know," Garrett finally spoke again, quietly reminiscing from across the campfire's last glow, "that little Jenny stayed by Dana's side in the hospital every minute, day after day, never giving up. Talking to her as if she wasn't in a coma on life support, reminding her all of the things they had done together, talking about all their good times and laughter. She told her she had to wake up because they had so many things planned, and talked about their to do list, all the places they still wanted to vacation together, and everything they needed to share together. Calling her back, holding her to life, demanding she wake from her coma because Jenny needed her. Then she would cry buckets, making herself sick almost, before squaring that determined little chin and starting all over to remind Dana of their past trips and future plans."

Garrett gave a weak chuckle, a wry twist to his mouth as he said, "That was probably what did it. The weeping. Dana would have recognized that was Jen all right! Would have known she was needed. And rushed back from the dead just to pat Jenny's shoulder and hand her box after box of tissues. Ah..."

Garrett paused another few thoughtful moments, cleared his throat, and tossed the last of his coffee on the fire. "Sorry man. Guess I got a little maudlin, there." He sounded embarrassed.

"No, it's good you have such strong feelings, buddy. Dana's a wonderful woman and everyone is glad you have her in your life." Rave stood and laid a hand on Garrett's shoulder as he stepped away from the campfire. "And Jenny, well, she could be your sister, you know? She did for Dana what you did for me, buddy."

And with that Rave had walked away into the dark while emotions and memories poured over him. He wasn't too proud to say more, just unable to, for the boulder that had lodged in his throat.

Garrett understood, calling a soft goodnight and heading for his bedroll. Each had sought the privacy of their own thoughts.

That, Rave recalled, heading back down the pass, was when he had changed his attitude about a very desirable and, as he had learned, special brunette.

The woman in his thoughts, with the long dark hair and cobalt eyes, was straight through the mountain from him, looking his direction—only miles away as the bird flies. A mountain divide blocked their view of each other. And the waterfall she was looking at would run down to the Pacific Ocean, while the ones on his side were trailing to the Gulf of Mexico. So close, but on different sides of the great divide.

Ranger Ravenwolf wondered how to heal their last encounter and bridge the gap when he saw her again. He would try to go easy, because now he wanted to. But he still wanted her. More now than before.

Unaware of the plans being made for her, Jen was enchanted with the west wall of the divide and the landscape that featured the five hundred foot descent of Bird Woman Falls.

A small afternoon rain shower was moving through, but all it did was brighten and enrich the colors. Stark gray rock faces dampened to bring out a myriad of subtle tones from white to tan and charcoal gray tints in cliffs that looked as if they had been scraped with a huge serrated knife, scored with parallel horizontal lines across their faces. Verdant vegetation, with only scattered copses of evergreens, emphasized the deep green bowl at the head of the valley they had just climbed up from, the Going-To-The Sun Road curving around the encircling cliffs.

It was like being in a massive coliseum, a huge green open air amphitheater, half way up the risers, already thousands of feet high. One end of the circle lay open running down toward the entry at the Lake McDonald valley. Almost level with them far across and midway up the cirque at center stage were three massive stone columned arches set into the wall, as if there truly was an ancient coliseum hidden underneath. From the snow sheathed charcoal mountains way above along the upper rim, the tangled web of sparkling silver rivulets of Bird Woman Falls fell down curving, carved staircases of rock to join their cool streams and reappear through the arches to fall into the green walled abyss.

"What's that white thing moving on the ledge over the stream?" Jenny squinted, pointing just where Dana had been focused. "Is that a mountain goat?"

"Over the arch?"

"Yeah."

"That's a white car, Jen."

"That tiny thing?"

"Yeah, that's the other side of this road. Where we are heading. Really gives you shivers at how huge this is, and what tiny little ant specks we are on the side of this cliff doesn't it?"

"I'm trying to savor the view and not think too much about the hanging off a cliff bit, just now," Jen responded.

They both turned behind them to check out the part they were hanging from. High above, the strange thin gray cliff wall continued to curve, looking even more like the partially collapsed and worn wall of some ancient place.

Dana turned back to the water stair stepping down the Garden Wall and pulled open the car door.

"I just have to get a picture of this, it's spectacular!"

Jen tried, but couldn't get the whole picture she wanted framed in just one photo. It was too much. Something she was beginning to realize might just be synonymous with Glacier Park. Everything here was too much, too big, too amazing, too special, each individual part enough to fill the senses alone. A snapshot at a time was the prescription so you didn't overdose on the whole panorama. How many years would she need to return here, to get another dose, learn another corner of all to be seen and experienced in Glacier? She chuckled to herself, thinking it was a tough job, but someone had to do it.

Dana heard her laugh, and sighed, smiling, "I know, isn't it—?"

"Yeah," Jen agreed. "Indescribable."

In Rome men built their 'ancient' amphitheaters of stone.

In Glacier National Park the Ice Ages carved their own immense stone walled amphitheaters from truly ancient rock.

It 753 BC, depending on the legend, the great nation of Rome was first founded under King Romulus. The city and nation state grew, battled the Carthaginians and others, gaining power and land and the Roman Senate, and the lives of Julius Caesar, Anthony and Cleopatra came and passed. After much of the city burnt during Nero's reign, when the Flavian dynasty came to power in AD 69, they decided to begin a program of public works to please the populace. Started under Vespasian, and completed under his son Emperor Titus around AD 80, one of these great and enduring works of man was what is known as the Roman Colosseum—though it was named The Flavian Amphitheater. Four encircling tiers built an open air arena that was large enough for the gladiators to fight, or to stage mock sea battles.

But nature can always upstage man's monuments. In AD 79, Mount Vesuvius exploded burying the south of Naples, with the towns of Herculaneum and Pompeii and their residents. Today tourists flock to Italy to visit both 'ancient' sights.

In roughly 16,000 BC, depending on the latest science, the Ice Ages had completed most of their work in North America and began in fits and starts to recede—the bulk of their carvings of stone amphitheaters complete. In that truly ancient time, the continental ice sheet of the Laurentide had extended south and east through Canada down to just shy of where alpine glaciers flowed off the eastern slopes of the divide of present day Glacier National Park. On the western side of the park, the Cordilleran ice sheet hemmed the western park border where the alpine glaciers flowed down and out of the valleys to join it, creating an ice dam backing up a massive glacial meltwater lake to the south.

Snow and flow, two words most associate with thoughts of glaciers, can be highly misleading. They just sound too soft and fluffy to get much hard work done, distorting the power of what they can create. Even trying to think of a bank of snow plowed aside and left frozen all winter is only a few steps closer to understanding an alpine glacier. Now if that snow was still there after the summer, we are another step closer. It is not how hard it

68

snows in the winter that is the first key, but how much is left to be snowed on again after a cool summer that begins the process.

Because of the cool climate year round during the thousands of years of the ice ages, snow continued to accumulate above the snowline. It froze and then refroze, changing its structure from fluff to grainy, denser snow pellets, continually losing air pockets and gaining density, becoming a recrystallized form more like the snow bank, known as FIRN. More snow and more snow layers were needed to weigh it down until one hundred and sixty-five feet below, FIRN was pressured into forming a solid sheet of interlocked crystals creating true Glacial Ice. A little more weight above and the solid sheet layers would begin to flow forward over each other downhill. In addition to this flow of deep ice over other layers of deep ice, the base of the ice mass would begin to move over the bed of rock beneath. The term is basal slip, but flow or slip, both words are too fragile for what is really happening. The words chew, grind, crowbar, bulldoze, chop, scrape, and scour are more accurate for the resulting two types of glacial erosion known as plucking and abrasion. We are talking demolition derby, not sanding a table, here.

So on the west side of the divide some small dip in the mountainside began to capture snowfall that never completely melted. It seeped into cracks in the rocks, then froze again, expanding, breaking the rock apart, so the next melt water could seep deeper and break more of its bed apart, creating an ever deepening bowl to gather snow and build ice. Even deep beneath a permanent snowfield, the earth's heat was enough to continue this freeze-thaw excavation. With the great time span of the Ice Age climate, a huge hole was pried from the mountainside—a glacial cirque had been started. And as soon as the depth of the snow was a couple hundred feet deep, it was moving downhill, continuing to attack the rock beneath and around it, finding the weak spots and layers, chewing them out, injecting moisture to freeze and pry out chunks (plucking) and boulders that it dragged scraping into more rocks, bulldozing shattered debris, but without the scoop of a curved blade, this bulldozer ground forward and shoved its burden down under its weight at the same time, gouging, grinding, crushing everything in its path (abrasion). And unlike wind or water erosion, ice doesn't drop its heavier debris as its velocity and force changes. It carries the whole grinding, scratching, rocky mess along with it to tear through mountain walls and down valleys. As it passes it chops the weakest spots or layers of softer rock out first, leaving the harder rock to stick out for *awhile, giving cliff faces a linear scored or stair step appearance, depending on the makeup of the underlying rock.*

When the Ice Ages were done carving, shattering, and sculpting, they left behind dramatic steep walled scored cliffs on three sides of huge bowls of open air amphitheaters, with the downhill side open to wide U-shaped valleys, filled with long fingers of lakes. In some places cirques on either side of the divide chewed so deeply they left razor thin fins of mountains.

Far above the McDonald Valley where the road climbed the cliffs around the rim of an ancient cirque, the work was done and overdone. The razor fin of the Garden Wall had been plucked clean through to the cirque on the other side, creating Logan Pass in the Continental Divide. Ancient monumental works, begun a hundred thousand years before Rome was a blemish in time, and completed tens of thousands of years before. In the early AD 1900s, men dangled from cliffs adding a few finishing touches, adding a span of three memorable stone arches to support the road and allow the silver ribbons of water to flow under the arches beneath the Going To The Sun Road into the natural ancient amphitheater below.

While Jen and Dana had been taking pictures of Bird Woman Falls, Jenny had been trying to describe the incredible scene in her own mind so she would never forget it. Over time her pictures would only be flat depictions and she wanted a more vivid memory to lock in her mind. It was the size of it all that was so hard to grasp, the grandeur that had first shocked her senses that she wanted to capture. She just couldn't get over the hundreds of stair steps that climbed so regularly down from above, before falling into the valley. The man-made triple arches the stream wove through, made it even more surreal. They blended so perfectly with the stair steps and landings above that they seemed to all have been made at the same time by some giant god or goddess from above.

That's when it struck Jenny what image she would forever carry in her mind of this place. It did look like some goddess had first stepped to earth to descend this natural stairway. This would be the magical place they would want to arrive, descending the stairway and the valley below and after blessing the western lands, they would place a source of water above, to flow down their staircase in an endless tumbling fountain to please the earth people below.

Yes. Bird Woman Falls was the staircase of a goddess, a native goddess. The most beautiful waterfall she had ever, or ever expected, to see. Rather than plunging with power and huge volumes of crashing water, it seemed to almost tiptoe daintily down the mountain wall, one step after another of fragile rock ledges, picking a path down the grand staircase.

And the staircase back up to the Continental Divide, the Crown of the Continent was now floating in the mysterious mists of the rain showers was a stairway back to the hidden heavens, if she had ever seen one.

Throwing her arms wide, Jenny laughed and told Dana, "This is what I'll think of from now on when someone talks about a stairway to heaven!"

She climbed back in the car reluctantly, it was getting late and dark and they still had a long ways to go to their lodge on the east of the pass.

"I want to come see this every day." Jen murmured.

An exhausted, but contented silence filled the car as it climbed the rest of the way over the divide at Logan Pass. Dusk was settling in, and the cliff walls were highlighted with the dying light from the west. The rain shower dampened and darkened the charcoal cliffs, the slanting rays picked out the strange parallel grooves that scored horizontally across the flat surfaces, like fine ruled writing paper.

These mountains looked so exotic, Jenny thought, lazily gazing out her window.

Her eye was trained to the Cascades. Washington had more conical peaks from chains of stratovolcanoes, many weathered, or doming on the top. Some had flattened tops from blown out erupted peaks and bulky, lumpy flanks, from lava, lahar, and pyroclastic flows. Jen smiled faintly to herself. Her eye had trained itself to the mountain silhouettes of home, but it was her friend that had trained her in the terminology and meaning of those landscapes.

Yet these mountains didn't even look anything like the ranges on either side of Paradise Valley, in Dana's new Montana home; and it was more than the different shapes that was nagging at Jenny. There was something weird about the texture of the rocks.

"Those mountains look really strange, don't you think, Dana?" she murmured.

71

"Strange how?" Dana asked, unable to take her eyes off the road for long, as shadows deepened when they started down the east slope of the continental divide.

"I don't know. Just seem weird somehow." Yawning hugely, Jen asked, "We're heading straight for the lodge now, right?"

Dana suspected her friend dozed off before she even agreed. Fortunately, Dana had her curiosity peeked to keep her alert on the long winding road. Jen was right. There was something very strange about the rock, and she couldn't help but wonder why it looked a little weird. It was an irresistible puzzle she could hardly wait to start solving. Rave hinted at a surprise for her here, but said she had to solve the mystery herself. Her dear husband refused to spoil it.

chapter four

JEN AND DANA WERE STARING at legs.

And not male legs, either!

"Did you see those calves?" Jenny whispered. "How old do you think she is?"

"I don't know, but I hope I have calves like that when I'm her age." Glancing down at her own long, slender, athletic appendages, Dana's forehead puckered into a frown.

" ... or even my age, for that matter!"

"No kidding!" Jen exclaimed with feeling. Noticing her friend's raised eyebrows, added hastily, "I meant mine, me too." She waved a hand at her own shorter, but shapely, version before turning back to study their guide. "Mine are all show, no muscle."

The attractive Interpretive Park Ranger had short, steel-gray hair as crisply styled as her impeccable summer uniform and manner. She had the slender and wiry strength and beauty to go with those steel-plated calves that had them wondering if they'd be able to keep up on the proposed trail hike. Her wide, warm and friendly smile made them relax and expect a fun and pleasurable time, but those calves warned otherwise.

Jenny watched Dana's face for reactions as the ranger told the group about the length and elevation gain to be expected. Dana had been an professional athlete. If she showed signs of concern, Jen knew she'd be toast and would be much better off sitting in the car reading a good book. Only they didn't have the car—or her book.

"Sounds like fun!" Dana grinned as the group started off. "I'm excited! Aren't you?"

"If you say so." Jen fell in behind Dana as they headed out for this game of follow-the-leader. Hoping, if she kept close enough, she could draft behind Dana. It worked for trucks.

It worked for Jenny, also, until the third time she ran into her friend's back when the ranger stopped to 'interpret' something.

"Would you mind walking on your own heels, instead of mine?" Dana complained, getting annoyed. "Better yet, you go in front of me. I can see what the ranger's pointing at over your head."

"You promised no short jokes this trip."

"When have I ever promised you that, Jen, and not lied about it?" Dana laughed down at her petite friend from her comfortable eight inch height advantage. "You know it's my favorite entertainment"

"Don't you think it's getting to be a pretty old joke?" Jen huffed.

Dana placed a finger on pursed lips and gazed up at the sky as if seriously considering the matter.

"Ah. . . No."

Smiling, she patted Jenny on the top of the head just to really annoy her, then pushed her onward.

Jen was already feeling a little grumpy today. Dana had caught her at a weak moment this morning and talked her into spending one night camping out. Jen seemed to think she had said 'maybe'. That isn't what her best buddy chose to hear.

Dana had driven over the Going to the Sun road back to the west side and pulled into a campsite on Lake McDonald, nagged Jen into helping her set up a tent, and then hustled her over to the free shuttle to go back up to Logan Pass to do a few short hikes today along the spine of the Great Divide.

It was clear that Jen was 'maybe' camping out tonight, whether she liked it or not! After exploring the Crown of the Continent, no less!

Why do I let her do this to me? Jen made a show of grumbling under her breath a little more, then sighed and surrendered. She loved Dana. She'd walk through fire for her friend. But she wouldn't ever admit that out loud.

Unless, of course, Dana was really, really, depressed, and needed cheering up.

Jen clomped her new boots along the raised boardwalk that led south from the pass on the Hidden Lake Trail, nearly jumping out of her skin when what looked like a foot long blur of brown shag carpet burst from beneath, suddenly scuttling off to one side.

"Ah," alerted by Jen's smothered shriek, "there you see one of the species indigenous to the sub-alpine," Ranger Legs explained. "A hoary marmot. They like to hang out and sunbath on the rocks.

"And, as I'd like to remind everyone once again, the sub-alpine meadows are a very fragile eco-system. The mosses and wildflowers you see here only have a two-month summer growing season and if crushed, can take years to recover." Adding with a wink and friendly smile to Jen, "So thanks for doing the broad jump in place."

Noting that Jen laughed easily with everyone else, Ranger Legs teased her a little more.

"Generally, if you hear an "eep!" sound like our broad jumper just made, it comes from another alpine species that hides out in rock piles—the charming pika. Pikas look like tiny squirrels without tails, have big ears like a favorite cartoon mouse, but actually are part of the rabbit family. Rather than hibernating like the marmot, pikas cut, cure, and stow their own grasses and hay to feed them beneath the deep winter snow cover. But you are more likely to spot the larger mammals that frequent the area, like the bighorn sheep, with their horns all done up in curls." The ranger calmly returned to her original presentation.

"Between the lush forests and mossy moisture of the west and the wind tormented grassy plains that stretch from the eastern base, Logan Pass sits at over six thousand six hundred feet astride the continental divide with a third climate zone, the sub alpine tundra and its uniquely fragile plant life.

"Off to the southeast there, by that pyramid shaped peak," Legs pointed, "is something quite unique. Most of us are aware that standing here at the Continental Divide, that the term means that all of the waters of the continent divide here and flow either to the east or west. However, Triple Divide Peak and Pass splits the waters to flow in three different directions: to the Pacific Ocean, to the Atlantic Ocean via the Gulf of Mexico, and amazingly up to Canada and to the Artic Ocean via Hudson Bay."

"Wow," Jen murmured, "I guess you could start there and get almost anywhere."

Dana agreed, a thoughtful look on her face. "I wonder if the ice sheets did that? I mean the big sheet down from Canada blocking and shoving the river draining to Hudson Bay down here?"

"Got me. Ask her. She's fun, don't you think? Even if I do resent her steel-clad calves." The group had already moved ahead on the boardwalk that climbed the meadows, and they listened carefully.

"The pass was shaped by rare forces where the cirques of glacial sheets on either side of the divide had bitten back into their mountain headwalls and chopped completely through, joining into a massive ice sheet that flowed over this mountaintop forming this open saddle at Logan Pass. "

"No wonder the Garden Wall stands up top like a high narrow fin!" Dana commented over Jenny's shoulder, as they waited at the back of the group while Ranger Legs spoke.

They had crossed the divide in Yellowstone, but it seemed so much more dramatic here, where it could be seen to rise suddenly in a thousand feet of sheer cliff walls before the open pass.

Squinting her eyes, Jenny looked all around them, trying to imagine sheets of ice so high they would have shaved both sides of that narrow, spiny fin, cruising along closer and higher, carving its sides deeper until just a sharp sliver of rock was left before its back broke and the sheets came together.

She looked straight up at the sky, trying to imagine thousands of feet of the space above her covered in blue ice, scouring this piece of land of all its soil and vegetation and warmth as it went. She shivered when the picture in her mind became too vivid and she felt the crushing weight and cold of that ancient monster.

It was humbling to realize that even this high in the sky, that even as a modern human with her cell phone and technology that could reach around the world in seconds, she would still be mere sand before a force of nature like that, to be ground to dust and buried for centuries. A chill ran up her spine as she wondered if they were only in one of those warm spots between ice ages again, or if the climate was really overheating.

Dana had shown her those zigzag charts of the climate swings, cold then hot over the long millennium. The great recycler, mother earth, constantly tipping from one extreme to another, throwing off species as she went, dabbling in new life forms ...

"Jen?" Dana's soft touch on her arm brought her back to present time and space. "What are you looking at up there?"

"Nothing," she shrugged, "just pondering the mysteries of the universe. You must be rubbing off on me, Dana, that's usually your job."

"Oh, I don't know about that, Jen. I tend to get captured in the details of how the universe or earth are put together, how they work. I'm the scientist type. You're the romantic, the dreamer, the soul, Jen." With a quick hug and fond smile, Dana added, "So please, ponder away for both of us."

Thinking it over quietly, Jenny wondered if that was true. She never had these thoughts, these dreams in the crowded city. She was always too rushed and busy, it seemed, to just hang out and think. But here...

"Hey, thanks, Dana," she said softly, turning to scan the horizon, "but much as I would like that to be true, I think it's just this place that brings it out in me. You just can't be here and not feel ... it. "

Too small a word to encompass all she felt without knowing what it was. Maybe 'it' was the soul of this wild, ragged, rugged landscape.

The trail from the visitor center had started as a gently rising boardwalk, then stepped up in terraced levels, like the outcrops of exposed rock slabs scattered amongst the glacier lilies. The sub-alpine looked more tundra than meadow, an expanse almost treeless except for conifers so windblown they looked more like flags caught in a stiff wind, or trees so stunted they grew more like mats close to the ground, than upright where they would get crushed and frozen by heavy snows or snapped off by winds gusting over the pass.

Yet a few amazingly delicate wildflowers clustered in the rocky soils. Along with the yellow star-shaped glacier lilies, she spotted the delicate pale blue petals of wild blue flax, that formed a cup for the dainty bright yellow pistols and stamens at their center. Jen identified the mats of sphagnum moss for Dana. The wildflowers wouldn't peak at the pass until late July, she advised, having studied the flower guides on the park as avidly as Dana would the geologic features.

They would climb about five hundred feet on the mile and one-half walk to an overlook where they could see down into the turquoise waters of Hidden Lake. They had already decided not to take the trail further that day—or Jenny had. They would have to climb down seven hundred feet just to reach Hidden Lake, tucked between Bearhat and Clements Mountains. Jenny knew she would never have the legs to get back up again after their hike to Avalanche Lake, the prior day. Her calves were already feeling like bruised marshmallows just looking at the ones the ranger sported.

But the view was exhilarating. Mountain peak after mountain peak marched north into Canada, and south deep into the U.S. from this vantage point on the spine of the Great Divide. The horizon to the west was even more breath-catching. As they climbed the open expanse, Clements Mountain, a matter horn, abruptly edged the meadow just above the drop to Hidden Lake, but elsewhere it was just open sky and air, where the land dropped three thousand feet down the valley to Lake McDonald—and the rest of the world.

Jen shivered, thinking of that drop and remembering the beauty of the Bird Woman Falls that fell, step by step, down it. She wondered if the waters had any idea of just how far they had to go to finally reach the Pacific Ocean.

She recognized that was part of the beauty of Glacier National Park. Everywhere you turned were sights that you not only saw with your eyes—spectacularly scenic in themselves—but also saw in your heart and soul. It made you not only admire and stare with jaw dropping awe, but shiver with wonder. Ponder, respectful of the great expanses of earth and time, and the great forces of nature, with mankind—or in her case, womankind—much like the delicate flax flower, barely clinging to its surface. Somehow she felt both smaller here, and yet taller, and more filled up with life.

She was falling for this place, big time.

Go figure!

Jen laughed self consciously at herself. She would need to buy some of those steel-plated calves, she decided, to really enjoy it all.

"Ready for another hike?" Dana asked, after they had gazed their fill down into Hidden Lake and returned to the visitor center. "Let's try the Garden Wall part of the Highline trail. It's just across the Going To The Sun Road."

"How long is it?" Jen asked, bending down to massage her calf.

Dana decided not to tell her they could take it all the way into Canada, or even to mention the seven some miles to the backcountry Granite Park Chalet.

"Ah… how about if we just go a few miles for the view and then turn around and come back, skip the steeper parts?"

Jen felt that frisson that was a mixture of anticipation and terror, that was becoming a familiar companion, with the idea of traversing across the front of that sharp, steep, jagged fin of mountain wall that had loomed over their drive up to the pass. She had seen a photo of people hiking there, and it had the romantic look of a dream outdoorsy vacation. It had also looked more like an across than up kind of hiking. Jen was not a mountain climber, but she seemed to be doing a lot of mountain-hanging in her first twenty-four hours in the park, whether by car or afoot.

"Okay, as long as we come back as soon as my legs start to tire. This wilderness doesn't do railings and I don't want to trip or stumble and go sailing. Let's use the restrooms and stock up on more water and energy bars first."

After passing through wind stunted and twisted Engelmann spruce and alpine firs, the trail began to wind around the walls of the cliff, through more stands of trees and tundra, with meadows studded with wildflowers. Jen identified the white of cow parsnip and the blues of gentian, with several pink varieties in the mix.

The most distinctive flower reminded Jenny of a cobra with its head raised and undulating high out of the grass. The flower had a thick neck-like stalk several feet high, topped by a thick flared head of numerous tiny white, to palest yellow flowers ending in a blunt pointed tip. The flowered heads swayed in the breeze, looking almost alive, but their puffs of soft flowers, made their texture, if not their strange shape, inviting. Though they were of the lily family, they were, Jen recalled, named Beargrass.

"Are these called Beargrass because bears like them, Dana? Do you know?"

"That's just what the Lewis & Clark gang named them. The first time they saw one, they saw a bear. "

"Oh. Good. What plants do bears like?"

"Well, I know they like Huckleberries and the tender roots of Glacier Lilies. What are those pretty yellow flowers mixed in with the Beargrass?"

Jen looked down at the pretty flowers about the color of daffodils, but with the flower hanging from a slender stem. The flower had five petals that were narrow and curled upward like the prongs of a crown over the bell shaped flower below. From a distance they looked like little yellow stars.

"Glacier Lilies," Jen replied with a gulp. Great. The flowers had looked so innocent back in the wide open sweep of the pass. That romantic hike photo she recalled did not have any nasty clawed bears in it, among the wildflowers. She was glad to be distracted by Dana.

"Look over there. See that quartet of white fluffy things scrambling over that talus slope?"

Sharing the field glasses, they took turns watching some big-shouldered mountain goats scampering on the steep, slippery rock face. They looked half-dressed at this time of year with their thick white winter coats, now peeling back and hanging in fluffs and flags from necks and flanks, as they slowly shed for warm weather. But the mountain goats tired of entertaining long before the girls got tired of watching, moving straight up into hidden crevices out of sight.

Almost an hour into their second hike of the day, they were feeling the effects of altitude and heat exhaustion on the relatively gentle grade along the cliff of the Highline Trail, when Jen suddenly stopped, guzzling down the rest of her water bottle and pulling another from her backpack.

"Remember how you told me once about those books you like? The ones written by that real park ranger?" Jen asked.

"Oh yeah, you mean Nevada Barr? God I love her books! I've got every one she's written. My favorite ... "

"Anyway," Jenny cut her off before she got going, "What I want to know is, is this the one? That trail?"

"What do you mean?" Dana stopped and turned waiting for Jenny to catch up and catch her breath.

"You know, the trail in that book, *Blood Lure*? The one where the grizzlies attacked? Is that this one?"

"I was kind of hoping you wouldn't read that book before we came. Of course it's not the same trail." At least she didn't think so. "Besides, that was fiction, Jen. It didn't really happen. It wasn't real."

Dana didn't see any point in telling Jen that this trail did lead to Granite Park Chalet, where the *Night of the Grizzlies* did happen decades ago, because they weren't going that far or staying overnight. Setting off up the trail again, she hoped she'd settled Jenny's fears, though now the hairs on the back of her neck were starting to tingle and stand on end.

"Grizzly bears are real," Jenny insisted from behind.

"Fine." Stopping again, Dana stepped to the side of the trail, motioning sternly to Jen.

"Then you better hurry and catch up with our guide before the group is out of sight, so you'll be safer."

Luckily, Jen took her suggestion and ran with it, striding up the trail as quickly as she could safely move. Dana stayed on her rear as if protecting her friend's back, trying to remember that falls killed way more people than wildlife. "Watch your step," she called out.

Jen came around a bend in the trail and stumbled on their group gathered around their guide and—a God!

Jenny felt her jaw drop and all the moisture in her throat dry as she gaped at the vision on the trail ahead of them. She wasn't the only awestruck female in the group silently checking out the rear view of the bronzed god communing with their guide.

The sun glistened off sweat-slicked muscles that rippled lean and sleek across shoulders flared wide, like a cobra's hood, before narrowing down the corded back to where his hands rested on lean hard hips, above jeans that rode low on all that tantalizing bare skin. Only the hard muscles of his well-defined butt seemed to be keeping those soft, faded, snug jeans from sliding down long legs and pooling around the dusty hiking boots planted in the middle of the trail.

Jen tried not to swallow her tongue.

She let her eyes roam the leisurely journey back from the ground, up those braced legs to the hard, hot ass, retracing the rivulets of sweat back up the channel to their source near the dampened red bandana, knotted around his neck, beneath gleaming blue-black hair. She told herself she was not thinking about the sensual joy of trailing her tongue down that warm, salty channel, or taking a bite out of that hard muscled butt, when she joined in the low, suppressed, communal female groan as the god shrugged a cotton khaki shirt across that display of hard, damp skin that must be prickling from such intense inspection.

Jen seemed hypnotically fixed where the view had vanished when the god turned, suddenly skirted past the crowd, and practically collided with Jenny's nose at about the level of his still bared and broad chest.

She felt strong lean hands come up and grasp her shoulders to avoid a collision, heard a deep, faintly amused voice, before she was able to raise her eyes from their fleshy feast and realize the god had spoken. To her!

"Well, hey, little wren! Imagine running into you like this?" He laughed. When his dark, sparkling eyes finally captured her gaze, he murmured, "I had dreams of us in this position, of course, but nothing quite so public." Then with a wink, and flashing grin, lifted his head, "Dana! Great to see you again!"

"Hey, Rave. You're looking ... hot." Unable to stifle a laugh, Dana added, "Are you part of the wildlife? Providing the tourist attraction and torturing the poor frustrated women today, are you?" She waved, motioning toward his still bare chest and the group up the trail.

"Hadn't planned to be," he grinned sheepishly at his buddy's wife, with a glance back over his shoulder, and a shake of his head.

"I was called to do some emergency trail repair, help remove a downed snag up above, or I wouldn't have been caught out of uniform like that." One hand still resting on Jenny's shoulder he started buttoning closed the front of his shirt with the other. Glancing back down, he gave Jenny's shoulder a little squeeze.

"So what do you think, little wren? Is this some incredible view, or what?" he asked with pride, his arm sweeping the expanse of mountain walled meadows below them.

"Terrific view!" She agreed with an enthusiastic nod, and then remembered to look out at where he was pointing. That was an amazing view also. They were so high up she realized that must be why she was feeling dizzy. She fell into a shy silence, unable to think of anything brilliant to say—or anything.

"Don't you remember me, Jen? Best man at Garrett's wedding?" he added, when she gave him a startled look.

"You weren't naked then!" She blurted before she could bite her tongue. Dropping her head to hide the hot flush she could feel burning her cheeks, she heard a chuckle rumble in the bare chest that was still too near her face for disciplined thought—or any thought.

"Well, I'm not naked, now, but," reaching out a finger to tip her chin back up so he could recapture those cobalt eyes, his voice lowered seductively. "As I recall, I tried to get naked with you then."

She didn't recall him trying very hard. Maybe he expected women to fall at his feet just at a glance from those sinful eyes. Though his gentle touch on her face and the soft growl of his voice did seem to make Jenny's knees feel like they had climbed much too high, too fast. She swayed and pulled her chin away from his finger so she could take a hard swallow, then another, as he let that finger trace up her cheekbone with a soft, feathery touch, before stepping back and releasing her with a pleased laugh.

"I was planning on giving you girls a call today after I got off work," he told Dana. "I'm just heading back in to finish up some paperwork now. I am taking tomorrow off so I can show you around."

"Sounds good. Text my cell," Dana suggested, ignoring Jenny's sharp glance. "We plan on camping out tonight near Lake McDonald."

"Want me to reserve a spot for you?"

"Already have it, and our tent is up, but thanks anyway, Rave."

He'd turned and his long, loose limbed stride had already carried him quite a way down the trail when he turned, waved and shouted back to a still rooted and dazed Jenny.

"Don't forget me, little wren! You'll see me soon. Soon, Jen."

Oh! Thank you for that image. Like I'll sleep tonight!

Jen stamped her foot, raising a cloud of glacial silt and dust and turned to hurry up the path, muttering about rude, arrogant, and way-too-hot-for-their-own-good almost naked men.

Dana waved the cloud of dust away from her amused grin and silently followed thinking this vacation was surely going to be even more entertaining than she had hoped. Whew! The sizzle she had noted at her wedding to Garrett, between these two, was showing signs of sparks and flames that just might blaze into a wildfire.

Glancing back, Jenny asked suspiciously, "What are you smirking about?"

"Wildfires," Dana replied, innocently

"And that makes you smile?"

"When it's connected to thoughts of Garrett, and lusty love relationships, it does." Dana judiciously skirted the truth with her carefully worded reply.

"Horny for your honey already? You newlyweds!" Jen snorted with disgust and huffed ahead on the trail.

Dana threw back her head and laughed out loud at her self-righteous friend, knowing exactly what thoughts were really in Jen's head.

"That's right!" she agreed letting her off the hook this time. A meadow clearing a while back had caught Dana's eye and brought thoughts of rolling in it naked with her own hot man, so she could hardly claim the high ground.

Of course, the specter of grizzly bears watching them crushing their lunch of glacier lilies, while rolling about au naturelle and defenseless quickly cooled those thoughts!

As soon as they were beyond sightline of Ravenwolf, and spotted a couple good flat trailside rocks, Jen plopped down, digging in her pack for water and a snack bar.

Lifting off their hats to let the breeze cool dampened hair and necks, pulling at their shirts to unstick them, they perched side by side to take long cool sips of water to restore their hydration in the cool, but drying mountain breeze.

"Do you suppose that second 'soon' Rave shouted at you referred to seeing you soon, or getting you naked soon?"

Fortunately the ground was cushioned where Dana landed on her back with an "Uff!" and laughter, when Jen knocked her off the rock.

Jen was not about to confess she had wondered that herself.

He had remembered her.

Called her "little wren". Not a nickname she was particularly fond of, but she couldn't deny the warm, fuzzy feeling that had shivered through her that he had remembered it—remembered her—at all.

"I'm hiked out, Dana. Let's head back to the shuttle. Two days in a row has just about crippled me. I hope you have a scenic drive planned for tomorrow."

Jen needed some quiet time to think, especially if Ravenwolf followed through on his threat to spend the next day with them. She needed to be cool and composed and clear about whether she would allow a vacation fling with him. If he asked. But he seemed so much more dangerous to her senses—and her sense—here in his element. A wolf in the wilderness. She might be wiser just to take pictures from a distance and avoid him; common sense to use around any unpredictable wildlife. Especially since he seemed to hypnotize her brain and zap all her nerve endings whenever he was close.

Before she saw him again, Jen needed to sort out if she wanted to take the risk. And, she thought wearily, it might be wise to write that decision inside her wrist also—just in case he zapped her and she needed a cheat sheet handy.

Dana hopped up much too cheery and energetic.

"Want to catch some fish for our supper?"

"Want to live until tomorrow?" Her dear friend snarled.

"Ah," Dana laughed, "then it's a good thing I brought hotdogs to roast." Adding, at Jen's groan, "Relax, they're gourmet hot dogs."

chapter five

THEIR CAMPSITE ALONG Lake McDonald had a fire pit and wood laid ready to burn. As dusk stole down on the lake, they lit the fire, settling on logs around the pit to enjoy the heat and ambience: the smell of a real fire, the soothing sounds of popping, hissing wood, and the scent, sizzle, and anticipation of hotdogs roasting on sticks.

Jen let the fire hypnotize her, her mind roaming back over the day, her thoughts flickered among the flames dancing across the tented logs. She remembered how she'd pushed Dana off the rock earlier that day from voicing the question that mirrored those circling in her own brain.

She sighed and tried not to dream about that god-like body totally naked and all hers to play with. She'd kicked herself more than once for letting him get away after the wedding. And he had only been a devastatingly handsome hunk in a tux tormenting her back then. Not a half-naked bronze god gleaming of sex in the sun! Her imagination had been bad enough. Seeing the real thing was downright scary!

She remembered how the minute she had seen him at the wedding she had wanted to run him down and jump him—until he made it clear how much he wanted to be caught, of course.

Then, true to form, when Jen found herself the prey instead of the pursuer, she had rapidly backed away. Why had she been such a goody-goody back then? She knew why. She had tried to sooth her frustration enough times by reminding herself that it didn't pay to play on impulse with a guy like that. And, Jen reminded herself, they hadn't really gotten to the point where she had needed to give him a firm 'no'.

Though she would have—possibly.

Jen decided that, when she did decide her course of action, either for or against involvement, she would write the word on her wrist. Then even if she got in a situation where he had zapped her mind and nervous system, and she found herself clamped helplessly against that hard chest ... um, she had lost her train of thought. Oh yes, helpless, hard chest, and her arms were wrapped tightly around his neck, she would be able to see, over his shoulder, her firm decision in bold letters there on her wrist, and respond correctly without needing a working brain.

Excellent. A woman needed a good defensive strategy with a man like that.

A guy used to women falling at his feet at the first meeting. A guy that could and did have any woman he wanted, whenever he wanted. A guy with a reputation so bad that even his best friend warned women off. But, a guy that hot got lucky because he was what every woman wanted, dreamed of having a fling with at least once in her life—even if she did get burned by the touch.

Wouldn't it be worth it?

Call it an adventure. But adventures could be dangerous. Impulsive acts could have long lasting consequences. Men like that should probably just be admired from a distance where they couldn't scorch you; using them only as fuel for wild, but harmless dreams and fantasies.

She had used those dark, dangerous looks for scores of her own fantasies! The nameless man had featured in some dreams of hers that had, very inappropriately, featured savage sex with a bronzed, fringed-buckskin clad man that had morphed into buck-naked sensual rites, lots of unclad skin peeking through long dangling, teasing leather fringes, and feathers stroked to tease and torment during repeated dark and delicious sex as his captive in a private and primitive forest.

Whew! Dana would have the PC police on her in a instant if she knew what kind of wicked fantasies Jen had been brewing with her hubby's best buddy.

"Jen. Jenny!"

She started, guiltily. "What?"

"Your gourmet hot dog is burning."

"Oh, thanks. I like them charred." Jen was so relieved Dana hadn't read her thoughts, she would say anything. Burned food? Her? Unbelievable.

After Jen managed to choke down her burned hot dog, making little noises meant to indicate how yummy it was, she got back to her private deliberations.

86

Now Jen sat in the firelight, in a primitive landscape trying not to think about that half-naked man! Yeah, good luck! Fortunately, it was a public place where he worked, no less, and he was just a notorious flirt and rakish charmer. He probably had all the women he wanted close at hand. He wouldn't have any real interest in someone like her, except to tease and torment, so she should be safe. He wouldn't waste time with a woman like her that was only wild in her thoughts and would want a serious relationship with a man, not just a wild night of heavenly sex. Though, ... she was on vacation ... No, cancel those thoughts!

Her willpower was feeling so weakened right now her best defense was that he was an unromantic man that wouldn't want to get himself tangled with someone as complicated as her. Besides. He had Dana and Garrett to worry about if he messed with her.

She'd just heaved a relieved, if disappointed, sigh, when a deep voice called out of the dark.

"Good evening, ladies. I just came by to make sure you had a legal campfire."

Jen recognized the excited tingles down her spine before the tall silhouette of the ranger of her dreams even stepped from the early evening shadows into the firelight.

"Hey," Dana called, "about time you showed up. Garrett asked where you were hiding. I told him we saw you earlier today for a few minutes. Pull up a log and join us. Want a hotdog?"

"Sure. You guys been enjoying the park?"

They shared their meal and all their tales about their hike and the sites they'd seen so far. Dana did most of the talking and Jenny did most of the watching, whenever those darkly inviting eyes weren't turned her direction.

Later, after the dark had fully settled in to close them in the intimate circle of light that surrounded the fire, Ravenwolf offered to tell a campfire story.

"I will tell you a legend that Chief Joseph supposedly told a white man in 1870 about the Nez Perce at Wallowa Lake in Oregon. It has special, ah … significance for me.

"Here is what he spoke. About the lives of two men long ago.

'My people were strong and had many warriors. Every summer they went to the lands east of the Big Shining Mountains to hunt the buffalo. The Blackfeet people lived in buffalo country, also.

87

'One summer Red Wolf, chief of the Nez Perce and a few of his warriors were hunting when a band of Blackfeet attacked and killed most of them. My people had been few and the Blackfeet many, but Red Wolf would get revenge for the killings. All that winter his people made bows and arrows and returned strong the next summer to take many Blackfeet scalps and horses. All our warriors returned from the fight.

'Every summer our people went to buffalo country to hunt and to battle the Blackfeet. Young boys grew to become new warriors and when the old chief died, his son Young Red Wolf took his warriors. The hunts and the battles continued.

'One summer night when we had many warriors hunting to the east, asleep in their buffalo camp, the Blackfeet attacked and killed many. My people fled the lands to return to our village, but the Blackfeet chased and killed them. Only a few and Young Red Wolf made it back across the lake, starved and weak, one dark night. The Blackfeet camped across the waters, waiting for day to come to the village and kill all men and take the women and children for slaves.'"

A log popped and broke in the campfire, making the girls jump and sending a shower of sparks spiraling up into the dark like fireflies. Ravenwolf watched the sparks to make sure they all faded out harmlessly a few feet over the fire, noticing a bucket of water sat ready beside the fire pit. The black night settled down over them again, the fire settling to a soft crackle and hiss. Leaning forward with his arms on his knees, he continued his story with an ironic twist to his lips and a soft hypnotic voice.

"'All night the Blackfeet warriors danced around big fires, shouting and strong. My people had no fires, wailing for all the young warriors that were dead. There was great sorrow. Young Red Wolf was weak, there were no men to fight the Blackfeet.

"'Red Wolf had a beautiful daughter, his only child, Wahluna. She loved her father and her people and saw they were weak, and felt great sorrow for them. She stayed by the willows near the lake and when all were gone she went to her canoe and paddled across the lake so no one would hear. She walked to the biggest fire and asked to speak to the great chief of their people. She saw the great Blackfeet warrior had the scalps of her people by his fire."

He noticed the girls shiver on the log across from him, their eyes wide and intent, the flames of the campfire reflecting in them. They were hunched forward, leaning into his story, listening with dread and fascination. He paused to use a stick to shift a log, letting the silence and suspense draw out. He almost hoped for the howl of a wolf or the scream of a mountain lion that hunted in the dark of night to punctuate his story and truly terrify his listeners. None of the local predators heard his call, so he continued before the girls leaped on him and choked the rest of the story out of him.

"'I am Wahluna, daughter of Red Wolf, and I come to plead for my people. They do not know I am here, but all our warriors are dead, we cannot fight. My father says you will kill us all in the morning. What good are scalps of women and children to warriors? I beg you to go back to your home beyond the Big Shining Mountains, and we will never fight you again. She lay down in the sand burying her face.
'The chief's son was a young warrior. Tlesca saw the girl was very beautiful. He covered her with his robe. You are brave, he told her, and love your people. I grieve with you and will never fight your people again. This angered the war chief, his father. He said Red Wolf's people were dogs, his son must pick up his robe, the girl would die also. But Tlesca would not remove his robe from the girl.'"

"Ohh, that's so romantic," he heard Jenny sigh and saw little stars dancing in her eyes.
Ravenwolf bit back a grin and continued.

"'Red Wolf is not a dog! He fought bravely for days over the mountains, starved with hunger, but brave of heart. My shoulder bears the break of his war club,' Tlesca spoke. 'Red Wolf is not a dog and his daughter is not a dog. My robe stays with her.'
"So the great Chief listened to the son he loved and laid his robe over his son's, on the girl. Wahluna's people were saved. She went to her canoe followed by Tlesca. You are brave and beautiful, daughter of Red Wolf. In twelve moons listen at night for the hoot of Great Owl and we will speak by the lake, Tlesca told her.
'Wahluna returned across the lake in her canoe and morning passed and there was no attack on the village of my people. She counted the moons, then listened for the hoot of Great Owl and went to the lake to meet Tlesca on that night.

89

'I am a great warrior, favored of Blackfeet women, but the daughter of Red Wolf holds my heart. I want Wahluna as my wife, he spoke to her. She cried that it could not ever be as her people would feed his bones to the wolves; as his people had feed hers.

'Tlesca told her to listen for the howl of Gray Wolf in the middle of the night in six moons, and come across the lake. They would speak again.'"

Ravenwolf had to smile to himself. He personally liked the way the young warrior ignored rejection, refused to beg, and just told the babe to be there later and he'd speak to her. Nice move, guy.

'"So the lovely Wahluna counted the moons and waited and when she heard the call of the Gray Wolf in the night, paddled her canoe across the lake to him. He had spoken to his father and told her that the great Chief and the other great Blackfeet chiefs and warriors would come to the village in the morning and smoke the pipe of peace with Red Wolf the great chief of the Nez Perce and his warriors. Then they would fish in this lake and her people would hunt buffalo in the country by the Blackfeet and no one would be harmed again. And when Wahluna told her father the next morning, and the peace meeting took place, the two tribes were like brothers.

'The great Chief of the Blackfeet told Red Wolf that his son was a great warrior and his heart was held by Wahluna. Tlesca wanted the daughter of the great chief of the Nez Perce for his wife. My daughter's heart is also held, by Tlesca. She may go to his lodge. So Red Wolf sent out runners to all the chiefs of my people and the Kookooskia and the friendly tribes of the Yakima and Cayuse to come to the wedding feast...'"

"Oh, what a lovely story! It's so romantic! Almost like Romeo and Juliet, only better, because they didn't have to die." Jenny jumped in, not realizing the story wasn't finished.

Seeing the dreamy look in her eyes that suited his purposes, Ravenwolf decided to leave out the rest of the legend and let it end on her happily ever after—not an ending that most native tales, intended to teach and warn, ever used. But his audience was happy, who was he to spoil it.

Dana had been silently studying the embers, rising she left them alone for awhile, promising to bring back the marshmallows, chocolate and graham crackers so they could make so' mores.

A while after she left, Jenny conquered a sudden shyness and glanced up at him across the fire.

"You said that the legend had a special meaning for you. What did you mean by that, if you don't mind my asking?"

"You can ask me anything, little wren." The look he gave her suggestive of something naughty he'd like her to ask for, before his face turned serious again. He leaned in to shift the logs in the fire pit around to the sides, leaving a flat, level circle of bright red coals glowing in the center. Picking up some green willow sticks, he pulled out his knife and began sharpening points on the ends, so they'd be ready to roast marshmallows when Dana returned.

"The legend has special meaning for me because of my background."

"Because you're a Blackfoot?"

He chuckled, then corrected her.

"It's Blackfeet, Jen, here in the U.S., even when there is just one of me. The term Blackfoot is generally used to indicate the whole confederation including the Canadian tribes. And yes, that's part of it. The Nez Perce were old enemies of the Blackfeet. Many tribes feared the Blackfeet. They were dominant warriors and superior horsemen across the buffalo plains.

"I belong to the Blackfeet Tribal Nation but I am only three-quarters Blackfeet. Here's the irony. One of my grandmothers was Nez Perce, and my mother was raised as a Nez Perce. I was never told about my mother's real father, but the man that raised her was Nez Perce and very religious, and she grew up near Lapwai, in Idaho. The legend was passed to her from my grandmother, and to me by my mother. And ... well, my mother named me Tlesca. "

"What? That's your real name? Why do you go by an initial?"

"I go by Rave, or Ravenwolf. The initial is for my legal birth name that I don't use, except on documents."

"Why not?"

He shifted uncomfortably, silent while he stirred up the fire, and when she asked if it was because it was difficult to pronounce, he agreed, and rose to help Dana with her grocery bags.

They shared more tales around the fire as they got fingers and faces sticky and gooey with the messy, but delicious, traditional campfire treat.

When he rose to leave, Rave pulled Jenny up from her log.

"Walk with me to my car, little wren."

She went along with him and his teasing, willingly walking into the darkness, leaving the light from the dying embers behind.

When they reached his truck, he pulled her into his arms, murmuring that he'd watched her across the fire, wanting to lick the marshmallow and chocolate from her face.

He tasted the corners of her mouth first with his lips, then gently sucked the sweet flavors from her lower lip. Tracing her upper lip lightly with his tongue, he teased her lips apart, then plunged into the heat and the taste of her, possessing her lips and raiding her mouth with all the fierce heat of a demon and all the force of a man that had waited too long.

He struck like a whirlwind, thrashing her senses, tattering her defenses, weakening her knees and legs and heart, with one hand tangled in her hair and the other cupping her hard against his heat and need.

Then just as suddenly, he was gone.

She found herself pulling in deep gulps of cool air, trying to balance on shaky legs as she watched the red of his taillights dim as he drove away. She lowered the arm still hanging in the air from where it had been clutched around a hard waist a moment before. An earring dropped down her neck and skidded inside her shirt. She remembered to blink and close her mouth.

Turning, she steadied herself and headed back toward the faint glow of embers before another wild beast leaped out of the darkness and swallowed her.

"Wow!"

The thought was hers, but the voice was Dana's.

"I thought you two had been swallowed by some wild animal!"

Jenny had had the same thought.

" I could hear you making those whimpering, moaning sounds in your throat, Jen, all the way over here!"

"Gee, thanks for sharing that, Dana. You know, it is polite to pretend that you didn't hear anything. But," she couldn't help the sigh, or control the silly smile, "You're right ... Wild, yes, and...Wow!"

"So, are you pregnant yet?"

"God, Dana, we were only gone a minute! A minute I'd like to savor *without* your pithy comments," she huffed. "I'm going to bed to go dream about dark haired savages that tell me romantic legends, and ... tell me all their secrets. 'Nite."

"Wait! What secrets?" But Jenny had her revenge, Dana was all alone at the campfire. She'd try to weasel the details out of Jen in the morning.

He had deliberately lied.

Or, at least, lied by omission.

He had deliberately manipulated his best buddy's wife's best friend's emotions. That should make him feel like a heel—if not worse. He had deliberately played his friends' friend just for a little clutch and kiss.

He was a dog. A truly harsh insult to a man of his heritage.

But his punishment would be much greater than the insult.

He would pay for his crime of omission, of manipulation, all night tonight.

He was actually afraid he might be paying much longer than that.

Since Garrett's wedding, he had tried to strictly discipline himself to thinking of Jen only as his best friend's almost sister, to add a little chill to his more wayward, more heated thoughts. Over the long windy, chilly winter since he first met her, first looked into those china blue eyes so full of fury, of passions, ever since he first touched her and felt the delicacy of her wrist, the heat of that elegant, petite figure beside his, he had tried very hard to remember that she was with 'them'—and all the rules that entailed!

But too many of those chilly winter nights, when the winds from the artic north hurled and howled down the east front of the Rockies, had been warmed, heated, and over-heated with dark, delicious, naughty if not nasty, always lusty dreams filled with what he wanted to do with 'their' friend.

It had been increasingly hard—pun intended, he smirked—to see Jen as 'theirs' when he pictured rolling her hot, damp, naked little body beneath him, seeing her dark hair flung across his pillow, his fingers tangled in the rich curls to hold her still for his ravishment of those pouted, panting little lips—and more, oh so very much more. He would play bawdy tunes on that sweet, lush little body, whispering to his little wren, groaning her name, *Jen-n-n-y,* as he buried himself in her, surrounded himself with her ...

Bliss. Fiery bliss!

His fiery bliss—his. That word he tried to forbid himself, when in his heated thoughts he caught himself feeling and thinking it. 'His'. She was 'theirs' he kept trying to remind himself—

forbidden thoughts, forbidden actions, rules of behavior. But he was very much afraid that subterfuge would not work tonight. He feared he would never even sleep tonight. One armful of her scent, her softness, her freshness, and his blood had exploded. He had all but short circuited his nervous system when his lips and body had come in contact with hers. He could still feel the scorched and raw nerves sparking, snapping, still uselessly seeking that connection, that completion. Oh no, he would not dream of her tonight, that was a hopeless thought, for he would never find sleep like this. But he would see her, sense her, beneath his closed eyelids, he would see her beneath him, and there she would be his. And he would be punished, and tortured all night for his little deception.

When he had seen her eyes grow dark and dreamy in the firelight, with the romance of his legend, he had wanted to keep her in that mood, keep her ready for his kiss, so he had let the story end where it would benefit him. He had manipulated her, manipulated the story, which like most Native American tales was not meant to have a happy fairy tale, or romantic ending.

So he hadn't told her that the wedded couple had gotten into a canoe to head off into the happy sunset and been eaten by a monster in Wallula Lake and disappeared forever. He hadn't told her that the tribes had seen this as an omen that the two should never have been joined in peace, and continued killing and raiding each other until the 1855 Fort Laramie Treaty forced them to get along, and share or lose the buffalo hunting grounds—though raids continued after that.

There was no romance in that, even in his own family. He still believed he had been named Tlesca more as a curse than as any kind of blessing. She didn't need to know those dark alleys and shadows in his life.

So he had stopped when she had sighed, and clasp her hands together at what she thought was a happy ending. He had lied by omission, manipulating her while she was soft and dreamy, taking her beyond the firelight when she would fall into his arms like putty. He was a dog! No doubt.

But she had already punished him.

Her lips were sweeter, softer than he had imagined. Her scent mixed with the tang of outdoors was more fresh and intoxicating. Hers eyes soft with romance, glowing in the moonlight, had swallowed him whole. And he had let them—forgetting to struggle, forgetting to panic, forgetting to keep his mind aloof, while his body played..

He had thrust his tongue into her mouth possessively, only to find himself sinking into her sweet, heated, honey, helplessly possessed. Realizing too late he was falling into a trap he couldn't convince himself to escape. And when he had tried to regain his dominance by pulling that small, soft body firmly against the hard need of his, she had nearly taken him out at the knees. He had felt a desperate need to own, and a desperate fear that he was not in control.

His heart had jerked in a panicked rhythm as if he had been jolted by a bolt of lightening rather than one petite woman that looked more like a doll than a femme fatale. His nerves had sparked and sizzled while his mind was in a lazy, shocked daze of pleasure.

God, it had scared the hell out of him!

It still did.

He was sure, experienced as he was, that he hadn't let it show.

He would take his punishment tonight. He deserved that. Then he would be able to scoff at the softer, more dangerous emotions, that he had imagined he had felt. He convinced himself he had just gotten caught up momentarily in his own spell of romance. He would be in control when he saw her again, guarded, his emotions cool, and distant, while charming hers into submission.

She could be his, for awhile—safely—without him becoming hers.

He planned to give her pleasure and a memorable vacation to take home with her. He was sure she was warned about him, and understood the rules. And as long as he was gentle with her there shouldn't be any problem with 'them'.

Yes, a well understood little fling was just what was needed.

He would charm her, tease her, steal a few coaxing kisses, then let her have him—if she wanted. And if she didn't, well then he would just have to work a little harder, a little faster, to convince her she wanted him. Temporarily. To top off her vacation, so to speak, with a little romp on the wild side in the wilderness. So she could return home smiling and he could go back to work— grinning. No strings, no heartache, just a little fun.

And maybe they would even find themselves compatible enough that whenever they found themselves together with their best friends, as they most likely would in the future, they could while away their spare time, spare nights, entertaining each other.

Playful, friendly, occasional lovers while the married couple, Dana and Garrett, were busy. Yes, it would make a convenient foursome, at times. It sounded ideal.

Then they would each go back to their own lives, relaxed and happy. He would return to his life and his ladies. He conveniently ignored the fact that he hadn't found the ladies as appealing since Garrett's wedding. None of them had seemed quite as interesting, as challenging, or smelled quite right, or fascinated with their figure, or had the right snap of fire in their eyes, blue eyes, when he teased them as.... Well, they hadn't been what he wanted, at the time.

Regardless. What he wanted right now was here.

He would give her a dream vacation. It would be fun.

And he would pleasure her. Generously.

She would be his.

For a while.

And as he drove home to face his torment alone, he didn't even consider he might be lying again—to himself this time.

chapter six

"RISE AND SHINE, LADIES," Ravenwolf called from the front of the tent.

No response.

Well, girls were usually picky about anyone seeing them when they first woke up. He ambled over to the logs around the cold ashes of the fire pit and sat down, carefully balancing the cardboard tray with two extra large coffees beside him, uncapping the third.

Pretty hot, still. He blew the steam off the top of the cup and breathed in the aroma of the strong brew before taking a wary sip. He sat and enjoyed the sounds of the early morning, listening to the busy hum of insects, the morning chirp and calls of birds, and sounds from other campsites stirring, but not a single rustle or murmur from the closest tent.

"Ladies," he raised his voice a little. "Dana and Jenny," he specified in a sing-song voice. Not a sound.

He waited patiently, sipping his coffee, thinking of spots to suggest that they might enjoy visiting today. By the time he had finished his coffee there was still no activity from the tent. He started to wonder if they had changed their minds about roughing it on the hard ground and had returned to their hotel. Was he talking to an empty tent? He spun around and checked. No, the car was here. Hmmm.

He glanced over at the other two coffees, but instead of reaching for one, pushed himself up and went to find a piece of deadwood. The multi-limbed broken off branch he found was just what he needed.

Stepping around behind the tent he rustled his feet in the underbrush and gave his best imitation of the snuffling and snorting sounds of a grizzly bear rooting around, then he scraped the branch like claws pawing the back side of the tent about where he figured the girls' heads were.

That worked.

He heard a muffled shriek, then a shaky but familiar voice whispering urgently.

"Dana! Dana, wake up. Wake up! I heard something. I think there's a B-E-A-R out there!"

He clamped his palm hard over his mouth and nose to hold back an un-b-e-a-r-like snort of laughter, even as he heard Dana grumble hoarsely, "Jenny, you don't need to spell, the bear doesn't..."

"Shhh! It'll hear you."

Dana ignored Jenny and called out, "Ravenwolf, is that you out there scaring the crap out of us?"

"Yes, ma'am." He responded cheerfully.

"What's your excuse for waking us like that," Dana called back, trying to sound angry and chuckling in spite of herself.

"The coffee I brought is getting cold."

"Well, why didn't you say so?"

Dana scrambled out of the tent before she'd even finished her sentence. Her long, lean athletic body was clad in a gray sweat suit, but her feet were bare. She seemed totally unconcerned that her hair was a tangled mass of auburn curls that stood up on end as if she had really been scared by a bear.

Tip-toeing over the rocky, prickly campsite, toes curled and little "ouch" sounds coming from her lips each time she took a quick hop, she didn't let it keep her from making a beeline for the coffee. She grabbed a cup and curled up on the log.

"Oh, god, Rave, I'm in love with you!"

Hunched protectively over her cup, she hoisted it two-fisted and took a deep drink, literally shivering with delight. After her first gulp she warned, "Don't tell Garrett I said that," after the first shot of caffeine reached her brain.

"Jen, get out here," she called. "I'm not bringing your coffee in to you."

"Though I might bring it to you for a price," Rave offered in a voice meant to curl little bare toes. He winked at Dana, then added, "What are you wearing in that sleeping bag, little wren?"

98

Jenny exploded out the flap of the tent immediately, fully clothed like Dana, but kept her head down and a hand shielding her face.

"Don't even look at me," she ordered, groping her way to the coffee. "I have a rule. I get to see myself in the mirror and scream first, in the morning, before anyone else does."

"I'll turn my back."

"Okay, that's good."

She waited a moment, sat down, grabbed a cup, then raised her head to look right into his dark, laughing, lying eyes.

He opened them wider, mimed a scream and put his fingers up crossed like the sign to ward off werewolves.

"You are so dead," Jenny growled, burying her face in her coffee cup.

Actually, he thought the little brunette looked pretty good in that warm, slightly dazed, rumpled, sexy, just-woken-up woman kind of way. He could get used to seeing that in the morning from a prone position, no more than a foot away from that cute, scowling little face. He started to share the thought, then stopped himself. She might get the wrong idea.

It was probably too early in the morning to start toying with her too much, anyway. She might toss that cup of coffee in his face, and he wasn't sure it was cool enough yet.

"Are you one of those disgustingly cheerful morning people?"

"Yes, ma'am." Oops, that was close, tone a little too cheeky. He'd seen her hand tighten around her cup and thought he might need to duck. He hoped she wanted to drink it too badly to waste it on him. "So, do you ladies have a plan?"

"Quit "ladying" us!" Well! Little Jen had quite the temper in the morning.

"Okay, what do you guys want to do today?"

"I don't know about, Jen," Dana stirred, "but that hike was a lot for me yesterday," she suggested diplomatically. "I'm pretty sore and stiff and still out of shape. Can you think of something we could do today that would be more riding and less walking, at least to start out the day?"

"Sure, I can think of a few spots that are remote but are accessible by road. We can start by heading up the west side of the park to an area called the North Fork. Grab some food or stuff for a picnic then check out some lakes, even take a road tour all the way back around the southern end of the park on highway 2. If you give me your keys, Dana, I know a guy at the station here that

99

will pack up your gear and deliver your car to your hotel, just for the ride to the east side. We can have dinner in East Glacier, or Browning. My treat. So go get dressed."

They just stared at him for a moment, then sucked in more nourishing gulps of coffee. Dana was the first to regain coherence.

"I'm not sure I followed all that, but it sounds good to me If you are doing all the driving and know where we are going. Jen, sound good to you?"

"No hiking?" She tried to shrug and sound nonchalant about a whole day stuck with the sexy ranger. "Sure, that sounds okay."

"The road is a little rough in spots, but we'll go to Kintla Lake, too. You'll be sure to want to see that, Dana."

"Why is that?"

"I won't tell you until we are on our way, so you female guys don't take forever to fluff and dress," he gave a wicked grin full of mischief.

"Okay," he relented. "One little hint. One of your science interests."

"Oh!" Dana jumped up and danced around, suddenly animated. Grabbing Jen by the back of her sweatshirt, she nearly dragged her to the tent. "Come on, girl guy. Let's get moving!"

The western side of Glacier National Park is roughly outlined from its southernmost tip to where it meets the border of Canada in the north by the Flathead River. The river overlays the fault that had etched this same boundary tens of millions of years earlier.

The Middle Fork of the Flathead River lays just outside the park, romping along beside the highway and railroad line on the southwestern edge up to near West Glacier.

Above that the North Fork of the Flathead River corrals the western line of the park and its free ranging wildlife. It is a place of unique and diverse environments and rare species. It is a home to many predators, including a few rare plants—some of the carnivorous variety. It is the home to the pygmy shrew that can eat three times its quarter ounce weight, and northern bog lemmings, the one ounce relic of the Ice Ages, along with pine martens, free ranging gray wolves, coyotes, wolverines, bear, elk, deer, mountain lions, and a couple thousand pounds of moose on the hoof.

In the Ice Age maximum, ice ploughed down the long trough of the North Fork Valley straight south out of Canada, where it was four thousand feet deep, to taper out south of current Polson on the south end of Flathead Lake.

It was fed from the east by the mountain glaciers coming off the western slope of the Continental Divide, carving their own east-to-southwest trending valleys as they joined the great ice tributary. The main flow south left behind a North Fork floodplain buried in glacial debris, and Flathead Lake, believed a remnant basin where a slab of stagnant ice melted.

The mountain glaciers that joined from the park left behind the near parallel stack of finger lakes above Lake McDonald: Logging Lake, Quartz Lake, Bowman Lake, and farthest north, the Kintla Lakes, surrounded by thick fir forests, interspersed with fen meadows full of wildflowers and grassland prairies.

Lower Kintla Lake curved up like a slightly bent left index finger between the Boundary Mountains barely separating it from Canada as it curved at the joint around a complex of peaks and cirques dividing it from Bowman lake to the south. Kintla Peak, is the highest, at over ten thousand feet. Separated at the next joint by a series of waterfalls and cascades, Upper Kintla was the remote eastern tip of the finger. North of the lakes was the border with British Columbia's Akamina - Kishinena Provincial Park on the border with Alberta and the Waterton Lakes portion of the International Peace Park joining the northeastern side of Glacier National Park.

The elevation gain and cascades between the Lower and Upper Kintla lakes had created another unique species, where the native bull trout had lived in isolation since the ice ages ended, ten thousand years before—or possibly even a few thousand years earlier.

Another rare feature of the North Fork Valley, in this modern day and age, were the potholed, washboard, dirt and gravel roads, and the small communities without electric power or phone lines, and residents more than happy to remain that way.

Once they dropped Dana's keys off at Apgar, at the west end of Lake McDonald, they took the Camas Creek Road inside the park northwest past the fens of McGee Meadows. They exited the park for awhile to take the Outside North Fork Road along the Flathead River, stopping about thirty miles to the north at Polebridge, at the historic Polebridge Mercantile.

The old store wasn't done up for tourists in faux-rustic. It was the real thing, with town dogs lolling on the front porch, no electricity, and fresh home baked pastries for a late breakfast. Gathering fresh baked bread, lunch and snack foods, drinks and juice, they checked out at the antique register, where $1, or $2 or other sign popped up instead of a digital readout. Rave had brought his cooler loaded with ice for their purchases.

From there they crossed the bridge back over the river onto dirt roads into the northern edge of the park, detouring to check out Bowman Lake, then heading further north. They rattled past the grasslands of Big Prairie, Round Prairie, and the bursts of bright red fireweed marking the path of prior wildfires on the rough inside road to Kintla Lake, near the border with Canada.

They had taken Ravenwolf's SUV with the canoe strapped on top. He knew it would get scratched and scrapped on the way to Kintla Lake, but he figured the girls might enjoy sitting out in the lake and soaking up the wilderness, maybe spotting some wildlife along the shores.

It was about fifteen miles of rough, rutted road, but Ravenwolf convinced them the bruises would be worth it.

"Hey guys, you should find this interesting. . Excuse me, I meant "ladies". Girls?"

"I don't mind being called a guy, or a girl. I know I'm a woman," Jenny piped up from the backseat without thinking, which earned her a wolf grin and wink in the rear mirror from Ravenwolf.

"Oh yes you are," he said seductively. "What was I thinking?" Continuing after being rewarded by a blush from her, "So, do you know how they figured out the timing on the melting of the major ice sheets in Glacier Park?"

Dana was all ears.

"Some of it was compliments of your home state, or former home state, Dana, of Washington. They believe the melting of the ice age sheets started about twelve or thirteen thousand years ago here. Maybe, like today, warmer temperatures were accelerated in the mountains, I don't know for sure if that was the case. But they figure by eleven thousand years ago, most, maybe ninety percent of the ice was gone in the park, based on patches of ground that did, or didn't, have certain layers. Layers blown in from Washington.

"Just like in 1980 when the eruption of Mount St. Helens blew volcanic ash into Montana, they know that Mount St. Helens also erupted eleven thousand four hundred years ago, and landed on bare ground in places in the park. On top of that, or alone, are layers of volcanic ash with the chemical signature of the explosion of Glacier Peak up by North Cascades National Park, also in Washington. And that ash pins that sediment to eleven thousand two hundred years ago, letting them piece together what land was still under ice and covered during one or both of those events."

Dana was digging through her pack looking for paper to make notes.

"But what will really tickle your toes, Dana, is the Folsom stone point found up where we are going. Were you aware of that?"

For a moment she didn't respond, just stared at him as if she hadn't heard him.

"Well, a while back an archaeologist found a Folsom point right at the Kintla Lake Campground. It was a surface find, possibly even carried then washed out of a glacier, so ... "

"Folsom?"

"Yeah."

"Did you say a Folsom Point?" Her voice rose as she grabbed his shoulder and shook it. "Do you mean an OVER TEN THOUSAND YEAR OLD Paleo-Indian type of point? One often found with extinct bison and camel bones type of Folsom Point?" She nearly screeched. Her green eyes looked like exploding emeralds, her auburn hair seemed to be about to burst into flame. Dana keep shaking his shoulder as if she was trying to shake the truth, or the stone point, out of him.

"I guess so," he laughed. "I'm not up on that stuff but I definitely know that the point that was found was Folsom and it was at Kintla Lake. We don't even allow people to dig to bury their tent stakes up there anymore. Though as I was saying, it was most likely not a site but washed or carried there from elsewhere."

Luckily they were pulling up at the lake access, before Dana shook whatever teeth he had left, after the jarring ride, from his head.

"Hurry, hurry," she said as he was braking the car, leaping from it while it was still moving.

"It's not still there, you know, Dana," he hollered after her, laughing.

"That's okay," she called back. "I just want to be there, feel it, sense it in the surroundings."

"Now tell me," he turned to ask Jenny, "do I know how to get a woman all excited and please her, or what?"

"That is your best friend's wife you're exciting and pleasing," she countered, sternly.

"And he will no doubt give me a big sloppy kiss for giving her such a treat," he returned unrepentant, "but maybe," he deepened his voice, "as her loyal best friend you should protect her and divert my skills and charms onto yourself?"

"Keep dreaming, fella."

Oh, I will, little wren. I certainly will, he chuckled to himself.

"Hey, I can't get out of this thing. The belt must have jammed from all the bouncing around." Jen was bent over trying to free herself.

He had put her in that seat on purpose, loading a cooler behind him, putting Dana up front and Jenny in the backseat, so they would each have a window on the side looking into the park, as he had adroitly explained, and Dana having longer legs, of course, should sit in the front.

He had been pleased at the little scowl he earned from Jen, but had managed not to laugh. He knew about Dana's short jokes. He could only imagine the fierce scowl he would get if Jen found out how truly devious was his intent.

He had wanted her there, where he could glance at her in the strategically angled rear view mirror, in the seat that had the perfectly good shoulder harness seat belt, except for the catch that was hard to unsnap, without assistance—his assistance.

As he rounded his car now, he schooled his face so the pleased smirk didn't show. Everything was going according to his plan.

Opening her door, he murmured, concerned, "What's the matter little one? Here sit up straight and let me fix it for you."

He tried to keep his eyes off where the belt divided and emphasized each sweet breast, though he wasn't beyond clumsily letting his cheek brush against one, as he bent over her working on the sticky catch. He pretended he didn't hear her little choked gasp or feel the bud tighten as he reluctantly freed the belt. As he drew back slowly, he captured her mouth, as if to steal a quick kiss, but his mouth came down on hers open, warm, to possess, to linger. Suddenly he jolted back as if his lips had been scorched by something hotter than expected, banging his head on the doorframe.

Taking her elbow gently he helped her slide out of the car, not looking at her, but reaching in behind to haul out the cooler.

"Go on ahead, I've got this." He heard the rasp in his voice, thankful when she took off after Dana like a startled deer.

"Shit!" He muttered under his breath. "How does such a little girl pack such a dangerous punch in those lips?" He shifted the lid off the cooler and scooped up a handful of melted ice water and buried his face in it.

He shook his head, straightened, and, confidence back, planted his hands on his hips, and grinned. Definitely *woman!*

Convinced he was back in control of the seduction, he hauled the cooler to the lake, and had the ladies return to help him steady the canoe while he hoisted it off the top of the car.

Ravenwolf had flipped the canoe down from his car top carrier, barely requiring any help from them except to balance the ends while he got a good grip. Jen wondered if he had really needed their help or had just wanted an audience to show how strong he was. When he had twisted the canoe off his shoulder and rolled it down to ease it on the shore, the muscles in his forearms and shoulders had pulled and rippled fluidly. Impressive. And the man had to know that they had noticed.

Jenny didn't seem too enthused about going out in the canoe, at first. He thought he should give her some incentive. As soon as he had placed the bow of the canoe into the water, he had turned toward them, saying something about the best view of Kintla being from the water while he had casually reached down and popped the button loose on his belt-less low riding jeans. Jenny had watched open mouthed and hypnotized, not hearing a word he said, as he unzipped his pants and started shoving them down narrow hips over some under clothing that was black, silky, and brief, his eyes fixed on Jenny as he slowly eased them down to his ankles. She hadn't been able to resist her eyes following his jeans down over those long, lean, thighs roped with muscles. Even though he wore black swim trunks beneath, the obvious mischief in his eyes as he did a slow strip tease for her had her throat so dry she could barely swallow. And all the while he watched her watch him. His black eyes soft, seductive, and ... amused, damn the man.

Dana just laughed and clapped, clearly unaffected.

"Well?" He looked in Jenny's eyes, "Are you coming?"

"Er ..."

Dana gave her a little shove from behind and started her toward the canoe.

"You two go," Dana said, "I want to sit here in the quiet without any distractions," she winked at Rave behind Jenny's back, "and think about the people that came here and left that stone point at the end of the ice ages. It's almost too much to imagine!

But I want to try. I can't thank you enough for telling me about it Rave," she said seriously, "and showing me this place where it was found."

Kintla Lake proved to be worth the bruises they'd gotten getting there. Dana was in heaven just being on the ancient site, especially one west of the Continental Divide. Most Folsom Points had been found to the east of the Rockies on the High Plains, and most theories held that was the only path imaginable for migration of early people at the end of the last Ice Age, in the Pleistocene.

Dana loved it when things didn't fit neatly into the old plan. She thought there were a lot of surprises still to be learned. Recent discoveries were finding Folsom points further west in the Rockies, like this one. Maybe ancient man, the Clovis ancestors of the Folsom culture, had traveled on top of the great ice sheets south, instead of in a corridor between them? It was something she wanted to sit and ponder.

More playfully, Dana added to Rave, "I'm just so excited and thankful I should give you a great big kiss! But Garrett would kill me. You kiss him for me, Jen."

"What!"

"You're closer."

Before Jen had even finished sputtering, Rave wrapped her in a strong arm and helped himself to a big smack on the lips.

"Mmm, thanks Dana," his eyes laughed into Jenny's. "Another? Sure," and he treated himself to another, but this time with less smacking lips, and more sizzle. He grabbed her around the waist and tossed her into the canoe, when her knees buckled.

Jen clambered gracelessly and a little dazed into the bow as Rave stood knee deep in the shallows steadying the canoe.

"I see you know where to sit but why don't you turn around instead before I push off. and kneel facing me. That way we can talk and I can point out sights to you. Don't worry, I'll be your slave and do all the paddling. You just relax and enjoy the scenery," he directed.

Great, Jen muttered to herself, ducking her head to hide the heat on her face as she gingerly shifted around and knelt with her back to the bow, tucking her oar down alongside her. She had been hoping for a bit of a respite from the scenery she had just been too thoroughly enjoying. Her nerves needed a rest. She flicked a glance at his sleek, lean muscled legs, flashing with droplets of water as he hopped easily into the stern.

Dana shook her head and gently shoved the boat out into the lake. "Toss me the car keys, Rave, in case any unfriendly wildlife comes to visit. And don't do anything to tip that canoe!"

They'd launched the canoe and glided silently away from the campground, into the center of the Lower Kintla Lake. It was still early enough in the day to see a few mists clinging to the lake.

The silence was so loud it was rich with the taste of a rare and sinful treat.

No jets flew overhead; there was no rumble, rush, or horns from a highway, or even the engine growl of a single car. No tires hissed over pavement or crackled down a graveled road. There was no background drone of lawnmowers, or the more intrusive teeth gritting pitch of pressure washers, no annoying buzz of weed-whackers or leaf blowers, or the angry hornet whine of circling jet skis or powerboats. The silence seemed almost unnatural, but so sweet without the ding of a microwave or buzz of a dryer finished with their tasks and demanding action, no phones ringing or cell tones singing for an immediate reaction. There was no blare of a television or blast of distant sirens. There was just the quiet peace of a much earlier century—blessed, rich, and beautiful.

She watched the paddle dip quietly into the sparkling water and, when it lifted for another stroke, she saw the droplets cast off, glittering like a rainbow of diamonds in the sun. It was so quiet she could hear the tinkling sound as the tiny gems dropped back into their liquid home. Off to one side she heard the soft patter and whir as a brightly colored harlequin duck tiptoed across the water and lifted off to move to a more distant spot on the lake.

As the day brightened, they could see the top of the Boundary Mountains, the Canada border here only about five miles north of Kintla Lake. Ravenwolf had quietly pointed out a moose browsing knee-deep, and a pair of foxes having a drink.

He later spotted a wolf for her.

His first cousin according to Jen.

She had thought it was someone's lost Husky, with its fluffy white furred face, and its pale gray mask and markings, when he had first pointed to it. Besides, it clearly was wearing a collar. He told her that the wolves had all been hunted out of the park at one time, just like in Yellowstone, until they had decided to capture wolves in Canada and release them back into that park in the 1990s. But in Glacier, the gray wolves had apparently already migrated back down from Canada a decade before, sneaking past customs and immigration in this remote backcountry. There were at least four wolf packs in the park now, two of which had radio collars. The Kintla wolf pack, along with the Apgar pack wore radio tracking collars.

"Speaking of wolves," Jen took a deep breath and squared her shoulders, girding herself for an unpleasant task. But she needed to have a talk with this man and get a few things straight.

"I need to talk to you about a few issues I have with you about your hit and run kisses. You do not even wait to see if I want ...," she paused, dropping her gaze. Mauled was too strong a word to use, because she actually liked his kisses, but she... "I don't feel like you have any respect for me and I will not be treated like one of your easy come easy go playthings. If you...."

"God, I am so sorry Jen. I didn't mean to make you fell harassed and disrespected. I thought I was being playful, stealing a few kisses, but I should have respected your space." Rave interrupted quietly.

His face was serious! Jen snapped her mouth shut, nodding. "Yes, you should have. I enjoy your company, Ravenwolf, but. . ".

"I've just been happy to see you again. You have been in my thoughts all winter, with Dana and Garrett talking about you all the time. I guess it seems like I know you better than I really do, and I took liberties that I didn't have a right to take. I like you and want to know you well, though I must still seem like a stranger to you. Again, I'm sorry. So, now you know that I respect you can I steal some more kisses, or should I back off, and keep my hands to myself?"

Well, damn, he had done it again— scrambled her brain, etc.

Jen lowered her head, unable to meet his eyes, she twisted her watch, then said, "No."

"No? No what?"

"It doesn't say. Just no." Jen muttered without looking up, continuing to twist and worry her wristwatch, trying to read a more detailed answer.

chapter seven

"NO, DON'T KEEP MY hands to myself, or no don't steal any more kisses?" He asked patiently, dark eyebrows raised.

Jen planted those big cobalt blue eyes squarely on his and started earnestly to explain. Or attempted to.

"I just, ... I need you to know I am ... selective about my ... ah, who I ... I'm not a ... I do like your kisses, they just need to ... I am not your usual type, and ..."

"No, you are not a type, Jen. You are a unique, fascinating woman. A woman to be respected. But I admit I like to tempt and tease you and watch that fiery temper sometimes. And I admit I want you in my bed. I won't lie about that. But I understand you are asking me to slow down, and no more sneak attacks. So I will try to broadcast my intentions so you have time to run."

"Thanks," she said weakly. "I think."

The hours on the lake, the silent slide of the canoe and wildlife going about their routines in the remote area, gave an almost spiritual solace to the day. Now that they had gotten past the awkwardness—she hoped.

Jen breathed deeply and enjoyed all the sights and silences. She sucked in the pristine air and let her breath sigh out with all the tension in her limbs and mind she had not been aware of before the soothing touch of silence. Her shoulders eased and her face relaxed into a soft, contented smile. She let her eyes drift half-closed and swayed with the gentle motion of the canoe as she listened to that one other soothing, yet fascinating sound.

The sound of his voice.

"They called these mountains the Backbone of the World, and they called themselves Nizitapi, the Real People, made up of many tribes and bands. They shared the Algonquian family of language, in various dialects. The earliest Canadian traders and trappers called them Blackfoot, or used the tribal word for that, Pikuni. The tribe that lived closest to where the Blackfeet reservation is now, were the Piegan."

His voice was a deep, soft rumble that blended in this other world as naturally as the light breeze brushing gentle waves on the surface of the lake. She let it wash over her, through her, take her back to a time when the stories of life and creation, the stories of the world around were explained by elders passing the knowledge off to their people down through generation after generation of time and travel. Travel between summer and winter camps and villages, and travel further in search of more abundant game, and berries, and bulbs, until the people arrived here, thousands upon thousands of years ago, leaving their flaked and fluted stone point on the shore.

The thick fir trees curved down the u-shaped valley that the glaciers carved until they met the edge all around the lake. The isolation, the remoteness, the suspension of time fascinated her. She could be looking at the present or that long ago past when she might have been one of the first women to gaze upon this scenery. It was a mystical feeling.

"It's so remote, so isolated," her voice was little more than a whisper. "The scenery is so beautiful, so exquisite, Rave."

"Yes, it is beautiful. And very exquisite." Something in the low tone of his voice had her glancing at him. He had taken his sunglasses off and she could see his eyes. Soft, intent. On her.

He set his oar crosswise and braced his arms on it as he leaned forward and brushed his lips gently across her forehead, along her cheekbone, then settled them lightly on hers, in a kiss of such tenderness that it somehow belonged to this moment and this magical place.

Then as if his heart had also stopped for a moment, before racing too fast, and seriously, he shifted back and gave her his trademark wicked grin. A distancing, of the tenderness he had just shared.

"See. Slower."

Glancing off to shore, his voice still teasing and playful, he said, "And here we are all alone out here. Back in 1910 when this park was first created, the legislation passed by congress said that Glacier National Park was intended as, and I quote, 'a public pleasuring ground' to be 'preserved in a state of nature'."

Turning those eyes sparkling with naughtiness back on Jen, he tipped his head toward shore, and dropped his voice to a wicked purr.

"Why don't we get in a state of nature and I will take you ashore and pleasure you. Endlessly."

As she stared at him, silently, he slowly slipped his shirt off over his head treating her to a mouth watering display of the sleek muscles on his broad and bronzed chest.

This was clearly the broadcasting he promised.

"This is how we were meant to be, Jen," he urged quietly, "take off your top for me. I won't touch yet, unless you ask, I just want to see those sweet breasts that nature gave you so that mankind could be fed the milk of life. Get in a state of nature with me, my sweet little wren."

And she was tempted. Very tempted.

"You know the native people worshipped the sun." He stretched his arms up to the sky for a moment, tipping his head back with his eyes closed, bathing himself, gilding himself in the warmth of the golden rays.

Jen suddenly felt overdressed in the purity of this wilderness. But she also felt shy in the bright sunlight, and slightly intimidated. His body was as perfect as a sculpture, with the broad muscles of his back flaring beneath his arms as he paddled, forming a wide vee that narrowed to that hard flat belly, narrow hips, his thighs strong and exposed by the side vents in his trunks. She could almost imagine him dressed only in a breechclout, with his blue black shiny hair longer and braided beside his face.

He looked like a man of ancient times, fit and muscled and prepared to test and prove himself against an unknown wilderness. So perfectly male, so tempting, but ...

She frowned and took a quick, deep swig from her water bottle to cool herself down, and tried to concentrate on the rest of the scenery, and the wilderness around her.

He slid a glance sideways at her, his expression turning to concern. "You look like you are in pain. You must be stiff after your hike yesterday. Probably ready to uncurl from the tight confines of this canoe. He trailed his paddle off into a J-stroke to turn the canoe back in a slow circle. "No?" He added at the quick shake of her head, "Then what were you thinking about?"

Sun burned nipples!

That's what Jen had been thinking and frowning about.

The painful thought of spending her vacation with sun burned nipples was probably the only thing that had kept her from whipping her shirt off.

God he was a smooth talking man! State of nature, hah! The handsome scoundrel had almost talked her right out of her shirt!

But ... for a moment there, she had seen it, pictured with her eyes and mind. The timelessness of this place, unchanged and uncluttered with man's presence and improvements. It was so damn beautiful in its natural state, without the wounds of roads and parking lots, without the annoying buzz of speedboats, with the wake of their canoe just a quiet swirl of water, barely intruding on the aqua wavelets dancing beneath the life giving sun.

She'd seen it, felt it, wanted to belong to its natural primitive lure.

She had looked at Rave and imagined him, his hair blowing in the wind, paddling her across the lake on some ancient errand, maybe to check a fish weir to catch and dry food to store for the long cold months of winter. Yes, she had felt overdressed and insignificant in this vast expanse of natural beauty, in the sweep of tens of thousands of years of time it held unchanged. .

But she didn't trust herself yet with this velvet-voiced rogue, even though she was seeing a depth in him she hadn't known before—probably because it unnerved her. It made him more appealing. And she really didn't want to have to deal with sun burned nipples!

But he was touching a deeper layer in her than before, not just a physical, sensual layer, but as a man, as a friend she wanted to know and understand. He was much more complicated than she had ever imagined. And she suspected that he was a private soul that hid most of what she—or anyone else—most wanted to understand.

He felt her focus on him.

He had felt the intensity of her gaze on him before, skimming his surface appreciatively. Used to that kind of female focus, he accepted it, even expected it, played to it. His appearance was his weapon—and his shield. Rave knew he was a lot more attractive on the exterior than he believed himself to be inside.

As soon as he had become aware of the effective diversionary value of his looks as a teen, he had used it mercilessly, and hidden behind it.

Except with Garrett, his best friend, his only true friend.

But he felt Jenny's focus now, differently. Her eyes were locked on his, and not with their usual half-wariness. Listening to him with an intensity as if all her senses were bent forward with the effort, she was looking at him, into him, with a depth that would make him leery with any other woman. Though even this woman peering into his soul was unnerving. Exciting, but discomforting. He wanted to open some of himself to her, but hoped to keep the dark shadows safely back in the far corners.

At her request he told her more of the early legends.

"The Piegan believe in an eternal spiritual being, the Creator Sun, that created earth and life forms from the dust of space and spit. See a lonely Creator Sun made a mud ball and blew on it and floated his bare mud ball in space, played with it, but still felt empty, so he made snakes to fill the his bare ball. But the snakes overran the mud ball so he made the earth boil from below to destroy the snakes. Only one small snake survived and he let her live. After the earth boiled it dried in pretty colors but was too hard, so the Creator Sun made soft green grass to walk on and add another pretty color.

"But, Creator Sun wanted more. A mate, and a family. So he made Moon for his lady, and they had the seven sons of the Big Dipper.

"Now, as in all good stories, there was a snake in the grass—and yes, there is a pun, also. That one female snake also had a son, named Snake man, and he wanted revenge. So he lured Moon and there are the most fascinating stories about her betrayal and the battle with her family. It involved all the natural forces as weapons, the banishment of Moon, and the second mate of Creator Sun, Mother Earth.

"Dana would be fascinated with them also, because they tell of the earth covered in water, and of mountains being built. But, back to the good part. When the kids got out of line, Creator Sun commands them to 'Be honest to life' and he made a leader to teach them all how to live on earth from a part of himself, and he was known as Oldman, or Napi.

"There are many, many tales and stories of Oldman, Napi, the disciple of the Creator Sun. And they are best told by a Blackfeet drum leader that at the age of sixty-seven did his best to write down the history and stories of his tribe, the Piegan, and the oral stories of the ancient Pikuni so the true ways would be known and saved.

"I'm learning these stories from Percy Bullchild's book, *The Sun Came Down*. It's fascinating to hear stories from his memory as they were passed down and told by the elders for generations. They are so much richer than the summary I've given you. And are authentic, instead of the white man's versions ... or my abbreviated one."

He could tell by the glow in her eyes, like the bluest sky, back lit with sunlight, that she was enchanted, not bored by what he had shared.

"If you are interested, the Blackfeet give jammer and bus tours of the park where they tell their stories, and there is a great program in the lodges called "Native America Speaks."

"I'm fascinated! Will you take me? I mean us?" She asked a little shyly.

He smiled at her hesitation, the soft flush on her face.

"Of course, " he agreed, though what he wanted to say was that it would be as a date, with Dana tagging along if she wanted. But, he decided to go slow as she had requested. Though he didn't ask himself why asking for a date seemed more touchy than asking her to strip and go play naked on shore with him.

"Thanks. I mean for everything, Rave." Her arm swept the lake and surrounding mountains and wilderness. "Hearing you tell me the stories, here in this place, this timeless place, makes it feel ..."

"Special?" He suggested.

"Very." She nodded, shrugged, looked out at the treed shore and said softly, "More. Mystical, magical. Right."

It did feel right, Rave mused, slowly paddling in the crisp, cool waters of the remote lake with a woman—*this* woman—to share the sights, the feelings, as if she was his mate and they were the ancient owners of that Folsom point. He had been so at ease, he found himself sharing, showing, maybe more than he had meant to.

He felt his lip twist in a wry smile. He had hoped to show and share some different kinds of feelings with her. Ones of a more basic and definitely carnal nature, but this was a woman that needed to be courted first, respected first.

He turned his head to hide a grin as he tried to imagine the look on that pert little face if he had courted her in a more traditional, more ancient way, by dumping a fresh killed deer outside of her tipi to show he wanted her as his woman and to prove that he could provide food and hides. A much more practical courtship than modern times. After all, who could eat a diamond ring? Or light it in winter for warmth? Or turn it into warm clothing without pawning it? Or...

What the hell was he thinking?

Diamond ring! Courtship? Mate?

He was getting himself lost in the fantasy of them being one of the early American peoples living along these remote shores, more than ten thousand years ago, confusing that with reality. That was crazy dangerous thinking! That he could even picture that fantasy much too easily threatened his peace of mind. She was wearing high end hiking clothes, he should be seeing her naked, not envisioning her in furs in the wilderness, smiling at him as he tramped into camp to their lodge at days end.

He was scaring the hell out of himself. He must have gotten hypnotized or something by the soft lulling rhythm of the lake rocking the canoe. Or the lights sparkling and dancing off the waters like the lights in her brighter-than-blue eyes. It was time to get back to shore, back to Dana. Back to safety.

But first... just one more taste of that crazy dream.

Jen had been puzzling over why Ravenwolf never called the Blackfeet 'my people'. He had done it several times, like an outsider looking in at a family he belonged to, but had never met, and didn't claim to represent. Or maybe it was just that he was telling stories of distant times so he used a distant voice, but this was not the first time she had noticed the seeming oddity. It seemed like too private a thing to ask. Until she knew him better, anyway.

As he slowly rowed them back across the lake, she wondered what he was thinking as she watched a myriad of emotions flicker rapidly across his sharply chiseled face. And then he steadied his paddle and lowered his head to her again and she was sinking under the spell of his kiss.

She told herself that it was just the magic of the day that sent sparklers zinging along her nerves at the bare touch of his lips to hers, shooting shivers down her spine, and everywhere else. It was just the silence of the day that made the passion ring so loudly in her ears and let her hear the sudden rapid thunder of her heart. Just the magic that made this moment seem so intense.

No kiss alone should slam through her senses like this sweet, sudden possession that made her feel like she was floating off on a gently rocking cloud. Her hand dropped limply to her side with a splash, and she jerked her eyes open to find her cloud was in the middle of the lake and dark eyes were smiling unrepentant at being caught. He kissed the tip of her nose, laughing.

"Sure you want to head back, or did you want to get in a ah, 'state of nature' with me first?"

"Take me back, now, you wolf!" She shoved him away, laughing, with little tingles skimming her nerves that were pure pleasure, not fear, despite the rocking of her boat.

"Dana probably wonders what has happened to us, and I need to get my cramped legs out of this canoe." Pretending his every kiss didn't turn her legs to wobbly liquid rubber.

He just gave her a knowing grin. Turning the canoe with deep strokes, he sent them gliding back to the western end of the lake.

"Remind me to lovingly massage those poor cramped legs for you later, little wren."

Once the rutted roads had disappeared in the dusty rear window, they headed south from West Glacier leaving the park to skirt it along the Middle Fork of the Flathead River, down and across Highway 2 below the southern boundary between Glacier Park and the north edge of the Bob Marshall Wildness, enjoying the scenic drive.

Part of the incredible impact of Glacier was the surrounding area, with massive tracks of wilderness and lightly developed reservation areas that amplified the view and vistas seen from within the park, and the landscapes that encompassed the Crown of the Continent.

To the north in Canada, Waterton Lakes Park and Glacier combined in the first International Peace Park and later a World Heritage Site. Along the western boundary of the park curved great tracts of land in the Flathead and Kootenai National Forests, Lolo National Forest, Flathead Lake and the Flathead Indian Reservation, Hungary Horse Reservoir, Swan River Wildlife Refuge, the Bighorn Mountains Wilderness, and more of the Lolo National Forest interspersed.

This met up with the Bob Marshall Wilderness to the south which included three separate wilderness areas: the Bob Marshall, the Great Bear, and the Scapegoat. Then the Lewis and Clark

National Forest completed the southern curve to meet up with the Blackfeet Indian Reservation which covered the whole eastern boundary of the park that held their sacred mountain places.

The Crown of the Continent as a whole was this abundant patchwork of natural lands, wildlife corridors, wild scenic rivers, and diverse ecosystems that made up the rare and treasured gems in the crown. Though it was not entirely free of man-made distractions along the margins, including the lines of the Great Northern Railroad that had first brought outside visitors to a park— to be preserved and appreciated by all—and now continued to bring visitors to the park via Amtrak passenger service.

The views north into the park, of seemingly endless dark blued- gray mountain peaks, with dazzling streaks and patches of crystal white snow, were spectacularly framed by the deep, dense greens of the forests, and the sparkle of water from the Middle Fork of the Flathead River. Even the concrete of the adjacent Highway 2 was colored dusty pink in places, reminding the traveler of all the rich, barn red rocks of the park, named for early explorer and proponent of its creation, George Bird Grinnell. He was the first to use the term 'The Crown of the Continent' in a 1901 article.

Looping around the southeastern end over Marias Pass, before they arrived in East Glacier, Rave pulled to the right down a road near the pass and into a parking lot.

"What's this?" They could hear the river rushing as they stepped from the car, and watched as a train whooshed past on an elevated trestle.

"Something you don't want to miss." He led them to the edge of the lot to look down a steep cliff to the river. "Over there." He pointed to a bare steep cliff on the opposite side, made of dusty pinkish-tan rock.

Then the cliff moved.

No, not the cliff, something on its face.

Several some things.

"Oh, my god, Dana! Look, Rocky Mountain goats! How do they do that?" Jen could barely believe her eyes. Disguised by the rosy tan dust that clung to their white fleece, mountain goats were running up and down the near sheer cliff, and grazing on something, as if they were on flat land! She didn't see any plants, but she did see…

"Babies! Ohh! Look at the babies, Dana." Jen gave her friend an excited shake, then darted back to the car to get her camera.

Rave's thoughtful dark eyes followed her.

Babies...He shook himself, realizing his mind skittered back to his crazy notions of a mate on the lake, realizing it could—would— get even scarier if he didn't watch his step with Jen. Damn! He'd had a miserable childhood. What was he even doing messing with a woman that had commitment and family written in every loving, nurturing part of her? But he knew, even when he tried to deny it, that he was as thirsty for that nurturing part of her as drawn by her beauty and body. Though he only wanted to borrow her sweetness, and he sure as hell didn't want to share it.

When she returned, Rave was explaining that this was called Goat Lick because the soil of the eroded cliff had exposed rocks of high salt content, which the goats loved to 'graze' on. Fought over, really, as soon became clear. While the girls gasped and held their breaths as a couple goats got in a tussle on the treacherous rocks, worrying the babies might get knocked off, Rave explained—almost desperately—that mountain goats were comfortable on a forty-five to eighty degree slope, and actually preferred it as a defense mechanism to protect them from other predators. So would they please quit panicking.

They could have watched the goats for hours, but it was late in the day. As more people arrived, they reluctantly gave up their viewing places.

Once they passed into East Glacier they were on the outer eastern edge of the park on the Blackfeet Reservation lands, which, since 1895, no longer included the east slope area that became part of Glacier National Park. But the reservation lands ran beside it all the way north to the Canadian border.

Ravenwolf worked north from East Glacier along narrow reservation roads, sometimes dicey with sharp blind curves around cliffs, that showcased the Two Medicine area, climbing high around Lower Two Medicine Lake and Looking Glass Hill, on Highway 49. He pointed out the dark forest of blue-green conifers, Douglas fir, lodge pole pine, and spruces rising up to the flanks of the slopes on the west side of the road.

On the east side of the road were quaking aspen groves where they had the open land and sunlight they needed. In the fall, the aspens would blaze into brilliant color along this drive with their ghostly-white peeling trunks. Many in the stand of identical looking trees turned color at the same time. Rave explained that the

118

extreme weather conditions made it hard for aspen to grow from seeds that lived only about a week without cover and nourishment, so they grew from suckers of ancient root systems instead— actually one plant with multiple sprouts. So what they were seeing were groves of aspen clones. Park grizzlies on the ground, or park black bears in the trees, often did a little of their own hunting and gathering on reservation land.

"Speaking of wildlife ... unfortunately, or rather fortunately, in your case, Dana, there aren't any buffalo left in Glacier Park. They all went extinct in the early 1800s, but they were a different type of buffalo than that Plains buffalo of Yellowstone that you tangled with. The ones that lived in Glacier were a more primitive species with curlier hair known as a Mountain or Wood Buffalo. They do have a small protected heard still up in the Canadian part of the park at Waterton though ... "

"I'm afraid I'll have to pass on getting a close-up of them," Dana told him.

Rave chuckled, "I would too if I were you! They are fenced in so you would be safe up there."

"Oh, it's not that! Actually, I'd love to see them, but Jen and I already decided to pass up the Waterton area this time and save it for a later trip. We just won't have enough time to see everything we want, especially now that you're given us a taste of how much more there is to get in and explore."

"Before you start doing any exploring, let me add this cautionary note since you are a known buffalo magnet, Dana. There is an exciting program that has begun on the Blackfeet reservation to restore bison that are direct descendants of the last herd here in the 1870s to reservation lands. It was only started a few years ago with the transfer of calves of those descendants from a Canadian conservation herd to a breeding program that will hopefully restore free-ranging herds to the east slopes of the divide. But I don't know the current status of that project. Just stay clear of trouble for me so Garrett doesn't have to kill me if any more beasts find you irresistible, okay?"

"Why that sounds wonderful. I swear to stay out of trouble."

"Thank you for that."

Continuing on his clearly appreciated road tour, Rave pointed out enough peaks to daze them, filling in with detail about trails and trips that could be taken and interesting tidbits on all the flora and fauna found in different areas, recommending an excellent book on the natural history of the area by David Rockwell to Dana, that he had gathered much of his knowledge from.

Winter winds blew hard down from the Artic. On the eastern park slopes they were monitored by machine and had been clocked blowing at a hundred miles per hour for up to thirteen hours straight. Once a gust over one hundred sixty miles an hour had registered just before breaking the equipment. But the winds also scoured snow off valuable winter wildlife grazing areas.

On a high dry ridge in the park he pointed out one of its toughest trees on the east side. The limber pines clung alone to high treeless wind-lashed ridges where only their drought-tolerant skeletal shapes could survive, leaning away from the direction of the wind with their twisted claw-like limbs stretched out as if grasping for something to hold on to, hard short-tight grayed-green needles furring only their witchy fingertips.

He told them about the Cut Bank area just visible to the northeast, giving them the stories behind the names of the peaks, telling them of Mad Wolf, and the legend of the Medicine Grizzly, the spirit reincarnated of a chief of another band slain by the Blackfeet, said to roam around exacting revenge.

Then he cut east on Highway 89 away from the Rocky Mountain front and headed over the prairie to Browning, the center of The Blackfeet Nation governance and culture.

"Dana, it's too late tonight, but there's something I'm sure you'll want to check out in Browning. The Museum of the Plains Indians. Which reminds me, have you guys talked about whether you can stay a little longer, yet? The North American Indian Days celebration is soon, in July. They will have traditional costumes, celebrations, ceremonial dances, horse races ..."

Jen caught that odd distance again in the way he spoke.

Dana heard a note of pride in his voice, saw a hint of plea in the eyes that caught hers in the mirror. She knew he'd already asked Garrett if they could stay on longer, so she suspected that he was hoping Jen would extend her stay also. Dana could only shrug and promise to talk about it and let him know their plans later.

Greeted by name at the restaurant he took them to in Browning, Rave told Jen this was home base for him now, even when based away from Glacier, he kept his home here on the reservation.

After finishing a leisurely dinner, the women headed for the restrooms while Ravenwolf went to the entry to pay for the meal. Jen and Dana were headed back around a partial wall that

120

shielded the entry when they heard an overloud, less than sober male voice calling out.

"Hey, Rave Man, how'ya doing? Where 'ya been, you sick man?" Turning the corner they saw the back of a short, stout young man pumping Rave's arm vigorously. "So hey, no dating the babes in six months, I hear. What's that about, man? What, you got the clap, bro'?"

Stopped in their tracks, they saw Rave's startled glance over the man's shoulder, but couldn't hear his low, terse response that sent the young man stumbling away.

The ladies' silence was both stiff and decidedly frosty as they passed him to get in his car—their only choice of transportation.

chapter eight

IT HAD BEEN A MAGICAL day. For the most part.

Before it became stilted and silent.

A day begun with the wonder and mystery of ancients that had left a Folsom point in the dawn of a new post-ice sheeted renewal of the land. A day eased into on the quiet, gently rocking glide of a canoe, to greet a fresh morning with private glimpses of wildlife along misty lakeshores. A day of breath snatching scents and scenes lush with dense forests and wilderness stretching for mile after soothing mile. A day filled with the throat aching beauty of nature left alone, unmolested, and the wish for even more un-constructed peace to enjoy.

It had been a beautiful, even intimate, day.

The trio had spent almost the entire long, lovely time in close quarters: in a canoe, the car, at the restaurant, seldom far apart. It had been a friendly, comfortable closeness. A shared closeness of talk, laughter, teasing, happiness, of shared sights and thoughts and, for Rave and Jen, even more. Much more. They had shared their lips, kisses, and warmth, felt the sudden jolt and excited sizzle of newly sparked passion, along with the shared stories and wonder, so each shared smile fanned hidden embers of heat and pleasure.

The day had not lost any of its scenic beauty.

It had, in fact, seemed to put on a last burst of furious color to cap off the glorious day.

But the intimacy was gone, they were no longer close—though still trapped in the same car. Each individual was alone in their own silent space and thoughts, on the previously planned and anticipated sunset drive on a short stretch from St. Mary to Rising Sun,.

As they reentered the park near the clustered tipi village at St. Mary, the skies cast their reflected blush on the white decorated canvases. The road was again Going To the Sun, though now it was chasing the sun west across the divide to where it would rest for the night. And, like a set of bookends, this end of the drive was also invitingly framed on the left by the rippling waters of a long finger of glacially gouged lake. Edged and etched more sharply this time by the east wall of the Rockies rising to backdrop the far shore in a serrated silhouette against the crimson, gold, and hyacinth tones of the sky.

Dana recognized the sharp saw tooth design as geologic features she had studied; the ones that gave the park its name and distinction as an architectural record of past glacial ages. It was exciting to see the dry diagrams of the textbooks grandly recreated in this stunning setting. It was like the difference between looking at blueprints and seeing a completed Street of Dreams home, as Jen would put it.

Individual cirques had formed high up in the divide where snow had gathered then flowed down the valley drainages in a series of almost parallel glaciers, shaving off the mountains on each side until they had made the peaks between them into thin knifelike spines. These parallel rows of spines and valley glaciers met at right angles with a massive main ice sheet that cut a huge glacial trough while casually slicing off each mountain spine and valley in cross-section as it passed, gathering in each of these side glaciers like streams as it plowed across creating the future trough where St. Mary Lake now nestled. But the lake was only melt water in the bottom compared to the height and size of the ice sheet that had chopped crosswise into the eastern edge of the Rockies. This left the far side of the lake with a steep wall of rock rising in elevation until it reached the saw-toothed trim of those sliced off mountains and valleys high above.

The narrow mountain spikes were called 'arêtes', knife-edges. The chopped off valleys were called 'hanging valleys', where the streams flowed toward the lake and then, instead of just entering, fell off the cliff face to reach it way below now. She also noticed the beaked-pyramid shape of a peak that was known as a 'horn', where cirques had formed high on three sides of a single peak and grown glaciers so wide that they had joined to chop the mountainside into a triangular-shape.

123

As she gazed at the arêtes and hanging valleys over the sunset colored lake, Dana automatically translated the geologic features in her mind to cooking terms to discuss them with Jen. She thought an old-fashioned homemade pie crust with its finger rippled rim looked like the setting. One once filled to the brim with vanilla pudding or cheesecake, that would represent the old ice sheet. But there was no way she was going to point out the features right now, and drop her words into the stiff silence in the car. She'd save it for later, taking only a photo now, wishing they had a real pie to commiserate over later when she and her best friend were alone again.

Dana slanted her eyes and thoughts to the silent man beside her, driving with one hand braced on top of the steering wheel. His arm was stretched out so straight and taut that he looked like he was trying to shove the wheel away, instead of steer it. Eyes locked on the road, face closed, the profile of his jaw was as sharp and hard as the cliffs except where a muscle jumped and clenched. Dana had no sympathy for the man, and bit her lip to keep from saying what she was thinking.

Let the silent treatment he was getting speak for itself.

As soon as they had gotten in the car, Jen had scrambled for the backseat. Shoving the cooler to the other side, she scooted as far as she could cram herself against the window behind the high-backed driver's seat—where she could not be spied on from the rear view mirror. She checked the release catch on her seat belt before putting it on, making sure she could make a quick escape—alone.

Jen was glad the sun was setting on her side, so she could gaze moodily at the crimson slashes on the lake, and the last golden light that caught a tree on a dainty isle in the middle of St. Mary Lake. The gilding and crimson brush strokes snuck through to the lake in the low spots between the peaks that shaded most of the lake as the sun fell behind the mountain range in the west.

The west where her home was and where Jen would much rather be at this *exact* moment in time!

She dug around in her bag and found a travel size bottle of Listerine and took a hearty sip and sat brooding, swishing it into every corner of her mouth, even swallowing for good measure. She ran her disinfected tongue over her lips, removing any lingering trace of him. Hopefully.

Ravenwolf gritted his teeth and cursed inwardly. He caught a whiff of medicinal mouthwash from the back seat, and scowled even more. The little brunette huddled so silently back there probably wished about now that she could sand her lips off and spit them at him, poor thing. Dana looked like she wanted to kick him, or worse. Her shoulder probably wasn't strong enough yet to backhand him black and blue, so he guessed there was that to be thankful for.

The great dinner he had enjoyed had turned to sour acid churning in his stomach; his day had turned to soot and ashes. It had been a beautiful, magical day. He couldn't remember when he had last enjoyed himself so thoroughly. While he worked in the park, and loved it, he often forgot to stop, step back, and see it through new eyes—first-time awed eyes—as he'd been able to today through Jen's and Dana's—especially those deep blue dreamy eyes of Jenny's. Hell!

It had meant a lot to him to share in that. To experience the closeness and bond he'd formed today with his best pal's wife and the lovely little wren that was capturing his heart and his mind. It had been just over six month's since he had first seen her at Dana's wedding. It hadn't been just the door she had slammed in his face that had gotten his attention.

Now the magic of this day, the beauty, the closeness that was just beginning, after so many months of dreaming and hoping, and waiting ... had all been shattered by a careless loud-mouthed drunken remark.

He felt as if one of those ice sheets had plowed right into his heated car, carving a frozen silent barrier between himself and the women. A barrier he didn't know how to melt, and even if he did, just like the destroyed landscape after a glacier had receded, he was afraid the friendship and trust they'd all shared would be ravaged. Drowned. Chopped off. And it would take a long time to bloom again as it had today—if ever.

"DAMMIT!" He pounded his hand on the steering wheel, nearly shouting through gritted teeth.

"I DO NOT HAVE THE CLAP! OR ANY OTHER STDS!" Rave roared in frustration.

"THAT IS NOT WHY I ... aww hell." He snapped his mouth shut as both women nearly jumped from their seats startled by his outburst, words he hadn't meant to shout out loud.

Another silent, strained mile passed as he tried to focus, get a grip, concentrate on his driving, and ...

"Wait a minute. Where am I? Did you say you were staying at the Many Glacier Hotel tonight?"

Dana gave him a curt nod.

He sighed, disgusted with himself, and eventually found a pull-out to make a U-turn and head back east.

He drove another ways before Dana spoke.

"My car?" Brief and to the point, but at least she had given him sound this time.

"Is waiting at your hotel as promised," he said quietly. "I had a text message that it was delivered."

"Good."

Well, he hadn't expected her to say thank you. He only had himself to be angry with. He had worked hard to earn a bad reputation, and now he was getting the payback. They didn't trust him, or believe him.

He drove back out of the park, turning north at St. Mary on Highway 89 toward Babb where the Many Glacier Road would cut west back into the park, on a branch that dead ended at Swiftcurrent Lake. Dusk was already on them and darkness fell rapidly on the east slope once the Rockies blocked the setting sun.

"What's it like staying in a tipi, Rave?"

He held his breath, hesitating before answering, unsure whether he had imagined that soft voice from the back seat, or if Jen had really spoken to him.

Of course, if he was just dreaming, those words wouldn't come close to what he would wish to hear Jenny say.

"Beg pardon?" And did he ever literally mean that!

"Those tipis we just passed again near the park exit. What's it like staying in them?"

God. She really was speaking to him.

Civilly. Calmly. Probably just to distract him. Afraid he would lose it again after his outburst, before he got them safely back to their lodge and they could escape the nut case—the allegedly diseased nut case.

"I have no idea. I have never lived in a tipi, Jen. No, wait, now that I think about it, once when I was a kid I went to a summer camp for a week and we slept in tipis. But, I really didn't pay much attention to them. At that age it's just cool to be out camping with a bunch of other boys, telling ghost stories and pulling dumb practical jokes on each other like running some guy's shorts up the flagpole.

"I remember the time there was this camp counselor we all really hated. He always made us put our swim trunks back on while they were still wet and had practically frozen overnight. Man, we got him good, we ... ah ...sorry. Tipis. Yeah, I remember it was brighter and much roomier than the tents we stayed in other times."

Jeez! She doesn't need you to babble your life story, idiot, just because you're excited she asked a simple question!

Silence swamped the car again.

Though it didn't feel quite as strained as it had earlier, it was still plenty chilly. Both women had fallen asleep long before they reached the Many Glacier Hotel on the shores of Swiftcurrent Lake—or, at least, they had pretended sleep. The curt "nite" from Jen, after such a day, told him he was not forgiven.

He had hoped for a long, lazy kiss good night.

He received the back of a very cold shoulder.

Their magic day together lay crushed beneath a few careless words and his own reckless, thoughtless reputation.

While Jen was soaking in the tub trying to wash away all her physical and emotional bumps, bruises, aches and heartaches, Dana's cell phone rang.

"Hey, how's my beautiful babe? Do you miss me?"

"Garrett, you know I do! How are things going there, hon?"

"Good, babe, but I've really missed the sound of your voice." A deep chuckle came over the line. "Along with all your other unique charms."

"Really?" She teased playfully, settling back on the bed, curling up against stacked pillows. "My charms? Like ... my cooking?"

"Hmm, well that wasn't the charm at the top of my head, no."

"Well, you did say 'unique'..." She grinned at his bark of laughter.

"Unique is the word. Nobody cooks up a plate of potato chips and packaged dip like you, babe." His voice was soft with affection.

"My brilliant mind and witty personality, maybe?" she teased.

"Exactly! And all that warm, luscious skin that covers them."

"Well, you do have the ... odd charm, yourself, big guy."

"It's not *that* odd!" He gave one of those hearty head thrown back laughs that she so loved him for.

"So, babe," he purred, once he stopped laughing, "I've waited, hoping to hear from you for so long I was almost wishing you'd tangle with some wildlife and end up back in the hospital so we could have some more phone sex."

"Garrett! We didn't," she scolded, mock scandalized, "we just pretended like we were for Jenny back then."

"Speaking of ... I hear you guys had a fantastic day today."

She heard the more serious note his tone had taken. Ravenwolf must have called him and given him a report.

"Hmm. Well, we were ... until your friend ruined it by hurting and humiliating Jenny! But it sounds like you already heard about that from a little bird with a heart as black as a raven's!" Dana let her frustration flare in temper.

"Hey babe, come on Dana. You know I love Jenny like a sister, too. I've also known Rave for years, just like you've known her. So talk to me, babe, no need to shout. Tell me what he did that was so black-hearted, so I can understand."

Dana poured out all her anger and frustration on his long-distance shoulder, then was ready to listen as Garrett spoke softly, fairly and calmly to her.

"Dana, I understood that you three spent the whole day together, starting with Rave taking you to a site where a Folsom point was found. Something he knew would have special meaning for you. Then they canoed and you all took a long drive around the outside border of the park, even got to see the mountain goats. Rave said it was really great for him to get to see it all new and share that with you guys, and he said how much fun he was having."

She admitted it. "We *were* having fun and he was being so nice unit—"

"Until," he interrupted, his voice never loosing its gentleness, "after spending the day getting to know and trust him, you let some loud-mouthed, drunken stranger shoot his mouth off and you automatically believed that, instead of trusting your own judgment of a man you'd just spent a whole fantastic day learning to count on."

"Well, when you put it like that, I guess so."

"Is that what happened, Dana, or is there something Rave left out?"

"No. I mean, yes, that's basically what happened, but Garrett, remember at our wedding? You warned me he had a bad reputation with women, remember?"

"I did, that's absolutely true, and he did have a horrible reputation. But it appears the operative word here is 'did'—past tense..."

"Oh come on now, Garrett, every woman has heard that 'I reformed' crap. I did not expect someone like you to defend it."

Ever patient and confident that Dana was not attacking him personally in her snap of temper, he continued as calmly as before.

"There's something you don't know, babe. Something I wasn't sure of myself 'til now. I wondered, but ... You see, every phone call I've had with Rave since our wedding, he's asked about Jen. Oh not directly, but kind of casually. I didn't really even notice at first, until I thought about it later.

"He'd say something that would get me talking about her, like one time he asked how you were managing so far away from your best friend. Naturally I talked all about how close you guys were, how you'd met, what she meant to you, stuff like that. Each time he called he managed to bring Jenny into the conversation somehow."

"I remember you said he'd asked if Jen and I were still going to Glacier, that time."

"Yeah, that was when your sling came off, I think. But Dana, he brought it up a lot more than that, but I didn't take it too seriously. It was your trip he was talking about after all, showing interest, concern. But he did say that if your arm was still bad he'd be glad to show Jenny around Glacier for you, so you wouldn't have to worry about disappointing her. I did pause a bit on that one, but Rave's always been a loyal friend and really considerate guy, even if a little wild with the ladies. As my wife, he'd do anything for you. But I started to suspect he might also be a little hung up on your best friend."

"You never told me that!"

"I wasn't sure, but ... "

"But, what?" Dana asked impatiently when he hesitated too long.

"Well, tell me, what would you think if your playboy pal just gave up the last of his cool and admitted he was desperate. If I told you he asked me to call you to plead his case with Jenny?"

"He didn't!"

"Oh, he did!"

"You mean he didn't call to bitch about us but to beg?"

"Actually, he did say he was begging me to help him."

"Get out!"

"I can give you the exact quote, it shocked me so much it's burned in my brain. Besides, I wrote it out after I hung up, to be sure I recorded it word for word."

"So it would be accurate for us. Thank you, hon, that was sweet of you."

"Ahh, well that too, of course. You're welcome. But truthfully I was thinking more along the lines of keeping it as evidence to raze him forever about," Garrett admitted, more gleeful than sheepish.

"Make me a photocopy. Why should you have all the blackmail power? Okay, Garrett, I'm calmer now. And I grabbed a pen and paper. Tell me what he said."

"He said, and I quote, 'Hearth, I need help. I know I razed you a lot for falling for Dana like a love sick puppy, but I'm the one yipping now. I didn't want to admit this, but Jen— Well, I've got a real case for her, man. Ever since your wedding I haven't been able to focus on another woman. I'm begging you to help me out' End quote."

"You lie!"

"Never lie to you, Dana. You know that."

"I do. Did you really fall for me like a love-sick puppy?"

"Absolutely!"

"That's so sweet! I'm so lucky to have you. Did you really admit it to your buddy, Garrett? That you were love-sick for me?"

"Right." He sounded a little impatient having to confess twice to his sappy phrase. "Which is the point I'm trying to get back to and make here, babe."

"Rave admitted to you, a guy, a buddy, that he has a case for Jen."

"Exactly. And for a guy like him, that's drastic."

"Tough." Hearing his sigh, she added. "Okay, I believe you. Wow, and all that. Drastic. So now what do we do?"

"We tell Jen that the part that loud-mouth said about Rave not dating for six months was actually true, and she's the reason why. The rest was bullshit."

"Okay, then?"

"Then, my dear darling bride, I suggest you leave it alone and don't push them. Let things go however they will after that's

130

clear. By the way, sweetheart, what's this I hear about you telling Jen to kiss Rave for your thank you?"

Dana smothered a giggle. "Too pushy, ya think? Okay, I'll just show my thanks myself then, hon, is that what you want?"

"Over his dead body!"

"Well, that wouldn't do Jen much good, but he is so darkly handsome," Dana faked a wistful sigh. "And you are so far away ..."

"Tease. You'll pay for that when I get there."

"Sounds like fun! I can hardly wait. I miss you, Garrett," she finished on a soft whisper.

"I miss you more, babe, and you're there hanging out with the handsome men while I'm home kissing our horses."

"Give them one for me. Give that rascal Corky two."

"Listen, Dana, Rave wants to take you guys up to Grinnell Glacier tomorrow and he already arranged the day off special so he could, and bought the tickets for the boat tour. Try and talk to Jenny tonight. Maybe she'll be willing to give him another chance tomorrow, but don't push. It won't hurt him to work hard for her. She's a special lady."

"He should, she *is* special. A special woman."

They strung out their personal goodbyes awhile then Dana hung up just after Jen came out of the bathroom in a cloud of steam, wrapping a towel around her hair.

"How's Garrett?

"He's the sweetest man alive," Dana smiled.

"Oh, well, of course." Jenny smiled back, then added in a tart mutter, "Probably the only one, too."

"Yes, well it appears that a little ... raven ... called him and begged Garrett to plead his case with a certain ... little wren."

Jen met Dana's recounting of her conversation with her husband with stony silence, until hearing that Rave had confessed to have a "real case" for her.

"Yeah, right!" She snorted, and clambered into bed with a book and turned her back to Dana.

Discussion ended.

"Ahh," Dana hesitated at the clear sign Jen wanted to be left to her own thoughts the rest of the night. "Just one thing... before I quit bugging you. The Grinnell plan okay? Or should I cancel?"

"I guess we can go," was Jenny's unenthusiastic mutter, before pulling the covers higher over her shoulder.

"Right."

Dana took out her cell and text messaged Ravenwolf.

GRINNELL OKAY but not B4 10 am!
REST ???'

Then turning down all the lights except the one by her bed, Dana gathered up a stack of books, including a couple of new ones she had found at the gift shop, and settled down happily to do some research on the park.

She and Garrett had done all they could to help their friends muddle their way through whatever was up between them. They would have to sort the rest out for themselves.

Or not, if Jen's attitude was anything to go by.

chapter nine

IT WAS A GREATLY subdued man that showed up at the hotel door the next morning. A subdued man, yet a quietly determined one. And an exceedingly polite gentleman. Requesting that he might be allowed to spend another day in the pleasure of their company in return for his guide services on a trip to Grinnell Glacier.

"I also offer up my worthless body to be cast in front of any grizzly bears to protect you both, if the need arises," he said soberly, deadly serious.

Dana smiled at the graceful apology. Poor man, he had clearly lost his virginity, so to speak, as the man about town that had a heart no woman could dent or endanger. He looked so pitiful.

He didn't look like a love-sick puppy yet, but he certainly looked like a kicked one. Dana couldn't imagine anyone being so cruel to a pup, so she took mercy on the man, setting a light and playful tone.

"Come on in, Rave, we would certainly appreciate that as long as you don't take my 'thank yous' too enthusiastically today," she winked at him giving a smile and a warning there was still some work to do with Jenny. "Garrett says I can only give you a thank you kiss of my own over *your* dead body. So you'll have to settle for paltry words today, I'm afraid." Another warning.

"More than adequate." He stepped warily over the threshold, relaxing slightly when he got a polite smile and greeting inside from Jenny.

"Good morning, Ravenwolf. There are fresh doughnuts on the table over there."

"Morning, Jen. Thanks. Turning to Dana he asked a little more heartily, "So, are you guys-girls-ladies-women ready for a little boat trip and some more hiking today?" He wasn't taking any chances on saying the wrong thing today.

Jen took a seat in the back of the lovely old wooden boat that would cruise them across Swiftcurrent Lake on the first leg of today's jaunt, watching the dock and the hotel recede in its wake.

The Many Glacier area was in a cul-de-sac of spectacular mountain peaks and lakes that snuck in behind the dramatic sheer rock fin of the Garden Wall they had climbed along on Going to the Sun Road, west of Logan Pass. This was the reverse side of that wall and the east of the Great Divide, accessed by twelve mile long Many Glacier Road from Babb, along Lake Sherburne, another glacial finger lake, up into the Swiftcurrent Valley.

The Many Glacier Hotel, once the grandest and largest hotel in all Montana—even in this remote location—stretched extensively across the flat segment of shoreline. Surprisingly, it looked as unobtrusive from a distance as a jumble of dark brown stained driftwood logs cast on the edge of the shore. Relative to the massive size, power, and drama of its setting, the huge hotel was about as significant as kindling. And, over the years, that is what the powerful elements of ice, wind, long winters, and deep snow had almost rendered it.

Opened on the fourth of July in 1915 and added to shortly after, heavy snows had attempted annually to crush it. By the time it was added to the National Trust's list of the eleven Most Endangered National Historic Places in 1996, the Swiss chalet style balconies had suffered so much damage, exterior steel cables had to be used to hold them up. All the roofs and gables where under constant maintenance.

In 2006, a destructive year of fire, flood, and avalanche that tore up many areas including sections of the Going to the Sun Road, November floods swelled Swiftcurrent Lake until it flooded into the hotel and spilled over the access road. Now a many years long renovation had been completed, giving the national treasure another lifetime. Subject to Nature's harsh challenges, of course.

Up close the hotel was massive with it multiple roofs, dark chocolate stained siding, and tiers of decorative wood railed balconies, with whimsical chalet gingerbread trimmings and painted stenciling. While inside the cathedral height and majesty of being under the forest canopy prevailed, with columns of great trees from the Pacific Northwest rising on all sides in the lobby, similar to the Glacier Park Hotel, but in the lighter natural tint of peeled wood.

But most impressive of all were the mountain peaks marching across the lake, as seen through the lodge's windows. Their size and majesty humbling, looming over man's slight achievement tucked on the opposite shore.

From the deck of the boat, Jen looked west at the peaks of the Continental Divide, lining the far shore. All were dramatic, each peak a distinct individual on the horizon. Furthest north a bit of the ragged sheer cliffs of the Ptarmigan Wall stretched into the distance from a great fin of peak, the snow streaked matterhorn of Mt. Wilbur—much too dramatic for its name. A distant look at Swiftcurrent Mountain was overwhelmed by the big triangular bulk of Grinnell Peak, centered in the foreground on the lake. As they moved further down the waters, the barn roof shape of Mount Gould, with its distinctive black horizontal line that seemed to mark the roofline, loomed closer and linked to the Garden Wall that backed up Grinnell Glacier.

And those were just the ones that rimmed the west wall of the lake valley that was encircled by peaks, many in the nine to ten thousand foot range.

It was simply stunning.

This was high living, indeed!

Jen smiled at her own pun as the boat approached the little hump of land. They would climb less than a quarter of a mile over to the next lake up in the chain, Lake Josephine, where they would board another wooden boat.

She drew in a deep breath of crisp air and gave a great sigh, turning her thoughts to the serious dark-eyed man watching, waiting to help her off the boat.

Jen was relieved, okay, *hugely* relieved that she had a good reason to give Rave a second chance—was even encouraged to by Dana. Especially gratified to know that it had been as important to him, at least according to Garrett, as it was to her, to clear his name and regain her good graces.

No matter how fun, or how handsome a man was, Jenny had vowed not to ever let that blind her, or let one walk all over her. The day before had been like a dream. She had seen sides to the dark devilish man that were tender, thoughtful, humorous, and deeper than she had ever expected from him. And his kisses ... well, she'd expected him to be good at that—and was he! Sweet, drugging kisses that melted her right down into her socks.

After the day they'd spent she had been crushed, had felt so uncharacteristically helpless, when she heard proof that he was the type of man she'd first suspected—expected—before he'd charmed her into believing he was different. It had been easy for her to take what she'd heard as proof when everything was already seeming too good to be true.

She would have been okay playing with a man that played by clear rules, but he wasn't playing fair. Instead of the expected dance of hot looks, hot kisses, blatant flirtation and fast seductive moves, he was being sweet, tender, telling love stories around a campfire. That was not what she'd expected! He'd sabotaged her by being nicer than he was supposed to be. She was relieved he was blameless this time, but nervous she was getting too hooked.

As least this day he seemed quieter, they could all just relax, slow things down, and ...

A strong bronzed arm curled around her waist and lifted her from the deck to the path.

"Watch your step, little one."

When she turned to him, he gave her a warm smile that reflected softly in those dark, normally dangerous, eyes. Her heart jumped like a fish on a hook, and her serene day trailed off in the wake.

He took both her hands in his and leaned close, capturing her eyes. "I want to apologize to you, but you deserve a full apology so I will ask you to be patient with me until we get to a better place to talk alone. Now we need to catch the next boat," and with a quick kiss to her forehead, he turned her and guided her up the path over the hump of the moraine that divided the lakes, his hand gently touching her back on any rough patches. When they got aboard the boat to Lake Josephine, he sat beside her.

"I discussed this with Dana, now I wanted to get your input," he pulled out a trail map and leaned close to point out features. "This is what is considered a 'moderately strenuous trail'. As in not easy. We have shortened the hiking distance by taking to the water, but there are still about four miles of hiking and some is pretty straight up, after we get off the boat."

"Roundtrip?" Jen asked. She was wise to this trick.

He laughed ruefully, "Ah, no, sorry, each way from the end of Lake Josephine." He saw her eyes widen. "But that's only if you want to walk right up to the glacier. You can't step on it anyway. And like I mentioned some of it is steep climbing. So here is the idea Dana had."

She tried to listen carefully as he leaned over pointing out the different trails on the map, pointing out options. There was a trail to the left that went only up to a tarn, Grinnell Lake, that was just under a mile each way and had essentially minimum height gain, with a short side trip to hidden falls if she wanted to see more, but the glacier was out of sight above. Dana had met a couple of experienced hikers that had offered to hike with her up the much longer and steeper trail to the glacier, if Jen wanted to take the lower trail with Rave. Otherwise Jen was facing a steep climb up to a path on the side of Mount Grinnell that started at over a mile high altitude and switch-backed up a sixteen hundred foot elevation gain, but she would see one of the largest remaining glaciers in the park.

Jen spotted the other trick she had recently discovered, right away. Elevation gain noted on trail guides did not mean up a specific number of feet one way, and down on the return. In this terrain it more often meant something like switchbacks, only done vertically instead of horizontally. Up and down like a jack-in-the-box one could easily climb two or more times the listed elevation gain—both ways! It was definitely a net amount of climbing, more an infinite seeming, than finite, number of feet. And like that trail length trick, once you got to the end, you couldn't just stay there and be done, anymore than you could keep from climbing back up each time you went down another dip. She was becoming quite experienced at this game, so it was becoming harder for Dana or Rave to trick her.

"Does this have one of those bar chart thingies to show *how* that elevation does its gaining?" She asked suspiciously.

"I can just tell you, trust me ... " He stopped at the abrupt arching of eyebrows that, despite their dark, dainty perk, clearly said 'do not mess with me, buster', and rummaged in his day pack for a guide with charts for proof.

Trying to analyze the information and choices, Jen took the map and sat back to study it away from the distracting heat, and scent, and nearness of the man whose silky raven black hair kept brushing against her cheek, as he pointed out trails. She needed to make a decision—straight up the mountain, or take the easy trail, miss the glacier, and be caught all alone with Ravenwolf?

Jen was not sure whether she picked the trail hike she knew was beyond her fitness level because she was stupid or scared. Scared of the talk Rave wanted to have with her when he got enough privacy. At first it had sounded promising, then on further thought she wondered why a man said to be innocent of the charge was so intent on not just a sorry, but a *full* apology? Sounded suspicious..

So she had been stupid instead, agreeing to the difficult hike. The stupid parts seemed to come to her naturally around this man. She suspected he fed her a dose of stupid with each of his kisses. She stumbled on the trail, earning a quick backwards glance from Dana.

"You okay?"

"I guess," Jen muttered crossly.

They were climbing up the flank of a mountain through a forest that had survived after a wildfire, with sub-alpine firs filling in the valley. Climbing sharply up from the head of the lake they connected with the dirt trail that had come along the side of Lake Josephine and around Swiftcurrent Lake all the way from the hotel. The trail for those dedicated hikers that wanted to walk eleven miles roundtrip. Jenny envied their conditioning, while shuddering at just the thought of what she had let herself in for as they continued to climb one sharp switchback after another.

She restrained herself from whining and asking Dana how many more miles, knowing her trial had just started. Apparently the plan was to climb up above the tree line and look down on all this while sauntering along the side of the cliff. She had seen a picture of people doing that saunter part of this hike. It sure hadn't shown this sweaty uphill part.

Jen thought she would have much more trouble keeping up with Dana in front of her on the trail, up the switchbacks, the steepness seemed unrelenting, but it was proving easier than she thought.

Easier to keep up with Dana that is—not an easier climb.

Dana kept stopping on the trail to gape at things, most particularly the subtle variations of rock color and textures. Jen just kept trudging upward, her knees near fainting, her calves aching, but each time she stumbled or tried to stop for a rest of her own, a big male hand covered her butt and gave her another boost

138

upward. The contact seemed to sear right through her clothes and apply a too intimate scorch to her bottom. Each time she leapt forward on the trail like she had been electrically goosed. The man had way too dangerous a touch, and he seemed to be doing way too much of it.

In places he didn't belong!

Yet.

She was afraid that if he ever did get private with her... well, she hoped she let him apologize before she jumped him. Which she definitely would not do! Or slugged him after the torture of this climb to remind her about being stupid. She just wished the man would keep his big hands off her!

Jen stopped a moment to catch her breath—and get another spark and sizzle to help jolt her up the trail.

They finally climbed into a more open area. The group ahead slowed and she could hear excited chatter. Rave had told her that she could expect to see big horn sheep grazing the upper meadows, to encourage her as she climbed to a vantage point. When she labored harder, and started to think about just rolling back down to land into that nice cool lake where they had started, he told her it was also a major area to see grizzly bears, encouraging her to get going and stay with the group. So she wondered now if wildlife had been spotted. Either big horn sheep? Or a grizzly feeding on it or some poor hiker that had fallen behind?

Dana was grabbing her camera. Jen's next gasp was not for air, but wonder, at the beauty below. Holding up a hand palm out to Rave with a stern scowl, to make sure he didn't do his grab and push thing, she leaned over, bracing her hands on her knees to catch her breath while she savored the scene below.

She had come to see a near extinct glacier—or mostly because Dana and Rave drug her along—but she hadn't come for this. It just leapt out at her like a surprise, a beautifully wrapped gift compliments of Glacier National Park, one of the most exquisite places, she was coming to realize, on this earth.

An artist could not paint the picture below and have anyone believe the setting and colors were of a real place.

"Oh, Jen," Dana breathed, "look at all the different colors!"

"I know. It's like a wonderland." But when she glanced up she saw Dana's camera was focused at an angle that would miss the verdant valleys below. She was focused on an elegant curve topped mountain that divided the valleys, and the subtle shadings of the strata that climbed its sheer face.

"That mountain is know as Angel Wing, Dana." She heard Rave explain.

"And that lovely little jewel of a lake?" Jen wanted to know.

"Lake Grinnell," he replied, "Now considered the lower one since there is one up higher."

It was hard to imagine the other one could compete with this view. A turquoise gem of a lake was set among emeralds of vivid grass meadows with a scattering of dark jade conifers to add richness. Sprinkled snow patches glittered like diamonds, softened by a whole meadow of the pale fluffy yellow beargrass flowing down the hillside. Dana's Angel Wing, with its red tinted base added the rubies, where it divided the bright treeless, endless green of the upper glacial valley that sloped to the dark jade green tree line below.

It was like a fairyland or what heaven must look like. Someone else must have thought so also to guard it with the wing of an angel. She stole Dana's camera and took a picture of heaven of her own to take home with her.

As they continued on the trail, able to stroll now for awhile, Rave told them about the other, higher lake.

"Upper Grinnell Lake wasn't actually here when George Bird Grinnell surveyed this area and first found the glacier that is named for him. And it wasn't here after the park first opened, either. It didn't form until about 1927. What is known as the Little Ice Age, when many of these alpine glaciers reformed in the cirques and valleys carved by the big Ice Age sheets, ended around the mid-1800s. When the glacier began to melt and recede, it left a terminal moraine behind, a big mound of rock and debris it had pushed and carried forward and dropped in a pile when it backed up. Behind that natural rock dam, the melt water left a basin of ice water, a tarn, which was given the name of Upper Grinnell, to distinguish it from the one left much earlier lower in the valley. Between are cascades and waterfalls dropping down from what is now an upper, or hanging valley."

"Like upper and lower Kintla Lakes?" Jen asked.

"Exactly. There are chains of those lakes all through the valleys that radiate out from Swiftcurrent Lake, in this many glaciered area."

"And that pretty turquoise au lait color comes from the ground rock flour hanging in the lake, with the sun reflecting off it, right?"

140

"I'm going to send you out to give interpretive tours soon, Jen, if you're not careful," he teased and tweaked a dark curl that had escaped her ponytail.

"Dana has had me in training for years on anything to do with rocks." She laughed back, smiling at her friend.

And Jen had enjoyed it, though she made sure to gripe about it so Dana didn't overload her.

Jen thought of heaven again, when a waterfall they climbed past sprayed her hot, sweaty, dusty body with a crisp shower. Then she knew she had reached there again when they came to a picnic area with logs to sit on, *and a chemical toilet*, and blessed shade trees. She plunked down and decided not to move for a very long time.

Or never.

If things like grizzly bears and mountain lions didn't exist, Jen might stay forever, or at least overnight to get her strength back. They snacked on water and energy bars, rested and cooled down, but when Jen rose to use the facilities, her legs were still shaking, her feet didn't seem to want to lift high enough to clear a pebble, and her ankles ached, something she had never experienced before.

When she found out she still had to climb over that moraine and go even further to get to the overlook to see the glacier up close with all its cracks and crevices, she told Dana to go without her and bring back lots of photographs. She'd wait right where she was and look at the glacier on the camera when Dana and Rave got back. But he insisted on waiting with her. All that climbing to escape a private moment for nothing!

No one in the group called Jen a quitter or gave her a bad time. The experienced hikers knew she needed to get the wobble out of her legs and be ready for the hike down, when she would need to place her feet just as carefully. The girl had been a trooper to get this far, and now she needed to be smart. So Dana set off with other hikers and Rave sat down beside Jen and gave her a wolfish grin.

"Alone at last," he sighed.

Great!

Resigned, Jen shifted on the log so she could see his face, and see if those dark lava eyes of his were lying or not. When he took her hand, she pulled it away, back into her lap, waiting.

"I understand that Garrett asked Dana to share some, but not all of this, with you already. That I am and have been perfectly healthy. The guy in the restaurant was telling the truth, but ... Wait," he caught her as she tried to stand and pulled her back to the log.

"Only part was true, Jen. The rest he made up."

She looked at his eyes, his expression, and saw only sincerity, but held herself silent and let him say his piece. Then she would decide.

Besides she couldn't walk well enough yet to flee.

"Do you recall the part about him saying I had stayed away from women for six months? Well, that part was true." His prior reputation was in a shambles because he hadn't dated, or hardly even flirted—it was little wonder those who knew him thought he was sick.

"Aren't you going to ask me why?"

No, her expression clearly told him.

"Okay, well at least listen to me." He hastily tacked on a "Please."

Rave took a deep breath before continuing but held his dark eyes steady on the narrowed cobalt blue of hers, trying to ignore the doubtful lines on her forehead, and tight set to her lips.

"I haven't dated," he continued, his voice dropping lower, a little husky, but his eyes steady, "because I met a woman a while back that seems to have knocked my interest in other women out of my head."

Jen held her face expressionless, but felt her mind, and maybe something else, cringe. He had fallen for some woman out there and was just playing with her until he could be with the other woman. No wonder he had only kissed her but not tried seriously to get her in his bed. For a guy like him, he probably considered a kiss about the same as a handshake for greeting women. She took a cooling sip of her water before steam started drifting out of her ears.

"I hadn't planned that, I mean I didn't consciously plan to quit seeing other women. Celibacy has never been a big part of my agenda."

Or any part! Jen thought, ignoring his sheepish little smile. She wasn't sure how much more of this 'apology' she could take, and tried to distance herself, at least mentally.

"I just never seemed to see anyone that could interest me, could hold my attention as much as the woman that was haunting my dreams. The woman whose face was the one that flashed in front of me all the time, whether I wanted it or not."

Okay, so he was trying to tell her gently that his days of flings were over and apologize for letting her chase him needlessly, though apparently he still felt free to let his lips roam at will, she snorted indignantly.

"Jen? Jen, did you hear what I said?"

"Sorry. Were you speaking to me?" Her voice all temper.

"I was saying that ever since I met a fiery little brunette at a wedding, she has been with me. Been In my thoughts, in all my dreams. The *only one* in my dreams."

Did he mean *her*? She frowned at him, narrowed her eyes more. But didn't pull her hands away when he managed to capture them this time.

"You, Jen, are the reason I haven't dated in six months, not some disease. Though you might be a new kind of disease that I couldn't find the antidote for—" Realizing immediately from her expression that he should have kept that joke to himself. He knew he was telling the truth, spilling his guts, really, and it was a little edgy for him. She was clearly having trouble buying in. He had to make her believe him, for a chance to see if they had something special, even if his Jen disease later proved chronic. As threatening as that idea was, he had to try. He wanted her, needed her, needed most for her to believe him at this crucial moment.

"Let me say this first. I know that it is my fault that you believed him. I apologize for that, deeply. I've built up a bad reputation, and I'm paying for it. I apologize for putting you in a bad, embarrassing situation because of my past behavior. You don't deserve that. Again, I'm truly sorry it affected you. Please, all I'm asking is that you let the past be past. And believe that you are the only woman I am seeing or want to see right now."

Naturally, as much as his words warmed Jenny's little heart, the ones that seemed to resound the most loudly were the last two.

Did 'right now' mean while they were on the hike? Did it mean for today? Or through the end of her vacation?

Who knew with a man like Rave? It was surprising enough to hear he was interested in just one woman at a time—or claimed to be. Why push her luck and hope her tenure in his affections would last beyond the present?

Even if she wanted it to.

Did she? Of course not! Jen scoffed at herself. She knew better than to let a man like Rave tamper with anything except her body. Her heart was totally off limits.

"Jen, are we okay?" His eyes pleaded sincerely along with his voice.

She turned to him with a cool little smile.

"Of course." But as soon as he grinned and wrapped an arm around her waist, she could not resist.

"For right now." She gave him her most angelic smile.

On the boat rides back to the dock at the shore in front of the Many Glacier Hotel, Jenny felt like she was back in high school.

She felt like a girlfriend, with her boyfriend's arm so casually draped around her, resting on the back of the seat. His fingertips sneaking in little strokes on her shoulder, playing with her hair, his thumb gently stroking her nape. Leaning close, to subtly keep her curled in the protective curve of his chest and shoulder, as they contentedly enjoyed the scenery and quietly enjoyed the comfort of being with each other—innocent pleasures.

Almost like a high school date—at least *her* high school dates. With that certain innocence that comes before carnal knowledge, when the focus is more on beginning a relationship, maybe even falling in love—puppy love, at least, though every moment seems dramatic or tragic—than on seeking a night of heated entertainment, or a short vacation fling that flares brightly before fizzling to forgetfulness—or worse, regrets.

Jen felt comfortable, and a little giddy. Their relationship had turned a corner it seemed. Just the fact that they could call it a relationship was new. She smiled, feeling young and foolish as his fingers caressed her lightly, and his voice murmured close to her ear about the changes he had seen over the years at the Grinnell Glacier, and the projections that the glaciers were on their last gasp.

Then he snuck a kiss, more a soft brush of lips, behind her ear, and Jen gasped at the slightly less innocent tingles it sent shivering through her nervous system.

chapter ten

AS PART OF HIS apologies for any embarrassment he had caused them, Ravenwolf brought Dana a book yesterday, before their trip to Grinnell Glacier. It was the Rockwell book on the natural history of Glacier that he had been telling them about.

Early this morning, Jen found that while she had spent the night tossing and turning over heated dreams of a dark and dangerous, apologetic man, Dana had spent the night tossing around her books, hot on the trail of the mystery of Glacier's weird rocks. She had apparently found gold in the one Rave brought, and spent her night turning pages.

"Oh my God, Jen. This is flat out amazing! No wonder it looked so strange. There is no granite here! None! Except for in the name of the Granite Park Chalet. Whoever named that must be *way* embarrassed!" Dana hooted, clearly delighted about something, before turning back to her books and muttering. "So that's why the mountains look like they have a flat, matte finish. There's no reflective mica, or... How could I not have known this?"

Jen had looked over from applying another layer of topcoat to her nails to where her friend sat cross legged in the middle of her rumpled bed, in a tank top and cotton pajama bottoms, bent over several books spread open on top her sheets, flipping from one to another.

Dana had made a another trip to the gift shop, plus the book Rave gave her. Dana couldn't go on a vacation without her books to study on the area, a collection that was now supplemented with her scientific texts for the courses she was going to take in Bozeman this fall. Jen preferred magazines and romance novels.

"Incredible!" Dana said, in that excited but whispery voice, soft with the wonder that shone in her green eyes, fixed, not on the wall, but on some infinite mystical sphere beyond. "Just incredible!" she said again before her eyes snapped back in focus and she turned to Jen with a cat licking cream grin on her face.

"And just what has my friend, the great book explorer, discovered this time?" Jen asked with an affectionate laugh. "And speak In English, not Science, please!"

"I've discovered the great mystery of Glacier Park, no less! A secret hidden, so to speak, in plain sight, but mysteriously little known to many who visit," Dana bragged, bouncing her auburn eyebrows, her smile bordering on smug.

"All these glacier carved mountains," she waved her hand toward the window, "are just the gorgeous distraction, nature's little slight of hand." Dana rocked back and forth on the bed laughing, too pleased and excited with herself to sit still.

Leaning toward Jen, she asked eagerly, "Haven't you ever dreamed of digging a great big tunnel deep into the earth Jen, so you can travel back in time and see what the earth was like in its beginnings? Find its mysteries?"

"Dig?" Jen glanced at her nails. "Can't I just get the DVD? Sorry. Just had to tease you a bit, you are way too pleased with yourself." She frowned thoughtfully a moment, then brightened.

"You mean like go back to the Jurassic or something?" Jen named the only ancient time she could recall, but was beginning to catch a little of Dana's excitement. "Sure, yeah. that would be cool."

But Dana just waved her hand, like brushing off a fly.

"Oh, that's nothing, Jen," she dismissed. "That's not that far beneath the surface east of the park. The Cretaceous, the end of the dinosaurs is nearly topsoil out there." She noticed Jenny's blue eyes widening at that comment. "Remind me to take you through Chouteau, to the dinosaur museum, on the way back after our vacation. But you do have the right general idea."

Dana shuffled through her books as she spoke, flipping pages furiously.

"You remember those charts that list all the periods of time. Here we are. A Geologic Time Chart." Dana ran her finger slowly down all the colored and labeled blocks as if she was tunneling down through time, reading off the strange names with the same ease as Jen would sort down through a sale stack of designer labels.

"Jurassic, Triassic, Permian, Carboniferous, Devonian, Silurian, Ordovician," until she reached the base of the named colored blocks. "And the Cambrian! Starting just over a half-billion years ago." Dana tapped her finger on the big blank block of time beneath and grinned gleefully.

"What if you could dig back in time and see *before* the Cambrian, see the earth before that? Huh? In this big empty hole of time between the earth forming about four and a half billion years ago, and the Cambrian, only half a billion years ago. I'm sure you've heard the term 'The Cambrian Explosion of Life'?"

Not recently.

"Well, this big blank area was believed to be blank of life, so they just called it all the Precambrian. The Pre-Cambrian.

Huh. Jen had never picked up on that before, before.

"Spooky time, huh?" Dana was on a roll now. "And over eighty percent of all earth time. Do you wonder what it looked like? I sure do. I've always wanted to go down to the very deepest depths of the Grand Canyon ... but that is still just a dry wall with all those pretty colors marking off ancient time on the outer edge. Just imagine, Jen, if you could squeeze in there and walk through one of those layers, walk on one of those layers, see it close up, not dry as dust but splashed with water and light?"

"But ..." Jen started then paused, a puzzled frown on her face. trying to assemble in her mind what she barely recalled of her less than favorite earth science classes. She recalled the fiery ball of earth, then cooling, vapor, water, then after that she drew a blank, until life forms—as blank as that huge blank block of time on the chart. The *Pre*-Cambrian.

"But what?" Dana prompted.

"It's just so ...," Jen spread her hands. "I don't known, *big* to try to think about, I guess. What all happened in that before Cambrian time? Do they know?"

"That's what is so exciting, learning how to fill in all those blanks. New tools and theories fill more all the time, especially about what past paleo-climates were like. A new frontier to explore." Dana had stars in her eyes, clearly dreaming of her own future opportunities.

"We are so used to Washington State, Jen, that we think about rock and mountains differently. Most of our mountains are volcanic in origin and so basically they were built up with new rock. Lavas and granite are all volcanic rocks, igneous, whereas in other parts of the continent we see long term build up of layers of sediment, usually newest on top, in sedimentary rocks. Those are

147

the ones that bury most of the fossils and artifacts of the ancient past over time, in a way we can find them. And it often takes a big hole, or deep canyon to see those layers.

"Say you go to Bryce Canyon, you can see layers of sediments stacked going all the way back into the Jurassic." Dana found another chart. "Then if you go to Zion Canyon you can travel even further back to the Permian, less than three hundred million years ago. If you then go to the Grand Canyon you can go even further back seeing layers from about where Zion leaves off down to the very bottom on the Colorado River you can finally see some ancient PreCambrian time rock—only it's a third type of recycled rock.

"So," Dana grinned, "do you want to know what the Precambrian looked like?"

"Er...," Jen was a little wary, not quite ready for one of Dana's hour long science lectures; her fingernails were not ready to be digging tunnels miles into the earth either—best pal or not.

Seeing Jen's expression—expecting it—Dana just laughed and jumped up, dragging her over to the window. She pointed at a sharp fin of mountain across Swiftcurrent Lake.

"It looked like that!"

Then turning, Dana pointed at all the peaks around the lake.

"And that, and that, and that! This whole park basically is ancient Precambrian time rock layers! Does that not just blow your mind? Or maybe I should say, doesn't that rock?"

Grimacing at Dana's pun, Jen said, "But that's not possible. Is it?"

"It shouldn't be. We should have to tunnel down to the lowest levels of the Grand Canyon—and I do mean tunnel, as most of what you see is Cambrian and earlier—to see any truly ancient time as is stacked here right in front of us. It's magical, don't' you think?" She threw her arm around Jen's shoulder and gave her an excited hug.

"And just think, we probably never would have known if you hadn't found the clue, Jen. You're brilliant!"

"I'm brilliant?" Jenny's eyebrows arched high in disbelief.

"Yes! You saw it. The clue. You said the rocks looked strange, different, weird. Boy were you ever right about that!"

Grinning, extremely pleased with herself, Jen said, "Okay, so tell me more about this great discovery of mine."

"See that black horizontal line that cuts across the peaks about a fourth of the way down from the top, Jen? The one that looks like some one drew a magic marker straight across it? It's darker in some spots and lighter in others, but looks like it was drawn with a ruler?

"Okay, yeah, I see it. Looks kind of like a layer of dark frosting in a cake. "

"Well that's a sheet of hot magma that squeezed in between existing layers, as in already there so they are older, right? It's called the Purcell Sill. It was so hot it baked thin layers just above and below it into white marble that outline it. It has been dated to ... And you will not believe this Jen ... One point two billion years old! Not million, B-I-L-L-I-O-N ! Or twelve hundred million, if you prefer."

Well that was pretty damn ancient!

It was the only coherent thought Jen could form at first, as she tried to process the information.

"But ... that's over twice as old as that Cambrian," she waved a hand impatiently, "That explosion of life thing starting. Right?"

"Yeah. For the big animal fossils they could see when they named it, anyway," Dana qualified. "And think about this. Talk about ancient. Do you remember about Supercontinents, when the lands were basically all crunched together?"

"Oh, yeah, Pana... Pan something, I remember that. "

"You thinking Pangea. But that was recent, that only happened a couple hundred million years ago, and had split apart long before the dinosaurs went toes up. Nope, this was *another* earlier Supercontinent."

"It happened more than once?" Jen hadn't known that!

"Oh yeah, several times they believe supercontinents formed. Rodinia is the one that was forming right about then. Once you turn your laptop on we can look at it on The Paleomap Project website. All the countries collided down near the south pole starting around one point one or two billion years ago. About the same antiquity as our black sill! Can you imagine where it was on earth and what forces it took to make that pretty little line? They figure North America was in the center of the pack with maybe Australia and Antarctica off our west coast—the *old* west coast before Washington State lands existed. If only we could have had a webcam wedged into the Purcell Sill .... What a wild and woolly world ... Wow! "

Jen laughed caught up in the fascination. "I think they used a fly on the wall instead of a web cam in the old days, Dana."

"Which only makes it so much more intriguing, because there weren't even flies back then—not for hundreds of millions of years."

"Okay, okay, I forgot where in time, somewhere on this planet, I was for a minute there." Jen tried to keep Dana focused.

"What I really want to know, Dana, is... Just how the *hell* did those billion year old rocks get from down in the middle of the earth to way up there? That's so surreal!" Jen was starring at the straight line across the mountain feeling like it was her only anchor—if just for her eyes to hold tight to—in a world suddenly swirling in strange and unknown destinations beneath her feet. It was one thing to *know* the earth changed, plates moved and subducted causing volcanoes and crumpling up mountain ranges, she'd spent too much time with Dana not to have *heard* it many times. But to try and accept the reality that those rock layers were hanging around the supercontinent Rodinia, was extremely disorienting.

"It's a little hard to wrap your head around, isn't it?" Dana said softly. "And as shocking, in our limited modern experience of how the earth acts, is how those layers got way up there. Glacier National Park used to be laying around in Northern Idaho, which at that time was... well, that's another long story... but, long story short, picture Spokane as a seaside resort—or more likely an underwater one.

"Anyway, a whole chunk of earth—that stuff being laid down just before and during Rodinia time—a bunch of sand, mud, and lime mud that was laid down in waters of a sea or old coastal shelf, must have had a good jolt and was popped up and slapped about 50 miles east, like a hockey puck, to land up here—up there.

Trust me, you wouldn't have wanted to be hanging out in Northern Montana walking with any dinosaurs when that ancient load landed on your head around 60-70 million years ago!"

"What?" Jen gasped, turning shocked blue eyes on her friend. Somehow she was much more comfortable with being on land that was like a big cruise ship wandering around on the ocean, than with the semi-solid earth beneath her feet doing such un-solid nasty things so recently.. She had seen the pictures of Mount St Helens exploding, and the massive and incredible destruction of that act of nature, but that must have been child's play compared to...

"How big a chunk moved?" Jen asked warily.

"One source I read said three hundred miles long by over 50 miles wide and up to four miles deep," Dana reported nonchalantly.

Jen suddenly sat down hard on a chair, saying weakly, "That's more than some of those small states back east, isn't it?"

Dana blew out a rude noise.

"That's more than two or more of some of them combined, Jen!. Take a couple of New Jerseys, or a couple Massachusetts, or you would probably need three of Connecticut. Pick your combination of anything totaling about fifteen thousand square miles."

"Oh my God!"

"Yeah. What was he or she thinking?" Dana laughed.

Wow, Chicken Little had been right. Her dino-bird ancestors probably told the legend of The Day the Earth fell from the Sky, or something...

"What are you whispering to yourself, Jen?"

"Um. Talk about a radical remodeling job," Jen answered.

"And then," Dana's eyes sparkled, "after that scare-the-hell-out-of-you part, along came the ice ages and ice sheet glaciers to chew it all up into what we see today."

"And that ancient layer cake?" Jen prompted.

Thinking Jen wanted her to finish with that topic and be done, Dana rushed a little. She tended to lose her audience when talking geology to Jen. "That ancient layer cake was all fine sifted stuff, there weren't any lumpy walnuts, or chocolate chips, or coconut to mess it up because there weren't any back then. Just fine smooth thin layers."

Jen blinked, then frowned.

"Dana, I'm not an idiot. Even I know there weren't chocolate chips back then. Really," she huffed.

"Just an analogy, Jen. There weren't trees or plants, or animals, or shell fossils, none of that lumpy debris to disturb the layers, just blank, thin, laminated ancient layers of sediment. Without life. Or so they thought."

"They thought?" Jen's curiosity picked up on the mysteries that had Dana's green eyes sparkling with excitement at discoveries made, and yet to be made from the ancient clues— maybe even in Dana's lifetime, or by exploring scientist Dana, herself!

The budding scientist would have been highly surprised by the thoughts going through her friend's head as she watched Jen

151

thoughtfully studying her nails, examining the thin laminated layers of colorful sediment for any flaws.

"The really special thing here in the park, I think," Dana pointed out, "is that normally you never get to see such nice billion year old layers. They are crunched down into the earth with everything on top, pressured and cooked and twisted into something unrecognizable, with lavas drizzled over the top or hot magma exploded through it. So it's not like this. It's not so eerily what it was so long ago." Too excited to remain seated, Dana jumped up.

"Imagine, Jen, looking at a cooked cake and trying to see what the flour and eggs, and other ingredients looked like before you beat and blended them and baked it. If you didn't already know how they appeared before, you could never undo it from the baked cake? It would be too late.

"But, amazingly, we have a piece of primeval history that landed on top, preserved for us to see what it was! It should be buried way down halfway to China, underneath the dino-dirt. But there it is! If you took an elevator down into the earth you'd not only pass the dinosaurs, but about five other mass extinctions, one in the Permian that made dino-death look like a blip.

"You'd pass reversed poles, and continents all floating around together, not once, but several times, you'd pass massive upheavals and ice ages, past the first plants, first shelled creatures, all the way back to early microbes, and you would see what's displayed in that mountain range."

"Well, Holy crap!" Jen was nothing if not eloquent.

"Really. Miraculous creation from microbe slimes, the holiest of all crap. And a lot of how it all worked is still mysterious. We know stuff happened to cause it all, but there are so many 'hows' and 'whys'. Like the mats of blue-green goo making some of our first air, trading carbon dioxide for oxygen, building up the atmosphere, when those mountains were laid down." Dana's voice was almost a reverent whisper.

"So it's like a we-were-there, or we-are-there in-time, almost?"

"Yeah, and I'm in heaven," Dana sighed.

"If you hadn't mentioned how unusual the mountains looked, hadn't seen it Jen, I would have missed it looking for glaciers instead of what's underneath. The glaciers are almost gone, the real story here is what they did, what the ice age did, but especially the chance at a billion year old view."

""Cool. Well, enough geology for now. I want to think about all this and get it clear in my mind. Thanks, Dana," she grinned sheepishly for her normal bored tolerance.

"I mean thanks, *really*, this time!" Jen insisted. "We better get moving though, before the ranger man gets here. I have no idea what the plan is today, so I'm going to wear those new pants I have that zip off to shorts, and my hiking boots. I can carry my thongs in my tote."

But a few minutes later, Jen startled Dana.

"I get it now!"

"Get what?" Dana's asked, her voice muffled under the top she was pulling on.

"I get what is so cool about all this geology stuff." Jen paused a moment putting her thoughts into words.

"it's like the earth out there is an on-going mystery thriller that still is only partially solved ...," turning to look at Dana. "No wonder you want to train to uncover the next clues. A detective on an unsolved case."

"No wonder you love this stuff, Dana!"

"Why is it *such* a big secret?"

Dana challenged Ravenwolf the minute he arrived that day.

"Well, not a secret, exactly," Dana motioned with her book, "but it's hardly well known." She was wound up and still energized on one of her favorite topics.

"It's all about the ice age glaciers, which, don't get me wrong, that's totally dazzling—and the current ones are worrisome—but ... Hey, this is like one of the biggest untold stories! It's huge! It should be plastered all over the brochures and media!"

Ranger Ravenwolf threw back his head and laughed deep and long, then rubbed a calming hand on Dana's shoulder.

"Garrett warned me about letting you have a love affair with Glacier's rocks!" he teased, seeing in her face all the intelligence and enthusiasm that Garrett had fallen in love with, in the beautiful indignant redhead.

"I agree it doesn't get much press," he said. "And not everyone goes through all the visitor centers, so it isn't well known, but it is hardly a secret. I happen to have come by the original 1937 official park booklet and there is a whole section on the geology of the park, in there. It is dated, but is gives the basics—

though they had no conception of *how* ancient the deposits were back then.

"But media focus right now is on the remaining glaciers that might not last out a decade. And you have to admit, Dana, that melting glaciers and the ice-age sculpture of the park are a lot sexier to the public than ..." The warning glint in Dana's green eyes froze his tongue.

Jen interrupted hastily.

"I don't remember the last time I saw a national media story about Glacier's melting icepack, myself. The last one I saw said they might be gone by 2030, or even sooner. How are they doing, Rave?"

"Not good, Jen," he answered soberly. "A recent study of thirty-seven named glaciers in the park since 1966 showed that only twenty-five still can claim to be glaciers, the standard being over twenty-five acres. But it's more complex than guessing how long it takes to melt that much ice in a warming climate. Too many other factors come into play on a regional basis. I think there are several on-going studies at the moment, trying to work it out. But I don't have a simpler answer for you, sorry."

"About my point about how important the rock story of Glacier is," Dana jumped back in. "I know everyone thinks the Grand Canyon is the 'sexy'." she made mocking air quotes with her fingers, "place to go to see rock layers. And I do agree its beautiful to look at—on a postcard from the comfort of your air-conditioned home. But do people even realize that by the time they go all the way down to the very bottom of the Inner Canyon on the River that—is by the way twenty degrees hotter than the rim—that there is something important missing? I know the base is recycled, reshaped schist at 1.7 billion years old, but oops, the next five hundred million years of sedimentary layers are missing?" Dana nodded. "And those aren't the only missing treads in that Grand Staircase. All that heat and exercise and still gaps in an important time in the early production of our oxygen atmosphere. Of course, they could come here and pull off beside the road and go lay their hand on a stromatolite."

After pausing for a smug little grin, Dana continued her campaign. "At any rate, you would think people would want to see layers that must hold secrets of how the air was created that we breath on our planet? Haven't you heard of the 'Green' eco frenzy? Hell, they sell everything these days just by labeling it 'Green'. And what, I ask, is more 'Green' than this? Not to mention more literally green than the desert ..."

Rave grinned, capturing Dana's jabbing finger before she hurt someone—most likely him. Jen was blushing, caught with "green" shopping guilt—especially at Dana's next words.

"How can people claim to be "green" and helping the planet if they don't even understand or care about the way it was built? The processes that make it work? The way the atmosphere was created? The way microscopic life began? The way ancient paleo-climates acted?

"And, yes, the fact that glaciers that feed watersheds that lead to three oceans are rapidly melting!"

Dana paused to catch her breath, then laughed when she saw the expressions on Rave's and Jen's faces.

"And you knew, Rave!" Dana huffed, narrowing accusing eyes on him. "Of course you did! Why didn't you tell me?"

"Garrett said you would have more fun 'discovering' it for yourself," he laughed.

Dana's eyes widened in anger. Then softened with love, murmuring, "He knows me so well."

"Okay. Well, I feel better now that I've had my rant," she said with a sheepish grin. "I just have big issues with fad driven versus knowledge based decisions about earth. I cringe every time I hear a plan to just bury some toxin." Dana snorted, "Don't they know the earth burps—or worse?"

She shook it off and grinned. "And, I confess, It just burns me that I could have driven the whole Going to the Sun Road and left, and never realized what I was missing. If Jen hadn't noticed the clue."

Surprised, Rave turned to Jenny, dark eyebrows raised.

"Weird looking rock in the cliffs," she shrugged, her amazing cobalt blue eyes wide with innocence.

He smiled down at her. "Smart girl," he gave a teasing tug to a dark curl, before wrapping his arm casually over her shoulder.

"How about we get outside and appreciate some of those rocks. And give you a chance to pace off some of that steam, Dana?" He just laughed when his buddy's wife took a half-hearted swing at him.

155

chapter eleven

"THE STORY OF THE LAYERS of ancient rock are told by the beautiful colored pebbles in all the lakes of Glacier National Park," Ranger Ravenwolf told them.

He had guided them from the lodge down to the shorefront, and seated them on a big flat rock. Scooping a handful of pebbles from the crisp, sparkling waters of Swiftcurrent Lake, he crouched down to tell the story.

"Now all these mountains around us are what are known as 'rootless' mountains. They didn't grow here, but were plopped down on top of the soil here like a lopsided layer cake on a counter. "Adding, with his devilish grin, as if he were the guilty one, "With a few bites taken out of the eastern side. "

He lifted one of his water smoothed and rounded pebbles, soft creamy tan in color.

"The oldest layers at the bottom of our cake are about one point six billion to one point five billion years old. Naturally things that old have taken a bit of a beating, so their outer weathered color can be different than the fresh color if you broke some off. So when you see these rock layers in the park, notice the fresh color where a chunk has chipped off recently, along with the color of the older skin, and it helps tell what it is.

"Now the very oldest layer is mostly buried on the west edge of the park, it's a very dark gray and was believed to have been deposited in a deep sea environment, and it's a mudstone. We will skip that name because you won't see much of it.

"Remember these layers are all sediments of sand, silt, clay, and lime mud, our different ingredients that are used in each layer. They call each layer a different name, and sometimes, I

156

swear, three different people named the same layer, so don't let that confuse you. As Jen here knows," he gave her a flashing grin and a wink, "the important thing is what the ingredients were in each layer and how they were prepared. That's going to tell us interesting things about the climate and such in a time a billion and a half years ago.

"This creamy golden tan rock is from the oldest layer, the bottom layer, on the east side of the park, called the Altyn. Its creamy white or steel gray fresh, then tans like this where you see it on road cuts. Look around you because the layer surrounds the Many Glacier Hotel. It's limestone with a lot of sand grains in it, which tells us it was laid down in warm shallow seas, and much of it has a lot of iron in it, so we call it *dolomite* limestone. You'll find most of the layers in our cake were rich in iron back then. And the colors will tell us about how that iron was ... prepared," another smile for Jen, "as in whether it was exposed to air, oxygen, or not.

"So, in the bottom of our basin, called the Belt Sea basin, by the way, the next layer to settle was, not lime mud, but clay rich mud. So something changed, otherwise the same thing would be falling in, right? Our mud layer is still rich in iron, that's the same. But there were more sand grains in that earlier limestone, now there's more clay coming into our basin. And," he plucked a new pebble from his palm, "it's green, suddenly, and a mudstone."

He showed them the pebble than clearly had very thin layers that shaded from a lighter green to a darker gray green repeating. He plucked out another more olive green pebble that was also of the group he called the Appekunny. He told them the green tended even darker gray green in this layer over on the west side of the park.

"Now the next layer is Grinnell, we saw a lot of that today, but here's a fascinating thing. For the first hundred or so feet, it's intermixed with the lower level, so the two colors alternate for a while. I don't have a pebble to show that, you'd need to see a chunk of rock, but here are two pebbles of the Grinnell. The more purple red is probably from those mixed beds. The most familiar is this one, the dark barn red of the bulk of the Grinnell formations. Interesting huh? Another big change, and for a while this green rock and this red rock alternated thin layers until it all turned purplish red. Again, why? How?

"Dana, try not to get so excited. Just spit it out. You don't need to raise your hand," their patient ranger teased.

"Exposure to oxygen!"

"Give the girl a gold star." He smiled at her.

157

"But," he held up a finger and challenged her, asking, "Was it changing sea levels, exposing the rock to air in shallow or dry seas, then covering it, like we would expect today? Or was it some special thing unique to the Precambrian? There are theories that the levels of oxygen were so low back then that there was only enough at first to oxidize some rocks, then more had to be created to oxidize more, and finally enough oxygen was produced to create an atmosphere. I don't know what the current scientific consensus or knowledge on that is, but it's a good mystery for you to research Dana. And I better talk a bit here about what a green color says.

"When rocks, mudstones rich in iron do not mix with oxygen for whatever reason, an opposite thing than rusting can happen, called reduction. The iron combines with silica and heat and pressure turn it into chlorite which is green, instead of rust red. Which makes our red then green rock story a little more intriguing.

"Okay, back to the red rocks of the Grinnell, probably the best known in the park. You must have seen a lot of it in Avalanche Gorge. And some clues to what was going on with the water levels, because beside the gorge on the trail there are Grinnell rocks with big mud cracks etched right into their surface. Even ones with rain drop imprints. You also saw those ones with the ripple marks of a shallow sea, on the Grinnell trail. You will also see along the road another strange mix of Grinnell with layers of white sand in between. The rusty red color tells us the iron was exposed to oxygen and oxidized, or as we like to say, rusted. The red rocks are another one of those muds rich in clay that hardened into mudstone that are known as *argillite* to distinguish them from the muds pressed harder into solid flat sheets known as *shale*. That's for your benefit Dana. I'm good just calling it mudstone.

"So we have creamy limestone, green mudstone, red mudstone with bands of sand in between, and clearly with all the mixtures we have some climate changes going on, we've also had something producing oxygen."

"I know!" This time Jen raised her hand, excited and blurted. "Those mushroom-shaped thingies, like in that bay in Australia!" Laughing at his pleased smile and nod, she asked, "Do I get a gold star?"

He gazed at her a moment, leaned forward and kissed her softy on the tip of her nose.

"Oh," she breathed out. Then with a cocky little smile said, "That will do." Then lowered her eyes lids to sultry level, added softly, "For now."

158

Rave shifted in his crouch and decided to sit down in the gravel in front of the girls instead.

"Okay," he cleared his throat, then grinning a little sheepishly asked, "Ah, where was I?"

"Stromatolites," Dana provided with a grin.

"Right." His lip twitched up, his eyes gleaming with amusement, "Officially known as those 'mushroom-shaped thingies'. But they came in more shapes than the mushroom shapes that we know ... and love, today." Rave flicked a soft glance at Jen, then a startled look flickered in his eyes before he quickly looked away, his voice brisk and all business.

"Above the Grinnell red and purple we have a thin layer of green again. And remember, I'm using the term layer like on our layer cake. Each group of rocks is made up of many layers, some thin as sheets of paper, or a single hair, some mixed with other layers as we have mentioned. They are know by another term to geologists, but we will stick with our layer cake."

He handed Jenny a thin rounded and water smoothed coin of aqua green that look like a hardened piece of the milky aqua glacial lakes.

"Here, I have photo of a boulder of this on my cell phone that will give you a better idea. This is called the Empire layer." The name seemed to suit the elegant looking rock in his photo. The aqua green of the rock alternated with a band of cream for about four inches, then another equal sized band of green, before turning to cream again, with a texture that made it look like pulled striped taffy.

"Oh, it's really beautiful," Jenny murmured.

"It starts out dark gray or green and weathers to this light green color. It's another mudstone mostly, with this pale band of sand, believed to indicate, coming after the Grinnell, to be a time of rising seas, as we have chlorite instead of rusty oxidation, then . . . "

"It looks like a tsunami layer," Jen noted, pointing to the creamy sand band.

Rave blinked and stared at her open-mouthed, looking back at the picture.

I have never," he said evenly, "in all the literature I have ever read on the Precambrian Belt Rocks ever heard the word tsunami mentioned. "When he glanced back at Jenny, she just shrugged, but gave him a look that clearly said "Well X-cuzz me, Mr. Smarty Pants!" He stared at her another moment and threw his head back and laughed.

"No, oh no," he said when he recovered, "that wasn't an insult Jen. Not at all. You know they're still arguing over whether the Belt Sea was a coastal tidal flat on the edge of the ancient continent, or if it was an inland sea? You should toss that idea out, let them chew on it."

"Well, I just thought it looked like a layer of tsunami sand, but I don't know anything." Jen said embarrassed.

"No, Jen, really," Dana jumped in, "he's right. Who is to say your common sense comment shouldn't at least be considered? After all you're plenty sharp about seeing the obvious that escapes one looking just at details. Who pointed out the weird rocks? Huh? Just because you didn't know they were a billion years old didn't mean you weren't right? and most of the main principles of geology were common sense, tested and applied."

"Oh, hey, thanks guys. When you are a geologist Dana maybe you can look into that. So what's the next layer, Rave?" Jen wasn't sure if she was more pleased or embarrassed so she changed the subject quickly.

"After the rising seas of Empire, we are back to limestone." He pointed this time to a chunk of rock that sat on the shore. It was a smoky blue gray where it was freshly broken, with a soft buff colored outer coating where it had weathered. This is called the Helena layer now, but originally it was called the Siyeh. And it can be found capping the top on Logan Pass from around Siyeh Bend to down the west side toward the loop, and up most of the sheer cliffs in the park. It's dolomite limestone, and it is cram packed with all kinds of fascinating things, like the Purcell Sill in its uppermost layers and our stromatolites fossils in great quantity.

"Above the four thousand or so feet of the Helena/Siyeh layer there is, of course, a lot of erosion of the top of our cake, so mostly it is the tips of the peaks where the uppermost layers are seen. We have the Snowslip that is about five colors with quartz icing on top. The seabed was exposed, then the sea expanded, then it shrunk, and so...," he leaned over and picked a rock off the shore about the size of a grapefruit. It had a pale maroon red color mixed with shiny white quartz, "This is Snowslip," then taking a sage green pebble from his hand, he added, "and so is this. The top of Mt. Wilbur over there," he pointed to the shark fin peak across the lake, "is capped with Snowslip."

Picking up a dark golden yellow rock from shore, he said, "Shepard. And see over here. This boulder that is broken is yellow where it is broken and a soft terra cotta color where it has weathered. This is on Yellow Mountain."

160

Pointing to the bright red Grinnell rock he had shown them, "This could just as easily be the Kintla rock, look for high peaks that are bright red on top and you are probably looking at Kintla, as the Grinnell layer is much lower down. Then two of the youngest top layers are almost non-existent anymore in the park due to weathering. Oh, and with some pink limestone also on top in some spots. Sorry, forgot the name of that one. So there you have your one point six billion to about eight hundred million years old layers of cake.

"And almost every layer has fossils of the most primitive plant forms of blue-green algae, fossilized into stromatolites of every shape; the cabbage look of mushroom-shaped thingies, ones in great cone shapes, ones like tall branching trees, there are at least six ancient species of the fossil that pumped breathable air for all the species to come. When these rock layers formed, stromatolites covered the world. Built by the earliest primitive forms of life."

"Amazing, "Dana whispered. "You are lucky it's late and time to eat, Rave, or I'd make you take us to see one of each kind. But ... I'm buying, where do you want to go for dinner, tonight?"

Jen knew one place she didn't want to go again for dinner, but outside of that, left the decision to Rave and Dana.

Jen came out of the steamy, vanilla scented bathroom after soaking what passed as her muscles—her *still* over-abused muscles from the prior day's hiking—as long as she dared in a soothing bubble bath. It had been a long day, and though they had only exercised their minds, neither Jen nor Dana had gotten much sleep the night before, for different reasons. It was decided just to stay at their lodge and dine downstairs in the Many Glacier Hotel.

Settling cross-legged on her bed, Jenny pulled the towel off her head and began trying to comb the tangles out of her hair. Dana was ironing a cotton blouse that had been too wrinkled to steam out while she had been showering. It looked like she was ironing her way through several other items while she was at it.

"You know Dana, if you pressed those and then rolled them, they wouldn't look so trashed when you unpack," Jen commented idly. "I'm surprised someone who has traveled all over the world for competitions like you have can't pack better."

Dana just laughed, not even turning to scowl at her friend. "Yeah, but that's my problem. I picked up bad habits. Spandex leotards never needed ironing. They were so snug that any

161

wrinkles they started with stretched out before the gymnastics meets began."

"Oh, right. I'd forgotten that." Jen worked with her hair silently for a while before asking, "Dana, what do you know about Rave?"

"He is pretty private actually, despite his public reputation. Why? What are you getting at?"

"I don't know, just curious I guess."

"It does take awhile just getting used to his stunning looks to get around to thinking about anything else, doesn't it?" Dana teased.

"That's an understatement," Jen muttered. "It does take a while for the brain to recover and start working again," she admitted. "But, do you known anything about his childhood, or, well anything?"

"I know he grew up in Missoula, not on the reservation. I know he has talked to Garrett about a lot of personal things that my sweetie very carefully explained that he was told in confidence and that Rave needs to share those things with me himself, if he wants. But I do know he was a very troubled guy when Garrett met him when they worked Montana road crews together in the summer when they were in high school. Rave has admitted that much to me himself. He said Garrett helped straighten him out. Garrett says he was just his fishing and camping buddy, and that Rave did all the straightening himself, and totally took charge of his life after that."

"He sure is a good teacher. Was he one of those interpretive rangers once?"

"I doubt it," Dana frowned. "He's a ranger for the nature, not the tourists. Garrett says he tries to get the backcountry assignments most of the time. But I wouldn't be surprised if he has a degree in that, too."

Then she answered the puzzled look on Jenny's face.

"Get this, Jen. Apparently Rave is very, *very* smart, as in not quite a genius, but no slouch in the brains department. He not only went to college on scholarships, and I mean Harvard College, among others, but he's got bachelors of everything, and even some masters degrees. I can't remember what all goes with what, but he was taking things like law, and economics, and engineering and... well, more." Dana lifted up her iron and motioned to the sky, then had to bend over and put the plug back in the outlet after having yanked it out.

"He might even have a doctorate in something," she added thoughtfully when she straightened, "But anyway, as if all that weren't enough, he took more classes at night in the summers when he came back to Montana and got back on the road crews. I guess as a resident he could get half off tuition at the local community college. He picked up mining and forestry management classes here, I think," Dana paused a moment, pursed her lips, then shook her head, giving up impatiently on trying to remember more specifics.

"Anyway, a lot of the community college classes are taught online now, or in hybrid classes, where it's mostly on line with just occasional classroom visits or field work, so it's easier to study around a job or from home. Garrett says he did most of one course from his bathtub, soaking off the grime and aching muscles after a day on the road crew, and the summer night courses didn't even cost him what other guys spent after work on beer!" Dana laughed. "So he could save most of his wages for his fancy colleges back east.

"I guess once he focused, he did it big time. Nothing distracted him until he got *everything* he wanted, which seemed to be to know some of everything. He's an extremely disciplined man."

Seeing Jen's brows arch high and disbelief she said, "What?" Before turning back to her ironing.

Jen snorted, "Well I can certainly believe he has some B.S.s in his pockets. The man can be full of it. But are you sure you are talking about Garrett's buddy, Mr. Womanizer? No sleeping with college coeds, playing around? Come on, Dana. Disciplined? That guy?"

Dana laughed. "Oh, yeah, well I guess that was my first thought and comment when I heard. also. But, Garrett said he was completely focused and totally disciplined. Rave didn't even sleep hardly, much less with any coeds during college years. He focused on nothing but college for about six or seven years, studying and working at it full time. And *then* ...ouch! That's hot," Dana thrust her arms through her blouse, and unplugged the iron.

"And then Rave gave his total focus and discipline to playing hard, and hot, and fast for the next set of years," Dana gave a wicked laugh.

Ending when? Jen couldn't help but wonder privately, as she tossed on fresh clothes and followed Dana out of the room to go down and meet Mr. Focused for dinner.

163

"Normally I wouldn't talk about bacteria while dining in the company of two lovely ladies," Rave lifted his wine glass in a silent toast, "but since you ordered mushroom appetizers, Jen, and asked me to tell you more about the 'mushroom-shaped thingies' ..."

"Sorry, I remember the name now. Stromatolites."

"Right, stromatolites. Well, I'm afraid I have no choice of a more appropriate dinner topic, in that case." He grinned and made sure they each had a fresh roll and chilled pats of butter before he started.

"Stromatolites are like the great palaces created by the ancient rulers of the early world—bacteria. For billions of years, bacteria was the only living organism to rule the earth, and it was everywhere— without competition. You've seen the colorful blue greens that surround the hot springs at Yellowstone? Those are the cyanobacteria, a later evolving form of bacteria that was photosynthetic and could convert carbon dioxide to breathable air—our essential oxygen.

"I thought I learned once that it was algae that did that? Did that converting. Blue-green algae, or maybe red algae?" Dana frowned thoughtfully.

Dana's question snapped Jen's attention back to the topic. She had been momentarily distracted by the speaker. Entranced by the way the candlelight played across the sharp masculine planes of Ravenwolf's face. The crisp white shirt and dark linen jacket he had changed into for dinner, gave him an elegance that only enhanced the dark, dangerous lines of his face, and the compelling dark depths of his eyes. Eyes that shone with intelligence, lit with pleasure in sharing his knowledge with interested parties. When Dana spoke, Jen reluctantly shifted her interest from the fascinating man, to the story. She *had* asked for the information after all.

Jen concentrated her eyes on buttering her roll, letting her ears focus undiverted from what he was telling them. His ease with the subject told her that everything Dana had told her about Rave's academic credentials—normally so well hidden—had to be true.

"Okay, first off the term stromatolite just means 'layered stone'.

They were first built by bacteria, or the original slime, if you will, capturing silt and sediment, and feeding up through it in

164

shallow seas toward the light. All of it was originally thought to be algae, Dana, until cells and gene sequences clarified the situation.

"Actually, bacteria and algae are in two different domains of life, though it seems that early algae stole a cell or two off cyanobacteria and swallowed it, incorporating it into its own cell membrane—maybe to get a head start, I guess. But, algae are in the same life domain as fungi, plants and animals and, of course, us.

"At some point green photosynthetic algae began to compete with bacteria in photosynthesis to green the oceans with plankton, but the exact details of that revolution are still being sorted out of ancient rocks. At least that is the way I understand the latest information." He shrugged, "It changes faster than I can keep up."

"But before our domain, before algae, there was bacteria and then cyanobacteria. About half earth's age ago, around two some billion years ago, the atmosphere of the air and the surface of the oceans began to change to higher oxygen levels slowly—all made by one of the most important life forms ever."

Dana offered, "I saw a chart on the computer that showed that oxygen crossed over to start becoming a higher percentage than carbon dioxide in the atmosphere somewhere just before the oldest rocks in the park formed."

"Right. Before that time it's possible that oxygen in the air and surface oceans was one percent or less than it is today—a totally toxic atmosphere for our type of life. But colonies, mats, and reefs of stromatolites were created one tiny layer at a time by cyanobacteria pushing their slime up to capture more thin layers of sand and silt in shallow seas to start to convert the planet to one that we can survive on. They took in carbon dioxide and breathed out oxygen.

"But once some oxygen was available, the photosynthetic algaes began to out compete the cyanobacteria, and a new explosion of algal stromatolites coated seas and built the first big limestone deposits of record by the time of the supercontinent Rodinia.

"Most of that heavy oxygen transition in the atmosphere is believed to have slowly taken place between about 1. 8 and 1. 2 billion years ago. The slab of rock layers that forms Glacier's mountains—known as the Belt Rocks— dates from 1.6 billion to 800 million years ago.

"So there are abundant *algal* stromatolite fossils in Glacier that tell that story of the transition of the planet to a new

165

atmosphere. Also about the early evolution of the life domain known as the eukaryotes, which includes algae and us.

"Those oxygen-only breathers, I call them the Eukes for simplicity," Rave added, smiling, noticing Jen looked like she was going to have to take notes if he threw more new science words at her.

She smiled her appreciation back.

"Okay, I'm with you. My older sister algae and I are the Eukes. We're the new kids on block. What's next?"

Encouraged, he continued. "The Eukes started to form multi-celled organisms and when there was enough free oxygen, they took off and started diversifying around a billion years ago. That microbe expansion was the precursor to the more visible fossils and explosion of larger life of the Cambrian a half billion years ago.

"So many of the big mysteries of early life and the key changes of this planet lie hidden in the layers of Glacier's mountains—or sediments of that same time period. Not just changing climate, but the interaction between that and the first multi-celled life. You're smiling, Jen. What are you thinking?" Ravenwolf asked.

"Oh, just a silly thought, really, but I was just picturing that dark, black horizontal line of the lava sill as kind of like an arrow, or highlighter." She grinned. "You know like a 'Buried knowledge treasure lies near here' marker." Jen shrugged, then smiled a little shyly when she saw his pleased grin.

"Yes, it does, doesn't it? Just to be sure to put a 'No digging in the Park' sign next to it," he chuckled. "You have a fun way of seeing things, Jen, that some people find rather dusty topics—excuse the pun." He winked at her. "Probably a necessary skill when hanging around with your buddy here," he teased, turning to address Dana.

"You'd be surprised to learn the timeframe here was once referred to as part of the 'boring billion' period, Dana. Which meant it didn't get as much grant money or research attention previously. There is a lot to still explore for future geologists, with high-tech tools that will be needed to eke secrets out of such ancient rock." He suspected Dana's excitement was already pointing her in that direction.

"I will try to make a list of spots fairly easy to get to so I can take you guys on a stromatolite tour. And now it's your turn to provide the conversation," he laughed. "I see our steaks coming, and I'm starving."

The conversation flowed between Dana and Rave discussing early life shown in stromatolites and the early environment shown in mud-cracks and wave rippled stone. Jen was content to listen, learn, absorb and enjoy the atmosphere—and being with two people she cared about. Her feelings for Ravenwolf had changed and grown and tended to scare her at times, but tonight was relaxed, comfortable, and she was going with the flow and enjoying herself.

Lifting her knife, she didn't feel quite as guilty this time digging into her rich, juicy steak—after learning that she was also loosely related to the broccoli and sautéed mushrooms on her plate. She just thoroughly enjoyed all her excellently prepared Cousin Eukes.

Jen caught him looking at her. Or maybe he had caught *her* looking at him, again. But it seemed every time she looked his way, as they finished their dinner, his eyes were on her. Dark eyes that seemed to brim with a molten heat as they met hers over the rim of his glass, above the top of the desert menu, when she glanced up licking ice cream off a spoon, she felt their touch like a silent caress that sizzled along her nerves and made her throat suddenly dry as a hot, dusty day.

Even when he responded to Dana, his eyes seemed to be speaking only to her as if some bond made only them real, everyone else in the room just a distant hazy blur. So when she rose to go for a moonlit walk with him along the lakeshore, she wasn't sure if he had asked her out loud, or if she had just read it in his eyes.

She barely remembered to say "goodnight" to Dana, until she heard him speak the words. Her hand was caught in the strength and warmth of his palm. She didn't even realize they had climbed down the stairs outside until she felt his arm come around her shoulders and the heat of him against her side. Heard the crunch of pebbles beneath her shoes, and felt the magic of the moon painting a romantic path across the shimmering lake waters.

His breath brushed warm and soft against her cheek as he tucked in close and asked, "Warm enough, little one?"

She was too enchanted with the night and the man to laugh about how she'd almost needed to use her napkin for a fan to cool the heat coming form his eyes over dinner. She managed a nod but let herself be curled in closer against him, enjoying the heat and crisp male scent of him.

"I thought we might stroll down the shore a ways and look for some of those pretty pale green pebbles you liked." His voice was dark velvet in the night with a soft smile buried in it.

"In the dark?" she laughed.

"Well, I'll just have to think of something else to give you to please you, I guess. Let me think." He seemed to mutter to himself, "Flowers, chocolate? I'll have to wait on that. What about … jewelry? Women like jewelry don't they?" Turning her into him, he asked her, "Do you like jewelry, Jen?"

She chuckled, delighted with his game. "Oh, I could be forced, but surely you can think of something else to please me?"

Dipping his hand into his shirt pocket he pulled something out and swung it in front of her face. The light of the moon glimmered off a small gold chain with delicate polished stones.

She gasped, "Rave! What?" Eagerly trying to snatch it from his hand.

"It's nothing fancy, just something I saw in the gift shop while I was waiting for you guys. It has tiny polished stones of the different colored rocks we talked about today. I thought it might be a nice reminder for you. It's a bracelet, but I have a small confession to make. When I saw it all I could think of was seeing you wear it clasped around your pretty little ankle."

He had watched her during dinner, fantasizing about having her lying naked before him and lifting her foot and gently placing the chain around her ankle then kissing it and nibbling his way all the way up her sweet, soft leg.

She shivered as if reading his thoughts.

"Maybe I should just put it on your wrist for now so we don't lose it." He lifted her hand close to his face so he could see to fasten the catch then turned it and kissed her palm, then her wrist. Pulling her into his arms, Rave captured her mouth in a kiss that was first achingly tender, then deepened with heat and need.

Jen felt the sweetness and then the desire spike and burn inside her. Pleasure seemed to fill her and seep into every part of her, filling, heating, shivering, melting as it went. Her knees gave way just as he pulled her up tight against him, and gave her his hard strength.

She felt like she could float in his arms and walk with him across the water on that romantic moonlight path. And then he eased her back, let go of her lips, and the cool night air suddenly rushed between them like a barrier.

"God, Jen." He buried his face a moment in her neck, and nuzzled breathing in her scent, while still holding her away from him by her shoulders. "You make me crazy. Too crazy, too fast."

"But ...," she realized she had no idea what to say to that.

She was only here for her vacation. Still caught up in the moment all she wanted him to do was get crazy with her a lot faster!

Maybe she was reading him all wrong. Maybe she couldn't think at all after his kisses. Maybe he just liked to toy with the tourists?

"I better go in," she murmured embarrassed.

"Thanks for the bracelet, and...," she waved her hand helplessly, turning away, "Everything."

"No! Wait!" He captured her hand and curled it in his, bringing it to his chest where his heart still beat rapidly.

"Listen, I ah... well, I really wanted to b ..." He couldn't believe how badly this woman made his normally smooth tongue stutter. Taking a deep breath, he tried again, more quietly and calmly.

"I wanted to be romantic, okay?" He shrugged, looked away a moment, but kept her hand trapped against his heart. "I didn't mean to bring you out here and, well, swallow you," he huffed out a disgusted breath. Taking both her hands in his he brought them to his lips.

"I wanted to bring you out in the moonlight and romance you like you deserve. I wanted to give you a little token of appreciation, and give you a few sweet kisses. But mostly I wanted to just sit in the dark and talk to you for hours quietly about ... things. Anything. Everything," his voice was just a whisper now.

"And just be with you, Jen. Just hold you close to me, and listen to your voice."

Jen had never felt so touched. Or had such a hard aching lump in her throat, as the one she tried to force words past now. She blinked her eyes hard trying to block the moisture she felt there from overflowing, finally croaking out, "Okay, sure."

And surely *that* wasn't the voice he wanted to listen to all night.

But it seems he did.

chapter twelve

THE NEXT MORNING WHEN Dana woke, Jen was already sitting at the table. Facing the window, her stocking feet resting on a chair, hand curled around a mug of coffee in her lap, laptop open and on, but her gaze focused outside where an early morning dawn highlighted the eastern face of the mountains.

"Mornin'," Dana croaked as she stumbled toward the bathroom, noting the miniature coffee pot was full, dark, and smelling delicious. Bless Jen, she'd made another couple of cups.

Filling her mug when she came back out, Dana sat on the end of her bed, pulling the blanket over her shoulders like a shawl, and joined a still silent Jen in gazing at the inspiring view. They sipped in comfortable silence as the sun shifted position and its spotlight on the angles and edges of the mountains.

"Anything wrong?" Dana finally asked, her quiet voice still roughened from sleep. "Not Rave, is it?"

Jen's lips curled up softly at the corners as she just shook her head slightly, took another sip of her coffee and spent more long minutes watching the day quietly unfold outside.

Rave.

She had not been thinking about him until Dana mentioned him, which was surprising as last night had been as novel as this morning's sunrise. He had tucked her against his shoulder and gently urged her to talk to him. It seemed as if she had told him and the moon everything about herself. Even about thoughts she hadn't known were there until they drifted out on the soft night. The fierce heat of their early kiss, their attraction, had turned down to a low, pleasant simmer, and last night he had been a caring, trusted friend instead of a lover. It had been more special for that, somehow.

But this morning she had been downloading the pictures from both Dana's and her camera cards to her laptop. When she had run a slideshow to review them she had been captured by other thoughts, until the dawn stole her attention away to the show outside.

Without taking her eyes from the window, Jen finally spoke for the first time that day. Her voice was soft, but the tone was oddly off.

"You know, Dana, I'm missing the half-yearly sale at my favorite department store. I mark the sales on my calendar each year so I never miss them."

Dana didn't seem to know how or if to respond so she just grunted and gulped some more caffeine down to get her brain working in case she needed it.

"I've been sitting here," Jen continued, in that same odd, calm voice, eyes still focused outward, "thinking about all the important dates on my calendar; all the things that mark the way my time is assigned during the year." Jen paused to take a slow, savoring sip of her coffee. "And at the ripe old age of thirty, I find I'm not happy really with the way I'm marking time. Because that is what it seems when I sit here, look at this. Just marking time until—" Jen waved a hand vaguely and shrugged. "Until ... what?" She fell silent.

Dana gulped her coffee and desperately refilled her cup. After a long while, seeing the laptop open, she ventured, "Um... so can you order the boots on line?"

"Of course." More silence.

Dana was eyeing the coffee pot, deciding to make another mini-pot, when Jen finally spoke again.

"I've been sitting here looking out at all those dainty little layers of time, of the billions of years that time waited for air to breathe, for life to evolve, waited for plants ... What were they anyway?" Jen looked away from the window finally, noticing Dana's confused, pre-caffeinated haze, she clarified.

"What were the first plants? Real plants like I could put in my garden?"

"Ahh," clearing the croak in her throat, Dana tried to remember. "I couldn't say but I know Horsetail Ferns came pretty early on. No flowers though, 'til way later."

"Horsetail Ferns. Hmm. Those things that look like asparagus with hair on the stems?" Jen asked. She received a nod.

"Anyway, Dana, I thought of all that time that all those little layers built into big layers, waiting for life, waiting for humans to evolve so that I could go to the half-yearly sale and get the latest season's trend in boots with just the right curve on the toe, and just the right stylish height heel for that month."

The silence told Dana she was supposed to say something.

"Okay," she offered cautiously, draining the rest of her mug and getting up to bring the pot over to the table to refill them both. "So... show me which boots you ordered online."

"I didn't."

"Don't you need some? For work or something?"

"It's never about need, Dana," Jen responded firmly, then turned and flashed a dimpled smile at her befuddled, not-a-morning-person friend.

"I decided I want to put on my old boots—old as in the two month-old boots that I brought—and get out there later this morning near those ancient, patient rocks."

Jen settled back more comfortably in her chair, soaking in the beauty of the jagged charcoal cliffs, covered on their lower sloping edges with a mossy vegetation that looked like soft emerald velvet rolling downhill to the deep green tree-shrouded band that touched the soft waters of the morning-stilled dove gray lake. Tiny waterfalls picked up the early sun, sparking and flashing like a delicate diamond chain cast down across the breast of a velvet gown. A small glacier high in a cirque, glowed with the brilliance of a large white diamond nestled in the hollow of a throat.

With a contented sigh, Jenny contemplated the beauty of the day and of lazing around in the morning having a quiet cup of coffee with her best friend.

While Dana curled around the steam rising from her cup and settled to enjoy waking without the stress of having to think or talk more before she was capable. The view out their lodge window was stunning, peaceful, timeless—and was working some kind of magic on her friend.

Something, or maybe someone, certainly was.

Unless she was still asleep and just dreaming.

Magic and dreaming. That's what vacations were for.

Ravenwolf's dreams were becoming more disturbing.

Somehow all those nights filled with hot, lust filled fantasies—tiring nights of tossing and turning, waking unsatisfied and frustrated—were becoming more appealing. Or less terrifying than the softer shape of the ones stealing into his sleep now. It was one thing to be in a romantic mood—occasionally—with the right woman—but it was unnerving when even his subconscious mind started tilting too far that direction.

A man had to keep his priorities straight and his fantasies and realities in their proper settings.

Yet it seemed that once he'd tasted the possibility of losing Jen's interest—from that guy's careless words—that something inside him he didn't consciously control had ... panicked. Even his smooth-talking skills had been lost as he stumbled for words, confessing, of all things ... the truth!.

Unsettling as it seemed, he'd meant what he said last night to Jen. Last night he had wanted romance, over sex, with her. His dreams had even confirmed that truth sub-consciously. It was dangerous, unknown terrain. Focusing on just one woman so intensely could suddenly leave one ... stranded. Abandoned. Alone.

He pondered that for a while as he stepped out and said hello to Creator Sun. It looked like it was going to be a gorgeous day in the mountains and for the picnic he planned to take the girls on to St. Mary Lake.

He tipped his head back and let the sun bath his face with soft morning rays. His gut still churning over that worrisome dream.

Maybe he should go see a doctor?

Or go talk to Shirl?

Naw, he was okay.

He still wanted the sex with Jen—in the worst possible way—so he was fine. He'd just wanted... more. That felt too strange.

Last night he had gotten more.

She had opened herself to him, for him, and he was having soft, scary dreams about romance. He could still smell the vanilla scent in her hair, feel her warmth tucked against his side, he could have listened to her all night. He recalled the soft tones of her voice as they sat in the moonlight, along with the way she shared her story with him.

"When we first met in college, Dana told me that I reminded her of a doll she had wanted as a girl. I sometimes feel only like someone's doll..."

173

Mine.

My little doll, Rave had thought, before tuning back in.

"But you know, I feel sometimes like my life has been like a Barbie's. That someone has just been moving me around without my really being in control of any direction. I'm probably not explaining this very well, but try to imagine girls playing with dolls. 'Send her off to college,'" Jen moved her hand like walking a doll," 'dress her in pretty clothes. Now put on her cheerleader outfit for the football game...'"

He knew it! Rave laughed, then abruptly squelched it at a scowl from Jen, but he had always suspected she'd been the pert little cheerleader type. She had just confirmed his guess.

" 'And here is our little Jen doll studying for her career.'"

Jen's voice had taken on that sing song tone that girls at play used to imagine the life their dolls were leading. "'A good career in marketing as a graphic artist and web designer. And here she is all dressed up in the latest professional woman outfit, getting in her new car and going off to work for the day. Here is her house, let's put little furniture in the rooms and move her around in it, and have her sit in a fashionable sports outfit out on the patio furniture ...'"

He heard the edge in her voice, and realized where the feisty, fiery part of her character came in. When you pushed Jen, she fought back on the spot, unconscious of her underlying frustration and sense of a lack of control over the direction of her life. But Rave knew better than to point that out—unless he wanted a demonstration of those fireworks.

"Do you have a house?" He said instead.

"Yes, with a great garden. I love gardening."

He'd pictured her in an apartment.

"Well, that sounds like you are in charge. A house, a good career?"

"Kind of. A college counselor suggested courses for good career prospects. So I took those classes. Then a recruiter came to the college and offered a good job, so I took it. I'm still there. Some raises and promotions let me get the house, but ... I seem to have missed a step. The part where you say, 'When I grow up I want to be—' The job, the career, just sort of happened, while I was partying my way through college. I was passive. Dana was always the goal oriented one. Now, ever since I've been doing something I'm not sure I chose or ever really wanted. I like it okay, I guess. But it is just what I do when I'm not off work.

"Do you see what I mean about a doll just letting herself be moved around? I'm thirty years old and I have no plan yet for what I want to be when I grow up."

He just nodded, thoughtful, then prompted with a wicked grin, "Then what happened with our little Jen doll?"

"Then we dress the doll for a date in a pretty party outfit, and she goes out with Ken in his convertible ..."

Rave's grin had evaporated and turned to a frown like a sudden summer storm on the prairie with black clouds boiling to blot the sun.

"But the best part was," Jenny continued, unaware of his mood change, "Dressing up for vacation with her best friend ... pajama parties and talking all night with the best friend... going places with her best friend that she'd never think of doing on her own." Jen paused and her voice turned somber.

"You know, Rave," she looked up at him with those deep blue eyes and he saw a hint of wistfulness in them. "I didn't feel like this, think like this really, before Dana married and moved away with Garrett.

"That's when I realized the rest of my life was just a routine. That's when I first felt like a doll being dressed up in different outfits and moved around with no real purpose, or passion. I didn't notice before when Dana was dragging me all over and talking me into doing things I always complained about. That was different, that's when I was having the most fun and really felt like I was living my life instead of just moving through it on some plan not of my making. As contrary as that sounds. But Dana has always been so vibrant and active, always with a plan or idea ready, always so much fun, and I chose to follow along, never bothering to come up with my own ideas. Her ideas, but my choice... I miss her."

Jen's eyelids closed, hiding her eyes behind those thick dark lashes, but he heard the slight catch in her voice. Her cheeks were luminous like mother-of-pearl in the moonlight, he wanted to plant a soft kiss on them, on her eyelids, her throat, her soft lips, but knew it wasn't the moment for that.

He lowered his eyes, toyed with the fingers on her hand, setting it on his knee, giving her a moment to compose herself.

"Have you thought about moving back closer to Dana?"

"Oh, sure, but ... Dana has Garrett and school and ..."

"Jen, you know Dana will always have time and room for you."

"I know. That isn't the point. It's that Dana is choosing a direction. Choosing a future she is passionate about and acting on it, making her life match what she wants. That's what I'm *not* doing. I'm drifting. I'm thirty, and I feel like I haven't grown up yet and chosen what I want to be, to do in life. I'd love to see Dana more, but that isn't the problem. I just did not see it until I watched her struggle with having to change her focus, her whole life, after the accident. Until she was gone and I had way too much time to think about my life and what it lacked. To think about the paths I haven't yet chosen for myself."

"So what are you going to do?"

"I don't know." She shrugged, turning earnest cobalt eyes up to his. "But at least now I'm realizing I need to think about it."

"Is there a different career that appeals more to you?" He held his breath, sensed it was coming. Jen was a nurturer, if she didn't say something like nurse or doctor, he knew ...

'Yes." She decided to be honest with him, but she had to turn away to speak the truth. "The most important one is I want to be a mom, and raise happy, healthy kids, so I need a job that won't interfere with that."

Yeah, that one.

The breath he'd held nearly strangled in Rave's throat before he could shove it out and suck in another deep one.

She didn't look up at him, and he sat there stupidly with a big lump in his throat, and the same flutter of panic that he had felt when she had sighed over the baby mountain goats. Babies! God. He knew it! He tried to tease himself around the issue.

"Ah, are you going to use a husband for that, or just find a stud service? I'd be glad to volunteer a few vials, or my body if you'd like the more personal delivery system?" He tried to laugh, but the attempt sounded more like a car cranking over trying to start with a half-dead battery.

After the silence had drawn out for what seemed many uncomfortable minutes—if not days—Jen asked as casually as possible, without looking up, "Do you want kids some day, Rave?"

"Err..." He tried again. "Ahh, I ah ... " And again.

"I, ah, confess I don't really think about it. Them. Ever." He added to close the subject. He should know better.

"Except when an old girlfriend comes knocking on your door three months later?" she teased, laughing and nudging him lightly with her elbow.

He laughed uneasily. "Never happen. I always use protection, if I'm getting your rude insinuation."

176

"You sound pretty sure there aren't any little Raves or Ravettes out there somewhere," she said quietly, questioningly.

"I am. If there were I would adopt and support them ,just to be sure." He'd caught himself, and shut up.

She had caught him, also. "Just to be sure ... what? Rave? I've just told you all my failings. Talk to me."

He sighed, struggled with it, then pinned her with dark, stormy eyes.

"Just to be sure they were protected from having a childhood like I did."

Then he stood abruptly and guided her back inside the hotel, done with the subject. But he had shared something he had never planned to. And she had soothed his heart with her good night kisses when he escorted her to her hotel room door, and left her, reluctantly.

He had gone home, gone to bed planning to have forgetful wild sex with Jenny in his dreams. But his dreams had gone soft on him. The only dreams about babies he wanted to have were about *babes.* Hot, curvy, adult female ones. Not little boys with raven black hair and Jenny's cobalt blue eyes!

Hell!

Well, this morning the day could only get better. He had a picnic date with a beautiful brunette and a lovely redhead. More his style.

As they drove south to St Mary along the eastern front of the Rockies, the landscape outside the car windows held more significance than the other times they had driven this route from their rooms in Many Glacier. On their right, to the west, the road paralleled the startling wall of mountains, one peak after another, running as far north into Canada as the eye could see, and south into the lower chains of the Rockies.

And not just a wall that was one range deep, but row after row of mountains fell in behind, rising high, then falling into valleys like the waves of an ocean. Dark tipped rock peaks had a white curled foam of glaciers and snowfields at their crests. Beneath the hard thrust of mountains were the rounded shoulders of lumpy, crumbling soft soils of the Cretaceous. Much softer, younger soils that fanned across the rolling prairies, covering the recent bones of dinosaur time—recent compared to that dominate slab of endless time. Time before life's workings visibly exploded into life, and a billion years before dinosaurs ended their sojourn on earth.

The leading eastern edge, where the great slab of ancient, rock layers had finally come to rest, was just inside the eastern borders of Glacier Park in a line that curved in where streams cut back, and out with hardened peaks, like a series of inlets and points along a coastline where younger soils met the ancient layered wall of deep time.

Chopped off and shoved solidly on top, the great mountain slab was so much more obvious and startling from this side of the range, as they drove along the rolling lands of the prairie that extended east into the vastness of the Great Plains. Such a shock it must have been to early travelers from the east after miles and miles of empty prairie.

Ravenwolf pointed out the rough line partway up the ranges where the lowest, oldest limestone layer of the Belt Rock slab sat rigid atop younger rolling layers, where trees and vegetation found purchase in the lower loose slope of young soils and weathered rubble. Jen and Dana could see how the ancient, ice-age scarred multi-colored slab perched above, looking east over the flat lands to the curve of the world on the horizon.

Their drive south from Many Glacier Road was along a section of Highway 89 known as The Blackfeet Highway that skirted the eastern length of Lower St. Mary Lake on the Blackfeet Reservation.

Inside the park, high on the continental divide rested the remains of the Blackfoot and Jackson Glaciers, melting at an alarming rate. The melt waters from glacial run off high in the divide gathered into the St. Mary River then left the massive ice-age glacial trough through the finger lakes, first passing through Upper St. Mary Lake inside the park beside the Going to the Sun Road. The river then flowed out of the park turning north to flow through Lower St. Mary Lake before continuing north to Canada, eventually joining first the Oldman, then Saskatchewan, before dumping into Hudson Bay and sharing waters flowing off the ancient rock slab with the Artic Ocean.

The scenery was incredible. The mystery and wonder of the massive earth forces that had come together over time to arrange and then reshape such massive expanses of land was humbling. They traveled the rest of the way south to St. Mary in a reverent silence for the majestic "Shining Mountains"—sacred to many—the source of awe in the journals of all the later trappers and explorers.

"That is where Garrett and I are staying tonight!" Dana pointed, at the tipi and resort as they passed through the town of St. Mary near the east entrance to the park.

"Jen, are you sure…?"

"Yes, I'm sure," Jen interrupted firmly. She actually wouldn't mind staying in a tipi for one night, she realized, but knew Dana's enthusiasm was as much about reconnecting with her husband. They were still very much newlyweds and Jen wanted them to have their time alone in the romantic setting.

Not to mention *she* would have the hotel room all to herself—hoping to connect with a little action of her own. She had been romanced last night. Now she just wanted something a little more wild and dangerous. And Jen just happened to have a "Tall, Dark, Wild & Dangerous" handy.

"What are you smirking at?" Dana asked suspiciously.

"Hoping your tipi is cemented securely to the ground," Jen teased. "Wouldn't want you to get into any embarrassing situations with your honey."

Jen ducked the map Dana swung at her head.

"Behave girls," Rave warned sternly, then laughed when they both chimed a very mischievous, "Must we?"

Their first stop inside the east entrance to the park and the Going to the Sun Road was at the St. Mary Visitor Center where Dana perused the geology exhibits while Rave guided Jen to the recent expansion of the Native American exhibits, telling her of additions since 2005 to encompass an outdoor tipi camp and area where the Two Medicine Lake Dancers and Singers could share the Blackfeet culture, with a platform for the popular Native America Speaks programs.

Rave reminded Jen that she would be able to see the dancers, and more bands at the annual pow-wow celebration soon, during North American Indian Days on the reservation.

He then suggested a more intimate setting for the speaker's program.

"Since Garrett is arriving tonight, I thought you and I might head back to Many Glacier and have a quiet dinner together, then we can hear a Native America Speaks program in the lodge this evening by the fireside. I would like to hear them myself," Rave admitted. "How does that sound?"

It sounded to her like a real date!

One with fascinating and intimate possibilities.

"Sounds perfect." She tried to smile without smirking—or blushing—as they went to rejoin Dana.

But before returning to the car, Rave lead them off on a short side trip, promising them the walk would be worthwhile as this was something they wouldn't want to miss.

chapter thirteen

THE DAY WAS PLAYING with glorious.

Achingly blue skies stretched from the mountains out across the great prairies that rolled in golden glory as far east as the big sky country promised. The day's early promise of heat was tempered by the near constant breeze ruffling the grasses in the broad valley. There was a sense of well-being to be strolling along the flats, wildflowers peeking from grasses, birds busily gossiping in nearby marshes, and a light frisky feeling and step with the day's and evening's promise when the trio would be joined by Garrett and pair off into couples. They didn't want to miss any of it.

Upper St. Mary Lake where they would spend the bulk of the day lay inside the national park boundaries, joined by a stretch of the river of the same name to the Lower lake on the reservation they had passed on their way down. The Going to the Sun Road bridged the river before curving along the scenic shore of the upper lake, but there was another bridge.

"So, what's the surprise?"

"A bridge. A rather special bridge."

"Why is that?"

"It's the best fishing on all St Mary Lake!" Then Rave laughed, delighted with the scowl on Jenny's expressive face.

"Did you ever watch the movie Forrest Gump?" He watched the scowl change and the light strike on her amazing deep-blue puzzled eyes.

"Many times," both Jen and Dana answered.

"Well, you are going to want to watch it again." He promised.

They had only walked about a third of a mile from the visitor center when they came to a simple rustic stone bridge over the sparkling, willow banked river, with the sharp cut mountain peaks framing the background.

"And when you do, you will see this bridge when he is running across America."

"No joke?"

"Seriously. You will recognize the bridge and a later view of Upper St Mary Lake. Remember when he told *his* Jenny that he had seen a mountain lake 'so clear it was like two skies'?"

His eyes had flashed to Jen's and held hers as he emphasized the word 'his', sending a burst of heat between them—until Dana ruined it.

"You mean when she was dying?"

They both flinched, and then Rave turned to answer Dana.

"Ah... right. Anyway, this is the bridge. And it *is* usually great fishing." Turning back to where Jen gazed over the side of the bridge, he slipped his arm around her waist, gathering her to his side with a reassuring little squeeze.

"So, does *my* Jen like to fish?" His tone was low and teasing.

Jen's breath caught then she huffed out a laugh.

"What is it with you guys? First Dana wants me to fish, now you?" She felt flushed, off balance—'*his* Jenny'—and tried to recover some nonchalance.

"The only fishing I do is at the carnival to hook fuzzy stuffed-animal prizes." Jen added full of disdain, "Do I look like the type to get my hands all smelly and slimy?"

Dark eyes glittered with amusement as he took in the soft, slender hands in question. Manicured, polished, graceful with rings and bracelets—even here in the wilderness. Soft white perfumed hands that he dreamed about having fluttering and roaming over his bronzed body. He gave her a feral smile, but his voice was softly teasing.

"I'm surprised, Jen. An excellent cook, such as I hear you are? Surely you would want to work with only the freshest fish?"

Well, he had her there. That did sound appealing.

"I'll teach you some day." He stated firmly.

Jen started to protest, but bit it back as the promising words 'some day' registered in her brain making her forget the point of the sentence. "That sounds nice," she murmured absently.

Dana swung her head around, startled, but before she could express her disbelief, Rave caught her eye and winked at her.

Already thinking that the freshest fish never smelled, Jen was dreaming up recipes. Maybe fresh trout with an almandine sauce?

She missed the silent exchange between them. And the next one.

"Maybe," Dana said casually, with a mischievous grin, "you should ask Rave if he knows how you can get that bear fat you wanted?"

This time he had to choke back a comment to keep from bursting out laughing.

"Oh, yes! What was that called again? Pemmican? I need some bear fat for a pemmican recipe, if you know where I can get some," Jen asked.

Biting back the obvious answer, Rave just smiled into Jen's hopeful blue eyes and promised to see what he could do to help her acquire something that would work for her cooking. Dana must have been sharing one of her favored books by the Gears on prehistoric people of America for that recipe idea to come from Jenny.

Dana turned away, slapping her hand over her mouth to quell a shout of laughter.

She could just about picture Jen fishing as long as someone else baited her hook and did all the messy stuff for her.

But bear hunting? No way, ever!

Besides, she didn't think Rave really wanted Jen to change her charming, ultra-feminine ways completely. He seemed to thoroughly enjoy them. Yet she could see him seducing her friend into expanding her interests a little.

One thing was clear to Dana.

Ravenwolf loved to tease Jenny.

But despite his reputation, she was surprised to see that his teasing of Jen was always laced with fondness, not mockery. Maybe he knew Dana was keeping a close eye on him to report to Garrett if he got out of line. Though she suspected the affection and charm were sincere.

Jen was an easy person to care for, so petite and sweetly feminine, pretty and friendly, and, okay ... a little fiery. But her outer charms couldn't disguise for long the special person Jen was inside. Deeply caring and interested in people, sharing and loyal, spirited, and a truly kind person beneath the shell she shielded her tender heart beneath. Dana suspected Rave saw and desired the whole package.

This could prove very entertaining, Dana mused, as she listened to the soft whispering of the wind bending the grasses as they walked back to the car. Jen gave back love to those close to her ten fold. Would Rave dodge and try to run from it? Or grab for it like a dying man? He might try to do both. But in what order?

Worried about her friend's feelings, Dana sensed that this was one of those times that she had to step back, shut up, and let Jen take her own risks.

Maybe even encourage her a little?

Like Jen had encouraged Dana to take a chance on Garrett, at a time when her life had shattered and left her feeling helpless. A risk that had remolded Dana's own life and future with a joy and belonging she had never known before. She wished for the same for Jen.

And even if it was only momentary pleasure, a vacation fling, she knew Jen would regret it if she didn't chance it.

No matter how well she had tried to hide it, Dana knew the man had been stuck in Jenny's mind—big time—ever since they met at her wedding. And Garrett seemed to think that his best pal had also been more than a little rattled by the petite and fiery brunette that was his new almost-sister.

While Dana encouraged and teased about the pair, Garrett didn't seem to know whether to protect Jen, or stand back and laugh if his lady killer buddy got himself roped and dropped like a helpless calf, by the pretty brunette.

In either case, if Rave wasn't careful with Jen, he knew Garrett would be coming after him, friend or not. And they both knew the fate of male calves!

Not to mention what Dana might do to him.

As they pulled out of the lot at the St. Mary Visitor Center, Dana smiled to herself, thinking about the annoyed look Jen had shot her at the bridge when she had—oops!—apparently interrupted a tender moment. She hadn't noticed the heated tension in the air until she had already opened her mouth and broken it—and been speared with a frosted blue glance from her dear friend.

She was looking forward to Garrett's arrival, she was tired of feeling like an unwilling chaperone. *Not* her style at all! Once she realized Ravenwolf wasn't going to swallow her friend in one bite, then spit her out, Dana had to admit she had been rather enjoying watching them dance around each other. Just wait until she told Garrett!

Rejoining the Going to the Sun road heading west, Rave spoke, capturing Dana's more serious minded attention.

"Notice how flat the land is here, Dana? We are still on the younger original sediments—about seventy million years old—along with a lot of mixed rubble from landslides and from the old scouring of the glaciers. But just past Rising Sun, we will start into the leading edge of the ancient slab that covers the rest of the park. And, ladies, you will magically be transported back in time over one and a half *billion* years!"

Driving by the lush grassland meadows of Two Dog Flats on their right, their attentions swiveled to the left hand side where St. Mary Lake began to parallel the road.

Soon they pulled off at Rising Sun, a rare, old-time motor court with campgrounds, cottages, showers, and a small camp store.

"Hang on, I need to pick up our picnic here, then we'll head up the lake." Rave motioned toward the Two Dog Flats Grill, a popular, busy place, where they could see a crowd standing in a long waiting line.

"Don't fret. I ordered our hiker's lunches yesterday for pick-up today, but it still may take awhile to get out of there with them. While you wait, why don't you girls/ladies/guys," he flashed his trademark wicked grin, "cross the road and check out the shore. There's a great view across the lake to Red Eagle Mountain. I'll holler when I'm ready to go."

They jumped out, eager to explore. Laughing when an appreciative wolf whistle followed them across the road. Rave was clearly feeling frisky today. They found a picnic area on the other side, then wandered down through an aspen windbreak to the shore, where a couple were launching their canoe. Moving further down the shore they saw a dock that serviced a tour boat.

The lake was fairly calm at the moment, but apparently it was better known for its wind and whitecaps—which was why the best fishing was down near the sheltered bridge over the river draining its base. Quiet like this, the lake was a vast reflective mirror. There was a tiny island in the lake that looked like a floating raft planted with wind-flagged evergreens.

Some distance south of Logan Pass, the north-south trending line of the great backbone of the Continental Divide takes a slow curve to the east at Gunsight Mountain, looping down to ten thousand foot high Mount Jackson, curling back up to Mount Logan, toward the Triple Divide, then dropping south and east again.

In this remote part of the Crown of the Continent, ice-age glaciers carved the drainage for the waters flowing off the east of the divide that today drain out through the St. Mary Lakes into the far Artic Ocean. Even today huge, but shrinking glaciers nestle in their cirques in the inner curves of this detour, notably Jackson, and Blackfoot Glaciers. But once this whole area was filled with ice that ground north east and joined the massive ice sheet that conquered and completely overtopped Logan Pass, plowing out the massive gouge where the St. Mary Lakes now stretch and shimmer so innocently.

But a clue to the power, and depth, and violence of that ice carver is in the sheared off broken pieces left behind. Today they create the dazzling and unique face of the upper St. Mary lakeshore. So scenic with its pie-crust like rim of peak after peak, sometimes with the glitter of waterfalls glistening like a string of tiny pearls down the sheer cliffs in between, that hide an almost unfathomable reality.

Picturing the Northern Rockies on a topographic map, one sees row after parallel row of north-south mountain ranges, with valleys in between. Imagine some great cleaving force chopping down across it east-to west, not just cutting down as deep as the lowest valley, but much deeper into the earth, and you will get a dramatic idea of what a hanging valley—those lower in betweens—means. Valleys in the sky leaking their waters out the broken open end, as if posing for a cross-section diagram.

Some massive force was not only powerful enough to chop those ranges and valleys off cold, but deep and high enough to shear them off way above where you stand by the lakeside enchanted by the view.

For a real chill down the spine moment, look up and feel the weight of the ice age sheet above you. Only the very tips of the highest surrounding peaks seen in the sky would have pricked the surface above it—with you under all those thousands of feet of hardened ice mass, at that bottom where former mountains were ground to dusty glacial flour.

Unfathomable power and devastation carved this setting that is so beautiful, especially at sunset, that it can make one ache with passion and pleasure.

In the foreground of their view across to Red Eagle Mountain, one in a line up of peaks, a pretty white wooden tour boat loaded families front and center. The sun burst through some scattered clouds, that had crept over the divide, to capture the flapping dazzle of red and white stripes of the boat flag with its starred blue square the color of the darker mountain shadows. It rippled on the bow as if to highlight the 'mountain majesty' of America.

Surrounding the lake were displayed flat-topped mountains, horn shaped ones, conical, finned, and the kind kids drew, even one that had three instead of two divides. You just didn't realize how unique mountain top styles could be until you saw the amazing selection that Glacier National Park offered.

It seemed to have one of every non-volcanic shape that might exist on earth—a breathtaking gallery. A catalog of majestic charcoal heights, streaked in buff, or green, or red, and trimmed in forests at the skirts of sheer cliffs. The high valleys were left to hang, with their streams literally falling off the cliffs to join the lake below. Lingering snow clung to steep sides in parallel horizontal rows like a plowed field, against the dark rainbow colored layers, and the occasional white specks told you those moving ornaments were probably wild and free rocky mountain goats scrambling high above all their natural predators. All of it reflected in the long, shimmering mirror of the lake below.

Jen couldn't resist the postcard perfection of the scene raising her camera to take multiple pictures. With the telescopic setting she could read the name on the side of the boat. Little Chief. She'd like to take this tour some time. Hearing Rave calling to them, she turned and caught a long distance photo of him, before hurrying back across the road with Dana to hop in the car. Jen would crop and enlarge it on her computer later, and label the close-up of the heart-stopping grinning male, Big Chief, or maybe My Big… No, better save that thought for later.

"Just past Rising Sun here, we are at the start of the ancient slab." Rave continued his car tour. "You should start seeing its oldest layer, the buff and gray Altyn dolomite limestone beside us in the road cuts. This is a layer, Dana, loaded with the stromatolites that were pumping oxygen creating earth's

187

atmosphere of the future. You'll want to examine it more later for the only fossils available at that time—mud cracks and water ripple marks from shallow seas, and the stacked laminated layers of the stromatolites.

"Then," he continued, "we will rise from deepest time up through the ancient layers as the road rises up to Logan Pass. But we are only going up a few layers today, to hikes on the upper end of this lake. We will see mostly the billion plus year old mudstones of the next layers: the green Appekunny, and over it the oxygen rusted purples and reds of the Grinnell layer."

"Works for me! "Dana piped from the backseat.

"I thought it would," Rave chuckled, then turning to Jen beside him, reached out to close his hand over hers, giving it a little squeeze, added just for her, his voice soft, "And we will see about some romantic waterfalls. For us."

When he turned his eyes back to the road, he kept her hand clasp in the warmth of his, while he turned his comments back to Dana's interests.

"You'll notice on the road cuts along here, the strata layers will be slanting down to the west—when you can see them through the vegetation. I'm going to drive up to the Jackson Glacier overlook so you can see several layer changes, then we will come back to the pullout for St. Mary Falls. As the thin layers within the colored groups start to decrease in age, as we rise toward the pass, signs of more oxygen producing fossil structures will increase. Whether we will see any stromatolites on our hikes today, I confess, it's been a while, I don't recall. But we will keep an eye out. You'll have first hand knowledge, Dana, when they start talking about all those synclines and anticlines, and overthrust faults when you start your geology courses this fall."

She thanked him with a big smile in the rearview mirror then glued her eyes and attention back to the roadsides.

Jenny looked out at the passing scenery also, but all her attention and nerve endings seemed to focus in her left hand. Then she gasped, excited herself.

"Look! It changed! Dana it's greenish-gray now!" She pointed out the window with her right hand. Jen was surprised at how fascinating she was finding the rock story, but not fool enough to mix her priorities and move that left hand.

At the upper end of Saint Mary Lake there were a number of hikes clustered fairly close together, ranging from nature trails to hikes with varied elevation changes, and extensions, or intersections with other trails. The day's exertions could be tailored to their stamina, interest, and time. They lingered longer than Rave had anticipated at the visitor center, so it was doubtful they would be able to do all the hikes that day. That was the beauty of vacations—the casualness of schedule, the lingering at points of interest, and the impulsive pleasure of side trips.

They drove up to the large pullout at Jackson Glacier Overlook, checking out the rocks along the roadside. The overlook had a large parking area as it was the only place a large glacier could be viewed easily from Going To Sun Road. It was also where one of the gates was located that closed travel over the road and pass during the six—or often more—months of the year when it was buried beneath deep snow and avalanches. An incredible task plowing out the road for summer visitors took place each year.

After viewing the glacier that was a major source of water, they headed back downhill to the top of the lake where those waters and others were gathered in. Parking at the trailhead for St. Mary Falls, they descended a few hundred feet into the valley. As they strolled along, sun freckled the path under the forest, and trails forked off that Rave told them could lead them up toward Siyeh Bend and over Piegan Pass into the Many Glacier valley leading back to their hotel, or down the far south side of St. Mary Lake all the way back to the Visitor Center where they had been earlier. It seemed they could get almost anywhere from here on trails if they were just willing to climb high enough and hike forever.

After a little over a mile, they came to the St. Mary River. Vastly different at this elevation and location, in force and vegetation, than where they had stood on the rustic bridge over its outflow. Just a way higher in the valley, this river coming down from the big glaciers was joined by Reynolds Creek draining off Logan Pass. The combined waters roared over St. Mary Falls. Their trail crossing the river just below the falls.

Deciding to continue on, they came out into the open. Cutting across the valley floor they could see Little Chief Mountain and Dusty Star, and the waters of Virginia Creek coming from the hanging valley between them. Following the creek a half-mile up the south side of the U-shaped valley they came up beneath Virginia Falls, where it tumbled down the cliffs at the intersection to the trail leading back along the south side of the lake valley. Less than two miles from the road, they had already walked across the deep trough of the ice-age glacier, and seen two lovely waterfalls, and a closer view of sheared off mountains and high valleys.

At each waterfall, Rave made sure he fulfilled his promise to Jen. Gathering her back against his chest, his arms wrapped around her waist, his voice close in her ear, he showed off his waterfalls, nibbling at the nape of her neck as he held her close. They were truly the most romantic waterfalls Jen had ever experienced. They left her breathless.

Back at the car, they drove down to the next pullout at Sun Point, and Rave hauled his cooler up the hundred foot cliff of red Grinnell rock where they could rest and enjoy the view, and a reviving picnic. Then they would decide if they wanted to do the Sun Point Nature Trail or head across the road and up into the Sun Rift Gorge.

All during their vacation, Jen had been in raptures over all the species of wildflowers in the park, asking Dana the name of each and every blessed one. In self defense, tired of feeling foolish by saying she hadn't a clue—each and every time—Dana had gifted Jen with a book from the gift shop on the flora and fauna of Glacier National Park. In addition, she now had Ranger Ravenwolf. Not only more knowledgeable, but much more patient answering all of Jen's questions plus adding a wealth of experience on the great number of species and biodiversity in the park. While he was explaining that the pansy-like petals colored marigold-yellow were called Prairie Violets, Dana excused herself, trotting off to answer the call of nature.

Dana had been gone so long, Jen began to suspect that the 'call of nature' probably had a different connotation where Dana was concerned. She had probably found some interesting rocks to examine, leaving the two alone to talk.

A discussion of habitat, climate, and elevation led into Jen telling Ravenwolf about her home state, Washington, and her home and garden there. He was mildly surprised to hear she had purchased her home, instead of just renting. She told him how she had bought the house new, and proudly bragged of how she landscaped the large yard herself, passionately speaking about the flower gardens and paths she had created in the private back yard, and the different types of plants that thrived there.

"Tell me more about your house." Rave requested.

Jen spoke at great length about the kitchen and the appliances and cabinetry she had seen at a home show that she hoped to be able to add when she remodeled the kitchen some day.

Nothing was wrong with her current kitchen, Jen admitted, but it clearly wasn't sufficient for real cooking and her growing gourmet tastes, and skills. Before she got too far along on a discussion of the sort of storage space she needed to add for some special fancy pots and pans, and just where she would like to have a drying rack for herbs she grew herself, he diverted her with a question about the rest of the house's features.

"Three bedrooms?" He asked surprised.

"And a study," Jen nodded.

"That seems pretty big for one person, isn't it?" Leaning back on one elbow to talk, his long, bronzed and muscled legs in khaki shorts stretched beside her, making Jen's senses start to buzz and flicker. She completely lost track of the conversation.

"I said, did you buy the house as a real estate investment?" He asked again, not sure if it was the sun, or those blue eyes caressing the length of his legs, that was causing him to feel the heat rising quickly.

"No, not really, though it is a good investment," Jen eyes darted away, distracting herself with chatter. "I bought it before the Real Estate bubble, and was smart enough to save until I could put twenty percent down. I went for a low-interest rate, but steady long-term mortgage, and didn't let them talk me into any risky balloon or adjustable rate options, thank goodness. And I didn't refinance, even when I was tempted, so I have a house payment much lower than most now, and better than I could rent a one-bedroom apartment."

Finally remembering his original question, and information she personally had an interest in, her voice calmed and slowed.

"But yes, three bedrooms and a study that could be another bedroom if I need it, because I really bought the house for a home, rather than an investment." She paused, then stated almost defiantly, not looking his way.

"My husband and I plan to have at least two children, three might be nice."

Ravenwolf's head snapped up, dark eyes narrowing, his lips thinned to a hard line as he studied her profile. There was a long, uncomfortable moment of silence before he spoke in a low, threatening growl.

"Husband? When were you going to tell me about your husband, Jenny? Last night might have been a good time."

Damn, Garrett should have warned him!

"Married," he spat, giving her a look of disgust. "Does he know you go off on vacation alone to flirt with and kiss other men?"

She turned and stared down at him a moment. Letting him wait. Letting him wonder, despite his thunderous scowl.

191

"I don't. I would never do that. I'm not married!" She stated crisply. Her cobalt eyes held a challenge when she added, firmly, "But I will be. Someday. And to a man that knows and acts like he is married and committed to only one woman for life. And not a lady's man, but one who could be trusted not to flirt with or kiss other women behind my back either. And he will love children."

He just nodded, hiding his relief, trying to squelch the sudden anger and panic, the stab of pain in his chest when he thought she was lost to him. He tried to expel the breath that choked in his throat slowly, quietly, so she wouldn't know what she had done to him. He recognized, belatedly, that her sudden attack and personal jab at his reputation was probably just a sign that he was getting to her, making her feel nervous; a warning to herself as much as him that she might be starting to care too much. He knew the feeling.

It had shaken him badly this morning that he had even been thinking about blue-eyed, raven haired babies. Hell! It surprised him how fierce he felt a moment ago at the thought of her having them with someone else! Some of his panic seeped back, and sweat beaded down the center of his back. Dark eyes intent and unreadable, he tried to respond casually. "Passing out your requirements list, Jen?

"Or was that a warning?"

"It was a statement," She said firmly, rising and dusting off her pants to go find Dana. Leaving him to gaze after her, chewing on a stem of grass, wondering if he had just been freed or was wandering into some dangerous trap.

The thought he might already be standing in the middle of the trap, just waiting for the jaws to snap closed was something he refused to think about at the moment.

He didn't usually worry about the future much with women. Live for the day, that was the only way. So he hoped it was just hunger for some solid food that was making that pang of queasy, hollowness roil inside his stomach.

"Get Dana. I'm ready for that picnic lunch." Rave stood and busied himself setting out a blanket and unloading the cooler. Scooping up a chunk of ice, he held it against the back of his neck for a few minutes, before shouting to the girls to 'come and get it'.

192

chapter fourteen

JEN NIBBLED ON HER cold chicken drumstick, covertly watching Rave. She didn't know what had come over her earlier, why she had felt she needed to challenge him and make her point so sharply. There had never been any suggestion that he had anything in mind with her beside a brief and heated fling. Until last night when he had wanted to 'romance her', as he had said.

Still, that didn't mean anything to him surely, other than just a little sweet foreplay before he closed in for the kill. But it had meant something to Jenny, gotten beneath her defenses. Now she was mixing up a short summer romance in her head and heart with something more permanent. The only thing more permanent she would ever have with him would be friendship, as they would see each other from time to time because of Dana and Garrett. She told herself she'd just been warning him that she had plans other than being his occasional lover in the future, when their paths did cross.

Jen heaved out a disgusted sigh. God, she hated lying to herself. Truth was she felt like one of those valleys left hanging, about to fall off a sheer cliff named Ravenwolf. The fall would probably be heavenly. It was the crash that was deadly. She huffed out another sigh.

"Stuff yourself too full?" Dana asked.

Too full of something, Jen thought to herself, nodding to Dana and pushing aside her paper plate. She had actually eaten quite a lot she realized, groaning as she stood and bent to gather up her litter. Even simple food tasted so much more appealing outdoors for some reason.

Rave had been answering Dana's question about the Blackfeet reservation and the upcoming North American Indian Days while they were eating. Garrett had planned his vacation not only to allow the girls some time alone, but so he could stay through for the pow-wow, a weekend of dance, drums and celebration that brought native people from all over the country.

After they had cleaned up and stowed everything from their lunch, Jenny's curiosity got the better of her. She had noticed it on several occasions, but had chalked it up just as a manner of speech. Now she was beginning to wonder if there wasn't something key that she was missing.

"Rave, why do you always say 'them' instead of 'we' when you talk about the Blackfeet?" It was asked lightly, but when he acted as if he hadn't heard her question, her interest sharpened.

Rave just looked off at the lake, chewing on a stem of grass, but there had been a tiny moment of absolute stillness that told her he had heard her question. She waited a moment to see if he was just thinking of how to word his response, then persisted and repeated her question.

"You always say Native Americans, or Indians, or Blackfeet. Why don't you ever say my people, instead?"

Rave turned slowly, but looked at Dana, instead of her.

"Do you suppose Garrett is on the road yet?" He asked her.

"Oh, I'm sure he is," Dana replied confidently, then glancing up at Rave, caught some message in his eyes that had her stop and peer more closely.

"Maybe you should give him a call. Make sure he didn't get caught in some construction delay or emergency. See what his ETA is."

"O-o-kay," Dana said rather uncertainly, but seemed to sense that he wasn't trying to worry her. "I guess I'll give him a call."

"Jen and I will give you some privacy, we're going to walk down a ways to the lake shore on the nature trail. I promised to show her more of those pretty aqua rocks and wildflowers, anyway. We'll catch back up with you in a bit."

Catching on, Dana grinned. "Sure. I'll give him a call, and…ah, just take your time. I'll be right here." Then remembering, "Wait! My cell doesn't work here."

Digging in his pocket, he tossed her his keys. "My sat phone is in the car. Help yourself."

Sensing his impatience, Dana couldn't resist teasing. Brows arched she mocked, "A satellite phone, Rave?"

He shrugged sheepishly, "Seemed like a good idea living here."

"Of course it did. *It's* a high-tech toy. *You* are a male."

Dana had to give him points for just rolling his eyes instead of growling at her. "Okay, I'm going. Almost gone."

Reaching a hand out for Jen, Ravenwolf gave her a tight smile pulling her along toward a path. Keeping her hand in his he leaned to look into her face a moment, as if to read her emotions, and gauge if she was angry with him for ignoring her questions.

"Okay with you, little one?" He dropped a quick kiss on the tip of her nose. A pretty shade of pink flushing her cheeks, intensifying the deep blue light in her eyes.

"Lead on," she said agreeably, waiting until they had climbed down to the lower trail to add, "You know, last night it seemed all we talked about was me and my family and childhood, so I thought today... Well, I'm sorry if I asked a too personal a question. I just hoped we could talk some about you today. But if you don't want..."

"Jen?"

She stopped and looked up at him. "Yes?"

"I'm going to answer your question. But it *is* personal, more personal than you realized. Something private for me ... "

"Oh, you don't have to ..."

"I want to tell you. Just in private. Okay?"

"Oh. I see. Okay."

They strolled down the trail in total silence, except for the sound of birds, and rustle of leaves and needles in the breeze and under their feet, the lakeshore peeking at them through the trees.

Jen just tried to relax, hold her tongue, and enjoy the walk. She looked at the lodge pole pines with branches flagged from the winds that could blast down the lake, stepping carefully over loose rocks in the telltale ancient green mudstone, glancing down a trail leading up to yet another waterfall.

Anywhere but at the uneasy tension in Rave's profile.

After about a mile, he led her off to a clearing near some cottonwood trees where Baring Creek entered the lake. It had been the site of an old ranger cabin that had sat beside the lake and housed a ranger and his family for decades during summer seasons after WWII. Now the cabin was long gone along with those times.

Rave dropped her hands, turned away and went to stand on the shore and look out across the lake, seeming unsure where and how to start.

"Is this something Garrett doesn't know?" Jen finally asked.

"Oh, he knows." Rave paused a moment then began to speak quietly, and more easily.

"Garrett was the only one I had, at the worst times, but was the best friend a guy could ever want. I owe him. He might have talked to Dana about me some." He shrugged and turned so he could look at her, but he didn't close the distance between them, holding to his place alone at the edge of the shore.

"I expected that when they married. He either kept my most private confidences for me to share, or made her swear never to mention them to anyone, including her best friend."

"She wouldn't, if she knew," Jen nodded agreement. "She has told me some things about you that she learned from Garrett, but now that I think about it, none of it seems of the confidential kind."

Jen smiled, adopting a teasing tone, "Though I have to admit, I was a little shocked to find out how many degrees you have. Do you have any initials after your name?"

He threw his head back and laughed away some of his tension.

"Unmasked, am I? Some initials I guess," he shrugged, but didn't enlighten her. The last thing he wanted was for her to be calling him Dr. Ravenwolf, or some such nonsense, because he had found economics a breeze and had taken it as far as he could.

"It was important to me once to get those initials. But I don't need them anymore. At least not to flash around." Then his wry smile seemed to falter along with his lighter mood, and his eyes darkened. She felt him mentally pushing her away again.

Jen wanted to go to him, to touch, connect, and comfort, but sensed this was not the time.

He stood silhouetted against the lake as tall, and proud, and sharply chiseled as the high mountains behind. But it was like watching a storm building across the landscape. His hands fisted, clenching the muscles tight in his arms, his shoulders were as rigid as rock. Long legs seemed braced against any assault to his balance or place by the shore. A gust of wind flipped raven hair into dark flags standing out from his tight, bronzed cheeks. Cheeks that were carved beneath in dark hollows, his nose a strong, arrogant blade between.

Dark inner storm clouds took the light from his eyes, turning them flat, black, and as hard as basalt. His lips had flattened, his jaws seemed clenched, chin firm, determined. Only in the strong column of his throat, where she noted a deep swallow, did any sign of vulnerability show.

The coming storm could be destructive, but it could also flush out any broken debris, letting streams flow clear and strong again. It could destroy. It could renew. But until it passed, there was no way to stop it or to know what the result would be.

Jen found a sheltered spot higher onshore and sat, pulling her knees up against her chest and wrapping her arms around them to quietly and patiently wait it out.

Crouching down on the shore, his rigid back angled to her, Rave raked his fingers through the pebbles, dipping them in water to bring out their color intensity, seeming to need his hands busy while he talked.

"You asked why I don't say 'my' people when I talk about the Blackfeet ... Yes, I am Blackfeet and Nez Perce. But I was not raised with them, or on a reservation, or in either tradition. I am the unplanned result, you see, of two teens meeting during a pow-wow for the first time. Unsupervised out behind the celebration on the dark rolling prairies, they were having a private party too close to smuggled in six-packs—and each other. When my mother's shame later became known, she was tossed out by her strictly religious band and family, along with her unborn child.

"I was raised in Missoula by a woman alone, whose bitterness consumed her. I like to think that she cared about me— or that she had tried to—when I was younger. But, mostly it seemed that I was raised literally on and by the *streets* of Missoula." His words had come quietly but a rawness edged their tone. His back shielded him from her reactions so that he could continue, and force it all out this once and be done.

"According to my father, he didn't know about the fate of his one night of play, until he saw some friends of hers at an annual gathering years later. He found her in Missoula. She hated him for what had happened to her. He drowned his sorrows, yada, yada.

"Whatever," he snorted his disdain.

"When I was about ten, after years of fighting, he finally convinced her to marry him so that I could be registered with the tribe and inherit his place. What a farce that was! His name was

197

Raven Chasing Wolf," he shrugged. "It was fitting I thought. He had black spirits flying around inside him and his life was nothing but a hopeless quest for something he never caught.

"But he changed it—just his name, not his life." His shoulders tightened in a stiff shrug.

"Whether to sound less hopeless or just to sound less Indian, I have no idea. But it was Ravenwolf on the marriage certificate and ever since. They never lived together, though he made the attempt. He would come to town and beg and she would scream and shout and kick him out. I hated it, hated them, hated myself. He always ended up in some local bar, then passed out in the gutter.

"He died in one." Clearing his throat, he found a milder, more forgiving tone.

"My aunts and cousins on the reservation said he loved her and loved me, and that he just couldn't get himself pulled out of the white man's spirit bottle long enough to fix anything. But ... I don't know what's true or false ... except the misery it all caused me. I had enough trouble, bullying, and prejudice of my own to battle on the streets and in schoolyards, at that time, without all their problems."

He shook his head violently, scrubbed his hands through his hair, "God, I hate talking about this. It all sounds so self-pitying, but that is what I was. I was a bitter, hateful, angry, self-pitying kid. I hated the unfair world, my parents, being taunted and bullied for being Indian and not having the power to change any of it—except with my fists. Or causing trouble that I called revenge. Or through oblivion. I was an ugly person growing up, Jen, I'm not going to lie to you about that. Brawling, booze, drugs, petty crime, you name it. And all I got for that was slapped back in the face with trouble.

"So I went after a different vengeance. I was going to be as good—no better—than all of them. I was going to run faster, be smarter, know everything, be everything that was valued, and steal their women right out from under their noses!"

The storm kept building and breaking in him. She could almost see the thunder and lightning slashes, then he seemed to try to step back, find a momentary calm, before the next wave, the next pulse of anger washed over him.

Pushing to his feet, he shoved knotted fists in his pockets, rolled his shoulders, and still looking out as if he was talking to the lake, started again in the calmer, quieter—almost weary voice—he had so much trouble maintaining.

"So, do not use me as an exemplar of a Native American, or the Blackfeet or Nez Perce. I was not raised as one, as either. Don't assume that I know anything more about their culture and heritage than what I have recently set out to study and learn for myself.

"I am more like an American that married into an Irish last name, and went and got books on the history of Ireland and traced their in-laws genealogy on a family tree. It does not make them a native Irishman, or feel like one, or truly understand that culture."

Or an American Scots-Irish, thought a silent Jenny McCallum to herself.

"I've grown up more apart," Rave claimed, "than *part* of any family or tribe—including my own. That is until I went to school and found out I *did* belong to a special group after all, based on just my appearance! One reviled by bullies. So I defended myself—and something I didn't have or understand—every day I was a kid. And I believed their ugly words and hated myself for a while. I won't go into more details, but it's a wonder I lived to go to high school.

"Then I met Garrett one summer, and all he saw was a guy he wanted to be friends with. An individual. And I began to see and care about that guy—myself—again also. If not for him I never would have listened when the school counselor talked to me about college minority scholarships. I would have said 'Go to hell!' instead of applying to Harvard." His laugh was more a harsh snort, at those words.

"There was no way I was going to go to college in Missoula. I needed to get away from a place that reminded me of black eyes, split lips, and cracked ribs and go somewhere new where I could believe in myself again—or for the first time—instead of feeling like I did growing up like a trapped and cornered animal. Aw hell!"

His voice had gone raw and gritty again. The memories beating at him like driving rain.

"After college and grad school, when my father died and I came here to the cabin he left me, I never felt more an outsider in my life. I don't feel like I have any right to claim the Blackfeet as my people because I spent so much of my life hating my heritage and difference. Resenting it. And now, here, I am different, and an outsider, again. But I am coming to realize that I mistakenly blamed heritage—for what was just bad parentage and prejudice—for my crappy childhood. So I have decided to study and learn and claim what resonates within me. But I will never be an example

199

one should look to as what a Native American man is, I can only be the strange mixture I am. And be settled and honest about it.

"Jen, I let you believe a lie, when you thought I was named after Tlesca for romantic reasons. I never told you the end of that legend.

Pausing to take a deep breath, he seemed to gird himself.

"See the young newlyweds went off in a canoe on Wallowa Lake, but a sea monster—or more likely a huge wave—swallowed them and they were never seen again.

"The two tribes took it as an omen—a bad one—that peace and unity were wrong. Hostilities started up again. Like many native legends, it does not have a happy ending, any more than many native lives had at times.

"My mother named me Tlesca out of bitterness, hostility, and hopelessness, Jen. There was nothing romantic about it. It was meant more as a curse. That's why I use an initial in front, instead of my name, and why once I was so desperate to have the degrees and the initials at the back of my name."

His tone had become as harsh and bitter as his words, and memories he was seeing, feeling. He stood and threw the handful of pebbles he had been collecting into the water, one at a time, hurling them as far away as he could. "I just wanted to clear that up. Let's go."

He was so closed up. His back so rigid, so cold.

Jen fought the tightness in her throat, the burn in her eyes. No, she thought, not cold, but ... hurt. Probably ashamed also, so unforgiving of himself. But he was trying. He hadn't needed to tell her. She wouldn't have known any better. Why had he, then? Now? Just because she picked at him over not seeming to claim his heritage? Or was it because she was talking about kids earlier—any talk of childhood would be such a bad memory for him.

She stood up and brushed off her pants, walking slowly over to him, stopping slightly behind him, so she could not see his face. Placing one hand gently on the center of his back, she spoke to him quietly.

"Thank you for that gift, Rave. The gift of your story and your honesty. But I believe that when I think of your name it will always remind *me* of a blessing, not a curse.

"The Tlesca of your story was blessed by trying to right a wrong, to share love and find peace. Even if everyone around him was caught in their own bitterness and revenge, he was still blessed—he tried to find the way beyond it. Just as you are trying to do. The name is right for you."

He did not react or move for a moment, then he spun around and she saw the ravages on his face. The fierce emotions his personal storm had wrought in the tightness around his eyes and mouth. New lines seemed to have carved themselves into his cheeks and brows and his eyes burned black in his skull.

Then he reached out and grabbed her and pulled her into him. Holding her as tight as a man falling off a cliff, grasping desperately for any anchor he could find. Crushing her ribs, squeezing the breath from her, before he took her mouth in a kiss fierce with pain and possession. Just as suddenly he jerked his head back, softened his embrace, and bent his forehead to hers, eyes closed, whispering,

"I'm sorry, sorry." Tiny soft kisses raining over her eyelids, her temple, burying his face in her hair.

" God, Jen, I'm so sorry my sweet little wren. I don't know …"

"Hush. It's okay, you're okay." Cupping his face in her hands, her lips soothed across his jaw, brushing, kissing.

"Rave, it's okay. It's past. You gave me so much. Shared so much with me. Just hold me now. Everything is okay."

She pulled his face into her neck so he couldn't speak, but just take the comfort he had spent a lifetime needing. Pressing her cheek hard against his, she slipped an arm around his waist and held him as tightly as he was holding her.

She refused to release him for the longest time—until she felt his tension ease and blow away on the wind. They had survived the storm together. Soon the sun would peek out again.

Heading back, Rave grabbed her hand and guided her over a log to another path they had passed previously. His playful tone made her wonder if he felt better, or was just skillfully raising his protective shields again.

"You have to see this Jen. Another waterfall. And three is a charm!" His humor and wicked grin were back again.

Looking at the Baring Creek Falls, Jen felt it was safe to ask, "So what do you want now, Rave?" She had been thinking of future goals, when she asked the question.

That grin should have warned her.

"I want a smart, sweet, sassy, brunette." His arms came around her waist, pulling her in, his voice turning seductively low, and husky, "With a soft lush body, and a loyal, loving heart. A dark haired angel with eyes bluer than the darkest sapphire, and lips like this."

His mouth was on hers before she could breathe, brushing her lips softly, then capturing then tenderly, before taking complete and utter possession—of her breath, her pulse, and maybe even her soul. She knew she had already lost her heart.

chapter fifteen

AS THEY WALKED BACK up the trail, the sun was coloring the lake and surrounding mountains with the first hints of day's end. As they strolled closer to where they had left Dana, they saw that Garrett had arrived.

Jenny tried to slip her hand casually from Rave's grasp before they were spotted by his friend, but he held on, murmuring softly, "No, my little wren, be with me."

When Garrett turned from Dana's welcoming embrace and saw them approaching, his eyes riveted on their linked hands, then narrowed as he took a step in front of Dana and squared himself with Ravenwolf.

"Well, 'ole buddy, just what the hell have you been doing for so long back there in the bushes with my new little sister," his voice radiated tension.

Ravenwolf's grin split his face.

"I have been a perfect gentleman."

He lifted the hand he held and kissed Jen's fingertips, his eyes glinting at her mischievously. "Have I not, sweet lady?"

"Yes, he has," Jenny answered. Damn him, she silently cursed, feeling the fires he had lit in her, and not quenched, burning in her face.

"Bummer," Dana said with a laugh, reading her friend's expression. Dana gave her husband a playful punch on the arm when he turned to give her a scowl—more mock, than serious—before Garrett turned to grasp Rave's hand and give him a sound thump on the back. Prying Jenny's hand free from his buddy's, Garrett gave her a huge bear hug, lifting her off the ground.

"How have you been doing, little one? Have you been behaving yourself?"

"Do I have to?" she teased cheerfully. "I've been having a wonderful time, and I'm still standing, if just barely. So I hope you brought your hiking boots. Your wife can torture you now instead of me."

He set Jen down. "There's a plan."

Garrett turned a smiling look on his wife that hinted that hiking wasn't the only torture he hoped Dana had planned for him.

"I'm starving," he announced, but his soft denim eyes were still flirting with the green sparkling depths of Dana's. His next words crushed Rave's hopes of finally getting an intimate dinner alone with Jenny that evening.

"But, I know the girls will want to soak off their hikes in bubble baths first, so let's get headed back up to Many Glacier. Dana needs to pack her things so we can try out those tipis for a few days. We'll all have dinner together at the hotel, and have a chance to catch up."

Rave wasn't sure how eager he was for his good pal to catch up on *all* his immediate plans with Jen, but resigned himself to waiting a little longer be alone with her.

"You're buying dinner," Garrett told Rave grinning as if he could read his guilty thoughts, delighted in frustrating them. Rave had to admit he had missed seeing the big blond cowboy. They did have a lot to talk over, but he hoped to keep it focused mostly on horses, and the upcoming annual celebration and rodeo.

After dinner, once he got Garrett and Dana on their way to their tipis, he had a date with Jenny to hear the Native America Speaks program at the hotel. After that his plans were mostly hopes, so there was no reason to share them with Garrett and get his own handsome nose busted for them yet.

Jen had ducked into the restroom as soon as the program ended. She spend as much time as she thought she could get away with combing her hair, freshening her lip gloss, washing her nervous hands, and putting the tiniest bit of fragrance at her pulse points. She didn't want to be obvious.

When she emerged, Rave was leaning against the wall, arms and ankles crossed, a thoughtful look on his face. The smile he gave her made her toes tingle.

"You know, I never knew that," he said thoughtfully when she joined him, commenting on the talk they had just heard. "I always thought that Hill, the railroad guy, just took advantage of the native people to promote his lodges and railroad, calling them the Glacier Park Indians.

"And he did. But that was an interesting perspective, don't you think? That while he may have been using them, in return they did get to keep their culture, stories, drums and dancing alive, that in those times where being harshly suppressed across the nation. That notion kind of surprised me," Rave said, wrapping an arm around her shoulders and guiding her towards the lounge.

"How about a quiet drink? I want to hear all about what you thought of the program."

His earlier intimate dinner plans screwed by his buddy, Rave thought he would never get Jen alone. Now he was determined to have his intimate time with her—or at least, start things in that direction—if he wanted an invitation up to her room later.

When he seated her in the lounge, leaning to brush the merest kiss on her nape as he pushed her chair in, Jen heard him turn and order their drinks before sitting across from her. It registered with her for the first time that his cool, frosty glasses rarely contained anything alcoholic. Before she had just assumed he was still on ranger duty, but now she knew it must be more significant. She realized she had rarely heard of him with more than the occasional beer shared with Garrett, uncertain now if it had even been alcoholic beer. Rave clearly didn't want to be like his father. So much more was starting to make sense to her now.

At the soft stroke of his fingertips across her hand, she shivered. So easily this fascinating, handsome, complex man could command her senses. He looked hard and chiseled, but he touched so soft and sensual. And when he shared—he gave it all.

They spoke softly, but tonight was a communication of much more than words. As much was said by hands and eyes touching.

Rave seemed to barely take his eyes off her lips as he listened to her thoughts on the evening, and anything else that came from her mouth—except to capture and hold the gaze of her eyes. He listened as if just the sound of her voice flowed soothingly over his senses, his hand slowly stroking her fingers and his thumb rubbing gently across her palm teasing the pulse at her wrist.

Jen was enchanted.

Rave's long, bronzed fingers touched her hair, brushed a chocolate curl from her shoulder, grazed her cheek, played with her fingers, while his dark eyes never left her face. His eyes didn't rove over the beautiful women in the lounge—and there were many—Jen noticed. He looked only at her, listened only to her, with his ears, his body leaning close. And those intense eyes that would fasten on her lips until she felt the heat dry them, and she had to lick them. Each time she did, she could see him swallow. See a slight flare in his nostrils, before he raised those caressing eyes back to hers. Even the cute over-friendly cocktail waitress could barely get his attention to place an order. And even then, when he spoke, he looked only at Jenny.

His intimate focus, the intense attention of this sensual, desirable male, was almost primitive in its gravitational pull and pulse on her senses. Her blood heated to a steady simmer in her veins. The constant, casual, caressing touches caused ripples and waves of anticipation sizzling and snapping along her nervous system; her heartbeat seemed to ebb and flow beneath his dark lava gaze. Awareness between their bodies seem to arc in the air, feeling much too visible to Jenny, too intimate for such a public place.

Or so she told herself when she heard her low voice ask him up to her room for a nightcap, after they finished this drink. Her palms dampened with nerves and anticipation at the thought of being alone in the dark with this dangerous man.

Rave set down his unfinished drink and rose immediately, his face solemn as he reached out his hand to raise her from her chair, dark eyes never leaving hers.

All Jen could think was that *finally* her handsome savage was going to ravish her until she melted or even died of pleasure—if she could just make it up the stairs on suddenly rubber legs. The soft little nibbles he was making on her bare shoulder while she tried to open her hotel door didn't make her any steadier.

The next day just the thought of the night before had Rave's body clenching. His heart hammered in his chest demanding more room. His mind drifted lost in a luscious, scented sensual fog.

It had been more than Rave had hoped for even when it was less than he had planned. It had been different than all his dreams of being with Jen.

There had been a terrifying, aching beauty that had transcended all he had imagined, but …

"Rave! Hey buddy, get your mind in the game here. So what do you think about this horseflesh?"

Garrett stroked the flank of a Spanish Mustang they were considering purchasing for a joint breeding program they had planned.

"Rave? This horseflesh?"

Flesh. Soft. Sweet. Supple. Vanilla scented flesh …

"RAVE!" Garrett shouted impatiently.

"Oh. Yeah sure fine. So fine."

She'd had no shortage of fantasies about what it would be like when she finally let that Handsome Savage get her in bed. She had dreamed it would be an earth shattering experience.

And it was.

The one thing Jen had never imagined was that she would be left disappointed.

Not unsatisfied, just disappointed. She had been satiated right down to her toes. Several times. Just the memory made her heart stutter, flutter, thump—and roar in anger.

"Jennifer McCallum, I am *totally* disgusted with you, girl!"

Jen snarled at her face in the bathroom mirror, then closed her mouth around her toothbrush, deciding things were bad enough. She didn't need to watch herself talking with a mouth full of toothpaste. She was already humiliated enough.

There was absolutely no way of denying or justifying her actions last night. She had become a cliché!

She had been felled by a notorious womanizer. Given herself up like all the other silly female lambs, one after another, to the slaughter. He was probably marking another notch on his belt as she brushed her teeth, trying to wash the taste of his tongue out of her mouth. She groaned a little. Couldn't look herself in the eye in the mirror while she recalled how good he had tasted, how…

Stop!

Her eyes flashed back to the mirror. Furious cobalt eyes glared back at her. She needed to keep that picture of him notching up another easy conquest on his belt foremost in her mind.

Of course he wouldn't notch the belt he wore with his ranger uniform. He was too professional for that. He'd notch his private, woman-chasing belt. Though … She paused, rinsed, and leaned against the counter. Now that she thought about it, she couldn't recall him ever wearing a belt on those jeans of his that hung precariously low on lean hips over that hard, ripped, bronze belly.

She stifled a shiver, trying not to think of how he had looked last night stretched out, hands cupped behind his head, the muscles under his arms flaring out like a cobra's hood toward broad, bare shoulders. Naked chest smooth, sleek with muscle, running down to that six-pack belly of his. Dark, arrogant, dangerous, eyes sensuous as he silently watched hers sliding down his body, devouring it. The top button on his loose, low slung jeans was so casually, and invitingly, undone. Jen gulped, realized her throat was dust dry, and grabbed a plastic cup, hurriedly filling it with cold water. She hesitated, not sure whether to fling it in her face, or swallow it.

Damn that man!

And damn her! She'd let it happen.

Okay, understatement. Begged for it, nearly.

She hated being such a fool, such a damn cliché! Especially since it was her own fault!

But she had been taken off guard. God, he had been so different than she had expected!

Jen had never known her skin could turn into liquid silk until Rave had melted it, slowly, sweetly, with lips trailing over every blessed inch of her. His long, sensitive fingertips had tenderly teased, cupped, framed, stroked, and trailed with wonder all over her, making her feel like a beautiful work of art. Treasured, then adored by the soft brush of his lips. She'd felt worshipped, languid. She'd felt exquisite. And just a wee bit impatient for the savage lover to be unleashed.

But he had given, and given, and given more. His lips had fluttered softly behind her knee, drizzled down the nerves in her leg, lapped at an ankle, kissed her arch, and then… God!…sucked each and every one of her toes. Thank goodness she'd had that pedicure just before she went on vacation, or she would have expired of shame on the spot.

All the time his lips worshipped, lapped and lingered, his eyes sought, captured and held hers hypnotically trapped in the serious intense black heat of his. It seemed as if he had held her suspended in a magic world for hours, days, when he rose up to capture her lips, his whole sleekly muscled near naked body coming in contact with her totally naked one.

Still he seemed to just revel in the sensual contact of skin to skin, luxuriating in it, stretching her arms out slowly to each side, framing them with his, curling her hands in his—porcelain twined in bronze, he had whispered. He held her mouth with his—possessing without pillaging. His chest slid across her breasts, his legs rubbed up and down and curled around hers, he pressed his hard belly against her softness, humming in her mouth with each slow, sensual touch and texture, hard against soft, firm against silk, hot against hot, just brushing, touching, sensing the differences, the tension exquisite.

Jen nearly screamed with frustration when he pulled back, pulled his lips slowly from hers, and began another lazy journey of lips and fingertips back down her body. Then she did cry out when he sent her climbing, exploding, soaring with pleasure, again and again, with just those tender touches. Always giving, savoring, not yet taking. No wonder he had such a reputation with the ladies, Jen mused, drifting slowly back to awareness in his arms.

When he gazed down at her, his eyes hot, dark, and possessive, she shivered with anticipation as his lips took hers again.

Now, she thought. Now her lover would take *his* pleasure. She could barely wait. This kiss was hotter, harder, deeper, unleashing darker passions when Rave pulled back, kissed her nose, rose and began gathering his clothes.

"What? Wait?" Jen's senses were scrambled and shocked.

"Gotta go, sweet little love," he just smiled down at her affectionately and pulled his shirt on.

"But, but... but, what about... what about that?" She motioned toward his clearly unfinished arousal still tucked in his jeans.

He chuckled at her sudden shyness, grinned at her, and quickly closed that tauntingly open button.

She couldn't believe it!

Reaching down, he trailed a fingertip across her cheek.

"Maybe I want to keep you coming back for more?" He suggested softly.

Or maybe you are full of bull, buster!

Jen was getting pissed off.

When he said he'd come prepared, she never thought he meant the two candles he had placed lit on the nightstand before turning out the lights, preparing a romantic atmosphere for her.

She didn't know for sure if he was prepared with protection in his jeans, but doubted that was the problem or reason he left.

209

Those jeans! That he had unbuttoned provocatively, but never shed. Jen's brain skidded off track momentarily.

The damn man was a blatant tease!

Seeing her disbelief and brewing anger, he'd sat on the side of the bed, capturing and stroking her hands.

"Ever sneak a fingertip of frosting off your birthday cake?" he asked her, startling her with the strange change of topic.

"Even if you know you're guaranteed the biggest and best piece of cake later, with the most frosting, there is just something irresistible and special about stealing a taste first. It builds the excitement, the expectation, makes you just drool for the piece of cake later. Don't you think, Jen?"

"But ..." Jen clamped her lips shut before she started whimpering. She had been drooling damn long enough. She wasn't buying his story and wouldn't give him the satisfaction.

He was already up and at the door.

"Dream of me." He winked, gave her that wicked grin, and pulled the door shut just before she hurled the pillow at it.

"They're called nightmares!" She snarled at the empty room.

Well! The nerve of that man!

She had expected him to be skilled enough to pleasure a woman first before satisfying his own greedy needs, but to worship her body for hours ... She'd turned and checked the digital clock ... yep, hours. To send her soaring time after time, to be so damn tender and loving ... Then to just up and leave?

What the hell was wrong with him!

Was he just one of those guys that thrilled to the chase and lost interest once his prey was captured and surrendered herself to him?

She worried that question through most of a restless night. Shortly before dawn she turned the question around and began to doubt and wonder. Had something been wrong, something lacking in her? Had he unwrapped the goods and changed his mind?

On that depressing note, she finally surrendered to sleep. He had treated her like a goddess, after all, maybe it would all make more sense in the morning, she had thought.

And it did. Oh, did it ever!

She was a fool!

A tourist for him to play with and send on her way. A cliché.

She was half tempted to find a whole frosted cake and shove it in that handsome, arrogant face!

chapter sixteen

THERE HAD BEEN A BRIEF thunderstorm that morning and the rain was still drizzling down beneath muddy, gray skies.

No one had made any advance plans for the group for that day, outside of a late morning appointment the guys had to see some horses they might purchase. Otherwise, since originally it was unknown how late Garrett would arrive the night prior, they agreed to go their separate ways until afternoon. It would be nice to have a morning off, to laze around, so everyone could just sleep in … or whatever.

Jen wasn't getting any whatever, or any sleep either.

Idly toying with the croissant on the breakfast tray she'd ordered from room service, she wondered how Dana and Garrett fared in the tipi with the storm. Tearing off a piece of the flaky pastry, she snorted.

They probably hadn't even noticed there had been one. Or more likely just mistook it as part of their 'whatever'. Jen laughed, imagining them wondering where the half-foot of water had come from. It wasn't really funny, but she had to amuse herself with thoughts that *someone* was having fun.

Picking up the TV remote, she clicked on to the morning news for something to distract her while she had her solitary breakfast. They were yammering on about fixing social security. That wasn't news, or new! They'd been on basically the same subject since Franklin Roosevelt first created it in the 1930s New Deal times. It had been illegal then, so that was the first thing they had to fix. And they had been 'fixing' it ever since. She highly doubted it would happen before she got back from vacation. Or was old and gray and needed it, for that matter. After just a few minutes, she shut the TV off again.

Her sigh sounded loud in the empty room. The outer world just didn't seem to fit here in Glacier, the news more an intrusion and annoyance, than a companion.

Jen jumped and scrambled for the room phone when it rang, trying not to sound breathless as she answered. But it was just the courteous staff from the kitchen calling to make sure the room service meal was satisfactory and asking whether there was anything else she needed.

She resisted the urge to ask them to send one Ranger Ravenwolf up. That probably wasn't included in the room service menu. Besides, she needed that cake before the next time she saw that guy. Inquiring, she found frosted cake *was* available by the slice on the dinner menu.

Good to know.

Finishing what she could eat, she put her tray outside and sat down at the table facing the window. The overcast was so low she couldn't even see the mountains across the lake. Pulling her lap top over, she thought maybe she would play some games, or check her emails to while away some time.

Leaning back to get comfy, she lifted her legs to rest on the edge of the table, ankles crossed, slumping back in the chair. Still in her robe after her bath, the motion bared her legs. Looking at them critically, she wiggled her polished toes. They looked normal.

"My weren't you guys naughty last night!' She addressed them. "Who knew? Remind me to stuff you in shoes today instead of sandals to muffle you so you can't squeal on me and carry dirty tales to Dana."

God! She must be loosing her mind! She was talking to her toes! The damn things still tingled from all the attention they received last night. She squirmed a little. So did all the rest...

Stop! She ordered herself again firmly. She was calm for the moment and wanted to stay that way. She turned on her laptop. She had already scrubbed a silly grin off her face once today—and more than a few scowls. She didn't have enough skin left to start all over again.

"Cake, my ass!" Jen muttered for the hundredth time that morning, clicking on the icon of her favorite computer game. Hadn't he heard about Marie Antoinette?

The computer game bored her, as did her email inbox. Casting about for something to do, she got her camera out of her pack and took out the memory card to download recent pictures to her computer and free up space. She hadn't meant to look at the photos from yesterday, but was unable to resist. After dating and labeling the file, she clicked on slide show and sat back arms crossed to watch.

Reaching out she stopped the show and brought up the prior image. She had known it was postcard perfect when she took it, but seeing it now full screen took her breath away. It was the photo she had mentally labeled 'America the Beautiful' of the flag topped Little Chief boat on the lake walled with mountains. When she had snapped the shot, she had been focused more on centering the photo. Now she saw all that she had captured. The light played on and around the mountains and lake picking out all the varied textures, highlighting the red tint and proud rugged face of Red Eagle Mountain. The setting pulled at her.

Jen sat back trying to identify what she was feeling.

She hadn't felt it in Yellowstone, like Dana had. That fascination with all those boiling pots, springs, and rivers, and the super volcano lurking underneath—all that explosive heat.

But she felt it here, in this land shaped by uplift, upheaval and ice, with its snowfields and forests, and razor edged peaks. It pulled at something deep inside her, created an uncomfortable need, luring her from her content and comfort zone with her own life and lifestyle, and demanded something more of her.

What, she did not know or understand, but she felt it tugging insistently at her. What was it?

It was more than her pleasure at being with her best friend again. Seeing Dana so healthy and happy was something she appreciated more than ever after the events of last year. That had been key to her coming on this vacation—but it wasn't the source of this feeling.

It was something else. If she could only pinpoint what.

At first she had thought it was just the lure of *him*. A potent attraction and distraction, but … It was something more, beyond, separate from the excitement and annoyance of being near Ranger Ravenwolf.

Something more than the people around her. Some elusive grip that this place seemed to have on her.

How many times had she stared out the window of the lodge, or the car, almost hypnotized by what she saw? When Dana would ask what she was looking at, she would feel the connection snap suddenly, quickly answer that she was just looking for mountain goats, or bear, or … something else. It was the something else that had her so entranced, yet was too vague to even try to share with her best friend.

213

What was I looking for out there? she asked herself. Why do I have this edgy feeling that I don't want to be just a visitor looking on, but need to do something? About it? Belong somehow?

Why did these mountains and forests pull at her so? Why did she look out on the dark scraped and scarred rock that hid the fossils of oxygen creation and feel ... what? It wasn't the science, like with Dana, though she had been surprised by how fascinating it all was.

She'd known intellectually, of course, that the early atmosphere had been different. All school kids learned that. But the difference between hearing something and standing before thousands and thousands of feet of deep time where those mushroom-looking things were pumping out air future life would require for breath—that was visceral. Immediate. Eerie. As high as these mountains rose, they never stretched high enough to touch the time most people thought of as life—when all the fossils big enough to see showed up.

She'd seen the Grand Canyon as a kid. Watched movies about traveling deep into the earth back in time. But this was totally different. Felt totally different.

A canyon was more like looking down from a cliff looking at the world's tallest tree from above. So what ? A treetop was a treetop. But this felt more like standing underneath that tallest tree and looking up. A very different experience and feeling.

Even Jen could feel the magic of the rock here—in this place already dramatic from ice age sculpture and its own wilderness beauty. And still something more pulled at her.

She couldn't pin it down. It was something more, a sense of unease, like you had when you had something you needed to do urgently, but you couldn't quite remember what it was. And the sense of guilt and unease that nagged at you to act. But what was it she was hearing so faintly, what was calling to her?

She tried to shrug it off, usually she could. Or she laughed at herself, telling herself the place was haunted and the ghosts of ancient spirits must be playing with her—even as she knew the unease she felt was not fear but some unnamed longing, some untaken action.

One thing was certain; it was a great place for a vacation because it could make you completely forget about all the things that had seemed important or worrisome back at work or at home. Yet she felt the pull of so much more. And an uneasy sense that it was shifting, changing something deep inside her, filling some hollow gap inside that she hadn't known existed before.

She shoved aside her laptop, stood at the window. The view felt like a deep breath. She felt a deep sense of this place, and its ... peace? Was that the word that she was looking for?

No. The chaos of its creation, carved everywhere she looked, didn't make her feel peace exactly. That wasn't the word she was seeking. She recalled feeling that indescribable something tug sharply at her subconscious on that canoe in the hushed, timelessness in the middle of Kintla Lake. It had been a feeling as if the air was sprinkled with magic, but a deep quiet feeling at the same time. Not peace, so much as patience. Patience with the passage of time, the passage of chaos that left beauty and silence behind, patience with the coming and passing of mankind, just a ripple of water left by a passing wake in the great span of earth time.

Yes, the patient timelessness this place made her feel was part of its pull on her. Something she felt, and could see in the ancient layers of rock built up over a billion years. But within that patience was that nagging pull for her to *do* something. She couldn't pin down *what* that was, but it certainly was thought provoking.

If this place had done nothing more, it had caused her to slow down and think about things she never bothered with, or had time for, in her busy rush from one thing to the next in her daily life—or things she usually left for Dana to think about for both of them.

But Jenny's normal routine and habits seemed almost foolish in the face of these mountains. They held the structures, the stromatolites that had been built maybe one inch a year, patiently, slowly, converting the toxic atmosphere into breathable oxygen, so that all this—so that *she*— could exist. And do what? What kind of ripple would she leave in the wake of time? And when would she start making one that felt like it mattered?

She sighed, turning from the window. Would she ever even *learn* patience? Teach me that first, she challenged the silent mountains and lake.

Jen knew she had the emotional patience of a firecracker. She had been that way all her life. She reacted impulsively, instantly, exploding in anger or drowning in tears, annoyed with herself afterward, for acting so childishly, without thought. When was she ever going to grow past those urges? She tried to shove the question and concern behind her, as she usually did, and tapped her laptop, to bring up the next picture.

She sat down and stared at it.

A devilishly handsome Rave grinned back at her.

The tug at her heart this time, was vastly different.

Speak of childish temper tantrums! What on earth had been wrong with her? Looking at his picture now she was lost in a soft, sensual haze of remembering his eyes, his hands, his lips on her body the night before. She nearly moaned at the memory.

And where had her patience been then, when he had asked for it? She had been furious ever since that he had not made love to her!

But was that fair?

He *had* made love to her yesterday. Twice! Well, on two separate occasions, anyway. She could count more than two times that she had been... well, sent into space, so to speak.

Yesterday, by the lake, she had asked why he never said *my people*, and what had he done? He had turned himself inside out for her. He had given, and trusted, all of his deepest most private pain and vulnerabilities to her. If that was not a gift of love making, it was hard to imagine what would be for as private a man like Ravenwolf.

Then again, last night, he had cherished every inch of her body—*almost* every inch, anyway. It had been love making. Sweet, drugging, unselfish love making. And she had been bitchy because ... Because she so long envisioned having wild, abandoned, thorough sex with him!

And that had made her furious?

Why? Because wild sex would be so much safer than the tenderness he had given her, a little voice inside her cautioned. That is what has you so scared and angry. Jen recognized the truth.

What Rave had given her—if she lost it— could tear her heart right out of her chest. The thought terrified her. She fought it the only way she knew how—fury. Senseless fury, she saw now. Thankful he'd left before she blew up and started spewing like one of Dana's volcanoes!

Standing at the window another minute, taking in the dampened scenery, Jen felt she had to take a moment to thank the mountain spirits for helping her find a little understanding—for sharing their patience and ancient wisdom.

216

The rain had stopped completely, and a glorious rainbow arched across the pale, gray skies.

The guys had taken off early that morning after all, according to Dana, to meet up with one of Rave's cousins on the reservation, to go look at horses. Dana called then picked up Jenny to go to Browning with her, and entertain themselves for the afternoon. They checked out some galleries in town that Dana heard about, explored the Museum of the Plains Indians there. Browsing the museum gift shop, they traded small credit cards for large amounts of bags—always a good trade, Jenny thought—then picked up tickets for the four day North American Indian Days celebration and powwow starting the next day.

Jen was watching the prairie, which always seemed so flat on the horizon, but rolled and undulated here. As they drove across, her mind rose and fell gently with the undulations, rolling over her thoughts and feelings earlier that day.

Dana had been raving about the night that she and Garrett had spent in the tipi village.

Listening with half an ear, Jen chewed her lip worrying over her own events of last evening—of which she hadn't breathed a word to Dana—as she was still so unsettled and conflicted herself. And grateful Dana had been so fascinated with the tipis, she planned to drag Garrett off to spend a few more romantic nights there.

Jen would be alone at the lodge, without fear of interruption, hoping she could make good use of the time and space. She couldn't help a private little smile.

She had spent her 'alone' time last night so languidly limp and helpless, under Rave's amazing skills, that she doubted she could have found the will to jump up and cover herself if a whole army had marched in on them.

Ah, Ravenwolf. Why couldn't she get him off her mind?

She had been fascinated with him from the first moment she had seen him. Fascinated with his male beauty, animal grace, virile body, Jen found it even harder to believe that she'd captured him.

Well ... almost.

Still she marveled that he had wanted her, that those lithe bronzed limbs had been semi-naked with hers, touching, pressing, caressing. It was hard to belief.

It was even harder to believe that cake and frosting story. More like pie in the sky, she huffed out a breath. He had probably just wanted to escape.

It was clear a man like that didn't need to worry about a woman being tempted to come back for more. He was temptation spelled in capital letters in every muscle and sinew in that body, even without the wickedly handsome face. Hell, he had a line around the block of women just waiting their turn for his attentions.

So why her?

Or more to the point, what was it that was wrong with her? Why had he held back from taking everything he wanted?

And where had he gone after he left her? Home?

Rave had his own home. They could have gone there. In fact, now that she thought of it, she had said something about wanting to see his place. He had just smiled at her and led her upstairs, murmuring something about her room being closer. Yeah, right. Of course. That way the guy could leave whenever he wanted.

And leave when *he* wanted, was exactly what he did.

Jen hated the jealousy crawling in her belly and poisoning her mind. What was wrong with her? It had to stop. Besides, she had no proof the man had done anything. Anything but give *her* immense and endless pleasure. Hadn't she just been discussing patience with herself that morning?

They were heading up to meet the men in the town of Babb, at the junction where the Many Glacier Road met the highway north of Saint Mary. With the powwow starting, serving alcohol was prohibited on most of the reservation, but they could still get wine with their dinner in the park, or in Babb. They all wanted a different dining experience after being too tired to go further than Many Glacier lodge, so they were going to check out the Cattle Baron Supper Club in the small town. They hoped to catch an earlier dinner and then take the sunset boat cruise on St. Mary Lake—a romantic end for the day.

First they had to connect up with the guys.

Dana reported that Garrett had called earlier to let her know they would be at the other bar in Babb for awhile, where they had gone with Rave's cousin. As Dana and Jen finished a bit earlier than expected, she planned to look for Garret there first, before checking to see if he was waiting at the Supper Club.

Just north of St. Mary they came to an area that reminded them they were on open range. Dana slowed for a herd of horses, scattered on either side of the road. It was a strangely unique experience. Not to see horses on both sides of the road, but that the highway was unfenced, as were the lands around them on the reservation. The horses were free to roam across and along the road, as they wished. Another of those novel juxtapositions of time these lands continually charmed the tourist with—never sure if they were in this century or some other. Somehow startled by something as natural as how it had once been, the senses paused to try and identify what was wrong with the picture, only to realize that it was unblemished.

Dana eased to the shoulder a moment so they could take pictures of these descendants of the Spanish Mustangs that escaped early explorers—sometimes with a little help—and had played such a part in changing native cultures by giving greater range and mobility to all the distant areas not accessible by waterways.

"Look, they are such lovely and varied colors, aren't they?" Dana asked. "Did Rave tell you about the breeding program he and Garrett are planning? That's where they've been all day. Looking at horses with Rave's cousin, that they are thinking of buying."

"No," Jen said absently.

She had been in a strange, quiet mood all day. Looking out the window at the horses, she murmured something almost under her breath.

"He told me about his childhood."

What? Dana was shocked, couldn't believe her ears, but managed to catch herself before saying anything. If she knew one thing from Garrett, it was that his friend didn't like talking about his childhood, and she was never supposed to ask him.

But he had told Jenny. Well, that was stunning. That he would be that intimate with her. Ah, well, Dana wondered when he had told her. After all, they had been alone last night together. Maybe all night. Being intimate and ... well, being really intimate? Dana stifled a snicker and wondered if she dared to ask.

She decided to save her questions for later when Jen turned from the window and asked, "What do you mean a horse breeding program?"

"It all started as a joke when they used to work together on road crews and go camping together. One time Rave took Garrett to camp in Yellowstone, and they rode their horses over the Old

219

Bannock Trail. Rave told Garrett that the Nez Perce used that southern route over the Rockies to stay clear of the hostile Blackfeet when they went to the buffalo hunting grounds on the plains.

"Well, one thing led to another. Garrett teased Rave about being part Blackfeet who used to steal the highly prized Nez Perce horses, and Rave said he planned to breed some mixed breeds, like himself someday. Garrett said that if they were as tough as Rave, part Nez Perce, part Blackfeet, he would go in on it with him. And even though it started as teasing, they never forgot the idea, or the bond of friendship they cemented on that trip.

'The Blackfeet have a breeding program here to preserve the remnants of the original Spanish Mustangs that created such a change for all the early natives when they spread to all the tribes in the early 1700s.

"The Nez Perce were particularly known for selective breeding of their Spanish horses that they traded for with the Shoshone, and for creating the Appaloosas—legend has it—from their first white mare and colt. Rave and Garrett have been dreaming of breeding the pure Spanish Mustangs back with Appaloosas, like the Nez Perce originally did for ages. And the guys plan to preserve pure strains of each also, if all goes as they hope.

"So Rave found Garrett's Appaloosa stallion for him in Idaho, from the revitalized Nez Perce breeding program. He will be the stud to start the program. Now they are looking for mustang mares here. You remember Blue Moon, don't you? Isn't he a handsome guy?"

Jen gave her such a vacant look that Dana wondered if she had even been listening to her rambling on. Though she usually paid complete attention whenever the topic included Ravenwolf.

"I do remember Garrett's gorgeous stallion, but I don't remember him having any Appaloosas," Jen finally said, with a puzzled frown, adding "Aren't those the ones with the cool spots and speckles?"

"Yes," Dana agreed slowly, "and no. Most people don't realize how many different coat colors and textures the breed has, or that you never know when you breed them what you will get—solid, spotted, or another mix like Garrett's. That's one of things that is so exciting about them. Blue Moon is what is known as a blue roan. His coat is not quite a solid color. If you look closely you'll see that it has a white-speckled undertone, and you probably noticed how pink the skin on his nose is. Other characteristics unique to the breed are striped hoofs, the skin under the coat mottled pink, and eyes that look like humans, because you can see the whites around the pupils. They also have other traits and are great trail horses, with long distance endurance and a comfortable walk—besides all being so gorgeous to look at!

"Anyway, they have been looking at land and horses lately whenever they get the chance. Their ultimate plan is to create great trail horses by mixing the two strains, but also sending part of the proceeds of the horses they sell back to the two native breeding associations for their preservation efforts of the original individual strains. I think it's a fantastic idea!"

Jen was impressed. Every time she thought she understood Ravenwolf, she learned something new that completely baffled her. Who was he? Certainly not the womanizing dog she had once thought!

But she had been wrong before.

chapter seventeen

CLEARLY UNABLE TO RESTRAIN herself any longer, when they reached Babb and were still alone outside, Dana finally had to ask.

"So what did you and Rave do last night?"

"Oh, we went to a program at the lodge," Jenny stalled. Knowing what Dana was wondering, she babbled on about the fascinating Native America Speaks program. "And then we had some drinks. I did anyway, Rave doesn't seem to drink much does he?"

Dana grinned, seeming to recognize the attempted diversion. "Oh, he is always ready to go to the bar for drinks. His just don't have any bite in them. But you were telling me all about your evening alone with Rave. Then what happened?"

Breaking down, Jen blurted it out, though she'd never meant to.

"Oh Dana, it was wonderful! And horrid!"

"Horrid? If he pushed or pressured you, I'll ... "

"No, no Dana. It was nothing like that. I asked him up, but ... "

"What? Don't tell me Rave pulled a wham-bam-thank-you-ma'am?" Dana's brows arched in total disbelief.

"No, he never bammed, or whammed, or... oh, forget that. I mean... it was just the opposite. Oh, Dana, I can't talk about it now," Jen groaned. "Forget I said anything. I'll explain it all to you later. Just as soon as I figure it out," she added. "Isn't this where we are supposed to meet them?" Jen asked desperate to stop the discussion.

"Yeah," Dana agreed reluctantly, recognizing she wasn't going to get anything more out of Jen right now. Wonderful, meant nothing too bad happened. Horrid probably referred to something that just embarrassed Jen. Relieved, Dana pulled open the door of the bar letting Jen go in first.

"We are a little early," Dana said, "but let's go in. I need to get off my feet and have a cold one."

The stormy morning had cleared earlier in the day with the last drizzle ending in a stunning rainbow before noon. The summer sun had returned to dazzle and reclaim the sky shortly after.

Entering the darkened bar now after the bright late afternoon sunlight outdoors, Jen took a few steps inside with Dana behind her then paused for her eyes to adjust, blinded by the change.

She thought she heard a familiar deep, sexy rumble of laughter as soon as they opened the door to the bar. The same voice that then gave a seductive croon.

"Come here, little girl, give me some of that."

Jen was startled by Rave's voice. Surprised that he had spotted her so quickly in the cool, murky bar after they were backlit by the blinding flash of light from outside. She took a few more cautious steps forward, with Dana following, hoping her eyes would hurry and adjust so she had more than his voice to guide her forward.

She stumbled into a solid wall of male flesh. A young, handsome man in native dress leather breeches, his muscular chest in a tightly stretched tee shirt blocked their path, as he hurried to push out the door. He was cursing under his breath, but uttered a brief apology as he squeezed past the women and out into the sunlight.

Regaining her balance, eyes squinting in the dim room, Jen carefully made her way around the dark silhouettes of patrons, seeking the source of the voice she had heard. Another burst of male laughter drew her eyes to the shadows in the back corner of the bar where she saw something illuminated beneath a beer sign that took her a little while to make out.

Her eyes first widened in shock, then narrowed in anger, as her vision and recognition improved. What had first looked like a heavy set man with a huge spare tire around his waist sitting on a barstool, turned out to be a very fit, lean laughing man sprawled back on the stool facing a very scantily clad lithe woman in his lap. Her arms were closed around his neck and long, slender, legs wrapped around his waist like a snake. She seemed to be trying to devour his face and neck with lips and tongue. Her hips squirming and pressing rhythmically against him. A male hand spread across her skimpily clad ass, gripping and holding her in place.

She had found Ravenwolf.

And he was laughing, the bastard!

So were his drinking buddies.

"Who-eee, you got yourself a hot one this time, Rave! Maybe you should take it outside."

"Hell, no," another hooted, "I'm enjoying the show. Maybe we'll all learn something from our local expert Romeo."

"Better get a fire extinguisher ready," that laughing, cheating, lying, Romeo bastard called back.

And he hadn't even noticed Jen yet, though she stood there frozen with steam hissing out her ears, and flames about to shoot out of her nostrils.

He was going to need a hell of a lot more than a fire extinguisher!

"Uh - ohh!" Dana breathed behind her.

Rave swiveled his chair around so he could stand, and slid the girl down his body to set her on her feet, his arms firm around her.

"It's bedtime for you, little girl," he chuckled, then glanced up and froze. His smile vanished as abruptly as his laughter.

"Jenny?" His voice as strangled as it was startled.

"You bastard!" she spit out. Too humiliated to speak past the angry lump choking her throat, she spun and dodged around Dana, blindly bumping into tables as she ran for the front door.

Dana just stood there glaring at him, disgust and disbelief clear in her eyes and face. She had never taken Garrett's warnings about his buddy too seriously, until now. But she had seen the ugly proof herself over Jen's shoulder.

"Dana?"

She heard the request for mercy and understanding in Rave's tone, saw the despair and pleading in his eyes. But she had no mercy for him in her heart now. It was a cold, closed door.

Without a word, Dana rushed after her friend. She called Garrett from her car, and told him to meet her at the lodge instead. She needed to get Jen out of this too small town, away from that cheating dog of a man, right now.

Rave cursed, turned around and slammed his fist down on the bar so hard it rattled everyone's drinks. He raked both hands through his hair, trying not to howl with frustration.

He felt something wrap around his waist again, tighter than a belt, and heard a slurred female voice asking, "Bed?"

Hell! Grinding his fists into his eyes he tried to figure out how to get out of this mess, then twisted around and ordered a double—a real one.

The laughter in the bar had died to uneasy murmurs.

Jen convinced Dana she was fine and just wanted a quiet dinner and evening in her room. Alone. Though she clearly was *not* fine, the way Jen unclenched her jaw to bite out *Alone!* had Dana in immediate retreat.

As soon as she had sent Dana back to her husband, Jen packed and caught the shuttle from Many Glacier to the Amtrak station in East Glacier.

She found herself unable to scare up a smile to join in the exuberance of the other tourists on the bus, but at least her anger was holding back the tears—at least for the moment. Her heart felt like one of the sharp, jagged, icy stone edifices that lined the route south as they moved along the eastern front of the Rockies, following the Old North Trail down through the reservation.

Jen wanted—needed—to think about anything but the image embedded in her brain of the man she'd let lure her into love—last seen with another woman straddling his lap, wrapped around him like moss on a tree.

Had his look of horror, when he'd noticed her in the dim light of the bar, been from guilt? Had he cared, even a little, about her?

Quit torturing yourself, she ordered, with a firm shake of her head, trying to hold back the moisture she felt welling in her eyes. Tightening her lips, she let anger and cynicism replace the pain. He probably was just freaked that Dana had witnessed it also, and therefore Garrett would know now that he had screwed up big time.

Good ! She hoped he'd have to pay somehow for making such a fool of her. She never would have let down her guard and trusted him, let him matter to her ... Dammit! Fallen head first in love with him, Jen admitted, if he hadn't been Garrett's best friend.

At least, she hoped she wouldn't have been such easy prey for Ravenwolf, if not for that. At least she wouldn't have met him.

Jen wished now she never had!

Enough!. He is so over.

But her firm chin had a quiver in it. She tried to tighten the tremble in her lips and swallow the lump building in her throat. She could not, would not, let herself cry now, here in public, or she would never be able to stop. And she would not allow the added humiliation of word getting back to him that she had cried her way out of town! Jen could not let that happen, she clenched her teeth and her will.

Salvage something good from this trip, she silently commanded herself.

Forcing her thoughts and view out the window to the land that had also caught her heart and imagination; the land that Jen was soon to leave behind, with all its bad memories. And its good ones with Dana, also. Jen sighed at that loss, focused on those thoughts.

They'd had so much fun exploring and discovering, as if they were the first to find this land and all its lesser known secrets and histories. When she had originally planned this trip with Dana, pouring over the website, she had expected it to be all about the glaciers and their carvings after the last Ice Age. Now, over a hundred years after the park's founding, ten to twelve thousand years after the retreat of the great ice sheets, the glaciers were almost all melted away, though the devastating beauty of their carved and sculpted works remained.

And the wilderness, so vast and well preserved for all to enjoy with its grizzly and mountain goat populations, unique plants, hundreds of miles of backcountry trails and fingerlike alpine lakes, were the other draw that Jen had looked forward to experiencing with her pal—some from a great and healthy distance.

But, as usual with Dana, they'd found such a vast wealth more to see and learn that went beyond the glossy tourist pictures to ancient secrets of the earth and ancient mysteries about the peopling of the land ... *this* land and possibly most of the Americas.

Jen gazed at that land rolling past her window—and it did roll, hugely. To the west, the stark shaved peaks dominated and raked the sky. Off to the east the Great Plains that Lewis and Clark crossed, rolled out—but that seemed such recent and overblown history.

In the middle, here, lay the real adventures of man on this continent. Here off the eastern front of the Rockies, was the middle of prehistory in this country, as Dana had shared the details with her—and this time Jen had been listening—for this had been the dividing line between the great prehistoric ice sheets of the last glaciations of the continent, ground zero of the last great climatic battle in the U. S.

The southern skirts of the Cordilleran and Laurentide continental sheets had met—or almost met—here, aided by the out flowing lobes of alpine and piedmont glaciers, to come within mere miles of each other. Here! Right here In this very place, so very long ago but mere moments past in earth's span of time.

Jen quirked her lip in a wry smile realizing how deeply Dana had infected her with an enthusiasm for the deep past. Jen, herself, realized the current "green revolution" was nothing but a fad unless one tried to understand first the kind of recycling that Mother Earth had done in the past, and would continue to do in the future—human species, or not.

Beneath the wheels of their bus, and the deeply rolling landscape, lay an even older past in the chalky layers of Cretaceous times, littered with the bones of the former rulers of this land—the dinosaurs. It was the time of the Ice Ages, though, that held Jen's attention, as she could see those effects out her window.

Dana had tutored her on this.

Glacial till had been dumped in mounded moraines by the retreating ice sheets, pocked by former boggy kettle lakes, and carved, curved and sculpted by the flooding of muddy melting outwash waters, to create this rollicking, rolling landscape between the Rockies and the Great Plains.

But what really captured Jen as the bus curved around climbing up and down over the terrain—and kept her blessedly distracted—was the "almost met" part. For this was where the famous ice-free corridor funneled early Americans from Siberia over the ice age land bridge through Alaska then down between the great walls of ice. It would have opened out right here in at least one of the great migrations thirteen thousand or more years before..

Jen tried to remember some of the ancient and amazing history she'd learned about the area.

The Old North Road, was once the great corridor between the ice traveled by mammoths and other massive, extinct and strange beasts ... and by man. Maybe in groups of men, women

227

and children as small as twenty in a band dressed in animal skins with only stone, bone, and antler for tools and weapons. No maps, no GPS, no concept of what lay ahead, on foot, without cell phones to call or text for help—or even anyone else to call on.

Jen shivered picturing that scene. It was both a terrifying and an awe inspiring image.

And Lewis and Clark thought they had it tough! Hah!

They weren't even close to the *real* voyage of discovery, but they got all the historic marker signs and glory for some reason, Jen muttered to herself, before turning her thoughts back to that ancient time and those ancient peoples that had first walked this land.

She wondered what they would have thought when they first looked south from one of these high hills and realized the land was opening wider between the walls of ice. Would they have realized they were leaving something and entering something else?

They certainly couldn't have known of the vastness and richness of all the land that lay open to them, or even trusted it was more than a temporary gap. Maybe it even scared them, so unfamiliar after the generations that would have passed as they lived in the close icy-walled canyons?

Now *that* was a really bizarre thought! The ice sheets were probably normal to them—their comfort zone—they must have been freaking out about global warming themselves! Even if they never knew they were on a tiny globe hanging out there in the middle of space.

But they had enough to worry about with the dire wolves and mammoths and saber tooth cats, and bears bigger than grizzlies and all their ice walls breaking up, receding and melting. So what had they seen and felt when they stood on this spot?

Only a few hundred miles to the south was Missoula, the city that lay in the scarred mountain walls of Glacial Lake Missoula. It had flooded repeatedly and catastrophically west to the Pacific across her home state. She'd seen the scars. Would the vista have been one of more melt water lakes than land? She tried to picture herself as one of the women standing on top of the hill thousands and thousands of years ago and ... the bus stopped.

Jen abruptly returned to the present, or at least to a mere century past in the early 1900s, as she realized her view had changed to the entrance veranda of the Glacier Park Lodge. She had intended to be let off across the street at the Railroad Depot, but had gotten so lost in her ice age journey, she'd forgotten her current destination. She might as well get something to eat and check out Glacier Lodge first, since she was here, and since it had been built from what she considered "her" trees.

And since she had to do something to hold back the tears until she could be alone.

Salvage something, everything you can. Jen tightened her will.

When he left Jenny's bed the night before. Rave had felt conversely both elated and nauseated. The elated part was easy. She was so soft, sweet, responsive, and lush he could have devoured her for hours. And he knew that it wasn't just unsatisfied lust that had twisted and tangled his stomach up like knotted snakes.

Fear. That's what it was. Or sheer panic caused the nausea.

He had done the only thing he could and lit out like he had evil spirits breathing down his neck, treading on his heels. As he drove home last night he had tried to talk himself down, calm himself, even tried to reason with himself.

And even lied to himself. No big deal. As soon as Jen went home after vacation and left him alone, then everything would be just fine. Just dandy. So he told himself.

Right. Then he could just die and wither away slowly without anyone noticing. Because that was the problem that had him cornered like a frantic animal.

He did not want her to leave.

Ever.

But he'd been afraid to claim her completely because that would have made everything harder and more complicated. For him. He knew if he'd taken all that she had so sweetly offered him—it would be his heart and soul that would be trapped. And that scared the hell out of him. So he had run to his den to lick his wounds and, hopefully, figure out what to do next.

Just like he had run from her after Dana's wedding.

And now he had a new problem to sort out and deal with. But Jen was so forgiving. He was sure once he explained she would understand, maybe even … No, scratch that.

But driving home tonight after getting his little friend from the bar safely home to her bed, Rave was convinced that after a night of explosive anger, Jen would be calm enough tomorrow to reason with.

As long as Dana or Garrett didn't find and murder him first.

Learning at the information desk that the train departed west only once daily, in less than an hour, Jen hurried back up the drive to the tiny, antiquated rail station dragging her wheeled, but still reluctant, bags across grass and gravel, only to arrive breathless at a near empty station.

The Empire Builder Amtrak Train had apparently been delayed leaving its Eastern Base in Chicago yesterday afternoon, then further delayed in the wee hours of the morning in St. Paul/Minneapolis for an inspection and transfer of passengers to a replacement sleeping car. By its stop in Minot, North Dakota, the train had been running almost three hours late, but according to the harried agent, hoped to make up time.

However, he continued, as Amtrak only leased track from the freight trains that had the right of way, whenever they were off schedule like this, they were required to pull to a siding for every freight on its regular schedule to pass.

It boiled down to an anticipated three hour departure delay from East Glacier. Subject to any changes, off course. He'd have a better idea when the train arrived in Havre, Montana, which it should have done by now, but hadn't quite reached yet, he scratched his head, so ...

It was at this point that Jen started inquiring about sleeping accommodations, beginning to realize that the term schedule, when applied to trains, was a nebulous concept. She didn't care how long it took her to get home, as long as she got out of here before anyone could find and try to stop her. Or she broke down. She selected a roomette, which looked like it might be large enough for a single person to travel in comfort, and had the added bonus of meals and—best of all—privacy.

The privacy alone was worth the extra expense right now, as she continued to beat back feeling, the only way she could avoid a deluge of tears to rival the ice-age floods.

Reassuring the apologetic agent that she was grateful the train was late, or she might have missed the once daily stop, Jen left her bags locked behind the station master's partition. Promising she would come back across to the station well before nine that evening, she decided she would be more comfortable in the lobby and shops of the Glacier Park Lodge while she waited.

Walking back across the drive and lawns to the lodge she tried not to look at the large tipi stationed on the vast front lawn. Or at the lengthening shadow it cast as the sun headed down to meet the top of the peaks behind the lodge, a reminder of the romantic sunset cruise she would never be taking now.

Clamping her teeth and her control tightly, Jen hurried up the front veranda and headed for a gift store inside. Shopping had always calmed her, but it didn't work this time. Everywhere she looked the souvenirs of Glacier just made her heart ache a little harder. She should be buying them to take back to her fellow office workers, but she couldn't do it. Going to the magazine section she selected three or four home decorating and gardening magazines, studiously avoiding any that might hold articles about relationships or romance. She added a large selection of chocolate candy snacks and headed for a secluded seating area in the lobby.

As the day and room darkened, she reached over to turn on the cute table lamp that had a base that was carved into a squirrel. Like many of the bent wood framed chairs and rockers, it must have been done by a talented artist. It was so beautifully detailed and realistic looking, she almost felt as if she could see it breathing.

And then the lamp base blinked at her. Amazing! Jen wondered how they achieved that detail. Then when her hand was just inches away, the squirrel leaped off the table and went scampering across the floor. Jen was too startled to even squeak.

The speedy little creature made a run for it across the wood plank lobby and leaped onto one of the massive columns that rose several stories. Columns that had been made of Jenny's Pacific Northwest trees, complete with their bark. And for the first time that day, she found herself laughing out loud, unable to stop herself.

How was that silly little squirrel to know he wasn't in the real forest, after all, with two dozen rough barked Douglas Firs planted around the open central lobby? Goodness, she thought, what if he had a whole family up there? Jen nearly giggled herself silly trying to imagine it all. She wondered where they hid the nuts for the winter?

Which reminded her that she still hadn't had any dinner.

After the help from her funny little lamp base, she felt ready to speak to people again, and headed back to the information desk, fronted by another massive chunk of one of *her* trees, halved and laminated as an enormous table.

It made her homesick. Or at least to desire her own nest to hide away in.

chapter eighteen

THE CONNECTION BETWEEN railroad expansion to the west and the early national parks is nowhere as evident today as at East Glacier, on the southeastern tip of Glacier National Park. Competition between rail lines for passengers created great benefits with the building of many of the grand park lodges by private railroad money, a fact not always recognized today. And only at Glacier does that original linkage still exist for modern passengers, able to take the train to the front door of a historic lodge and hundred year old national park.

While the rail line built the access and accommodations to one of the nation's most beautiful and unique remote national parks, its wonders built the strength of a rail line that continues today with Amtrak's Empire Builder Tour from the Pacific Northwest to Chicago, along the scenic southern border of Glacier Park.

Arriving at the depot in East Glacier, the view out the front is a stunning vista of the snow stained, ragged charcoal peaks of the Northern Rockies, so startling after a long journey across the plains. The immense lodge is almost hidden against the backdrop, nestled low beneath like part of a wooded foothill, blending into its natural setting—an unusual concept for the time.

Great Northern wanted luxury hotels that fit the setting, and had this main lodge modeled on the idea of huge trees for columns like the Forestry Building built for the Alaska-Yukon Pacific Northwest Expo of 1909, in Seattle, Washington, with a touch of Swiss Chalet thrown in the exterior for their American Alps theme.

Exterior columns were massive tree trunks and the lobby was created with an inside-the-forest feeling, using trees so

233

massive that they could only be found in the Pacific Northwest forests, and brought in on their railroad.

The interior lobby alone required twenty-four trees, forty-eight feet long, and tapering from four to three feet wide, found in the five to six hundred year old Douglas Firs of the Pacific forests. The trees were cut in winter so that they could stand around the inner lobby with their rough bark on, as if they grew there supporting the balconies of the three stories that rose to light filtering atrium windows.

The native people called it "the Lodge of the Big Trees". No trees of that size existed anywhere near, with such massive girths.

The lodge opened with steam heat, individual showers in rooms, a plunge pool, and other amenities that made it the height of luxury in such a remote wilderness. Hotels and tours were advertised from one to five dollars a day in the 1920s.

The depot at East Glacier is like a small museum and time capsule of those earlier days. The enclosed wooden counter has an old lift up window, with glass that looks like it is made of frosted ice crystals, and it clearly states its purpose—TICKETS. Around the corner is another area, designated "Conductors". This back room is now given over to glass cased displays of the clothing, moccasins, breastplates, feathered headdress, and beaded ornaments of the native people that once greeted visitors with their drums and song.

Jen was glad it was getting dark so she didn't have to see the park she have come to love. She hated saying long, sad goodbyes. But even in the moonlight, the mountains haunted her, with ghostly white snow fields glimmering up high where the shadow of the mountains rose against a star engorged sky. She would see neither once she got back to the city and its artificial light hiding the brilliance of the open night sky.

Turning from the train window, she figured how to work the metal contraption they called a tray table, that so far had just been useful for bruising the side of her knee. But with the glass door closed and her curtains draw, she was at least private and alone, at last.

Putting her laptop on the tiny table between the seats, she had a duty to let Dana know she had disappeared, so she wouldn't worry tomorrow morning. She emailed a message to Dana's cellphone, brief and to the point.

Dana - Don't worry, went home on train.
Have fun with hubby. I will write or call
when ready. Love & thanks, Jen

She had just finished when her attendant ushered her out of the tiny cramped space to set up the bed. As soon as the bed was made to crisp hospital corner specifications, Jen sat on top of it and managed to squirm her way into pajamas in the tight space.

Emotionally spent, she laid down, buried her face in her pillow and let the tears she had held so long, leak down her cheeks, let the racket of rails drown her sobs, until the rocking motion of the train finally helped soothe her grief wracked body to sleep.

He knew he shouldn't try this by phone, but he wanted to catch her early before they met up with Dana and Garrett. He just wanted to arrange breakfast with her at the lodge. He'd save the rest of what he wanted to talk to her about to discuss then, face to face.

Shifting his phone to the other ear, in case he had misheard, he asked the desk clerk, "Are you sure? This early? Can you page the coffee shop?"

"Not in the hotel? Okay, did she leave word for the friends she is meeting today what time she will be back?"

He quickly changed ears again, neither of them seemed to be working so hot this morning.

"Checked out? She can't do that!"

"You are right," he clenched his teeth trying to remain polite despite the desk clerk's sarcastic response.

"Yes, I should have notified her myself that she was not allowed to leave your hotel. If you could just tell me one more thing, please. What time did she check out this morning?

"Yesterday?" he roared, cutting of the clerk in the middle of telling him that in future he might want to keep better track of his women.

He quickly sent a text message to Dana.

"Jen with U?"

It only took a minute for a reply, which Dana didn't bother to abbreviate, just to be sure he was crystal clear on her meaning.

"Jen not here, ASSHOLE!"

Garrett even sent him some additional information from his cell.

"DITTO!"

Rave felt panic begin to scramble around in his gut. If Jen wasn't at the hotel or with Dana, where was she?

He headed for his truck to go find her. Without a car she must be on one of the tours, either by boat or jammer. He hoped she wasn't dumb enough to try hiking alone, just to get away for some private time. But she was probably in a temper.

And she probably switched hotels, just to avoid him. He'd check them all. And he should give Shirl a call later, maybe she could give him some advice on how to handle things when he found Jen.

On his own he had just done a damn fine job of screwing up! Even his best friends hated him!

But when he had a chance to explain, everything would be okay.

He was sure of that.

Once he found Jen ...

Breakfast on the train was yogurt, juice, and a cinnamon roll in her little private space. Jen was glad she had spent the extra on her fare, so she could avoid the dining car and people curious about her trip and her swollen puffy eyes and face. She wasn't hungry, but she had ordered so the helpful attendant would go away. She hoped the food might help fill some of the bleak hollowness inside her.

It didn't seem to help.

She had woken up that morning when the train began to climb back up into the mountains. Her mountains, this time, the familiar Cascades, built of volcanoes and lumpy gray granite mostly obscured by deep, heavy evergreen forests. With the delays, it would be close to midnight by the time she arrived home. Too late for her other mountains, the far distant snowy Olympics guarding the Pacific coast, to welcome her. But even the familiar was painful now, bringing back the loss of the unique, sheer chiseled cliffs of Glacier, and a chiseled male face and form that made her heart ache.

She shoved her thoughts away from him, thinking instead of her departure last night from the depot. She had wandered the displays at the historic train depot, reading every typed description, admiring the brilliantly colored primary blues, reds, and yellows, used in the native clothing and beadwork worked into geometric designs. There had been a deerskin shirt and bone breastplates, and everywhere colorful braids, beading and feathers.

All things that took time, and care, and patience to create. Like the patient mountains and prairies around them. She had found, then lost, her patience in Glacier. Jen sighed, and tried to distract herself again, trying to keep hurt and anger at bay.

She recalled seeing even more dazzling colors and attire with the passengers arriving and unloading at the depot, carrying their best, beautiful native costumes for the celebration that started tomorrow. Today, now. The Blackfeet powwow brought people from all over the country to celebrate together each year at the North American Indian days.

Jen was going the wrong way, at the wrong time. It had helped her secure accommodations on the train, but she would miss the annual weekend celebration she had really begun to look forward to.

When she had been in Browning with Dana just yesterday, though it seemed far longer past, they had seen glimpses of some dancers practicing, and they had heard the sound of the drums. Those drums were unlike anything Jenny had ever experienced. She had thought she had seen it all, felt it all, on TV and in movies. But she had been wrong, so wrong.

It was like the difference between seeing a picture of white water rafters, and being a tiny soul in the violent grip and at the heart pounding mercy of a powerful river. On that vast edge of the prairies, with the sky so huge above, the beat of the drums was so primal, like a giant heartbeat that pulsed from the earth, through the body, the very beat of life itself. Jenny lost words to describe it. It was like air, so elemental it had to be drawn inside, and felt.

The bright blues, and reds, and yellows, and greens of the dancer's costumes against the vast seared grass of the prairie was spiritual in a way that could never be felt from a glass case in a museum. She had been captured by the life and breath and pulse of the scene, and had been reminded of the rainbow she had seen earlier that morning.

Those basic colors, so bright, and dazzling, and right, but special, wondrous, worked on stark white buckskin against earth's natural backgrounds. Life was a celebration of color: the colors of the ceremonial native dress, the colors of the rainbow, the colors of the ancient rocks and pebbles of the mountains and lakes of

Glacier. She remembered thinking that all rainbows must end in Glacier's colored rocks that morning, when she was contemplating love; that same afternoon she had see the rainbow colors gathering in the native peoples of the reservation, when she had felt the beat of life and the pulse of hope.

But rainbows never lasted.

Hers had been shattered by a man.

Ravenwolf had not met them at the powwow as planned. Dana thought it was a very wise decision. There were just too many handy tomahawks around to keep her out of jail.

The only way Garrett had convinced her to come was by reminding her that Jen was missing it and needed someone to take pictures for her and tell her all about it later. Dana knew Jen meant her words, when she told Dana to have fun with Garrett. She wanted them to enjoy their vacation and leave her alone. Dana would respect her wishes—for as long as she could bear it. Damn that Ravenwolf! She wanted to kill him and send Jenny his scalp!

"Good, you're smiling again," Garrett wrapped his arm around her waist, never knowing just how bloodthirsty his lovely redhead could be when it came to her best friend.

But the drums began, and the sound, and colors, and the cheerful ceremony, mixed with jokes and laughter, turned even Dana's anger to joy and fascination, celebrating with Garrett, and the many gathered nations.

Late that evening, after they left the celebration and returned to the hotel, Garret had gone to seek out his old buddy and get some answers.

Lifting her head from the geology book that she had been studying, Dana smiled fondly at her guy when he returned.

"Did you beat him into pulp like a paper mill, honey?" she asked cheerfully.

"Nope."

"You didn't? Oh, how thoughtful. You left some pieces for me to tear out of him, didn't you honey?"

"Nope."

Putting her book down she frowned and studied his face more closely.

"Garrett? I know he's your best friend, but you warned him! Jenny's crushed! You can't—"

He stopped her with both palms out, then gave her a huge grin.

"What? You did something more painful?" she asked hopefully.

"Yep."

Jumping up she grabbed his hands, shaking them impatiently.

"Tell me!" She insisted.

"I just said one word to him," he said, clearly proud of himself, blue eyes twinkling.

Dana thought a moment trying to guess, then growled his name threateningly in frustration.

"I said," he paused, laughing, enjoying teasing her, "J-E-N-N-Y. I spelled it out."

"Jenny? Wow, you're scary. Remind me to handle it myself next time!" She was surprised and very disappointed in him, for the first time ever. Stepping back she braced her fists on her hips and glared at him, but the damn man was still grinning.

"Hey, babe, it's all I had to do. It's amazing!" He was gleeful.

She didn't understand. Garrett had connected to Jen long ago when Dana had been in the hospital unconscious after her injury. He'd taken Jenny under his wing like a sister. When Dana moved and married him, Garrett had even finished a small cabin on their property, supposedly as a model for his construction company. But he had put in the cabinets Jen had admired, and told Jen she would always have a place there of her own to stay when she came to visit them.

So Dana never would have expected this response from him.

Sure he was loyal to his own long-time friend, but he'd even told Dana that he'd warned his buddy off from ever hurting Jen. And now the jerk had broken Jenny's heart and Garrett wasn't doing anything. Except grinning!

"Hey babe, it's okay," realizing his error, Garrett tried to gentle her. Reaching out he wrapped his arms around the angry redhead before she took a swing at him. He really shouldn't have played with her, not where Jenny was concerned. She loved her self-adopted sister. So did he.

"Listen, it's okay. I went over there, said Jenny's name and he grabbed a half-empty whiskey bottle from the table and took a big gulp and just curled up and told me to go F-off."

"Which you did!" She accused angrily from where he had her face scrunched against his chest.

"Don't you see? What's so amazing is that Rave doesn't drink! Ever! Didn't you notice he was just drinking plain tonic water at our wedding?"

He got a better grip on her and kissed the top of her head. Man, his woman was pissed off! It was kind of funny, but he better hurry and get himself out of trouble.

"No, Dana, when we were young and the road gang would get someone to buy us a six-pack of beer, he'd never take a drop, even though we all razzed him. Only non-alcoholic beers. He didn't care. He told me that with his Indian blood, drinking booze was about as smart as swallowing arsenic. He knew first hand. He even used to say that white men had used the poison of alcohol to subjugate and take away the will of his ancestors. Hey, he was totally serious about it. So the guy has never had a drink as long as I've known him, now you say 'Jenny" and he glugs a bottle? It was rotgut crap, too! Well regardless ... don't you get it? He's miserable. He's drinking what he considers poison, he ... "

"So did you at least go buy him a few more bottles?" She interrupted furiously.

"Dana!" He scolded. "Shame on you! Don't pretend you'd want to poison the guy just because you want to kill him right now."

Logic clearly was not the issue.

"Look what it means? Rave is obviously in love with her!"

"Oh sure!" she replied sarcastically, jerking out of his grasp. "He has a fine way of showing it, now doesn't he? Jen is drowning in tears, he's drowning himself in the bottom of a bottle. Perfect!"

"It is perfect, or it will be soon. He's in love and he's drinking because he's scared to death because he knows he's hopelessly trapped and doesn't want out. I know this guy stuff, trust me on this."

"I did trust you, Garrett. For everything. Even for my own life!" Dana's anger was turning to hurt, confused hurt, "But now ... "

He pushed her back now enough so he could look into those stormy green eyes as he spoke.

"Now, now that we know he is punishing himself, we can only step back and let them start to sort it out, Dana. We can't let it come between what we have. Babe, come back to me, please," He was relieved when she burrowed back into his chest on her own and let him comfort her. This was the first time that they had fought over anything since they'd married. It was important they could use their love for each other to keep it from pulling them apart.

And he would see to it that his pal paid for this, too!

"As I was leaving, I told him Jen had grabbed the Amtrak and went back home. Hell, he damn near lunged off the couch and tackled me to demand if he'd heard right, if she was truly gone. Then he tossed me out and slammed the door in my face," he confided to her quietly as he rocked her gently in his arms.

"He's a mess, Dana. He'll do something, he'll fix it, he has to for himself. We just have to wait and let it happen. Now that I'm sure he loves her, we have to let them work it out, babe."

"He's got one week," she muttered through clenched teeth, "then I'm going to go break every single bone in your buddy's body starting with that arrogant face!" she promised.

"Good. I'll help you, babe."

"And Garrett?" Dana turned her face up to his, "I love you. I'm sorry I got mad at you just because your friend is a heartless jerk."

"I love you, too, and it's okay. You'll forgive him as soon as Jen does. Besides, right now, I have a way for you to make it up to me." His eyes had a decidedly naughty twinkle in their blue-denim depths.

"I thought you might," she drawled with a little smile, wrapping her arms around his neck and threading her fingers into the thick blond hair. "So ... show me," she whispered pulling his lips down to hers. "Now!"

"Yes, ma'am!" He scooped her up and carried his wife to the bed.

Jenny was home, tangled in the sheets of her own bed.

She was curled in a ball, her face buried deep in the damp pillows she used to muffle her sobs and sop up the tears. Tears that seemed endless.

Every time she thought she'd gained some control she'd crawl into the bathroom, soak a washcloth in icy water and slap it completely over her red and splotchy, swollen face. Little hiccups of sobs still coming through the wet mask with each attempted breath.

It never lasted long. Then the anguish, the pain, and the betrayal, started the flood again.

She hated him! Or wished she did. She loved him, dammit! Why didn't he love her? She was a nice girl, not bad looking, smart, a great cook ... and miserable. She didn't deserve this. She needed to get mad, get angry. Maybe then the tears would stop. She needed to hate him. He deserved that. She needed anger. She needed rage!

So she would try to hate him—in a minute.

She needed to cry some more, first. She had a lot more hurt left in her, and not enough energy to hate him yet. Besides, she loved the ass, dammit! But how could she?

Ravenwolf never made it to his own bed that night.

He was passed out, sprawled half on half off his couch.

He'd managed to stagger into the kitchen and dump the rest of his whiskey down the kitchen sink after Garrett left. Just before he crashed, the second time.

The first crash had been the wall he'd slammed into when he realized his little wren had his heart in a steel vice— permanently.

Then Garrett told him she'd left town with it. On Amtrak.

He'd gone off an abyss, all hope splintering as he fell.

chapter nineteen

RAVENWOLF WOKE GROGGY, heading first for the bathroom and the medicine cabinet. After failing the child-proof-lid test on the aspirin bottle, he stumbled into the kitchen searching for something to chop the top off the bottle. Seeing the coffeemaker, he decided he needed that first before messing around with sharp things.

He measured in the water, but splattered coffee grounds all over the counter trying to fill the filter. He felt like shit and couldn't seem to get his hands to stop shaking.

With a broad palm he brushed the grounds into a pile then scooted them across the counter into the sink and rinsed his hand under the faucet. Good enough for now. He had bigger worries than polishing his kitchen.

He spent more than enough time at work being spit-polished and sharply creased. His personal life was his only chance to be a lazy, not always neat, guy and focus on the stuff that mattered to him. Right now that was his future.

Picking up the phone, he called Shirl and told her to tell the Park he wouldn't be in for at least a week—personal leave.

"Tell them I called in dead." She was convinced.

Robbing the first partial cup from the coffeemaker, he sucked up his first lukewarm drips of pure caffeine, trying to jam the pot back in place before the rest of it ran out all over the counter. A bigger gulp from his raided cup had him grimacing as he moved over to his desk.

Lifting off trays of feathers and half-tied fly-fishing lures, he dug down to his laptop. Blowing away the dust on the cover and batting away floating bits of feather fluff, he plugged it in and perched on the edge of his chair, scraping a spot clear on the edge of the desk to set his mug.

After logging in, he went first to the Amtrak site, checking schedules and stops, deciding right away he'd probably need the freedom and flexibility of having his own wheels available. He'd best take his truck—no telling how long this was going to take.

Switching over to his email, he searched through saved messages and tracked down the email Dana had sent when she had forwarded photos of the wedding party after her and Garrett's wedding. Just as Rave had hoped, he was able to snag an email address for Jen from the carbon copy line. Pulling up a blank message form, he addressed it then sat back and just stared at the screen.

Was this really a good idea?

What could he say?

Even more pressing, what could he put on the subject line that was either good enough or tricky enough to get her to even open the message and read it—instead of just deleting him unread.

Folding his arms across his chest, leaning his chair back, the monitor waited patiently as he calculated his chances.

Picturing Jen, he tried to visualize her reaction to seeing an email message with his name on it and a subject line that said, "I'm sorry!"

He snorted. That was pretty easy to imagine.

He could see her snarling in response and muttering, "You sure are!" Probably setting up her junk mail filter to automatically block and delete anything coming from him. She might even stab the 'delete' key so hard she'd break one of those pretty, polished little fingernails.

"Forgive me? " *Never you jerk!* Delete.

"I'm a jerk?" You're just figuring that out? Delete.

"re: Dana emergency"? No, he better delete that idea himself, right away. It was cruel and ... would probably work, but ... Too low. He *was* a jerk to even be tempted. Yes, he was a desperate jerk ... Suddenly he leaned forward and typed in the subject line,

" I LOVE YOU, LITTLE WREN."

That should make her pause for a minute and at least think about reading the rest of the message.

244

Hell! It made *him* pause!

What was he thinking? What was he feeling?

Did he...?

Was he sure?

Swiping sweaty palms down yesterday's jeans, he decided he better take a shower and think it over before he sent this message. He left the line he'd typed on the screen for now. It looked so solid. Much more solid than he felt at the moment. He was feeling pretty shaky—especially since he wasn't sure how those words got on the screen. Just a gut reaction.

And he had no idea what he wanted to type for his message, deciding a slight delay while he cleaned up, sobered and cleared his mind was needed before he sent anything.

Jenny rose that morning determined to put some steel in her backbone.

When she kicked her covers off, she stripped the bed down completely, so she wouldn't be able to crawl back in and wallow in misery any more. She was tougher than that.

Tossing her sheets at the washing machine on her way to the kitchen, she turned the water on until it ran icy cold. Filling the coffee pot, she plugged up the sink, letting it fill while she ground fresh coffee beans and started her morning brew. Turning around, she shut off the faucet, gathered her long, dark chocolate strands of hair in one hand and plunged her face into the chilled water. Coming up she gasped for air, but her face felt taut and firm..

Jen was *not* in the habit of washing her face in the kitchen sink—but it was the only one that didn't have a mirror staring back at her. If she had a good look at herself this morning she might burst out in tears of horror. That was something she was not going to do today. She'd need tear duct organ replacement surgery if she didn't stop this nonsense immediately.

She marched over to the washer and quickly loaded her sheets and the whites from the suitcases she'd dumped out, and set the washer going. Sorting the rest of her dirty clothes into piles, she carried the empty suitcases to the garage and stored them neatly in their proper place. By the time she went back in the kitchen, her coffee was ready. After plunging her face in the cold water once more, she took a cup and sat to make an intimidating to-do list for the day.

List and coffee done, she dressed quickly in old jeans and a tee, threw on concealing sunglasses and a large floppy straw hat and was ready when the washer quit spinning to reload and take her sheets out to hang on the line. That task checked off, she grabbed her garden gloves and tools from the patio and attacked her flower beds. There was no weed too small this morning to escape being drawn and quartered.

By noon, Jen had all her laundry done, all her flower beds groomed to perfection, and half of her house vacuumed, dusted, waxed, and pillow plumped, with fresh cut flowers still quivering from being plunked down in a vase on the dining room table.

She hadn't cried even once, though her jaw did ache from keeping her teeth gritted for so many hours. Tossing ice cubes in the water in her sink, she plunged her face again, took a Tylenol for her stiff jaw, and set about making herself a gourmet lunch fit for a queen.

Who needed men, anyway?

They just got in the way and left a mess behind.

They were especially good at messing up hearts!

Since Garrett had brought his laptop with him, Dana decided to email Jen. But she wasn't sure what she wanted to say to her friend.

Should she ask her if she was okay? Say something about Garrett going to see Rave? Or would hearing his name just be more upsetting? Probably.

Maybe she should just send something chatty and distracting. Let her know she was thinking about her, missing her company. Then when Jen replied, if she replied, if she wanted to talk about him, they would. Okay, that was a better idea.

So, what to say that was distracting? She could tell her about the powwow, but that would make her think of Rave. But if Jen knew they hadn't gone with him maybe it would let her know Dana was on her side. Solidarity. That might be good. So she sent a quick note, but held back any pictures for now.

By late afternoon, Jen cleaned everything she could think of, including the inside of her car. She had dunked and chilled her face until it was presentable with the help of eye drops and makeup and was ready to go out and run her car through a wash and wax and do what she did best—shopping.

Fortunately for her—if not for her credit card balances—some of her favorite half-yearly sales were still on. At her favorite mall it seemed strange, as if she had been gone for ages. Jen had ventured to a strange and foreign world—and been burned. She was safer here, stronger here, with the familiar routines that had become habits over the years. She didn't need to think, she just did her normal 'Jen doll' things. Maybe they weren't so bad, after all.

She bought two pair of boots because they had the latest heel design, and were 65% off—off of what didn't matter. She found new clothes she didn't really need, but they were on sale. On the way back to her car, while she was stuffing everything in her trunk, she noticed the bookstore near where she was parked.

Wandering over, Jen was thinking she would get something to read, or just look around to kill time. She saw books she would normally want everywhere, but the 'romances' were just too painful right now. Thinking of Dana's birthday in a few weeks, she went to browse the non-fiction science section, somewhere she'd never checked out before. Maybe she could find a good geology book for Dana.

She found the perfect thing. A coffee table book filled with photos of the geologic wonders of the Northern Rockies, it featured Glacier National Park prominently. She paged through it slowly, scanning the pictures, biting her lip when she recognized some of the sights she had seen and experienced herself. She closed the book with a snap.

It was too soon. The memories were too sharp and fresh. But she purchased it for Dana.

Spotting bright yellow spines of books that looked familiar, she hesitated and pulled one out to check. Yes, these were like one of Dana's books, a row of roadside geology books by state, Dana had the Montana one. Skimming her finger along the row, Jen found the one for her state of Washington, and pulled it off the shelf.

It was arranged by highway and between towns, so as you drove along and saw the sides of the road, you could stop and lookup what you were seeing, and its geologic significance and age, or how it had been made.

It would be like having Dana along on her drives.

Once her friend had told her that Washington state didn't used to exist. That the coast had once been along the Idaho border and the whole state had arrived in chunks and chaos and basically been rammed onto the edge of the old North America.

Jen didn't recall much more but she remembered hoping they had used super glue, so it *stayed* stuck together! But it *had* tweaked her interest at the time, though she had soon forgotten about it.

Maybe I should get this book for myself? Checking the price, Jen was horrified to find she could educate her mind for less than the price of one of her sale tee shirts! She had vacation time left, and a mind to fill with something besides that jerk, so she'd take a few of the roads listed and see what was going on in her local area—or had once happened.

Would that ever shock Dana!

Jen surprised herself a bit, also. She was actually starting to be interested in some of the science stuff Dana told her. She didn't remember it being as interesting in school as Dana could make it sound, or maybe it was just that there was so much worry now about climate change that it was more interesting to know how the world was before, and all its changes. Apparently it had been doing some pretty wild and dramatic things all along. She'd known that, kind of, she really just never paid attention before. Though she remembered feeling uneasy whenever they spoke on the news about just burying all the toxic things deep in the earth. But anyone who lived in an earthquake prone zone couldn't help but worry what a quake might burp up, right?

Anyway, it wouldn't hurt to check it out. Swinging over to her favorite section, she found another cookbook that looked good and headed for the grocery store.

She was going to fix herself a special dinner, then bake up a storm. She could start testing some of the recipes in her new cookbook. July wasn't too soon to start making and freezing cookies and fruitcakes for Christmas, was it?

Then maybe tomorrow she could go out and drive around and find some of those geology things in the book. It would be like she was still enjoying her vacation.

It would give her something to write Dana about, so she would think Jen was doing okay—even though she wasn't. But if she faked it long enough, tried hard enough, maybe she might even fool herself.

*   *   *   *

Subject: I LOVE YOU, LITTLE WREN

Message: Listen for the hooting of the Great Owl outside at night when the sun has turned two circles in the sky. I will come to you to speak.

Tlesca

He looked at his screen, took a deep breath and hit the send message icon. He didn't know if she would read it, but it was the best he could do.

He wanted to leave immediately, but he knew she'd need time to calm down. She might even send a reply. Doubtful, but he left his computer on while he went to sort laundry and throw a load in to wash so he could pack.

Digging clothes from the closet and hampers, making stacks of his colors, he debated with himself over whether or not she would read his message. Untangling a white tee shirt from inside a red sweatshirt he came to the conclusion that even if she read it, her anger would cause her to pretend she hadn't. He should have sent it with a notification to tell him when she opened it. Too late for that now.

So *if* she read it, she probably wouldn't act like she had seen it, and wouldn't reply. What if she did reply? What if she told him to stuff it, not to come, not to speak to her—never to speak or email her? That seemed a likely response. What then?

Well, he would just have to pretend *he* didn't get the message.

Carrying a load of whites to the washer, he dumped the pile in front of the machine and went first to shut down and unplug his computer. Finding the padded carry case, he packed the laptop and cords and set it beside the door to take with him. Nothing was going to stop him from going after her.

But he was under no illusions that, unlike his namesake, he would have to do more than just speak to his woman. Rave suspected it would take a whole lot of begging! Even a grovel or two.

*   *   *   *

Jen had managed all day not to cry, or think, to stay busy, to stay tough, to resist checking for any emails. But that night when she sank into her bed, with her crisp sheets dried in fresh outdoor air, she couldn't block the pictures, the memories, or the crushed hopes, anymore.

She would need to wash her sheets again in the morning, and hang them and her pillows back out in the cleansing air. She had rained all over them again, and she didn't even have a pretty rainbow to show for it—or to give her the promise of a bright world of color and joy at its end.

All her rainbows had faded now.

chapter twenty

SUBJECT: EYE ROLL ATTACK
Dear Jen- You will never guess what I just learned about? They have something called an Ice-Patch Archaeology Project here. Apparently the idea is that ice-patches in sheltered shaded areas can outlast melting of annual snowpacks, even glaciers. Remember me telling you about that atlatl (throwing stick) with a stone point that melted out at Yellowstone? Well, the way the idea runs is that past artifacts, either human, animal, or plant and pollen species that tell of past climate and cultures might still be recovered from ice patches. Even today animals use ice patches to cool when too hot, and as a reliable source of water, so ancient paths between ice patches traveled by animals, followed by hunters, etc., a great resource for information. It's more complex than that (I sent a website link) but the cool part is that the program here was one of the first projects in country to combine not only all disciplines of scientists and several universities, but also to involve the cultural councils for all the native tribes that were on this land at Glacier. I think that is fabulous!

It's a long term project but they have already found some ancient extinct bison bones that apparently grazed high up in the mountains versus plains!

Anyway, just wanted to touch base and let you know what I'm up to and how badly I miss having my buddy here to tell all this stuff and watch your eye rolls! Let me hear from you. Get even and describe your latest recipe! Love, Dana

"She's not answering her emails, Garrett. I'm worried. She didn't even open them yet. Jen isn't answering her phones. She has caller ID, she has to know it's me that's calling. What if ..."

"Whoa, Dana. Calm down. She told you she would call or write when she was ready, didn't she? She isn't ready. Jen is an adult. You are too linked in her mind with her experiences with Rave. Give her the space she needs, honey."

"I know, I know. You're right. But..."

"Just keep sending her emails, Dana. Let her know you are thinking of her, that you care, and when she is ready, she'll respond."

Garrett hoped he was giving the right advice. "Maybe you should look at the email I got today from Rave's cousin."

"I don't even want to hear you mention his name right now, Garrett."

He raised his hands palm out, in a peaceful gesture.

"No problem, I understand." But if he knew his lady, the next time she sent Jen an email on his laptop, she'd sneak a peak without telling him. He never knew a more intensely curious woman than his wife.

Dana cast about for a topic that would not connect with any dastardly dog she might name, or not, and came up with something that was a typical topic for her, and probably provide Jen with more eye-rolling entertainment and distraction. She'd prefer to call and talk to her best friend direct, but after this long email, Jen might just pick up the phone to avoid getting any more of the same.

Subject: Missing my rock-detective buddy
Hey Jen--
I've been studying up on our geo-mystery.
I've found out there is an amazing place on the

northeastern edge of the park. It's called Chief Mountain.

Remember that slab of ancient Precambrian Belt Rock that got shoved east over Glacier toward the plains? Well, picture the far eastern edge of it, up north near the Canadian border, with its connection to all the mountains behind it erased (like the glaciers did) and you have this amazing isolated pillar. The mountain pillar stands up like this cool geologic layer cake, because everything around it is eroded so you can really see the layers!

The top third of the Chief Mountain pillar is made of the billion year old Precambrian layers of mudstone and limestone on the Lewis Overthrust Fault, then beneath are the soft layers of the young Cretaceous layers (dino-dirt). Pretty cool, huh?

A picture of Chief Mountain is even in my geology textbook! That's how I found out about it. Apparently it's called a "Klippe", which is a remnant of a thrust sheet isolated by erosion, a very special type of geologic feature.

It got its name from the native people as it looks like a chief out in front, leading his warriors—the other mountain peaks—out onto the plains. For thousands of years the mountain has been a spiritual place for vision quests and other ceremonies. Isn't that a fascinating concept? (I have to admit from the picture I've seen that it looks more like the conning tower of a submarine jutting up from beneath the prairie like it got lost under there and is looking for the closest ocean!)

Anyway, Garrett is driving me up to explore and see it tomorrow. I can hardly wait! I'll take pics and email them, but don't worry, it's something I'm going to want to go and see over and over again. So we can go see it together sometime.

And, guess what else I found out the other day? I was reading about these layers they found up on Logan Pass that have fossil ripple marks from shallow water in them and wait until you hear about the conophyton zone! I'll have to send you a whole detailed email on that after I investigate. Love for now. Miss you. Please write or call, Dana

Dana couldn't resist a grin when she hit the send button. She had put enough techno talk in there to choke a horse—not to mention the threat of so much more. If that didn't get Jen responding in self defense, she didn't know what would.

Before exiting, Dana sneaked a peek at that email from Rave's cousin and gasped. She was glad she had already written Jen, or she might have gotten in trouble with Garrett for interfering.

Since distraction wasn't working anyway, Jen finally decided too many days had past since checking her email.

The latest one from Dana brought a wobbly smile to her face. It felt just like hearing her talking, all excited about something new she had discovered.

Jenny had actually seen a picture of Chief Mountain, just the day before yesterday. Of course she couldn't tell Dana that, it would ruin her birthday surprise. And she couldn't write back yet, she was too upset, because when she had finally checked her emails she had seen the one from Rave.

The subject line was hard to miss.

How could he do that to her? Hurt her the way he had and then mock her feelings, like he could just say something she wanted to hear and she would fall under his spell again?

Tears started to fall again, as she stared at the screen, trying to stop herself from opening his email and subjecting herself to more torture and torment. She'd wept over him all yesterday, despite her attempts to distract herself. Wasn't that enough? Why couldn't he just leave her alone to heal?

She couldn't survive more days like the last few.

Jen didn't think she had cried so hard or so long since Dana was in the hospital after the attack in Yellowstone, and she had been afraid her beloved friend was going to die.

But this was a different kind of death, a different kind of grief, yet rending despite the shortness of time the bond had formed before being cruelly snapped—her fragile dreams smashed.

She hadn't even made it out the door to go exploring with her new book as even the pictures of rocks and pebbles had suddenly blurred her eyes as she remembered strong, slender, bronzed fingers holding colored pebbles, telling of their long and fascinating stories. Remembering those same hands on her body cupping her face, stroking her hair, touching her tenderly everywhere, she had lost her will to forget and ignore, and lost the day to drowning tears and pain.

Jen kept trying to find her anger, to shield herself, to turn the hurt like an arrow and aim it where it belonged. But when she brought the picture to her mind of that girl wrapped around him, this time—instead of just his betrayal—she recalled the look of pleading in his eyes when he saw her.

As she tried to focus on all the stories of his heartless philandering, seeking her rage, Jen kept picturing him facing St. Mary Lake that day, facing all the pain of his childhood. Shaking in her arms afterward.

Everywhere she turned to find the kindling for her fury, her mind and heart skidded to a tender moment, a special look, burning only with memories of the heat when their lips touched or his arms came around her. How could she be so weak and let him own her heart like this when she knew they were probably all just calculated steps for an experienced seducer? She should scorn him. Hate the betrayal. Shout with rage at his arrogant manipulation.

But she had only summoned more pain yesterday, not anger.

Taking a deep breath, Jen moved the cursor to highlight the email from Rave, with the provocative subject line. She didn't have the nerve to open it; but she couldn't bear knowing it was there and not reading it. She clicked it open and read the message from Tlesca. She stared at the screen, reading it over and over, letting the message sink in, remembering the reference to the legend he had told around the campfire about the warring tribes and the lovers.

And Jen had no trouble finding her anger then.

"Why that dirty, low-down, lying, cheating, sneaky, arrogant dog!" she growled, out loud, her voice rising with her temper. "If he thinks I am going to fall for this bullshit, he doesn't know as much about women as he thinks he does. The nerve! The absolute, arrogant, male nerve!"

Wasn't that just like a guy? Never using those words "I love you" unless they were desperate and needed them as a lure of last resort? Did he murmur them when she was naked beneath his hands?

No! Of course not!

He might get trapped, commit himself, give her the "wrong" impression. But now, when he wasn't *quite* finished with her, when he still needed to rack another notch on his belt, he tossed them out like candy to a starving child! Dirty sneaky dog! Well, it is not going to work this time buddy!

And did he really think she would turn into mush if he tried to use that story she had thought so romantic to weaken her? Did he think she would be reading this thinking "Ohh, *that is so sweet!"*?

Hah! Nice try! And did he really think it was romantic to use a line now, after he had cheated on her, that basically said, "Hey babe, when I whistle you come running."? The absolute bloody nerve of the man!

Well, he could hoot until his ... whatever fell off. It was time someone taught this man a lesson!

Sucking in a deep breath, Jen growled with the sheer pleasure of feeling alive again, and strong in her rage.

Late that night an owl hooted in her front yard.

Jen threw her head back and laughed like a maniac then turned up the sound on the DVD she was watching about ancient British woman warriors, drowning all outside noises out. Feet curled under her on the couch, she dipped into her bowl of gourmet popcorn. She had her old comfortable, ratty robe on, no makeup, hair a tangled mess, and all the doors and windows locked and shades drawn. She made sure she stayed up very late watching movies loud, with all the lights on, just to give the jerk false hope. She had never felt so in charge of her life.

The next morning she got up early and smiling. Packing herself a picnic lunch and her roadside geology book, she bounced out to her car. Hitting the garage door opener, she backed out on her driveway and glanced up the street before starting to back into the road. When she turned to check traffic from the other direction, she slammed on her brakes instead.

There was a raven haired man sitting cross legged at the base of her steps; and she happened to know the dog's name.

"Dammit!" Reversing direction she headed back into her garage to get away, barely remembering to hit the opener to raise it again before the door slammed into her windshield.

"Lunatic! Had he been out there all night?"

Hissing with anger, Jen stomped back into the house.

The siege was on.

chapter twenty one

IT HAD BEEN ONE THING to pat herself on the back last night and claim victory for not letting her heart betray her by surrendering to even a peek outside.

But by the time she finally fell asleep, tensing each time a car passed by on the street, doubts were already crawling around in her mind.

Jen seriously doubted the man would bother to drive all the way here without any encouragement. He probably just assumed his words would have her eager to go back to him, or at least talk to him. Give the lady the three magic words and make her feel like they were the legendary lovers and she would be like instant putty in his hands. Just a ploy he never meant to need to follow through. It was making more sense than him driving all the way here to hoot in her yard!

The embarrassing truth was that it had probably just been a real owl she had heard. There were owls around, she just never had her ear tuned to hear them.

But this morning, when she had actually seen him, it was a shock. He was so damn handsome. How could she have forgotten what just the sight of him could do to her. She had panicked. He was really here.

For her?

Or just to win? Or make a token try at making up to pacify Dana and Garrett?

It didn't matter, she told herself. He had shown his true colors and she was done being a pushover for him.

She huddled inside all day trying to convince herself he wasn't there. Right outside her front door. He had probably given up and left by now, but she didn't want to peek out and check. Just in case.

She had fallen for that pretty face once. She had to remember it was just the mask of a rake, a rogue, a womanizer, a dog.

"He does not exist for you!" She said out loud, to better convince herself.

Having already done all the chores she could think of to fill the last few days, she got her laptop out and decided to go through and label the pictures she and Dana had taken on vacation. She should be able to handle that task now. Anything disturbing in her photos could just be deleted, unlike the disturbing thing that might still be sitting in her front yard. She refused to check.

Organizing her photos into the date they had been taken, she started at the beginning, the safest place, when it had been just the two of them—best friends on vacation—adding titles and captions.

When she reached one of the pictures taken on the shore of Lake McDonald, Jen lingered. It was an incredible shot. She remembered trying to capture the dazzling variety of blues in the lake when she took it. Was this the scene where she had first fallen in love with the primitive beauty of Glacier Park?

She tried to imagine what it would feel like to be the first person that had stumbled through the forests and found that gleaming jewel. Maybe it was a woman seeking water?

Jen recalled something she had read in the newspaper once that had captured her attention.

It had been one of those filler sections that she had skimmed over once about how so many decades or hundred years ago on this particular day, a historic event happened. This one mentioned an expedition. She immediately assumed it was to the artic or such, but had been surprised to see that it was practically in her own back yard.

It was about a Press Expedition that had been formed because people on the east side of Puget Sound were so curious about what was behind the snowcapped mountains they gazed across the water at everyday on the remote peninsula. What was back there—spirits? What great unknown lurked?

So they set out to find out, and what Jen had loved and laughed at was the attached black and white photo. To her delight it showed not just men, but women also, posed on top of a massive glacier. And the women were in frilly long dresses, dressy heeled half-boots, large feathered hats, and parasols! Just imagine! What captured her was that they were just as curious and adventurous as the men.

She had shared it with Dana. It could have been Dana and Jen a hundred years before wanting to see first, what no one had seen before. At least no non-native woman.

In a film they'd seen in a visitor center, the Kootenai that still held reservation lands in the Flathead area east of the park, told of how in the past their people always had their winter camp near Lake McDonald. Each year in the dead of winter they would hold a huge gathering in a sacred place by that lake and dance the renewal of all the spirits. They talked of the great cedar trees hundreds of years old that watched their ancestors dance for each year's renewal.

And before that, Jen thought—not in historic, but prehistoric times—there was that stone point found to the north telling that over 10,000 years ago, people had been beside the lakes of Glacier. What might it have been like to be that first woman? She had felt that tug in Glacier.

Thinking about those women, first to see, she looked at the exquisite picture on her screen of the lake. Words began to slither and whisper through her head. Pulling up a word processing screen, she quickly typed them down in the form of a poem. It didn't rhyme but that didn't matter. Rereading it she realized it was meant for Dana. Jen applied some of her graphic artist tools, and a few minutes later sat back pleased. She had taken the lake picture, superimposed the poem, and at the bottom on the colorful pebbled shore, drawn the back of a woman dressed in furs, sitting facing the lake by a campfire, as it might have been ten or eleven thousand years before when first seen.

She labeled it "First Woman". It would make a great poster for Dana's office back home. Jen had felt bad about leaving so abruptly, about not returning Dana's emails. This would be her gift for her friend—in thanks and apology—a shared memory and very personal souvenir of their vacation. Attaching a very brief note, she emailed it to Dana.

Then that damn owl in her front yard hooted again.

Jen tried to ignore the tiny flip of her heart, an unwanted first reaction. His siege was getting to her already. She could feel herself weakening and dug deep trying to find her anger again. But she was just too mellow after making Dana's gift.

Lake McDonald had been on the first day of their vacation, when she was only anticipating a maybe fling with the dark, sexy man she had met at her friend's wedding. That man of dangerous dark eyes and reputation.

But the man she had later come to know was different—or so she had thought.

Resigned, Jen opened the picture file for their day at Kintla Lake, letting herself recall the man that had opened his arms to Creator Sun. He had been primitively handsome and sensual. She had wanted him, but ... He had been so much more, she had felt so much more, in that timeless place, that she had wanted more for herself, and from him. She had not wanted a casual fling with him then, despite the fact her body had hummed with yearning for his male touch, his male scent ... God!

Okay he mattered too much now. She felt scared, shy, afraid of losing everything with him, as that part he shared with her, he shared too freely with too many women. But did he tell them what he had told her? Let them see all the shadows of his past, the hurt in those dark lava eyes, the longing for some part of his history, culture to shape into his own?

Jen heaved a weary sigh. Not trusting what she did or did not know.

It would have been better if she had just let him take advantage, a few nights of wild sex, then ignored her and let her go home from her vacation with a few heated memories of a good time. That is what she had expected. But instead, he had tortured her, left her unfinished, longing for something that wasn't ever expected, but when glimpsed caused her unending torment.

She hadn't expected the tenderness, the romance, the emotional sharing. It had broken through her defenses and left her vulnerable and needy for something she knew she could never have—something she hadn't needed until he gave her a sample, then snatched it away before she could taste it. Brutal, uncaring, devious devil. God she hated him!

Or wanted to hate him—needed to hate him. Jen didn't want to love him—refused to let herself believe it. The ache in her heart was just humiliation; the tightness in her throat did not come from memories of drifting in a canoe on Kintla Lake sharing ancient times—but from a summer cold. The tears that kept seeping silently down her cheeks couldn't be from loss, as she never truly owned—but just a sudden allergy.

Jen sniffed, blinking rapidly, brushing the dampness from her cheeks, firming her lips and her anger. She wanted to go rip some weeds from her garden to calm herself.

But he was out there.

Instead she pounded on her homemade bread dough, twisting the kitchen blinds so they were completely closed, trying to resist bending a slat for a single peek at her torturer.

Still there.

As evening neared, still pacing, and edgy, she was muttering to herself. He had been there all day. He was making her insane! Finally she stomped over to her front door and flung it open.

"Is that a peace pipe?" she shouted, sarcastically.

He grinned, delighted at finally being acknowledged after camping on her lawn since yesterday. He raised the long, slender, decorated and feathered wooden object in both hands toward her from where he was seated cross legged on her front lawn.

"Symbolically," he said earnestly.

She didn't slam the door on him, or even step down off her porch, but she did plant both hands on her hips and take up that cute little furious and ready to fight stance of hers. Her eyebrows were raised in impatient question.

"Well?" Her toe tapping on the wooden boards.

"Ah, since there are many tribal rules for the use of special pipes," she was glaring at him again, so he tried a lighter note quickly, "And since you don't smoke..."

"Oh, no?" she asked archly. "I am quite sure that there is smoke pouring out of my ears right this minute! You are embarrassing the hell out of me. All my neighbors drive by staring. I am never, ever forgiving you, you heartless bastard, so get out of my yard, my life, and go home!"

He assumed that the door slamming so hard it almost bounced open again was sign language that she was not speaking to him again. He looked down at the flute in his hands, one he had made himself, and shrugged.

He wasn't going anywhere.

By the next night of the siege, Jen could have torn out her hair. He was still there! He must have left at some point. He had changed clothes, but she didn't know when. She couldn't do a believable job of ignoring him, if she kept peeking. But she wished she would have known and made her escape to a hotel—or anywhere else.

He was still hooting, and making some god awful noise tooting on that piece of wood in his hands. She was no pushover for his tactics, but she *had* been pushed just about over the edge!

He thought he would hoot, toot, and speak to her?

Well, *she* would show him who would do the speaking!

She went to the peephole again. There he sat with that fake submissive posture. Sneaky man!

She was surprised he hadn't just come and stormed her door—that was more his arrogant way! Well, if thought he'd melt her little heart into a romantic puddle with this little stunt ... She could feel the rivulets started to drip from her not-so-glaciated heart even as she was denying it—he looked so ridiculously pathetic—but, she was not weak. She *would not* be weak!

Except just a bit in the knees, it seemed, as she saw his head drop to his chest, bowed in anguish, his shoulders slumping with dejection for a few moments before slowly his raised his head, tried to square his shoulders and gave the call of the Great Owl again.

This time it sounded more plaintive, this time she saw the raggedness of his features in the streetlight. The pulled down corners of the mouth without its trademark grin, the hollowness of his cheeks. His black eyes looked haunted in a way that she had only seen them once.

She turned quickly, leaning her back against the door, arms folded defensively across her chest. She wouldn't look. It was all an act. Jen struggled to re-freeze her heart against him. It worked for a short time.

The owl hooted behind her, its calls becoming softer, hoarser. She held out a little longer and the silence stretched out. Maybe he'd left. Good, she thought; No, an ache in her chest moaned.

"Who-who-whoooooo. . "

She spun around and yanked open the door.

"Get in here, you jerk, before you wake up all my neighbors!" She snarled at him, satisfied with the way he leaped to obey her command. This was a much humbled man, or ... just faking it to get his way, she warned herself.

If the hooting mating call of the owl hadn't woken her neighbors, the way Jenny slammed her front door, after he scampered inside, surely did. The whole house shook.

She stopped him from stepping towards her with a rigidly out thrust palm and a furious glare, then stabbed one painted and pointed finger, like a steel stiletto, toward a chair on the far side of the fireplace.

"Sit there and don't even open your mouth. *I will speak* to you, mister Tlesca! And you better pay close attention!" She stalked over, all but snarling out her words.

"You think that because I like to cook and grow flowers, and like girly things and pretty clothes, and polished fingernails," her voice rising in volume and pitch, that steely pointed finger emphasizing every point. She sucked in more air for ammunition, "And romantic legends, that I am WEAK? You think I am a soft woman, a silly woman, a weak woman, you arrogant beast? Well. You. Are. Wrong!

"I may cry buckets like a baby, but I. Am. Strong!" She thumped her chest, to be sure he got the message.

It wasn't necessary, he was already intimidated by the fury of the tiny woman towering over the chair where he sat. All five feet of her. She was furious, proud, strong, like a female cougar snarling before she leaped on him, with tail twitching and sharpened claws. He'd been mistaken. For all her soft, sweet, dainty looks this woman was no little wren!

"Look around you, arrogant man! This is my house, my home. I worked for it. I purchased this shelter for myself. I take care of it, I nurtured the lawns and made the gardens and care for *my* lands!"

She thumped her chest again, the pain just increasing her fury.

"I created all the beauty inside. I fill it with the smells of savory meals. I provide all my food and shelter.

"DO I LOOK LIKE I NEED A MAN HOOTING ON MY FRONT PORCH?" she roared down on his head.

He ducked as sparks flew from her eyes like lightning strikes.

She was a lioness, he saw, a leader of her pride, strong, snarling, and so beautiful and complete. Way more of a woman than he had bargained for. She challenged him—made him need to become a better man to earn her. She was glorious! That thought made him quit shaking his head in awe, and smile.

It was a mistake.

A very big mistake.

"Out!"

There went that finger again.

First, 'sit', now 'out', she directed him with that steely digit with the rosy pink painted nail.

"Get out, now! Go and think. Think hard, miserable man. Then in two turnings of the sun, I *may* call and *speak* to you." She stalked him to the front door and shoved him out. "And I may not!"

Turning just before she slammed the door, he asked, "What call will you use? The owl?"

"The cell phone, you idiot!"

WHAM! The door slammed, the house shook. Then all the outside lights snapped off.

He was alone in the dark. Again.

But he had hope.

He would think, think hard, and wait, and wait for two turnings of the sun. And hope.

He'd left the flute on the chair for her. It was a gift, part of his hope. As long as she didn't hang it on her wall like a scalp that she had taken, he thought wryly, and never called or spoke to him again.

But for the next two days, hope survived.

chapter twenty two

Hey Jen, hope you're okay. Sure miss you. Thanks for the gift. I loved it!!.

Rave was supposed to take me stromatolite hunting but he seems to have disappeared from the area. But he did email me a list of places to look, so we are heading back up to Logan Pass to revisit some of those trails now that I know what and where to look.

Ah…Rave did call last night to warn me and tell me to look for his email. God, he sounded horrible! His voice was all raw and hoarse. He mentioned he had gone to try and see you. I hope you aren't making the poor man cry.

Please write or call me, Love Always, Dana

Cry? Hah! She was the one doing all the crying! Jenny scowled at her computer screen. "Poor man my ass!" she snorted.

He probably just caught cold from sitting out all night on her lawn, embarrassing her in front of all her neighbors.

The nerve! And just how did he get on Dana's good side again?

So he had a cold, maybe he'd leave now.

Was it her fault that she forgot her automatic sprinklers came on at night?

The flute sat on her living room chair where he had left it. It was an exquisite piece of Native American art. Hand carved, feathers hung from one end with leather wrappings, it was painted with symbols around the openings. Symbols that were beautiful but mysterious to Jenny. It must be worth a fortune! She wouldn't have any choice. It was much too valuable to fail to return to him. He'd probably done it on purpose so she would have to call him, see him to give it back.

Left on her chair it reminded, accused, called to her each time she passed by it in the room every day. Sometimes she even thought she could hear it calling to her.

You are proud, it seemed to say, but you love him, you know you do. He deserves the chance to speak to you of what is in his heart, it seemed to say.

But that was ridiculous! She snorted. Now she was believing in magic talking flutes! The man would be the death of her. Jen was so stressed she was imagining things—or giving herself an excuse to weaken.

"You've been listening to too many romantic legends lately, girl. Get a grip." Jen admonished herself.

She headed for the kitchen to sooth and calm her nerves with the feel, the smells, the pleasure of baking away her worries with another tasty confection.

She'd already canned up boxes of pears, peaches, and cherries. She'd pickled and canned beets and dills, baked cakes, cookies, breads, rolls, and a soufflé or two. Her pantry and freezer were overflowing, but her heart was still empty, barren and restless.

She heard voices out front. Female voices and giggles. Cranking up the blind she looked out. Rave was half turned smiling and talking to two pretty young women standing in the street.

What was it with that man? He seemed to attract every woman in sight! Including her, she scowled. It was probably just a

267

pheromone thing in her case. The damned man seemed to have the master key to every damn woman's pheromone code!

One of the women was about to step onto her lawn, but spotting Jen glaring out the window, quickly backed off with a laugh and wave, continuing her walk down the street with her friend. Wondering what exactly they'd been laughing and talking about, Jen was thankful they'd left before she did something stupid like opening her window and yelling at them, "Get your own stalker!"

She waited an hour, then curiosity took over, snatching up the flute she went outside and shoved it at him like a sword point to his chest.

Taking the flute in both hands, Rave looked down at it a moment before speaking.

"In Blackfeet tradition, young men play flutes as part of their courtship ritual." Looking up at her, gauging her mood, he continued. "They play the flute outside the tipi of the lady they hope to woo."

She studied him a moment, not letting him see if his wooing was making her knees go all woozy or not.

"The way you play Rave, you might be lucky if you can woo a moose or a cow."

A definite not.

He just smiled, nodded, and continued to tell her the courtship tradition. He had seen those lovely blue eyes soften when he told her he was wooing her.

"You know, I'm supposed to dump a fresh killed deer or buffalo on your doorstep now," he tried to keep his voice sober, his eyes solemn, despite the adorably scrunched nose and expression on his lovely little wren's face.

"To show you that I can provide for you and supply the food and hides for clothing and shelter that you will need for the winter. Not that *you* need it," he added and emphasized quickly, "so I didn't think you would appreciate it. But a Blackfeet man is supposed to show he is worthy."

Dipping his head while he rummaged to pull something from an inner pocket, he allowed himself a quick smile. She had the most expressive roll to those deep cobalt eyes, it was hard to maintain the seriousness of his courting.

He *was* seriously courting her, but she looked like she would murder him right there in the yard in front of the whole stuffy neighborhood if he laughed right now. God, she was so cute when she was thoroughly pissed off!

He sensed he was softening her up. Her hands had gone from fists braced angrily on her hips, to arms crossed under her breasts. She was definitely warming to him.

"Here," he glanced up with his most soulful look from where he was still seated submissively on the grass before his fiery beauty, handing her a crumpled envelope with the name of a bank stamped on the return address.

"I brought my bank statement, instead. Less messy," he added with his most sheepish and charming little boy grin that worked every time.

With one exception.

She just scowled at him and didn't move to take his letter, her foot starting to tap impatiently, if not loudly, on the dew-dampened lawn. Then her lips started to twitch.

"Less messy? Damn you, Ravenwolf! Get up off the grass. You look ridiculous. My neighbors are either staring and laughing or calling the police."

He dipped his head, coughed weakly a few times, patting his chest. "Sorry," he mumbled rising slowly, stiffly, painfully, to his feet.

"Oh, get inside before you get pneumonia!" She whirled and stomped off, almost catching his triumphant grin, when she turned again.

"And don't try anything! This means nothing. I'll give you some hot coffee, then you are out of here, buster."

Bluster. He could work with that. He'd slip into the bathroom and use his cell and get some flowers rush delivered, then stall until he could get her in his arms.

She didn't let him stay that long.

His coffee was in a go cup.

He was beginning to feel like a dog that was put out at night.

And he received a very strange look from the guy that came to deliver the flowers.

Too late, buddy, he muttered to himself.

It had been two turnings of the sun, when his cell phone rang. He snatched it up before the first ring tone died.

"How's it going, buddy?" Just Garrett.

269

"She is a warrior. I plan on surrendering and being her slave if she doesn't eat me first." He admitted to his friend, his voice sounding hopelessly hopeful.

"Harsh. Well, good luck." Garrett hung up, adding to himself, "Man is he toast!"

It seemed like hours before his cell rang again. Jen!

Her call consisted of just one impatient word. "Well?"

He felt like hooting.

"You are right, little wren. You do not need me."

Jenny felt her anger ratchet down a few notches. He'd obviously listened and thought about her words. But she held her silence.

Tlesca wanted to speak to her?

Well, this was his chance.

"You don't need me," he repeated, his voice softly sincere. "I've given that a lot of thought since you showed me your strengths and your lands."

Lands? Jen tensed, was he mocking her? Or just dehydrated? Then she recalled she had used the word, a tad dramatically, to mock him first.

"You don't need me, little wren. But I do need you."

She drew in a shaky breath at the tone and the timbre of his words. She heard—not mockery—but a soft plea. One she longed to believe.

"I love you, Jen," he said softly. "I hope you want me just a little," he continued, "and will let me speak with you, at least. Can we meet?"

Did he mean it? Were these just words? She needed to read his eyes to know for sure, she needed to be with him to know.

"I need to return the flute you forgot, again, anyway," her voice clipped and cool. "But we will meet in public, not here. You can buy me dinner."

"The flute is my gift of apology to you. I brought it to give you. I made it myself. I hope you will accept it and keep it in your home, as a reminder that once we were at least peaceful friends."

Somehow this surprised and touched her more than his words of need had done. Guys always needed, they didn't always give, she thought cynically. But this was special in a big way. Not only as a beautiful piece of art for her, but that he was also giving her all the careful hours of its creation, all the times his hands had carved, smoothed, and shaped. Clearly it was lovingly made. And given?

Jen felt a lump forming in her throat warning of a downpour soon to come. Without responding fully to his words of need, she rushed to get off the phone before she broke.

"Meet me tonight," she briskly gave a time and location, then hung up, and ran for her emergency box of tissues.

Disappointed Jen hadn't seemed to soften much, Rave held on to his hope. She had agreed to let him speak.

She had designated a public place with tables instead of slide around booths. She had wanted a place where he couldn't get his hands on her, weaken her, without drawing public notice.

Right. Her you-are-lying-to-yourself alarm bell rang somewhere inside her conscience. She hated that bell. Just when she was feeling good and self-righteous, it had a bad habit of going off like that annoying dinging noise her car made when she left the door open.

Open to self-deceit this time, apparently.

"Okay," she admitted, trying to turn off the conscience ring, "what I wanted was a place where I wouldn't be tempted to surrender and paw or jump him! Satisfied?"

Great. The conscience bell had stopped, but now she was talking to herself out loud. While lying.

She had surrendered long ago. And this wooing business had really gotten to her. But she put a stern, patient face on when she entered the cafeteria and sat down across from him. Face to face like this with him, on level ground, she felt his dark male beauty hit her like a physical punch to her solar plexus. Swallowing hard, waiting for her breath to return, she firmed her chin, raised her eyebrows and let him speak first.

He cleared his throat, and took the opportunity granted.

"The day you and Dana went to Browning, Garrett and I had arrangements to go look at horse breeding stock with my cousin on the reservation. He is very knowledgeable about horses, and about who has what stock available.

"He is a good man. I have become close with him in recent years. He had a hard youth and was a teenage alcoholic at one time. He was in and out of treatment centers as was his girlfriend at that time. He managed to get out, get his life on track.

"She didn't. And he realized he had loved to party with her, but not the woman she was. He had to break with her so she didn't

271

drag him back to that life. That was five years ago. She moved away but hasn't changed and never accepted that he has.

"Two years ago, he found a woman to love that brings light to his life. He has never been happier than since he married her. They have a new baby at home, and every thing is perfect. But his sweet woman is also jealous. It has caused problems when the old girlfriend gets drunk and calls his happy home, though he told her repeatedly, it was over long ago. But she has returned before, during powwow days, and stalked him.

"He is so afraid it will destroy his marriage, he has moved his family and changed his phone to protect the life he has now.

"After Garrett left the bar to go down to the restaurant to wait for you two there, she came into the bar in Babb, drunk, found my cousin there and cornered him. She was crawling all over him. He wanted to escape without harming her physically, but I could see how desperate he was.

"I tried to draw her away from him. And I did, so he could get out of there and she wouldn't be able to follow him. And then I looked up and you stood there. And I saw my own happiness and hopes shatter."

Jen could not breathe. Could not speak. Staring into his eyes looking for deceit, she saw none there, only sorrow.

Finally she pushed her voice past the tightness in her throat.

"Why didn't you just say so? Tell me. Why did you put me, put us through all this?" She was shaking, from pain or anger, she didn't know.

His reply was quiet, rather than harsh.

"Because it took more words than you have let me speak, than you were ready to trust and hear. And remember, little wren, this is not the first time you have condemned me though I was not guilty as you thought."

She was about to concede the truth in that, when he demanded, a tinge of temper in his own voice, "Why didn't you fight for me?"

Stung, without thinking, she responded defensively, with a dismissive wave of her hand.

"It was a vacation, Rave. Carefree? Fun? I didn't go there for stress, or to fight over anything. I left so I didn't ruin Dana and Garrett's vacation over something that would just amount to a summer fling, regardless." Her shrug belied her thoughts.

272

And what if I had fought and lost? She asked herself silently. Then I would just be more miserable. At least her way there had been a chance that they would meet again—inevitable as Dana and Garrett's best friends. Maybe later, after he had sown all those wild oats, he might have given her another look, another chance.

Why should she have risked it all when he was the only man she could see in her future?

Ravenwolf seemed crushed by the words she spoke, hurt by his own attitude flung back at him.

Just a summer fling, not worth fighting for. When had that changed? When had he changed?

He looked down at the table for a while, turning his coffee cup around and around in his hands, before raising serious eyes to her face.

"I was not unfaithful to you Jen. Then, or even since you came to the park. It has been only you, though I know my past gives you little reason to believe, that *is* the truth."

He scrubbed his hand back through that shining black hair, his next words less firm, almost hesitant. "Since I met you at the wedding?" He paused and looked at her carefully.

"Yes," she said slowly, uncertain.

"I wanted you then, you know."

Jen just waited.

"Then I came back here and checked out the ladies, looking for some play. But I found myself comparing them to you, and well, I just didn't want them." He looked embarrassed. Jen wondered if he was saying he hadn't been with anyone else since he met her? He had implied it once before.

He gave her a comical little smile, a shrug.

"It ruined my reputation you know, waiting for just the right one." Taking her hand, "I'm glad I did," he kissed her fingers. "Come back with me, Jen. Give us another chance."

The words were spoken so soft, so low, so unexpectedly, she wasn't sure he had said them.

"What?" Disbelief. "To my house? What are you saying?"

"It's too late to leave tonight. To your home first. Then come back with me to Glacier. Come finish your vacation. Come stay at my house. Come stay longer than your vacation, if you can, or come back weekends, but give us a chance, Jen. I think we

273

have something too valuable to not take this next step. Please, Jen, come with me. Come to me. Let me love you."

"I will agree to tonight, for now." Jen could not believe her own next words. "But, just to be clear, are we going to just be dipping into the frosting, or do I get a piece of cake this time?"

Rave stared a moment, then threw his head back and roared with laughter.

"Ah, little love, I'm surprised you remembered that. You didn't like it at all when I said it. I could see the lightening and thunder in your eyes when I told you. But I promise the whole cake this time, with frosting and candles with sparklers," he chuckled, his dark eyes gleaming with heat and laughter. His voice softened, darkened and the wolf grinned at her. "Or any other fantasy you want. Let's leave this place."

A blushing, smiling Jen hustled him out of there past all the fascinated diners attempting to eavesdrop.

Rave slipped into the hall bathroom with his backpack when they got back to her place.

Turning when she heard the door open, "Would you like a …," and the breath froze in her throat, her heart slammed hard against her ribs.

He didn't need to speak with those sensual lips, what he wanted was clear in the dark focus of his eyes, as he strode down the hall toward her. He was wearing a wide beaded collar at his throat, a wider leather band low on lean hips, with a soft red cotton breechclout pulled through it that hid none of his desire. Just acres of bronzed, lean, tautly muscled male skin, and nothing else.

"I believe you wanted to be ravished by a Handsome Savage?" He spread his arms wide offering himself.

Oh, yes! Jen thought.

With a shriek that sounded more like a choked laugh, she ran for her bedroom in mock terror, only to be caught by a fleet footed and determined warrior, and pinned to the bed with the weight of all that lovely naked masculine flesh.

"Stop giggling, you're ruining the fantasy," Rave grinned.

"I can't," Jen laughed.

But she could.

Then his mouth came down on hers, intent, tender, owning, and jolting in its power. The laughter and games stopped, and the loving began.

This time he gave her all of himself. His heart, his soul, his passions hot, sweet, and erotic, and—much to Jen's delight—every inch of his body. He made sure he surrendered any and everything she demanded, over and over until she was limp and dazed with satisfaction.

He had promised her cake and sparklers. He gave her a gourmet feast and a Fourth of July fireworks explosion.

And a most thorough ravishing—though more sensual than savage.

chapter twenty three

RAVENWOLF MADE LOVE TO HER that night with all the reverence of a man who had sought everywhere to fill a need he didn't understand. Until he found it all in one tiny vibrant package— his little wren held the world and his heart in her hands.

But so far, she had not even promised him tomorrow.

As she slept, he held and stroked her precious body. His lips reassured themselves she was here and his, kissing her cheek, her eyelids, her throat each time he woke from his doze. He was unable to believe his luck in finding this one woman that could bring him everything he longed for, and help him understand and shake off the bitterness of the past. He hadn't realized that bitterness was still guiding his actions, the wound hidden deep like an organ bleeding internally, until Jen had brought it into the light where it could heal.

He had never played 'Indian' in the cowboys and Indians way of kids. It was a role he had hated as he had blamed it for all the pain and misery of his broken home and life. A bitterness he thought he had risen above by leaving, by trying to educate and degree himself past and beyond. While he thought he'd conquered that old insecurity, he saw now it had just been buried beneath a façade.

Until Jen asked her simple, innocent question, that made him ask himself who he really was.

And he realized he was just a man.

A man with frustrations and hurts from the past that he no longer needed or wished to drag around behind him. A man that had every opportunity, was trained to do whatever he wished. And a man blessed with true friends and a heritage, and history as a Native American that could only enrich his life if he reached for it..

And best of all he was a man with one woman to love, to replace old bitterness with playfulness, share hopes and dreams, heal pain and find laughter—if he could hold on to her longer than just tonight or tomorrow.

When Jenny woke the next morning, she found a serious man beside her.

"There's just one thing I want to know right now, little wren." He grabbed her in his arms for a long, slow, devouring kiss.

"Will you come home with me today and give us another chance?"

She pursed her lips thoughtfully, her fingers lightly exploring his bare chest, "I do have more vacation time left ... "

"Great!"

Her eyebrows just rose, his grin faded.

"And I think I am falling in love ..."

He held his breath.

" ... with Glacier."

That was good, if not what he hoped.

"But you ... I will have to consider more. After I interview your cousin."

He thought that was fair.

"And...."

Uh-oh.

She rolled sensuously on top of him, "And, I think I might need a little more ... persuasion."

Much later they talked about calling their friends to share the news. Rave started to dial, then closed the phone with a snap, and gusted out a sigh.

"Maybe you better call. Dana has been a little rude to me recently."

Jenny giggled, "What did she call you?"

"A dog."

"Which you are." Jen pointedly reminded.

"Which I *was*," he corrected, running a fingertip down her soft cheek, "until you leashed me." He gave her an affectionate smile.

"Just remember, pal, that leash is attached to a choke chain."

"Thanks for the warning!" he laughed, then cupping her cheeks in both hands, his face turned serious again, his voice soft as he held that sweet, sassy little face close so he could look long and deep into her eyes.

"But it doesn't matter." He leaned in to brush a whisper soft kiss across her lips.

" I couldn't breath anyway, when I thought I'd lost you."

Somehow they got distracted and forgot all about calling their friends.

Before any other plans, they needed to return to Glacier.

He had already mowed her lawn to detailed specifications. His help wouldn't be needed until it was time to load her suitcases in his truck—though he might need a U-Haul for the few essentials she felt she needed for the next week or two.

He had no complaint, he would be happy to haul all her clothing back to Montana and hold it hostage to keep her there.

So Rave lay on Jen's bed, fully dressed to not distract her from packing, ankles crossed and arms behind his head, he shared some of his thoughts with her while she prepared.

He talked about the horse breeding program he and Garrett had been planning for a long time. A dream that had first been hatched around a campfire on Blacktail Deer Plateau in Yellowstone—and seemed an impossible goal for 'one day, when they were older'.

Over the years, Rave had found a purebred Appaloosa stallion, with excellent bloodlines, for each of them. He had found a blue roan, Blue Moon, for Garrett. Rave had what was called a blanket Appaloosa. He explained it was a dark chestnut horse with a blanket of white draped over his rump and hips with big oval spots, called halo spots, in the dark chestnut.

"He sounds gorgeous!"

"Wait 'til you see him, Jen. He's a big muscular, handsome guy."

"Two of a kind," Jen whispered.

"What was that?"

"What's his name?"

"Apikuni. It means Spotted Robe. Do you like horses, Jen?"

"Rave, I think every girl goes a little horse crazy when she is about twelve or younger. I certainly was, but I've rarely had much chance to ride. I need to be re-trained."

278

"I'd love to make you my favorite and only pupil." The look they shared almost delayed the packing, but Rave's stomach growled, and his gourmet girlfriend sent him off to plumb the depths of her treasure packed fridge and cupboards.

"Grab some coolers from the garage and load them with all the home cooked foods you want to take along," she called after him, pleased to have someone to spoil. "There is another freezer and home-canned goods on shelves in the garage."

Ravenwolf went exploring in Jen's kitchen and garage and found what amounted to paradise for a bachelor. After loading up Jen's two coolers and a couple boxes he found, he hot footed it out to his truck to bring in his coolers, also. Leaving his stack of treasures in the garage to stay cool until they were ready to go, he strolled back into the bedroom, wrapped his arms around Jenny's waist and pulled her out of the closet, and kissed her dizzy.

"I think I'm falling in love," he murmured against her lips.

Leaning back, she frowned. "I thought you fell already?"

"That was *you* I fell in love with." He gave her a rakish grin. "This is for the sexy cook."

She laughed and pushed him away. "Go eat, Mr. Distraction. Then come back and talk to me some more while I finish in here. I like hearing your thoughts and dreams."

"I want to do things, Jen," he said later, sprawled against the headboard, pleasantly stuffed. "Do something with all the education I have. But not money making things, helping things, you know?

"I still want to ranger, but I don't need to. I would be just as happy," he paused a minute, "happier, taking the horses and going up into the backcountry with just the two of us."

"Camping?" she asked.

Uh-oh, maybe not he thought.

"It could just be day rides," he suggested.

"That would be fun," she agreed. Turning to look down at him thoughtfully, she continued softly.

"I never camped or fished growing up, Rave. So It has always just seemed scary and messy to me. But when you took me out in that canoe at Kintla Lake, I ... " She shrugged, and sat down on the bed beside him.

"Well, I just felt something different. Like I wanted to try it. Like it was basic and real, instead of messy. And I would never be scared if you were with me."

He rolled and captured her waist and pulled her over for a brief, but tender kiss. Not a sensual kiss this time, but a kiss to celebrate the ache in his chest her words had caused him.

Rolling off the bed he picked up the suitcases she was finished with to load them on the truck—before he was tempted to ask her for too much before she was ready to hear it.

From the road, Jen called Garrett's car phone.

"Dana there?"

He just handed the phone across. "It's Jen."

Dana took the phone with a worried look on her face, and cautiously put it to her ear.

"Jen? You okay?"

"I'm more than okay. I just wanted to let you know I'm heading back to finish our vacation at Glacier. So don't leave. See you soon."

Minutes later it rang again, Garrett just gave it to Dana to answer.

"Jen?"

"FYI, Dana? Rave is bringing me back. We are coming back together. We will be at his house. At least for awhile. We'll see you tomorrow. Bye, again."

Grinning, Dana turned to Garrett.

"Well, it looks like you owe me twenty bucks, big guy. I might be persuaded to ... negotiate ... your payment."

The sultry tone and glint in his wife's green eyes, just about had her hubby running off the road into a ditch. He may have exceeded the speed limit back to their tipi.

Thank you, Ravenwolf!

After they left the traffic congestion behind, crossed over the Cascade mountains, and traversed the long bridge over the stunning Columbia River Gorge, the highway east rose onto a plateau for a seemingly endless straight stretch of mind numbing road.

Pouring more coffee from the thermos she had brought to keep them alert, Jen asked Rave to tell her more about the plans he had been sharing with her before.

"You talked a little about the horse breeding program and said something about wanting to do other non-money making things, but we got, um, distracted before you finished." She prompted. "Or said whether you still planned to be a Ranger at Glacier."

"Right," he smiled remembering. "You never looked at the bank statement I offered you in lieu of a deer on your front porch..."

"Ah, yes," she laughed. "You definitely have the most unique style of wooing I have ever seen. Quite ..."

Annoying? Distracting? Embarrassing? Impressive? All of those plus very touching, in retrospect. Jen gave up trying to fit a word to all the emotions she had felt. Throwing out her hands, laughing again, she finished, "Quite indescribable."

"It worked," he answered softly, with a smile for her. "That's all that mattered to me. I was a desperate man."

They drove a few miles in contented silence before Jen urged him to continue telling her about his plans.

"Where was I? Oh, my non-deer offering. You never looked at my bank statement, so I guess you don't know I'm actually pretty well off. Wealthy, actually. When I was getting my doctorate in economics, I practiced some of my own theories on the stock market. They passed the test, and are still doing well, so I'm free to do whatever.

"About Glacier ... Remember when I told you about how much of an outsider I felt when I first moved to my father's house on the reservation?"

She just nodded. She would never forget the pain he had spoken of.

"But I always felt like I had gone home in the summer when I went to work in the park, on that land, in those shining mountains. I don't know if they were born in my blood, or if I have some genetic imprint, or whatever, but the park was *my* place. It just felt right, that land of open plain and mountain wilderness was *my* tribe, *my* heart.

"I'm trying to learn the Blackfeet history, the stories, and understand how it all connects for me. But I try to avoid all the park and tribal politics and issues to just focus on who my people are and were. So my interest in helping doesn't lay in the political realm or power struggles, but in the pathways to achieve an individual's destination. Especially through education.

"I've personally detoured around a lot, and lost the trail many times seeking what it is I want, what destination I'm seeking. But each time I've picked up the trail again it has been through learning, and claiming what resonates with me whether it was through college, travel, or cultural studies. I believe the combination is important, and I'd like to figure out a way to create some kind of scholarship program that encompasses all that for Blackfeet children. So far I have only funded some technology equipment, so that all grade levels will have the resources needed. But I want to do more to help. I'm just don't have all the what or how sorted yet.

"Anyway, I don't work in Glacier because I need the salary, but because the park feeds something in my soul."

What an amazing man lay hidden beneath the handsome, if shallow surface, he had been presenting to the world!

No wonder I love him, Jen thought.

"I do understand. I've felt that enchantment myself." Her voice was sober, then she laughed, adding, "And I happen to be crazy about one of its rangers."

The mountains were silhouettes backlit from the west, but night shadows were already claiming the east front of the Rockies when they arrived at Ravenwolf's.

His headlights picked out the square stone house and the outbuilding where his horses were stabled. He had made an attempt to create a windbreak along the north of the buildings, but the trees were small and struggling against the fierce winds that funneled down the front range. Any other landscaping was left to what nature planted and allowed to grow and thrive on this drier east side.

There was no real yard, Rave realized, or shrubs except for sage, and certainly no profusion of colorful flowers. Compared to Jenny's home, his suddenly seemed wanting, too stark and barren a setting for her. Glancing nervously to the side to see her reaction, he was relieved to see that she had fallen asleep. He would have the golden light of the morning sun to soften her first impression tomorrow.

Letting her sleep, he quietly unloaded the truck and straightened the inside quickly before lifting her in his arms and carrying her into his bedroom. Exhausted from the long trip, his little wren barely roused when he undressed her and slid with her under the covers, except to cuddle into his chest and murmur some soft words that made absolutely no sense to him at all—except for his name on her lips. That was enough for him.

Smiling, he pulled her closer and was out like a light after his own string of sleepless nights sitting vigil on her perfect damp emerald lawns.

Jen slept late the next morning and Rave was gone, though she had a memory of waking momentarily to a kiss on her cheek and him saying something about horses and chores, and telling her to go back to sleep. Padding into the kitchen she found notes and a half pot of cold coffee. The sticky note on a big mug placed nearby had an arrow pointing one direction that said 'microwave', and an arrow pointing another direction toward a pottery canister that said 'fresh ground coffee beans'. She opted for the immediate fix. While the microwave was running she found the bathroom and another note on the mirror. 'Good Morning Love'. It warmed her insides more than a hot mug of coffee. Propped on the sturdy wood trestle table was another note, 'Gone to get fresh milk and eggs to go with all your homemade pastries. Before she could explore further, she heard the truck outside. Right outside the front door, she found when she went to investigate. The tailgate was backed up to the front steps and Rave was unloading two huge planters filled with colorful flowers to either side. Grabbing another bag and bundle from the truck he started up the steps before he noticed her standing there. Stopping, he set down a bag and unwrapped the bundle.

"You look beautiful in the morning, Jen. These are for you."

He pressed the bundle of fragrant cut roses into her arms with a sweet, drugging kiss that took the rest of her breath away.

He'd brought her flowers! Not just romantic flowers for today, but thoughtful flowers for tomorrows. She buried her nose in the bundle of white, yellow, and light and dark pink roses to hide the moisture in her eyes, taking deep shaky breaths.

Rave grinned, gently stroking her hair, probably knowing she was already watering her flowers.

After breakfast, Rave invited her to come with him while he stopped in at work, he said he had someone anxious to meet her.

Jen had gone with him into West Glacier to park headquarters while he sorted out his schedule and took more leave time. She met an asshole named Earl there, and a lovely woman with a smile and laugh that brought sunlight to a room, named Shirl.

Rave easily confessed to asking Shirl to marry him every time he heard her laugh. He clearly adored her and it was obviously mutual.

Shirl beamed at Jen and winked at Rave and nodded. When she said she'd heard so much about her, Jen knew

283

instinctively she could believe and trust her. After all she'd learned of his mother, Jen was glad to know Rave had such a warm, caring woman as his confidant.

By late morning a thunderstorm had grumbled and rumbled in, lightning streaks making outdoor activities too dicey. They had gathered at Many Glacier Hotel, where Dana and Garrett were now staying, to spend the rainy afternoon together—unless there were lightning strikes and Rave was needed for emergency fire crews.

Jen had brought along some of the home-baked foods that Rave had raided from her fridge, so they had a gourmet picnic for lunch with the help of the microwave. It was quite a treat after eating out so many days. And then, of course, there were brownies, blueberry cheesecake—only slightly tumbled from the trip—and an apple and almond strudel for dessert.

Jenny also brought along her laptop where all the pictures she and Dana had taken on their trip had been downloaded. After connecting up to Garrett's laptop and transferring all the files, they all sat around, stuffed and happily groaning, to slowly review the pictures one at a time—with colorful commentary by Jen and Dana.

"It's a pity cameras can't capture that amazing smell," Jenny commented as the first picture of their entry into the park came up.

"Or that incredible sound," Dana commented, when they looked at the shots of thundering Avalanche Gorge. "We should have used video, Jen."

"Um, I have not quite figured that out yet on my new camera," Jen confessed. "Rave will show me. We'll just have to go back and see that again."

When they laughed over their bear panic after seeing the grizzly warning sign on the Avalanche trail, both men were quick to comment.

"Good." Rave said firmly, squeezing Jen tight to his side. "The sign is meant to be taken seriously. There are literally hundreds upon hundreds of grizzlies in the park, and you need to always be responsible and conscious of your surroundings. Though bear attacks rank low in fatalities compared to falling, or slipping into the water and drowning, often just to get a better photo. The word park makes many people forget this is not a safe playground. Too many people forget that the wilderness is hazardous, every moment is at your own risk, much as it was for the first people here."

"And you can not count on cell phone coverage to get you out of trouble," Garrett added, sternly. "I brought the bear bells along that you should have taken with you, Dana. And the bear spray." He frowned.

"You are right, Garrett. Thank you for caring, honey."

"Rave made us wear bear spray belts. He told me they are the latest park fashion." Jen smiled up at him.

Chastened, but appreciating the caring spirit intended, the women continued to entertain them with their slide show.

When they got to the pictures they had taken after the Loop, of the dramatic cirque amphitheater, Jen rhapsodized about all her romantic thoughts about beautiful Bird Woman Falls, falling beneath the Going to the Sun Road, through the arches. She had taken photo after photo of her favorite spot. Ravenwolf and Garrett stared at the photos then looked at each other a long, silent moment.

Jen had frozen the screen on the shot centered on where the water fell beneath the arches into the cirque, with the red signpost saying 'Bird Woman Falls' in the foreground. Her stair steps to heaven in the background.

"Doesn't Bird Woman Falls remind you of a romantic stairway stepping up to heaven?" She asked the room.

Dead silence.

Rave knew it was up to him.

But it pained him greatly to have to do it.

Jen was not the first to make the mistake, but she was not going to take it well. Especially not with romance and heaven all tangled up in the mess.

"Um, Jen, sweetheart, I don't know exactly how to say this ..."

Rave struggled for some kinder, gentler way to word what he had to say, glancing up to his buddy for help only to get a you're-on-your-own look.

"Little Wren, I'm sad to say that you, ah ... I guess you didn't notice there is another interpretive plaque at the roadside?"

"There were too many cars to get closer, and it's so steep I didn't try going around. An interpretive sign? Does that mean there is another special meaning for Bird Woman. Is it named for someone? I'm not surprised. It's so very special." Jen was so excited.

"Um," he held a palm up to stop the flow of her words before it got any worse. "I'm very sorry to have to inform you that that," he pointed to the waters centered in the picture on the screen. "That is not Bird Woman Falls." He would have breathed a sigh of relief, but the worst was not over yet.

"But the sign says—"

"The sign is actually referring to the waterfall all the way across the cirque, the one not beside any road." Leaning over he tapped the touch pad a few times, then paused, pointing to a picture where a silver ribbon dropped straight down the cliff wall far across the gulf at the head of the McDonald Valley.

"This is Bird Woman. This falls almost five hundred feet. I think the exact number is four hundred and ninety two feet down this sheer face. That has to be more than twice the one at the Grand Canyon of Yellowstone, isn't it Dana?"

Dana just shrugged without speaking, foiling his attempt to divert the conversational hot spot over to her.

And inevitably Jen asked him *the* question.

chapter twenty-four

"BUT ... IF THIS ISN'T BIRD WOMAN," Jen flipped back to her favorite, "then what are these falls called?"

He could already hear the disappointment in her voice.

It would get worse.

Taking a deep breath, Ravenwolf muttered an answer.

"What?"

He cleared his throat.

"Ah. Haystack."

Jenny stared at him like he had just kicked her puppy.

"Did you say, haystack?" She seemed to choke on the word.

Total disbelief.

"That's outrageous! That is the ugliest, most unromantic name, I have ever heard! How could they name something so beautiful, so dramatic, that? It has no inspiration. I do not believe you, Rave. You must be pulling my leg."

He would love to.

Seeing what he needed on the dresser, he opened a map of the Going to the Sun Road and showed her the name under the points of interest. Watching the emotions crossing her face as she stared at the evidence, as if willing the words to change, Rave feared a flood was imminent. If there was any way he could change the name for her, he would do it in a heartbeat. Maybe he could petition Congress? Maybe ...

"Well," Jen declared, chin up and firm, cobalt eyes fierce, "That is just blasphemous to call that lovely, spiritual vision that ... name!"

Had they been outside, he was sure she would have spit on the ground after saying the word. The only thing that kept him from laughing was knowing her dreams of a favorite place were being crushed—and he felt like he was the one hurting her.

"I will not stand for it. I refuse to use it! That will *always* be Bird Woman Falls to me. So do not *ever* breathe that other word around me!"

Ravenwolf, and everyone else in the room nodded vigorously. Dana tapped the computer, quickly moving on to their pictures of the mountain goat at Logan Pass, on the Hidden Lake Trail.

"This alpine scenery reminds me of when I read Heidi as a young girl," she offered cheerily.

"Jen, are there any more of those brownies? My those were scrumptious!"

Disaster and potential flooding were averted.

All it took was total denial.

In one declaration, Jen changed over a hundred years of history and possibly even accomplished a geologic feat to even astound Dana. Though no one was quite sure whether Jen had moved the falls, or left two with the same name—and no one was about to ask for clarification.

Jen was cheerful again, and seemed to have settled the issue to her satisfaction for good, so nothing more need be said on the subject.

When Ravenwolf took a bathroom break he texted a quick note to Shirl at Park Headquarters, notifying her of the name change and warning her of the moratorium on the use of that other (bleep) word.

Shirl sent him back a madly grinning emoji.

By the time they left their friends to head home, night had fallen. The storm had passed through as had the rain that followed, and a bright moon lit the sky.

"I have an idea. Do you mind taking a drive, little wren?"

"In the moonlight and starlight of such a huge sky? I'd love to."

He headed south and then west up the Going to the Sun Road. They drove slowly, pulling into turnouts whenever an impatient set of headlights appeared in the rear view mirror. The roadsides were alive with nightlife, the headlights catching freeze frames of deer, mountain goats. a fox rushing home to its kits with something for dinner in its mouth, and even a grizzly galloping ahead of them to dive into the forest. The moonlight picked up reflections on the lake, but most dramatic were the stripes, and patches, and blankets of snow that glowed in the light from mountains that were mere ghosts in the darkness, turning the scene into a photographic negative of itself.

They didn't talk as they drove slowly up to the pass, just watched and absorbed the magic of the night. All the windows were rolled down to inhale the fresh, pungent scent that the rain-washed woods and meadows seemed to exhale.

Crossing the crest at Logan Pass, Ravenwolf continued a short way down the other side to the Mt. Oberlin overlook, and angled the truck into the middle of the deserted parking area. Sitting still for a few minutes, looking all around and listening for sounds, he turned the key lock to roll up the windows, then rummaged behind Jen's seat to pull out a stack of wool blankets and the duffel that held his flashlights, cans of bear spray, and weapons.

"Come," he said softly to Jen, pulling her out his door with him. Setting his blankets and duffle in the truck bed, he reached over and wrapped his hands around her waist, easily lifted her into the back.

Climbing into the truck bed after her, he set a folded blanket down as a pad and sat with his back braced against the cab. He motioned her to turn and sit in front of him, pulling her between his knees until her back was snug against the warmth of his chest. Wrapping the other blankets around both of them, they cuddled in a warm cocoon.

"Look up there." He spoke quietly against her ear, his face nuzzled in her hair. "There are your Bird Woman Falls. They are most beautiful after they are filled with rain or snowmelt."

"Oh!" She breathed, enchanted.

The moonlight sparkled off the rushing water, making it look like buckets of diamonds spilled down steps.

They sat long and quietly in the night, under the blessing of the moon, with the warmth of shared joy, cuddled close in their own heat.

"I love you, Jen," Rave breathed in her ear, his arms wrapped tight around her.

"And I love you for this," she whispered back, tipping her head back to press a soft kiss under his jaw. "Thank you so much. You don't know what this means to me."

He did know.

"We need to go back now," his voice still a soft breath against her ear, "but there is something I want you to be thinking about on the way. I love you, Jen. I don't want you to leave at the end of your vacation. I want you to stay here with me so we can do this anytime. Stay at my home. Be with me. Please. Think about it."

He kissed her tenderly, deeply, letting her feel all his longing and hope.

Then he lifted her from the back and helped her into the truck, tucking a blanket across her lap and keeping her hand cradled in his as they silently and slowly made their way back down the moon glazed mountains.

He'd offered her more time with him. Offered his home. And, as clever a man as he was handsome, he had tossed in this magic moonlit park. How was she supposed to think with so many emotions swirling inside her after such a heart-breakingly beautiful night?

And he had asked her to think, not just spit out an answer to such an important question. That touched her, also.

Disciplining herself, Jen focused on the easy part first.

On the practical side, there was her job and her house to consider. She could use up more of her backlog of vacation time at work, or even set up a network log-in and work on projects from here if necessary. Her house was okay for the moment. She had already prepped it more than necessary to be gone longer, and she'd packed more suitcases than needed just for the balance of her vacation. She hadn't explained that decision to herself at the time, nor would she now. The main question she needed answered from a practical standpoint was—stay how long?

On an emotional, relationship level, she was a hopeless mess.

Yet the first question that ruled and began to untangle all the rest was still the same basic need.

How long? How long will you want me?

Because there was no denying to herself that she wanted him—without time limits.

Which was *not at all* the same as for an indefinite time.

Jen didn't feel secure enough to share the whole of that with him yet. But there was one little item that it was time to address.

She recalled the first time she'd met him at Dana's wedding.

Jen had never gotten his name—just a bone searing kiss.

290

But he had called her 'little wren'.

She hated it. *Lie!*

Actually it had made her feel quite warm and ... fluttery.

Until she looked it up finding it was just a common brownish gray bird. She hadn't felt very flattered or fluttered after all, but insulted by that man that couldn't seem to remember her name—and would not share his!

Then she had come to Glacier many months later and stumbled onto a half-naked handsome hunk of male god on the trail ...

Don't you remember me, little wren?

OMG! She had nearly fluttered into a faint at his feet.

Jen sat on the side of his bed in one of her feminine sexy lace and satin nothings that always enticed and challenged him into new ways to slide them off her lovely body. This one matched her eyes—cobalt blue jewels—and set off the contrast to her porcelain skin, that was so silky it almost shamed the satin.

"Why do you call me 'little wren'?"

Wrapping his arm around her waist he pulled her down beside him, curling all that soft, scented sweetness against his naked chest. Sweeping thick dark chocolate hair off her nape, he planted tiny kisses on her neck, nibbling his way across her shoulder until he nuzzled the satin strap to slide down her arm.

"Rave?"

"Mmm." His lips crested her shoulder and he started his assault down her chest to the sweet slope of her breast, rolling her back a little for better access. He felt her question vibrate in her throat, raising his head a moment.

"What, sweetheart?" He nibbled her ear lobe and across her cheek while he was in the vicinity. Just before he reached her lips they moved again.

"Ravenwolf," she gave a little sigh that seemed half pleasure, half annoyance, "I asked you why you call me 'little wren'?"

"Because you are so delicate," he kissed one corner of her mouth, "and sweet," he kissed the other, "and that's my name for my little Jen." He brushed his lips over hers capturing her lower lip in his mouth, a pouty little treat to savor.

She rolled to face him and he felt something stiff against his chest instead of her soft breasts, and heard the crackle of paper.

291

"What's this?" He leaned back, planning to remove the barrier and toss it on the floor, but she clenched her hand around it.

"This is a little research I did. I was curious about why you chose to call me a wren, so I looked it up."

"I see." All he could see and sense was her skin, but he waited patiently for her to enlighten him and share whatever they were talking about.

She sat up and read. "A wren is a small stocky bird ... "

He frowned and raised up on one elbow. It might have been more romantic if he had turned down the lights sooner, but he loved looking at her, watching her eyes lose focus as he loved her...

"With a stubby tail ..."

"What?" He sat up scanning her sheet over her shoulder. "Ah, but it says its tail is perky." He wrapped a big hand around her hip, squeezed gently, dipped his head to the shoulder he had bared and let his lips pick up where they had left off.

Ignoring him, she continued, "A common brownish bird ..."

He reached up and brushed a thick sweep of her hair out of his path. "Nothing common here," he murmured, his lips sliding across her skin. "Just rich dark chocolate brown on my little bird, with pink tipped highlights." He edged the loosened neckline down with his mouth, almost freeing one breast.

"But this is the real beauty ... "

"Oh yes it is!" He gave a little nudge and a pretty nipple appeared.

"The species name. Let me spell it."

His tongue circled his target, teasing ...

"T-R-O-G-L-O-D-Y-T-E"

Caressing that sweet tip with his tongue it took a moment ...

"What!" He lunged up and snatched the paper from her hand. "Let me see that." He knew she was just teasing him, but ... "Oh hell!" There it all was in black and white—and brownish gray.

Ravenwolf could not believe his eyes—or his stupidity!

He had tried to charm and seduce a petite beauty by calling her some kind of primitive ape man? What kind of idiot was he? Why didn't he know this?

"Jen, sweetheart, I had no idea!" He looked up but her back was turned to him, her shoulders shaking. Oh god. "Listen love, I don't know birds. I can tell a bald eagle from a seagull, and a bluebird from a robin, but that's about it. We have naturalists that

292

handle that stuff." The words rushed out of his mouth, helplessly trying to undo the hurt.

"You would think someone that was half bird would know something about them, *Raven*wolf!" Her voice sounded tight and choked.

"Oh Jen. Sweet, precious, Jen. I am so sorry!" He grasped her shoulders, gently turning her to face him. "How can I make it up . .."

Shaking, she raised her eyes to his and they were filled with ...

Laughter?

"You are really losing your touch as a lady's man, Rave," she got out before slapping a hand over her mouth to stifle a giggle. Her bright blue eyes danced with mischief.

He shook his head in disbelief. On this day when he had wanted so badly to romance his lady he had given her Haystack Falls and called her his little troglodyte—over and over.

He threw his head back and roared with laughter. There was nothing else to do. Jen joined him, collapsing into his arms, laughing so hard she had tears running down her face.

When they finally wound down, gasping for breath, little chuckles still erupting spontaneously, he wrapped her tightly in his arms, his cheek on her silky head, breathing in the vanilla and spice scent that seemed a natural part of her, he held and cherished and knew he was a lucky man. A *very* lucky man!

He doubted any other man had called his lady a troglodyte and lived—much less laughed with her after. A chuckle rumbled in his chest.

"What would you like me to call you sweet Jen?" he whispered.

Raising her head from his chest, she kissed under his chin, saying softly, "I want you to always call me little wren."

His heart warmed.

"And then, if I ever get furious with you I can shame you for calling me the other, again." Her soft laugh ticked his throat.

"Ah," he grinned, "I did notice something on that paper about fierce and aggressive protecting their territory. That part fits. I love it when you get all fierce."

"You do?" She asked surprised.

"Oh yeah. You toss all that dark hair back, your eyes flash, your tiny little chin goes up, and you go into your fighting stance.

Legs braced apart, palms planted on your hips, shoulders back and lovely breasts thrust out. I fantasize about getting you naked and having you standing over me reading me the riot act all the time." He gave her that wicked wolf grin and ducked when she swatted at him.

"You are *so* ... '

"Wait. Take this off and stand up and give me hell."

The little shiver that went through her told him that she was almost tempted. He almost told her he would love a good tongue lashing, but held the humor and turned serious and sober.

"You know Jen, the first time I saw you at Dana's wedding ... a petite little beauty all perfect and elegant ..." His voice went soft as he pictured, remembered,

"So sweet and lovely coming down the aisle, then as you came closer I felt a physical impact when your eyes met mine, and I saw all the life and passion in those sexy blue eyes." He smiled. "And then they roamed all over my body like a cobalt laser. Whew!

"I swear Jen, if I had been a girl I would have fainted!" He laughed, automatically dodging her hand.

"Girls don't faint more than men," she grumbled, but she was smiling, her cheeks a soft pleased pink. "Or if they do it's because they have all the child bearing and monthly stuff that totally short circuits their body chemistry all the time, so who could blame them?"

"Exactly! You completely short-circuited my body chemistry and I almost fainted." He grinned. Then scowled. "But do not ever, and I mean ever, tell Garrett or Dana I confessed to near fainthood when I saw you!"

If that muffled sound was a giggle, he was not reassured.

"Anyway, serious now, Jen. I think something in me must have known I would need you, love you, from the beginning, but was too arrogant to admit it."

He expected a comment about his arrogance, but Jen was completely still and silent.

"But you had me flustered, unsure how to get close to you, mentally scrambling for words to charm and seduce you. And I don't know how to explain it but you were so petite and delicate I thought of a tiny-boned bird, and wren was the only little bird my addled brain could come up with."

"I find it hard to believe you were addled by a mere woman," she said quietly, but not accusingly. "You looked completely confident and in charge of your arrogance to me."

"I have a lifetime's experience keeping my face from showing my feelings,' he answered low, "but I was a mess. I think Garrett suspected. If not then, later, when I asked too many questions about you. But I could bide my time, play cool, I knew Dana would bring you to Glacier. Then I would know if I still felt the same."

She didn't voice the question, but he answered. "It was worse. Like when I kissed you the first time. At Dana's."

"I *beg* your pardon?"

He laughed. "That didn't come out right. Let me back up. I wanted to seduce you, get rid of that nervous edge you gave me. I thought that was all I needed to level myself out, so to speak."

She had a frown on her face, but he hurried on. Now was the time to bare his heart. He didn't want to be interrupted and have to start all over.

"When I had you pinned against the door in the cabin, kissing you ... remember?"

"Hard to forget." she muttered.

"The shock you gave me when I saw you just became worse, more intense, more dangerous, more ... compelling. I knew if I took things all the way, I would break something. Something precious, something very special that I wanted to save and hope to savor longer later. And I couldn't bear losing that chance, so I walked away. I waited."

Silence.

"Then when you came back to the park, my god, danger signs flashed all over the place but I could not resist. You were already in my blood, my dreams, my fantasies, and creeping into my heart. Jen, I *know* now. I need you, I want you, I love you. Please say you will stay with me.

"Please?"

He turned and pulled her snug, his forehead against hers, his lips against her cheek. "Stay, little wren."

She was silent for a long time before she spoke, then it was a hesitant whisper as if she didn't really want to say the words. "For how long, Rave?"

"As long as you can. As long as you want. Always works for me." He laughed nervously when she stiffened in his arms. "Ah, that was a proposal, an awkward one, little wren, but ..."

Why didn't she say something? What was she thinking? He must have really botched this ... He waited. And waited.

"Jen?," he pushed her back a little desperately so he could see her. "Say yes, dammit!"

Her deep blue eyes lifted to his, welling with silent tears. She swallowed, seemed to try to speak, then nodded.

Thank God! His breathe exploded out and he could breath once again.

chapter twenty-five

JEN'S VOICE CAME in a breathless rush over the phone.

"Dana, I couldn't wait to tell you. We're going to be happily-ever-afters too! Rave and I. We're getting married Dana, isn't that ..."

A hiccupping sob sounded.

"Jen, that's ..."

Dana was cut off, "Wonderful."

Unless she missed her guess her friend was probably drowning in tears of joy at the moment. No point calling her back and listening to that on roaming charges long distance.

Ravenwolf was there to absorb the flood.

And Dana could not claim to be surprised—only thrilled.

"I'd like to have our wedding atop Chief Mountain," Jen said suddenly, while she was preparing a salad to go with their lunch the next day..

Well, no need to worry she would change her mind, she was already planning the wedding.

But Rave tried not to groan out loud. He'd just gotten used to giving up the life of a bachelor. He supposed weddings like the type Jen would want were one of those tests a man had to pass to prove his staying power. A test, an ordeal of patience rather than battle.

"Sweetheart," he said quietly, cautiously, "that's a pretty tough climb. I just can't see you making it, especially not in a wedding dress. You'll get all dusty and sweaty," he added, sure that would squelch the plan. "And there isn't enough room for all the guests."

He wasn't going to be stupid enough to expect his Jen to plan a small wedding.

"I really want it to be up there. I want the pictures taken up there. I can just see the pictures, they'll be fabulous! I'm thinking of a series of aerial shots of just us on top, the wind blowing my dress and veil, from a distance showing the whole mountain top, then closer and closer until its right over the top of us, shooting down on us laughing and looking at each other."

Rave was speechless. *Aerial?*

"We need the distance shots for the drama of the setting. And for Dana, of course. She'll be disappointed if it doesn't show all the colored layers of time in the mountain. And just think, all those layers of time will be symbolic of the layers of life we will live together." Jen let out a dreamy sigh.

Rave felt his eyes cross—though the symbolism bit was nice.

"And of course since we will need a helicopter for the aerial photos, they can just drop us off on top first, so we don't get messy climbing."

Helicopter? He was feeling a little shaky.

"It will be perfect," she gave another deep sigh, and turned those wide, cobalt eyes on him. "And what's so special about it is that in all the years to come, for our children, and every generation after, I want them to have and save those photos, to tell the story of how we fell in love at Glacier. But mostly to remind them of their heritages, and the traditional lands of their father's people. They'll be so proud!"

Rave leaned over and grabbed her, and kissed her blind.

He'd get her a helicopter. His bride, the mother of his future generations, deserved anything her little heart wanted.

And thank God he was wealthy because the woman definitely knew how to shop and spend it! So far he needed a helicopter, a new canoe, an Appaloosa mare—she wanted a leopard spotted one, but fortunately had decided a Dalmatian dog wasn't necessary as a matching fashion accessory—then there was the high dollar wedding.

He wondered if she needed any new clothes—besides the mandatory designer wedding gown, of course. Now there was a dumb bachelor-type question! Those days were gone forever.

And thank god, Ravenwolf smiled.

"Garrett will be my best man, of course," he offered his contribution to the planning, "but I want Shirl to give me away at the wedding."

This time it was Jenny that was speechless.

Since it was now certain that she would be staying past her vacation, Jenny unpacked the rest of the suitcases she had brought along. As was becoming their habit, Rave sat on the bed out of her way, and they talked and shared plans as he watched her graceful, efficient movements.

They didn't even know yet where they would live after they married, just that they would be together.

When Jen suggested she would put her house up for sale, Rave refused to let her—at least not until she thought it over more.

"Look what you have created there? That will always belong to you Jen, as long as you want it. There is no need for you to sell it, I can easily afford to throw deer at you doorstep," he grinned at her.

"And if we don't end up living there, at least part of the year, you can always rent it if you want. Or we can even keep your home and watch our grandchildren living there in your beautiful yard with all the trees grown tall, and tell them you created it all with your own hands.

"Something else to consider also, Jen. I need to buy some good ranch land for our Appaloosa Program. We could live near Dana and Garrett if you want. What do you think? What appeals to you, Jen?"

She paused a moment with a stack of delicate, lacy underwear in her hands that made Rave completely forget the question he had just asked.

"Would we need to live there year round?"

"Where?" he asked, his eyes intrigued by a bit of black lace.

Laughing she put the distraction down. "At the breeding ranch."

"Oh, no, unless we want to. We will have ranch managers, so we aren't tied down. But lets look for good land between Glacier and Garrett's, and keep our options open."

"Perfect. But I wonder, Rave. Tell me what you would do if you stayed on the Blackfeet Reservation."

"Well, we have a community college now in Browning. I had thought of maybe trying to teach some classes there. I could work with the kids during the school year, and still be a seasonal ranger in the summer, if I felt the need to. But I would have to learn the Piegan Language first, as it is an immersion school ... "

"I want to learn too." He raised his head to look at her.

"You do?"

"Yes, with you."

"Seriously?"

"Totally. How else are we going to be able to teach our kids?"

He was still discovering what a lucky man he was. After a lifetime of prejudice, every plan this woman made was to celebrate and honor, now and in the future, what he had been scorned for. He and his future generations were blessed.

"Now that I have you to help me find and focus my direction, what works best for both of us, is what I want most, little wren. I want to be together on things, but ... I've never had any examples of how that's done. I don't want to smother your interests, or drag you around in my pocket, but Jen, I want us to share things so badly. You can't know what that means to me."

But she could. The man who had always felt apart, wanted to make up for the closeness he had missed.

"I want that too, Rave, the sharing, the closeness. I need it, I expect it. We will find a way to make our lives together because it is so important to us both."

With Jen beside him, he saw his future opening to a long life of happiness, commitment, blue-eyed, raven haired kids that he could teach to love the wilderness. And, he grinned, even fights with his fiery wife followed by great make-up sex. He heaved a deep contented sigh, scooting down so he was prone on the bed.

"You're working too hard, sweetheart. Why don't you slip into that black lacy thing in your hand, and come lay down with me for a little nap?"

It was his wolf's grin that did it to her.

Straightening, she tossed her dark chocolate hair back over her shoulder, raised a delicate, porcelain arm to drape the back of her wrist on her forehead, and sighed dramatically..

"You know, I do believe I'm feeling a little faint."

So was he when she picked up the black lace and sashayed slowly out of the room to change.

Lightning and thunder flashed and crashed outside the little stone house that night. Though the occupants were oblivious until the ranger's pager and phones started going off.

Late summer storms were a danger throughout the west, especially in the heavily wooded and remote wilderness. Lightning strikes could start dozens of small fires that had abundant fuel and

300

no easy access, hiding in the maze of mountains while they grew more and more dangerous.

Ravenwolf rushed to help in any way he could to put out widely scattered blazes in the early hours before outside help could arrive, staying to aid the fire crews day after hot windy day.

When he finally arrived home filthy for a few days break after several days out in the wilderness on the fire lines, Jen fed him first, then sent him off to shower.

"Rave, there is something we need to discuss."

He'd come out of the shower, only a towel around his hips, hoping to find her waiting for him in the bedroom. After coming home exhausted, day after day from the fire lines, all he wanted was to spend this blessedly rainy evening in bed in a state of extreme bliss with Jenny.

But he found her out in the living room, seated in an armchair, fully dressed, and looking and sounding much too serious. The glance she gave his towel made him feel uncouth and unencouraged.

"Sure, what is it sweetheart?"

"Please have a seat." She seemed to marshal her thoughts a moment before starting in.

"You know women are known for changing their minds ... Well, women allow that myth actually, to gain an advantage and reserve the right to change if they wish ..." She stopped, straightening her shoulders. "And that is what I wanted to talk to you about. I have changed my mind ... "

Dread sank so deeply in Ravenwolf's chest that he could barely breath, much less hear what she was saying. It had seemed too good to be true and now ... *I have changed my mind* Jen had changed her mind and life just seemed to stop inside him.

Interrupting whatever she was saying, whatever excuse she was making, he said, "But I asked you. You agreed!" Hurt and disbelief edged his voice.

Jen looked up at him, blinked, then continued calmly.

"You see, Rave, it is just so sacred. I've come to realize that and I just don't think it would be right to go through with this."

She was so earnest that Rave felt it like a dagger had been plunged into his heart—sudden, fatal pain.

"But you promised me!" He would fight for her, for them.

"Actually, it was you that made all the promises, I believe. But I don't want the helicopter..."

"What? What's a helicopter got to do with it?"

301

"It's one of the changes," she said patiently.

"Wait. Backup. What exactly are we talking about?" He held his breath, braced, but hopeful.

"The wedding. It just won't work."

"Why not?" He needed clarity to prepare his rebuttal. "Why can't things stay like we planned?"

"I'm sorry, I just don't feel right about it, Rave. On top of the mountain? With a helicopter? No, it's just wrong. I just don't want that now."

He started to breath, warily. Rave hoped she meant just the helicopter. It was a no fly zone.

"All of that fuss and glamour is wrong. Wrong for what I really want—and wrong for Chief Mountain. It is a sacred place, Rave, for generations! It deserves more respect. I would feel like we were desecrating it with those wild ideas we talked of before.

"I would like to have its beauty and strength and meaning as a part of my wedding, but not like that. This is what I'm picturing, tell me what you think."

He thought the lovely woman would surely drive him mad some day—and he would happily let her.

"I see us getting married below, in front of Chief Mountain, in a very simple ceremony—except for my dress. I'm going to wear a gorgeous dress and veil that will billow in the wind, and dazzle your eyes, and make you think you are the luckiest man alive." She already glowed with excitement. "But no flowers except our bouquets. And no altar, except that we will be facing the mountain. There will be a minimum number of chairs, mostly for elders or those that need them, but I want them set back," her hands motioned, gracefully drawing pictures, as Rave listened with a small smile on his face.

"The area behind us is where I want everyone we invite to stand in a semicircle, surrounding us with their support of our union." She smiled a little mistily, seeing their friends and family in her mind.

"But first they will stand to the sides and watch. First Garrett will escort Dana forward and they will stand to either side as our best man and woman. Then Shirl will walk you down to join Garrett and stand behind you, in her rightful place." She gave him a teary smile, acknowledging Shirl as Rave's surrogate mother figure.

Then with a little laugh, she added. "You know you have always wanted her at your wedding, Rave, you've asked her enough times! But I'm afraid she'll have to take second place, as

302

my father will when he brings me forward to take your hand at your side. And everyone will gather close behind us while we say our vows.

"Hopefully, you know someone with a lovely voice that can sing a song a capella, then we will turn and have our picture taken by one photographer, and go somewhere else to have the party."

She clasped her hands together. "What do you think?"

"I'm a bit surprised, Jen." He smiled fondly at her. "Why the change. I promise you can have any wedding of your dreams, because I know you have probably been dreaming of, and planning, your wedding since you were a little girl. You can have anything you want. Ah, except a helicopter in a no-fly zone, but..."

"Oh, Rave. You're right. I have dreamed of a huge, extravagant wedding since I was small. I played it through with my dolls over and over, embellishing it more and more over time.

"But... I'm not playing dolls anymore, and I am not going to play the doll—that doll—anymore. I've spent too much of my life coasting on childhood fairy tales that no longer match how I feel now. I don't want to be a caricature of myself.

"I am growing, changing, stretching into someone more than the limited vision of my youth. I want more, I want to explore who I can be, what I want. And one of the things I love about you is that you make me feel free to be whatever woman I can become."

"You are free, my love. I never want to hold you back. I know what it is to change and seek a brighter, happier future." He gave her his wicked grin.

"I chased you down, didn't I?" he teased. "But, seriously, I love the image of our wedding you just painted, but it's your special day and it will be exactly as you want it. Whatever it is. As long as I come home with the prize. So if you change your mind again—about the *details* of the wedding," he clarified, firmly. "I'm good with that."

"There *is* something else." Jen put her arms around his neck and leaned in close. "About the mountain. I still want it to be part of our plans, just in a different, quieter, more meaningful way. I want us to climb up to the top, sometime the week before our wedding.

"Just the two of us, no cameras, in our outdoor camping clothes. I want us to spend a night together on Chief Mountain, watching the stars and the moon, watching the sun rise at dawn, just thinking on and sharing what we mean to each other, what we see for our future. Our spiritual time before the wedding."

Rave gathered her in close and just held her to him for the longest time, absorbing how special she was and they could be, together.

"Yes," he agreed, "I want that most of all."

"There is something I've always wondered. What was that cake and frosting crap all about? Why did you leave me that first night?" He drew her close, his forehead and nose touching hers as he spoke in a low, caressing voice.

"The second first night, actually," he admitted. "Much like after Dana's wedding, it was because you were so special and it scared me. The second time, was even more intense. I was so humbled by the way I felt about you when I held you against me, kissed you, tasted the sweetness of your skin, traced the beauty of your lovely little body with my lips and fingertips. My sweet little wren, so precious, so delicate, so delicious. So very special.

"I did make love to you in all those ways, and I had meant to make love to you in every way. But it didn't seem right somehow to claim you completely until I was sure we would stay together. That you could count on me. And I was afraid to receive too much from you and have it taken away at the end of your vacation.

"I was terrified I'd take too much, too fast, and lose myself in you, and maybe lose you, before I figured out what it all meant. For once, with you, the woman was more important than the act. And the wait and anticipation would be just as sweet while I sorted myself out.

"Love had never captured my spirit before you, Jen."

Rave took her to their room, laid her gently on their bed, and kissed, and tasted, and made love to her in all the ways he had that first night—and more. Knowing this time that it was a true, lasting love that he was feeling and receiving.

Yet as pleased as Ravenwolf was with the new plans—and the love making that followed—he found he could not shake the dread he'd felt when he was reminded that she could change her mind at any time before their wedding after Labor Day, at the end of the tourism season.

The woman had nearly given him a heart attack! Now he knew why it was named that.

The wariness he felt when he knew that his life seemed just too good to be true, lingered. Worrying some fluke from his past might bite him and destroy Jen's confidence in him again. He needed to reinforce his devotion to her, show her how very special

304

she was. Reassure her—and himself—that she had no reason to change her mind about marrying him.

He slipped out to feed and water the horses, and make a few quick private calls, calling in friends and favors.

When Garrett's car phone rang this time he handed it to Dana again to answer—it was becoming his habit recently.

"Get Garrett," the deep male voice said abruptly. Handing it over, she listened curiously to the one sided conversation.

"Sure. Yeah, we can do that. Two cameras? All right. Of course I'll check the batteries." That last sounding a little annoyed and indignant.

"Got it. Rising Sun, just before dawn tomorrow. Bye. Hey, good going, buddy."

"What's up?" Dana was dying of curiosity. She was, for maybe the first time, unsatisfied by her husband.

"We have to get up early tomorrow." And despite her wait, he refused to say anything more. Except, "Don't ask Jen."

Men! she thought. They could be *so* insensitive at times.

Jen grumbled the next morning when she was rudely shaken awake while it was still dark outside.

The rest of last night had been a long, sweet tender night of loving, and being loved—near to exhaustion! Jen couldn't believe how inconsiderate Rave was being this morning to force her up and out after just a few hours rest!

It was barely brighter than total blackness as they headed over to Going to the Sun Road. Jen couldn't see anything but looming dark, and darker, shadows. As they came down the east side, just a tinge of pink light lurked on the horizon, promising the sun and a fresh day.

Jen said nothing when Rave pulled in at the Rising Sun motor court. She was too distracted hoping he was taking her to the Grill for an early breakfast to notice the cars parked in the murky but brightening light.

When she stumbled out of the truck, and started to trudge across the lot toward the restaurant, Rave just hooked her arm and spun her about, and pulled her across the road.

"What?" She protested.

"Hush, little wren. We are going to see the sun bring the new day first."

305

Jen, didn't suspect anything different until they started down a dock and she saw a few people waiting beside the Little Chief boat. "I didn't know they had sunrise cruises, also."

"They don't."

Then Jen was almost tackled and squeezed to death by a shadow that turned out to be her best friend. "Oh Jen, I'm so happy for you," Dana cried. Rave and Garrett shook hands, and watched the girls for awhile grinning, then broke them apart and got them on the boat.

"Right in here," Garrett patted his backpack patiently when his buddy started to nag again about cameras, "with a fresh pack of batteries, so cool it."

As the surprisingly empty boat moved out into the center of the morning still lake, the sun started to kiss the mountaintops, then shimmering pink tinged gold light spread to glisten on the lake. And that is when Jen and Dana forgot they had ever complained that men could be insensitive, or inconsiderate.

The boat engines dropped and the boat stilled in the center of the lake. As Rave took Jenny's hand and took her to the stern of the boat, Garrett passed a camera to Dana.

With the whole exquisite dawn of a new day glimmering in the lake and mountain panorama behind them, Rave turned to face Jen, captured those bluer than sky eyes of her, and holding them, slowly lowered himself to one knee before her.

He had asked her once, but it hadn't been quite right. He wanted everything right and special for his woman. Cameras began to flash and capture the moment, and he heard Jen's gasp of delight.

"Jenny, my love," his voice was as soft and quiet as the morning. "On this new dawn when the sun comes to bless the world, I kneel before you and cast my heart at your feet." A moment's humor flickered in his dark serious eyes and at the corners of his lips.

"To cherish, or stomp on, whatever your pleasure, but I ask that you keep and own it forever. Will you be my love, my wife, and share all the new dawns to come at my side?"

And again Jen was speechless. Nodding jerkily, tears sparkling and streaming from her eyes, she dropped down to weep happily in his arms.

Reaching around to his back pocket, he pulled out a wad of new handkerchiefs he had bought just to have them to hand to his woman. She was a little waterworks, but she was his lovely little fountain.

Muttered from the side of his mouth, he questioned his buddy. "Did you get it? The perfect pictures for her? Check, and make sure."

"Yes," Garrett gritted, Dana too choked up to respond. "They're perfect."

Good.

There was no way in hell Rave was going to leave those future generations to imagine this glorious moment when she confirmed her acceptance of him. He shuddered to imagine her telling them he called her a troglodyte then proposed like an awkward ass.

Jen deserved better. She would want pictures she could proudly handcraft into a satin, lace and ribbon record for her children. So feminine and petite, but she would build and bond and nourish their family and future.

That was how his little wren was—and how he loved her to be.

"Will you love me, forever, Jen?"

She paused for an unnervingly long time, dried her tears, then pushed back so she could look in his eyes.

"I will love you with an intensity that will make you stumble around in a daze; I will love you so happily that I will constantly cry tears of joy all over you; I will love you with such strength that your favorite mountains will shake; and I will love you so softly that your heart will almost break; and it will take me at least until forever, to think of all the other ways I want to love you."

"Really?" He felt his own eyes glimmer with moisture for a moment, before he cleared his choked throat and flashed her his familiar, wicked, handsome savage grin. He was looking forward to her proving those words.

Once his fierce and gentle Jen's weeping slowed to light showers—hopefully, before the sun finished rising—they'd take a few more photos as he put the antique diamond ring on her delicate finger.

The baguette emerald-cut diamond antique ring wasn't an heirloom from his family. It was one he had selected to be an heirloom representing their own future.

A future as bright and promising as the varied colors of the light rising and blessing them.

They were going to the sun.

Together.

307

author's notes

Going-to-the-Sun is the correct spelling for the specific road, but I used the longer, un-hyphenated form in this book to also describe a journey.

The Aftermath—The Fires of 2017—After this journey, devastating fires again reshaped Glacier NP. From news releases out of Glacier.

6-29-2017 Going to Sun road fully open

8-7-2017 GNP record breaking 1million visitors July 2017

8-11-2017 Storm causes 150 lightning strikes-multiple fires reported.

The Sprague and Adair fires burned between Lake McDonald and the Going-to-the-Sun Road, and the Sperry Chalet. Rangers started hiking tourists out of threatened backcountry areas and then had to hike 39 people out of the Sperry Chalet across the Continental Divide 13 rugged miles (10hrs) to the east of the divide. Except for some stone work, the historic Sperry Chalet was burnt and closed until it can be rebuilt. By the 3rd of September, an evacuation order was in place from the foot of Lake McDonald to Logan Pass on the west side. The Going-to-the-Sun Road remained open on the East side of the divide up to Logan Pass. By Oct 21, 2017 the road reopened to Avalanche on the west, was closed for the season over the pass, and only open from St.Mary to Rising Sun on the east. It is important to always check current conditions before planning a trip because while it is called a park, this is a wilderness, and nature rules. Park website https://nps.gov/glac for current conditions.

Re: the Science:

I have no academic training in the sciences, though I self-educate rigorously. I wade through technical papers, non-fiction books, educational Dvds—often scratching my head and muttering a lot—until I track down what appears to be the basic consensus of my focus. Then I try to explain what I've found as simply, clearly—and often humorously—as possible. I'm bound to make mistakes—any corrections are deeply appreciated at email bett@bettboneauthor.com.

And sometimes I Intentionally cheat in the interest of a simple, memorable overall picture.

I describe the Belt Rocks here as sedimentary rocks for the mental impact of layer after layer laid down over hundreds of millions of years in the deep past. I avoid cluttering that image back up in the case of argilites and silites by not detailing that they are "lightly metamorphosed", as they retain the sedimentary character. For those who want the details, specifics, and professional word, references are included at the back of this fiction book.

About Ravenwolf:

Ravenwolf, as he proclaims himself, is not representative of a Native American, and is not meant to be a portrayal of his Blackfeet/Nez Perce heritage, or to offend cultures I respect.

What he is meant to portray are universal issues of a hard childhood, prejudice, youthful rebellion, resulting self-destructive acts, followed by seeking, growth, maturing to a desire to know about his ancestry and finding harmony and purpose in life. I hope I have accomplished at least a part of that goal.

I did not set out to create a Native America character, but several ideas I wanted to write about someday came together with Glacier National Park and a man of partial Blackfeet heritage was naturally born. Tons of research later I realized the bulk of information is from European versus native viewpoint, and secondly, I am not qualified to correct or understand traditional cultural history and give it the respect it deserves in the scope of this story—but merely offer hints to spark others to seek that wealth of unknown, untaught information. So Ravenwolf of necessity had to have a childhood off reservation and non-traditional, though I refused to give up my descendant of the First Americans and what his presence reminds us all.

I would encourage readers to seek better knowledge and understanding from a work commissioned by Glacier National Park in 2008, developed from the gathering of a mass of archival information, and oversight and input of the tribal cultural councils of the people to either side of the divide in an exceptional (and much needed) historical work called

People Before The Park: The Kootenai and Blackfeet Before Glacier National Park, by Sally Thompson, Kootenai Cultural Committee, Pikunni Traditional Association, ©2015 Montana Historical Society Press, Helena, MT

It tells a rich and fascinating story of Glacier before, and is an excellent source of references for further information.

Thank you so much for going to Glacier National Park with me. Bett

About the Author

Bett lives in the beautiful Pacific Northwest near what is now known locally as the Salish Sea and just an hour—or so, depending on the ferry lines—from the Olympic National Rainforest. Just a short drive in any direction brings plenty of scenic inspiration.

But she loves traveling to the National Parks of the Northwest, and developed a particular passion for the rugged mountain wilderness of NW Montana.

This is her second book in the National Park Road Series.

Please enjoy the journey to Glacier National Park. For photos taken by the author in the parks, please go to her website at:

https://www.bettboneauthor.com

To receive word on the next National Park journey please email a request to:

Bett@bettboneauthor.com

Hey, thanks for reading!

Coming Next

Look for Book 3 in the National Park Road Series ...

road to mazama
A CRATER LAKE PARK LOVE STORY

by Bett Bone

for notification when the next book is available
email "let me know" to
bett@bettboneauthor.com

Partial List References/reading list

Alt, David D., D. W. Hyndman. Roadside Geology of Montana. Missoula: Mountain Press Publishing Co., 1986.

Alt, David D., D.W. Hyndman. Northwest Exposures: A Geologic Story of the Northwest. Missoula: Mountain Press Publishing, 1995.

Alt, David. Glacial Lake Missoula: and Its Humongous Floods. Missoula: Mountain Press Publishing Co., 2001.

Bullchild, Percy. The Sun Came Down: The History of the World as my Blackfeet Elders Told It. Lincoln: University of Nebraska Press, 1985.

Hazen, Robert M. The Story of Earth: First 4.5 Billion Years to Stardust. New York: VIKING Penguin, 2012.

Knoll, Andrew H. Life on a Young Planet: The First Three Billion Years of Evolution on Earth. Princeton and Oxford: Princeton University Press, 2003.

McDonald, Douglas H. MONTANA Before History: 11,000 Years of Hunter-Gatherers in the Rockies and Plains. Missoula: Mountain Press Pub Co., 2012.

McClintock, Walter aka adopted son of Mad Wolf Beaver Bundle holder of Blackfeet. The Old North Trail: Life, Legends, and Religion of the Blackfeet Indians. Pittsburgh: MacMillan & company, 1910.

McMillion. Mark of the Grizzly 2nd Edition. Guildford, CT: Lyons Press: Imprint Globe Pequot Press, 2012.

Meltzer, David J. First Peoples in a New World: Colonizing Ice Age America. Berkeley: University of California Press: Regents of the University of Calif ©2009.

Minetor, Randi. Death in Glacier National Park: Stories of Accidents and Foolhardiness in the Crown of the Continent. Guildford, CT: Rowman &Littlefield, 2016.

Molvar, Erik. Hiking Glacier and Waterton Lakes National Parks. Helena: Falcon Guide, Imprint Globe Pequot Press, 1999.

Moylan, Bridget Ellen. Glacier's Grandest: A Pictorial History of the Hotels and Chalets of Glacier National Park. Missoula: Pictorial Histories Publishing Company, Inc., 1995.

National Geographic DVD. "GLACIER NATIONAL PARK." National Geographic Parks Collection. NGHT, LLC, 2010.

National Park Service. "2013 NPS Geologic Resources Inventory Program for Glacier National Park." GRI digital geologic-GIS Ancillary Map Info Document. 2013.

National Park Service, U.S. Dept of Interior, Glacier National Park. https://home.nps.gov/glac. n.d.

National Park Service, U.S. Dept of Interior, Glacier National Park, articles .https://www.nps.gov/articles/ (re:bison-bellows/ice patch)

National Park Service, US Dept of Interior. AT HOME IN THIS PLACE: Blackfeet,Kootenai,Salish, and Pend d'Oreille Perspectives on Glacier National Park. 2011. DVD.

Nield, Ted. Supercontinent-Ten Billion Years in the Life Of Our Planet. Harvard University Press, 2007.

Olsen, Jack. Night of the Grizzlies. orig 1969/2000-2004 Crime Rant Classics. EBook.

Parratt, Mark W. Fate is a Mountain. Whitefish, MT: Sun Point Press, 2009.

Raup, Earhart, Whipple, Carrara. *Geology-Along Going-to-the-Sun Road Glacier National Park, Montana.* prepared by USGS&NPS: West Glacier, MT: Glacier Natural History Association 1983

Rinehart, Mary Roberts. *Through Glacier Park in 1915.* Boulder: Roberts Rinehart Publishers, 1916/1983.

Rockwell, David. *Exploring Glacier National Park.* Guilford,CT: Falcon Guide, Imprint Globe Pequot Press, 2002 Natural History.

Schultz, James Willard - aka Apikuni, Spotted Robe. *My Life as an Indian: The Story of a Red Woman & White Man in the Lodges of the Blackfeet.* Ed. forward 1907 by George Bird Grinnell. Vol. orig series Forest & Stream called "In the Lodges of the Blackfeet" pen name WB Anderson. San Bernadino, CA: Doubleday,Page & Company, 1907/2016.

Schultz, James Willard. *Blackfeet Tales of Glacier National Park.* Riverbend Publishing, Helena, MT 2002, 1916/2002.

Tarbuck, E.J, F.K. Lutgens. *Earth: An Introduction to Physical Geology -* 7th Ed. Upper Saddle River: Prentice Hall, 2002.

The Paleomap Project. http://www.scotese.com/Rodinia3.htm.

Thompson, Sally, Kootenai Cultural Committee, Pikunni Traditional Assoc. *People Before the Park: The Kootenai and Blackfeet Before Glacier National Park.*Helena: Montana Historical Society Press, 2015.

U.S. Dept. of the Interior. *Glacier National Park [Montana}.* Washington D.C.: U.S. Government Printing Office, 1937.

USGS Professional Paper. —"294- The Overthrust Fault." update 2008— . "296- Geology of Glacier Nat'l Park, Flathead,and NW Montana Region." update 2008.

Waggoner, George A. *Stories of Old Oregon/ A Legend of Wallowa Lake* . Salem, OR: Statesman Publishing Co., 1905 Public Domain

Fiction mentioned in this book

PEOPLE OF THE WOLF by W.Michael Gear and Kathleen O'Neal Gear, N.Y., TOR, 1990 .

BLOOD LURE by Nevada Barr, N.Y., Berkley Books 2001

www.ingramcontent.com/pod-product-compliance
Lightning Source LLC
Chambersburg PA
CBHW020407260626
47156CB00007B/2279